Once Upon a Winter Wonderland

SUSAN MAY WARREN

WITH

RACHEL D. RUSSELL

MICHELLE SASS ALECKSON

ANDREA CHRISTENSON

Sunrise
PUBLISHING

AUTHORS' NOTE

Thank you for reading *Once Upon a Winter Wonderland*! When we thought of this crazy set of novellas, we wanted to invite readers to Boone and Vivien's wedding...but we also thought, well, it can't be that easy. So we envisioned a massive snowstorm—and everything ensued from there.

But we also wanted to give you a magical holiday in Deep Haven, a Christmas story that might bless your season with the thought that, despite the storms we encounter, God cares. He wants to carry our burdens. And He wants to remind us that we are not alone. Ever. In fact, that's the point of Christmas. Emmanuel, God with us.

We hope that wherever you are this Christmas season, you discover a moment after, or during, the storms that is magical and glistening with hope. And in that moment you see God walking in the wonderland with you.

Merry Christmas,

Susie May, Rachel, Michelle, and Andrea

PROLOGUE

SUNDAY NIGHT

*I*t didn't *look* like the storm of the century.

"Just a second, let me go out onto the porch." Romeo Young put the call from his cell on speaker, then opened the door to the Evergreen Resort office and stepped out into the brisk, northern Minnesota, December air.

Sure, a few flurries drifted down, settling upon the evergreens lining the driveway, joining the snow already layering the grounds, frosting the handful of cabins and the roof of the resort truck, adding a festive, Christmassy touch to their northern wonderland.

But no blizzard of the century that his boss and manager, Owen Christiansen, was suggesting from his perch in southern Florida.

"Skies are a little gray, but the sun is out, and it looks all clear," Romeo said.

"All the flights into Minneapolis are shut down," Owen said. "We arrived at the Miami airport, waited six hours, and they finally canceled our flight. Jace and Eden decided to drive to Orlando and go to Disney World. The rest of us are going to wait it out in Key Largo."

Of course they were.

Romeo had checked the weather in Minneapolis, but that, too, didn't seem out of the ordinary. He bit back a spurt of annoyance. "I'm sure it'll open by tomorrow."

"Maybe. But we looked at the radar, and there's a huge storm front coming down from Alaska. You're about to get socked in."

Romeo walked over to the massive resort garage and retrieved the snow shovel stuck by the door. "Can you rent a car?"

He didn't want to sound inept but, well, with less than a week to Christmas, the resort was about to fill up, and…

Okay, he was just peeved, really, that the entire Christiansen clan had deserted him for two weeks for fun in the sun. Not that he should be—he'd given up his smokejumping gig in Alaska for exactly moments like these, when the family escaped and they needed someone capable to handle the resort.

Check in guests, keep wood chopped, handle small problems.

No biggie.

Probably a part-time employee could handle it. Which meant he could have joined the family for their belated Thanksgiving escape to Miami where Ingrid and John had docked their fancy boat after sailing the blue for a year.

Except, he wasn't part of the family, was he?

"Ten of us in a car for thirty hours? And that doesn't include Darek and Ivy and their kids—no thanks. The resort is in good hands." A chuckle from Owen. "You won't be setting any fires, right?"

Oh, ha ha. If he was referring to the nativity scene that caught fire the Christmas he spent with Uncle John and Aunt Ingrid— "That wasn't my fault. Besides—I *put out* fires, if you recall." Or had, for the past three years. Sometimes he wished he hadn't said yes quite so quickly to Uncle John's request to help run the resort.

Especially when "help" turned out to be less management and more errand boy to one Very Bossy Cousin Owen.

He supposed Owen had something to prove, what with the family legacy soundly on his shoulders. Still— "I can handle it, Owen."

Another chuckle. "Of course you can, Rome. But this means you need to keep an eye on Vivien Calhoun's wedding this weekend at

Wilder House. Casper says the venue is all ready for the rehearsal dinner and the ceremony, but you might need to let Vivien and her team in to decorate. And Boone's best man and a bridesmaid are staying at the resort—they're in the books. And some of Pastor Dan's friends—the Browns. He called right before we left. They arrive Tuesday. Oh—and don't forget Gerald Karlson. According to Darek, he's been a regular over Christmas for the past sixty years. His wife passed last year, so this is his first season without her. He always stays in cabin six, so make sure you put him there."

Romeo let out a breath, breathing through the fist closing over his chest.

"Oh, and when it snows, you'll need to plow. And not just the resort. I have a contract with the city, so you'll need to go down to the city garage and make sure the streets are clear."

That, probably, he could do.

"Fine." Romeo had returned to the lodge. Inside, the place didn't have a hint of Christmas cheer, terribly void of Aunt Ingrid's touch. No soaring white pine under the vaulted ceiling, no handmade stockings hung up the banister or a crackling fire in the hearth of the stone fireplace. No fragrance of cookies baking or siblings laughing as they worked on the annual puzzle.

And outside wasn't much better—no lights on the towering evergreen that had survived the fire so many years ago, no wreaths on the doors of the cabins, no wonderland skating rink, not even a bonfire to make s'mores.

For a guy who'd spent most of his Christmases eating a frozen pizza with his hungover mother, creating Christmas cheer just might be over his head.

"If it doesn't snow, I'll know you just wanted to spend Christmas on some beach," he growled.

"The snow will be there. Just keep the place running. We'll be back as soon as we can."

Romeo bit back a *hurry up*, because yes, he could do this. Even if he wasn't one of the *superstar* Christiansens.

He hung up and went to the sliding glass door that overlooked the snow-covered lake, the sun breaking through the pewter sky to skim the surface in gold.

It *wasn't* going to snow. It was just another dismal, gray Christmas alone.

A Beautiful Sight

RACHEL D. RUSSELL

CHAPTER 1

The howling wind outside was nothing compared to the howling inside Vivien Calhoun's head. How could her beloved town of Deep Haven betray her like this?

"There has to be at least ten feet of snow out there. I wanted a white wedding. Not a white-out wedding."

The room swayed in an unnatural and violent fashion no matter how hard she willed it to stop. She reached out a hand to steady herself, her fingers glancing off the cool, dark leather of a wingback chair before finding purchase.

"You've got to breathe, Vivie. Are you with me?" Megan Barrett's voice sounded tinny and distant, her hair a blonde blur and her eyes a soft hazel-brown smudge. "Why don't you sit down."

Right. Breathe. She could do that.

Vivien slumped into the wingback in the Wilder House library. She'd imagined Casper Christiansen's event center would be perfect for a winter wonderland wedding. But it should be more enchanting snow globe than Arctic freeze. She closed her eyes against the dark swirling walls of books.

Inhale…two…three…four…hold…two…three—

"Vivien?" Megan's voice reached through the tunneling darkness. "Are you okay?"

Vivien opened one eye. Stared up at her wedding coordinator. "You told me to breathe. I'm breathing." She wrinkled her nose. "And can I just say, it smells like musty paper in here."

"Right—but you went silent, and when you go silent, I'm not sure what that means. It kind of alarms me because it's so…*not* you." Megan was the queen of all things nuptial, but apparently her duties also included couples counseling, life coaching, and respiratory therapy. She stood there in her dark leggings and tall boots, her purple turtleneck snug against her neck. A pillar of calm and order.

Everything Vivien was not.

Because in three days she was marrying Boone Buckam. And that thought both quickened her pulse and seared dread into the core of her being. So much vulnerability entwined in that commitment. So much…risk. "What was I thinking, wanting a Christmas wedding?"

"It's the most wonderful time of the year?" Megan cracked a toothy grin. She gestured toward the elegant Christmas tree that stood like a sentinel in the far corner of the room—one of several in the large estate house. Two wooden nutcrackers flanked the fireplace, and pine and cinnamon blended with the bookish scents.

"Seriously, Megan." Because what Vivien couldn't admit, couldn't say out loud, was that fear and doubt had started to strangle her dreams. The storm had disrupted her carefully made plans—from the catering to the travel arrangements for guests. If she couldn't get the wedding right, how would she get the marriage right? And if she couldn't get the marriage right, then how could her life with Boone last any longer than her parents' life together?

Vivien lifted her eighteen-point checklist—her very own risk management plan. "With all the disruptions this snow has caused, there are a lot of things that need to come together for this to all work out."

The library door swung open, and Ree Turnquist blasted into the room. "Sorry we're late. Matron of honor and bridesmaids reporting for duty. Time to set operation Wedded Blizzard—I mean, Wedded Bliss—into motion." She pulled off her earmuffs and fluffed her short, blonde hair. "Word at the *Herald* is we'll see a reprieve before the end of the week."

Vivien wasn't buying that story.

Beth Strauss followed Ree and shook the snowflakes from her light-brown hair. She paused, her head bobbing up and down at the floor-to-ceiling shelves. "Wow—look at all these books!"

"It is pretty incredible," Ree agreed.

Beth turned back to Vivien. "Is your phone on the fritz again, Viv? I've been trying to call you."

"My phone? It worked earlier this morning, but I haven't used it since we talked." She drew the phone from her pocket. "Lovely. It's turned off." She pressed the button to restart it. "I haven't had time to get a new one. It's been a wee bit feisty lately."

Ree set down her purse and sank her fingers into the fur of her earmuffs. "We would have been here sooner, but the snowplow left a berm in front of the driveway, and then we got stuck behind a tourist who must be from a warm climate, because we could have walked faster."

"Did I miss anything?" Courtney Wallace came in behind Beth and Ree, carrying a box of silver, glitter-coated reindeer statues. "I brought these for the table settings."

The strawberry-blonde had gone from rising star in the community theater to one of Vivien's closest friends. Well, it was hard to spend that much time together and not grow close.

Courtney plopped the box on the floor and tugged her hat off.

"You're all just in time," Megan said to the crew of bridesmaids.

"For what?" Ree unwound her scarf and shrugged off her coat.

"To talk sense into our girl Vivie." Megan used her thumb to point sideways toward the wingback. "She's developed a severe case of Pre-wedding Panic."

"Hello," Vivien answered, waving her hands. "I can hear you." She tapped her Sorel boots on the rug.

"You're denying it?" Courtney asked. "You *aren't* in panic mode? Because you sounded a lot like you were panicking when you called us here. I believe you used the words *disaster, catastrophic,* and *emergency.*"

"And she has a list," Megan added.

"A list?" Ree asked. "We all know what that means."

Vivien ignored the knowing looks exchanged by the other four ladies, went to the window, and palmed the fog off the pane. "It's been a blizzard, ladies. A blizzard." She turned from the unsavory winter snowstorm. "How can I not be in panic mode? Is this not a calamity?"

"It'll be okay. It's just a little snow." Megan gathered her blonde hair into the band off her wrist, twisted it into a messy bun, then rolled up her sleeves. "It simply means we have our work cut out for us." She scooped up her binder and clicked her pen.

"A little snow?" Vivien pointed at the window. "Have you looked out this window?" She stared at the deep blanket of snow outside. Someone had plowed a berm the size of Everest at the end of the parking lot.

Ree laughed. "It's Deep Haven, Vivie. A white Christmas wedding was pretty much a guarantee."

Vivien pointed a finger at her friend. "Not helpful." And yeah, a white Christmas should have been expected—and Vivien was all for it *after* everything and everyone was in place for the big day.

"It's actually warmed up, and the worst of it is over," Beth said. "I got here with no problem."

"Well, that's something. Hopefully all the guests arrive on time. Good grief, it's been dumping snow for three days straight." Vivien turned and paced the antique area rug that covered the library's original hardwood floor. "And the flowers? What about the flowers?" She turned to Megan. "Did Claire get her delivery?"

"She's on my list to touch base with."

"Everything has to be perfect."

Megan blew out a breath. "I understand you have a vision for your big day but having some flexibility can really help smooth out the bumps."

Bumps were not an option. "What about catering?"

"I already spoke to Grace Christiansen. A few orders were delayed, but she'll get back to me with the details and alternatives as soon as possible."

Vivien checked her phone. "I still haven't heard from my mom." Her phone screen dimmed, and she re-started it again. "Her flight was supposed to land in Minneapolis today."

Megan gave her a gentle smile. "We've got this, Vivie."

Ree pulled a *Bridal Trends* magazine from her bag. "I was wondering if Zuri could do something like this with my hair." She flipped open the magazine to a tabbed page with an elaborate curled style.

"Oh, yeah—we're supposed to do hair run-throughs with Zuri too." Courtney fluffed her long, strawberry-blonde hair. "Mine needs some oomph. We don't all have thick, dark locks like you."

Vivien pointed to the magazine photo. "She can totally do that. Wait—where *is* Zuri?" Seeing her friend Zuri Milano arrive from New York had been one bright spot in the snow-bound saga.

"We saw her on our way in. She was checking out the accommodations," Courtney offered. "She wanted to see the space she'll be working in."

"Shouldn't she be back down by now?"

Megan placed her hands on Vivien's shoulders and gave a gentle squeeze. "It's all going to be fine."

"Well, at least I'll have my hair and makeup done right. Zuri is like the Michelangelo of makeup and hair." Vivien mentally checked that off her list.

"And you have the perfect gown. It only took us three hundred trips to Minneapolis to find a shop to sew your design and fit it," Beth said.

"I think it was actually three hundred and seven." Ree crossed her arms. "Not that I'm counting."

"Ha ha." Vivien laid the magazine down on the side table. "You're right. It isn't a Margaret VanEaton, but I do know I designed the perfect dress." The perfect dress to become Mrs. Boone Buckam in.

There went the swirling room again.

Beth picked up the magazine. "Didn't you say she was a designer for the rich and famous?"

Deep breaths. "She was—totally amazing. She doesn't design anymore, so the dresses are crazy expensive. Even more so than they were originally."

"Yes. Speaking of the dress—you've already picked that up?" Megan looked up from her binder, pen in hand.

"No. Kate was steaming it."

"Okay, I can stop and pick that up for you." She tapped her pen against her lips. "I'll make some calls and make sure everything is on schedule and that no one missed a plane. Ree, if you can follow up with Grace that the catering adjustments are good to go, I'll get you that number." She made a note in her binder. "And Courtney and Beth, if you two can reach out to Claire just to verify she doesn't need any extra help"—she glanced at Vivien—"and that everything arrived as scheduled."

The girls nodded.

"And then I'll pick up the dress when we're done."

"You're all doing more than enough. I'll pick up the dress. Besides, I'm anxious to have it in hand." Vivien took a deep breath. Stood. "Has anyone heard from Amelia?"

Ree's head gave the slightest shake, and she reached out a hand to squeeze Vivien's. "I'm sorry. She isn't going to make it. She tried to call you."

"Really? But—but—" Vivien closed her eyes. Score one for the storm.

"She tried." Ree twisted the earmuffs in her hands. "She couldn't get a flight."

Vivien blew out a breath. "I knew it would be hard for her. I'd just hoped…" Oh, and there she went, hoping.

"That also means we're short a bridesmaid," Beth said. "Does that matter?"

Megan flipped through several pages. "Practically speaking, you could either have one of your groomsmen walk solo or have two walk with one of the bridesmaids."

"Too bad they aren't single. I'd volunteer as tribute," Beth said.

"Duke is," Ree announced.

"That's true—but he's walking with you, smarty-pants," Vivien answered. She wrinkled her nose. "Oh—I know. I'll ask Zuri. I'd be honored to have her step in."

Megan scribbled a note in her binder, and Courtney, Beth, and Ree jumped into a conversation about Zuri, hair, and makeup, none of which Vivien could focus on.

Because tentatively resolving her bridesmaid crisis hadn't quelled the storm within. "I need some air."

WEDNESDAY, 9:30 A.M.

Boone Buckam was going to throttle someone with a string of Christmas lights if they didn't finish hanging them soon. He still had to drop off the new radios at the Crisis Response Team headquarters.

He tugged at the twisted strand and hooked it into place before stepping off the ladder. "Is there such a thing as death by twinkle lights?" At this rate, they might blow a fuse on Wilder House before the day was over. He picked up another wad of lights.

Cole Barrett released a burst of laughter and stepped down from his ladder perch. "I would have found out by now, so I assure you there isn't." He gave Boone a teasing whack on the chest with his palm. "Toughen up, man."

Funny coming from the former Army Ranger who was wearing what was likely the second ugliest Christmas sweater. And an antler headband on his high-and-tight.

Boone chucked the extra strand of lights to Seth Turnquist and shook his head. "Easy for you to say. You aren't getting married in three days—after a snowstorm swamped the airports with thousands of passengers who missed flights and a fiancée with a very long list of items to chase down." And when it came down to it, all Boone wanted was to step into his life with Vivien as husband and wife. To have a lifelong commitment. To truly belong to someone—and not just anyone. Vivien. His Vivien. He didn't need the twinkle lights or potted white birch trees or mirrored centerpieces with reindeer and pine boughs and whatever else it was.

"But I *am* wearing the ugliest sweater." Cole gestured to his sweater with a reindeer riding shotgun in a Jeep, four-wheeling with Santa.

"You both know I've got that beat," Seth answered. He tugged the sweater taut across his lumberjack frame. "I mean, come on—a Holstein cow wearing a beanie and its own ugly Christmas sweater? This is a classic."

Caleb Knight walked into the room, hauling a potted dormant birch tree on a dolly. "I knew I forgot something." He set the dolly upright and stood looking surprisingly normal in a long-sleeved thermal.

"Oh, you did not forget." Seth gave Caleb a friendly jab.

"This—*this* takes the prize." Boone puffed out his chest for a full display of his 3-D metallic garland and shiny miniature ornaments on a background of kelly green with sparkling white snowflakes. He pressed the button on the hem to activate the lights on the sweater. The embedded audio box played "O Christmas Tree" while the lights flashed, not quite in sync with the beat.

"No way. We'll just see how the votes come in." Seth extracted himself from the strand Boone had tossed him and smoothed out the wires. "Remind me how it is we ended up roped into this?" he asked. "No pun intended." Seth scooped up a second strand and snapped the two sets together.

"This is other duties as assigned for the groomsmen. It was on Vivien's list, and I figured this was better than chasing down a snow-bound florist, caterer, gifts, or musicians."

"Her list?" Seth asked.

Boone closed his eyes. Nodded. "Yeah. Don't ask." Because Vivien had been adamant that every single thing on that list was necessary in order for their wedding to be considered a success. And that particular success mattered to her for reasons he, apparently, could not understand. Which might be the reasons those whispers of doubt kept heckling him.

You're not good enough.

"Where's Duke?" Cole grabbed his water bottle and took a drink.

"He picked up Zuri from the airport yesterday and is getting the Mustang detailed today. I already saw him this morning—"

"Zuri?"

"She's Vivien's makeup-slash-hair-stylist-slash-friend from New York."

"Wow. Okay. And you're hauling the Mustang out of storage in this storm because…"

"We really wanted to do some fun photos."

Cole raised his brows.

Boone held out his hands and shrugged. "Come on—it's once in a lifetime that I get married, and I trust Duke to take great care of her. He'll wash her up, and she'll be safely back in the garage as soon as we're done."

"I still don't know how we ended up doing lights."

"Megan's with the ladies getting all the other stuff sorted out. I think, specifically, Cole offered us up to figure out the lights." He nudged his friend with a teasing elbow jab.

"It seemed like the right thing to do," Cole said, dodging the poke and straightening his antlers that had drifted forward.

Yeah, the husband of the wedding coordinator probably had spent his fair share of hours hanging lights.

"We aren't actually complaining," Seth answered.

"Aren't you though?" Cole teased.

Seth shrugged. "I'm just maybe wondering why this couldn't wait until Friday."

"You do realize tomorrow is two days before the wedding?" Caleb asked.

Boone ran through his mental notes of Vivien's list again. How would they possibly pull off the wedding with everything they had to track down due to the storm? "As long as we don't get a callout, right? The team's either in the wedding party or attending." Boone tried to tamp down his fears.

The Crisis Response Team already took up enough of his time. Case in point—he'd been on call for twenty-four crazy hours during the blizzard. Last thing he wanted was a callout interfering with his wedding day too. Not when the tension between family and duty already left him torn.

Family. He and Vivien would be *family*.

Cole nodded. "Relax. Jack's got it covered."

"I won't be relaxed until Vivien and I are sitting on a sunny beach and this whole wedding thing is behind us." He looked out the window. "They did say we were due for a warming spell."

Caleb crossed his arms. "I think you mean cold snap. You have beach weather on the brain. Seriously, I do hope the CRT isn't activated. I told you one of those destination wedding things would be the best idea. Somewhere warm."

"No kidding," Seth answered. "I'd go for that right now."

Boone grabbed his tall coffee cup from the floor and surveyed their handiwork. "You know, we might be pretty good at this." They'd crisscrossed long strands of twinkle lights across the high-ceiling room, creating a warm glow in the space. Chairs had been lined up in rows, with a center aisle, and more twinkle lights would go on the birch trees Caleb was bringing in.

"Don't tell Megan." Cole laughed.

Seth closed the lid on a box of leftover lights. "How's Vivien doing with all the snow and wedding plans?"

Boone had no idea how to answer that. "Good?"

"You answered my question with a question."

"I think it's all okay." Even he didn't seem convinced. Her voice had been drawn tight, uncertain how all the wedding details would come together. Which was exactly why he was stringing thousands of twinkle lights with the groomsmen.

He needed to figure out a way to help her relax. Unwind a bit. Let loose.

Seth patted Boone on the back. "It's okay to go touch base with her. I think we're almost done here."

"Probably just the stress of it all. Megan sees that with a lot of her brides," Cole offered.

"Well, her mom and my parents are supposed to arrive today," Boone answered. "Maybe she's still worried about them traveling. I'm going to go find her." Because Boone needed to make sure Vivien had the wedding of her dreams—that she knew she was his priority as they entered their marriage together.

CHAPTER 2

*V*ivien clutched her list and ducked into the Wilder House sitting room.

The octagon-shaped room held several armchairs and a loveseat along with a richly decorated tree. If only they could get a reprieve from the winter storm. Though the snowfall had weakened, the forecast called for more in a day or two. That didn't bode well for her wedding guests.

She'd always imagined a bright, beautiful Christmas wedding. It was a season of hope and celebration and, even in the dark days after Dad had left, it had brought her joy.

The Living Nativity. The Dickens carolers. Light displays.

But so far, the clouds still clung low and heavy over Deep Haven.

She shoved her to-do list into her pocket. Nothing would stand between her and the wedding of her dreams. Not even—she glanced outside—ten-foot snow drifts.

And so what if Zuri didn't know she'd need to be filling Amelia's shoes? Literally. She'd say yes. She had to.

"Hey—you hiding out in here?"

Vivien turned to meet Emma Hueston's blue eyes. She wore a thick down jacket over jeans. Snowflakes faded to water beads on the tops of her boots and dripped onto the rug.

"Maybe. I just needed somewhere to think." She pulled the list back out of her pocket. "You can still play at the reception, right?"

Emma nodded and unzipped her coat. "I'll be there, though I'm hoping Kyle doesn't get called in. This weather's been rough on our plans." She nodded toward the window.

Yeah, she imagined it must be hard to be married to the sheriff, who also happened to be the band's drummer.

"Don't worry—I have a backup if need be." Emma gave Vivien a wry smile. "And hopefully the CRT doesn't get activated, right? We don't want Boone missing his own wedding. There's no backup for that."

Vivien laughed. But even to her own ears, it came out thin and hollow, and her pulse quickened. "Right." She paced across the room. "I mean, that wouldn't actually happen, right? He wouldn't have to miss our wedding?"

Emma rested a hand on her hip. "Kyle didn't miss our wedding. Okay, to be fair, he didn't have as many responsibilities back then. I will say I've spent my fair share of anniversaries, birthdays, and holidays alone, though." Her pensive look spread into a smile, genuine and confident. "It's what we signed up for. The entire family serves. He's really good at what he does."

Vivien remembered her first birthday without her dad. Just her and Mom and two sad little day-old cupcakes.

But this was different. Boone was different. Once they were married, she'd take her place at the top of his priority list.

Wouldn't she?

Emma shook her head, still apparently musing over married life. "I wasn't sure he'd make it to our first child's birth, though. There'd been a huge wreck on 61—this was before the CRT—and my water broke. So there I was, alone on our bathroom floor, in dire agony—"

Emma's voice faded behind the din of Vivien's thoughts. Images of being alone in Boone's lakeview cabin—their lakeview home. Snow on the ground. The bathroom floor. Cold. Alone. Pain.

She shuddered.

Emma's soft laugh reconnected to Vivien, tethering her back in reality. "…yeah. It was quite memorable. We laugh about it now, but I was not laughing at the time," Emma finished. She pulled her beanie from her head and ran her fingers through her hair. "How are the wedding arrangements going?"

Considering a portion of their wedding party might not make their flights and their guest list was likewise compromised and she might not ever, truly, be Boone's priority— Terrible. Awful. Dreadful. "Good."

Emma gave her a sideways glance and a gentle smile. "You don't have to pretend. Getting married is a big deal, and you just had a snowstorm dump on your parade."

She blew out a long breath. "It's a mess." She waved her list. "But I've got this. I'm going to pick up my dress, and then everything will fall into place. Megan and the girls are busy working on it too."

"Well, I'm glad to do my part. I'm really happy for you."

"Thanks."

"We'll make sure your reception's rockin'. Hey—I heard you had a friend fly in from New York. That's pretty cool."

"Yeah. My friend Zuri Milano. She's around here somewhere. I'm so glad she made it." The thought made her smile.

"I never thought you'd end up staying in Deep Haven. I'm glad New York didn't get to keep you."

Vivien felt her smile fade just a little. Just a little pang from the past. The life she'd expected. Her big dream that didn't work out.

Emma hooked her coat and hat over her arm. "Well, I should go take a look at the reception hall setup so I can make sure we have all the equipment and cords that we'll need."

"Sure," Vivien said. "Thanks."

Emma disappeared, and somehow, Vivien felt worse.

She pressed the power button on her phone. The start-up screen sprang to life. "Finally."

It buzzed with a new text message.

Mom.

In Minneapolis. Barely. Rough trip. Long story. Can't wait to see u. Exciting news to share.

Vivien clicked the button to call her mom. That wasn't the kind of message to leave hanging.

She waited for it to ring. Nothing. Looked at the screen.

Dark again.

Add that to the list. Who had time to go buy a new phone?

She stretched her head back and tried to knead the knots from her shoulder with her fingers. If only she could stamp out the voices from the past that had grown louder with the passing days.

Memories of her parents' broken marriage and all the shards of life it'd left behind.

How many times had she heard Mom cry herself to sleep after Dad left? How many times had Mom told a friend that if she'd just done more, maybe he'd have stayed? They'd have been his priority.

And then there was the day a boy broke Vivien's tender, teenage heart. Her mom had drawn her close, wiped her tears away, and looked her in the eye. *Oh, sweetheart, don't ever give away your whole heart. You've got to protect yourself.*

The words had started beating in the back of Vivien's mind like the rumble of a snare drum over the past few months, the sound turning to timpani when unchecked.

But she had control of this. Her perfectly planned wedding. Her future with Boone.

She looked back out the window. The clouds had thinned, the pale blue sky beyond them maybe even holding the promise of clear roads and easy travel for her guests.

A hymn floated in the back of her mind, not quite forming in its completeness.

I lift my eyes; the cloud grows thin;

I see the blue above it...

Yet somehow, it did nothing to ease the maelstrom swirling within.

Maybe the anxiety would quell once she picked up her dress.

WEDNESDAY, 10:00 A.M.

With Operation Light Bright completed, Boone searched Wilder House for Vivie. He needed to find a way to calm the anxiety that had rolled off her in waves when she'd realized Old Man Winter had dumped some serious snow. And, okay, maybe with all the pressure of the wedding, he really just wanted to know everything between them was good.

They'd hung the lights and set up chairs. He'd even managed to flatten out the floor runner after Cole had rolled it out.

He'd left the guys watching the football game and wandered Wilder House, not exactly sure which room the ladies were using as mission control.

He wove through Wilder House until he came to the kitchen doorway.

Seth's wife, Ree, sat at a massive granite counter, pen in one hand, phone in the other. Megan paced the far end of the kitchen, and Vivie's friends, Beth and Courtney, scribbled frantic notes on what appeared to be a guest list set on the table in front of them.

"Good morning, ladies."

"Oh, wow—nice sweater." Ree snickered and set down her phone. "I see you're giving Seth a run for his money."

"It's not even close. Light-up garland? Come on…" He clicked the light-activation button again.

She covered her laughter with a hand. "You guys. Awfully competitive. I'm not sure what the actual prize is."

He held his arms out to his sides. "Bragging rights."

"Is that something you really feel you need to pad your résumé with?" Megan winked.

He dropped his hands back to his sides. "Hey, you never know when this kind of thing will come in handy."

Ree wrote a note in her spiral notebook and turned to Beth. "Nothing new on the Deckers."

Beth wrote another note on the list. "Are you here trying to sway votes? Because I think you're going to end up in a three-way tie."

He tugged on the hem of his sweater to straighten it out. "I'm actually looking for Vivien."

Courtney set down her pen. "She left a while ago."

Boone looked at his watch. "Oh, wow—have I actually been hanging lights for three hours?"

Megan ended her call and set her phone on a chair. Walked over to join the group. "Must have been a lot more talking than light hanging going on." She crossed her arms and winked. "Doesn't take me and my usual crew that long."

"Well, we might have been distracted by the Vikings game coming from the study."

"Uh-huh." Megan smiled. "We know how it goes."

Boone ran his hands through his hair. "Did Vivie say where she was heading?"

"She was supposed to pick up her dress," Beth answered.

"But—we came together. I'm her ride."

Megan snagged her phone from the chair she'd dropped it on and scrolled through several screens. "I've tried her cell a few times to ask her about a substitution for the vegan meal option, but it's going straight to voicemail."

"I'm sure it's fine," Ree said. "I'm sure she's fine."

Ree, Beth, Courtney, and Megan exchanged a look. One that knotted his stomach. Like something was wrong.

"What is it you're not telling me?"

Ree tugged at a thread on her shirt hem. "It's nothing. You know, the snow. The wedding. Probably some nerves."

"Vivien's nervous?"

"No, no—she just seemed a little distressed. Amelia isn't going to make it. Some adjustments like that. I'm sure she'll be fine once she gets her dress."

"Distressed isn't better than nervous, and she should have come to find me to get the dress." He searched their faces. "She must be here somewhere."

He clicked her icon on his cell and walked out the door.

This is Vivien. Leave a message.

"Hey, hon—call me."

He retraced his steps and returned to the main room hall. Emma Hueston stood near the fireplace. "Has Vivien been through here?"

"She went upstairs a little while ago."

"I'm right here." Vivien came down the stairs.

"Your phone isn't working."

"Yeah, I need to replace it. I was just about to come find you."

"Here I am. Your knight in shining armor."

She gave him a once-over. "It's hard for me to take you seriously in that sweater."

"Well, you look like you could use a good laugh."

She closed her eyes, swallowed, and looked away.

He drew her into his arms. "What is it?"

She placed her palms on his chest and looked up at him, her bright blue eyes a little gray beneath her dark lashes.

"Vivie?"

"It feels like everything is going wrong. I just want our wedding to be perfect, and it feels like everything is falling apart. The gifts I ordered for my bridesmaids didn't arrive. Megan says Grace is stuck in Florida with the storm...I mean...how am I going to have a wedding without a cake? Maybe it won't matter—our guests won't make it anyway. I don't know if my flowers arrived before the snow hit or if—"

"Stop. Wow. It'll be fine. Everything will come together. The guys and I put up the decorations. The ladies are placing calls to follow up on all those things, right?"

"I know. It just doesn't feel like it."

"Well, how can *I* help you?" he teased, leaning in.

She held up a piece of paper in her hand. "I have the list. Can we get my dress?"

The list.

He had imagined something more along the lines of holding her. Maybe kissing her. But a dress? Sure, they could pick up the dress. "Of course." He took her hand. "You'll see. Everything is going to be perfect."

CHAPTER 3

WEDNESDAY, 10:15 A.M.

Once Vivien had her dress, everything else might fall into place. The food, the flowers, the music. And then she and Boone could focus on each other.

Then they could get lost in this season.

Because even she had felt the energy drop between them when she rushed out the door, leaving him standing there.

He sat in the F-150 beside her, turned up the truck's defrost and adjusted the temperature.

Even in that silly sweater, he looked every bit a hero. Lean. Strong. Those pale blue eyes that set her heart aflutter. Dark blond hair she loved to muss up. The one person who always knew how to ground her.

The man who made her heart feel like it could explode into a million pieces.

She reached over and put a hand on his. "I'm sorry." She leaned across the center console, gave him a tug.

He shifted in his seat to meet her kiss with his own. Sweet. Tender. Adored.

His hands warmed her cheeks, and his kiss heated her core.

"We'll get that dress of yours and then—" His phone rang.

He turned off the ringer. "Where were we?"

"A kiss? A dress?" Vivien sat back and buckled her seat belt.

"Right." Boone lifted his phone. "I'd better check this message." He listened, his lips pressed tightly, then he shook his head. Blew out a breath. "I'll have to stop by headquarters at some point to drop off the new radios." Boone adjusted the truck's temperature.

Vivien's heart sank. "Today? Seems like we have a lot of other stuff to focus on today." She waved her list—her eighteen-point list. And tried not to feel a little jealous of the team.

"I know, but I can squeeze it in." He backed out of the parking spot and steered the truck down the plowed drive.

Right. "Maybe Jack can take care of it for you."

"Jack's the one who needs me to drop them off." He reached over and placed his hand over hers. "Where are we heading?"

"To Kate's Alterations. On First Avenue West." Dropping off radios wouldn't take too long, right? And she'd have her dress—which was the absolute most important item on the list. She shrugged off her conversation with Emma. She wasn't in this alone. Boone was *right here*.

"Got it." Boone turned toward town.

The roads had been plowed again since they'd headed to Wilder House earlier. She wanted to appreciate the bright white cover, but the deep drifts weighed as heavily on her as they did the trees and shrubs they passed.

Boone turned down First Avenue West. Deep Haven resembled a Christmas village, the drifts reaching window-height on several houses.

Heavier snow filled the side streets, and children ran about several yards, joined by snowmen with offset eyes and wild, angular arms.

Boone pulled up in front of Kate's. The walk to the red house had been shoveled, but a thin layer of freshly falling snow was erasing the bare cement.

Vivien hopped from the truck. Well, she wouldn't even care if they had to swing by headquarters once she had her dress. She waited for Boone, wove her fingers into his.

"Thanks for doing this." She inhaled the woodsy-spice scent of his aftershave. So familiar. In four days, she'd be waking up on their first Christmas morning as husband and wife.

"Of course." The warm timbre of his voice thrummed through her.

Boone held the door, and she ducked into the alterations shop ahead of him. They each paused to wipe their boots on the floor mat.

The shop smelled like cinnamon and apple spice, and Vivien drew in a long breath, shook out her shoulders, and clasped Boone's hand, giving it a squeeze before releasing it. She shucked off her gloves and unzipped her coat.

"Kate?" Vivien walked farther into the shop, drawing Boone alongside. Several bolts of fabric lay on the cutting table, and a dressmaker's mannequin stood with pinned-on cut fabric.

"Be right there." Kate's singsong voice called from another room before she came through the doorway. She wore jeans with a blue-and-burgundy Fair Isle sweater that made her look Hallmark-movie ready. Her long, dark hair had been left down, and it framed her olive complexion and brown eyes. "Vivien!" Her hand flew to her lips. "I forgot to call you—I'm so sorry."

A knot clinched Vivien's gut. "Sorry? What's wrong?"

Boone put a hand on her shoulder, gave it a little squeeze.

"Oh, no. Nothing's wrong. It's just, I meant to call you. My steamer quit on me, and I sent your dress over to the dry cleaner on Monday to get it pressed for you."

Vivien rubbed her palm against her chest. "You scared me!"

"I'm sorry—nope. It's fine. But I understand completely." She rounded the cutting table and gave Vivien a hug. "It's in good hands. No need to panic."

"It's been a little rough with the storm disrupting so many things. I'm just so...so...I don't even know what I am."

"It's pretty normal under ordinary circumstances for the bride to be a little edgy as the date draws close and all the plans need to fall into place."

"I appreciate everything you've done."

"It's a beautiful dress, and you'll be stunning in it. I can't wait to see the photos—I've been stalking your Instagram page."

Vivien laughed. "It's kind of ironic—I started posting to keep my name out there while I've been offstage, and I think I've had more followers watching the wedding plans than ever cared about my acting."

"Gotta love social media."

"Well, kind of a love-hate, right? But we're going to do some fun photos with the Mustang."

Boone wrapped her hand in his. "You know it's true love when I'm willing to pull out the Mustang in a Minnesota winter for her."

Vivien winked at him. "And they say I'm the dramatic one."

"Sweet." Kate grabbed a dress from her work rack. "Let me know if you need any last-minute fixes, but it should be just perfect after that last alteration."

Perfect.

"I will." Vivien turned toward the door. "We'll see you later. Thanks again, Kate, for all your help."

"Anytime."

A cold blast greeted them outside, and they both zipped their coats up, tugged their gloves back on.

Boone looked at his phone. "Unfortunately, the cleaner doesn't open for another two-and-a-half hours."

Argh.

"Hey, you two!"

Vivien turned to see Caleb Knight and his wife, Issy, standing next to their truck just down the street. She looped her hand through the crook of Boone's arm, and he led her down the snow-covered sidewalk.

"What are you guys up to?" Issy gave Vivien a big hug.

"We were picking up my dress, but Kate said she had to send it over to the cleaner, so we have to wait until they open. What are you guys up to?"

Caleb shook snow off his hat. "I finished placing those birch-tree things at Wilder House and checked with Megan to make sure they were right."

"Thank you. Did Megan say anything about the flowers? The food? What about the Christiansens? Are Owen and Scotty going to make it back?"

Caleb held up his hands. "Whoa—I'm not sure about all that. Right now, we're going to take a bit of a snow day. We're meeting up with a few of the players for some winter shenanigans."

Vivien snapped a look from Caleb to Issy. Back to Caleb. "Where are your priorities?" Vivien tried to add a bit of teasing jest to her voice to soften her point. But still make the point.

Boone placed his hand over hers. "What she means is, have fun."

Right.

Issy winked. "We'll see you both later."

Boone and Vivien returned to his truck. Puffs of breath filled the cab.

Vivien shook off the chill and adjusted the climate controls.

She'd definitely, totally, one hundred percent have the wedding of her dreams.

Boone's phone rang and he clicked it to hands-free. "Hello?"

"Hi, it's Ronnie. Sorry to bug you, but did you ever drop off the new radios at CRT HQ? I've looked all over but can't find them."

He looked over his shoulder into the back seat of the extended cab, where two boxes sat. "I'll be right there." He disconnected.

She knew what was coming before he even said it. "So, we're going to HQ now?" And okay, she probably hadn't kept the agitation out of her voice very well.

"It won't take long, and we have some time to kill." He reached over and gave her hand a squeeze. "You okay?"

"Yeah. Just stressed." And worried. And somehow maybe even a little jealous that he was heading off to help the team while she wanted him focused on the wedding. On her.

Which was stupid and silly and totally juvenile.

But somehow, knowing that didn't make it any easier when he turned up First Avenue toward HQ.

Because Emma's words didn't feel so far from the mark.

So, there I was, alone...

WEDNESDAY, 10:45 A.M.

Vivien might not know it yet, but she was about to get her own rescue. Boone hadn't missed the waves of frustration coming off her when they detoured to the CRT headquarters.

But the stop had worked out, because he'd been able to quickly pass the radios off to Ronnie and snag a sled Cole had left behind. He'd get Vivien's mind off her stress. Off the dress. Off the waiting.

Boone parked in the makeshift lot at the base of the hill at the edge of town.

"What are we doing here?"

"The cleaner won't be open for two hours. We're going sledding."

"It's too cold." She gestured toward her clothes. "I'm not dressed warm enough."

He reached behind the seat and pulled out a duffel he'd snagged at headquarters. "I grabbed snow gear from my office. We've got everything we need."

Boone exited the truck, grabbed the sled from his truck bed, and opened her door.

She eyed him, a gleam of suspicion in her gaze. "I suppose that's where you got the sled?" She nodded toward the bright red one in his hands.

"Yes, ma'am. I slipped it into the truck bed while you were...pouting." This time he grinned. Gave her a wink.

"For the record, I wasn't pouting. I just thought someone else could have stepped up and gotten the radios."

He raised a brow.

She stepped out of the truck, and her boots sank into the white powder. "What?" She threw her gloved hands into the air. "I wasn't pouting."

"Well, then I also submit *for the record*, everyone on the team chips in. The radios were my responsibility, and I wanted to make sure they were delivered."

"Uh-huh." She tugged her knit hat down. "Well, still. We can't go sledding."

"Why not?"

"Wedding plans. The list." She looked up at him. "It has to be the priority."

"It is. We can't pick up your dress yet, and Megan's probably already taking care of several items on your list. That's why you hired her." He stepped closer. "Come on. It'll be fun." He held out a hand to her. Waited. "And you seriously look like you need some fun."

She narrowed her gaze and pressed her lips together, stared at his outstretched arm. He could see the smile she was trying to pinch closed. He bent down and scooped up a handful of snow, started packing it. "Unless you'd rather have a snowball fight?"

And then she grinned, bright and beautiful, with tease lighting her eyes. "Don't even think about it."

He dropped the snow and stepped closer. Snowflakes clung to the dark waves of hair that had escaped her knit hat, and the cold air painted a rosy wash over her cheeks. He unwrapped his scarf and lifted it over her head, then settled it around her shoulders and drew her close.

Her jasmine perfume warmed him from the inside out. Their breaths frosted in the air between them, and she wove her arms around him, looked up at him.

He could get lost in a moment like this. No plans. No schedule. No emergencies. No responsibilities.

Just him and his bride.

He tugged off a glove and ran his fingertips across her cheek. Their eyes met.

"Race ya!" She ducked out of his arms and snagged the sled's towrope.

"Viv!" Cold air zapped his body, and he missed the warmth of her against him.

A twitter of laughter drifted across the snow to him. She bolted up the hill, waving a gloved hand in the air. "Come on!"

He pulled his own glove back on and ran after her, gaining ground by running in the flattened snow. At the top, they doubled over, sucking in the icy air.

It probably should have hurt, but joy filled his chest.

"You're getting slow." She stood, wiping her eyes and pulling his scarf back over her cheeks. Delight colored her eyes with mischief and probably a little mayhem.

"Shall we?" He swung his arm out to present her with the sledding run.

"We shall." She stomped her boots to knock off the extra snow and then set the sled into place at the top of the run.

He swept the fresh snow from the seat and climbed onto the sled. He held out his hand to her, and she slid down, nestled into place in front of him.

He pushed his hands against the ground, walking them forward to the edge of the slope.

"Ready?"

She nodded.

He gave a final shove and sent them over the side, zipping down the hill. Vivien squealed, her laughter vibrating against his chest.

They came to rest at the base of the hill, her giggles still filling him.

"I don't even remember the last time I went sledding." She stood, wiped away the tears reaped by the wind, and held out a hand to him. "Let's go again."

He stood, watched her clamber back up the hill.

Yeah. He could do this all day.

A bright thread of sunlight lined the edge of the clouds, and maybe for once, the local meteorologist was right about clearer skies ahead.

He'd get Vivien her dress, and they wouldn't have any more interruptions from the CRT.

And his bride would have the wedding of her dreams.

CHAPTER 4

*I*f Vivien let herself admit it, sledding might actually be the best thing she'd done all week. And okay, yes, of course she'd been pouting.

She was pretty sure the Bridal Rulebook allowed for it.

She could demonstrate she wasn't a maniacal bride. She could have fun and reconnect with Boone.

By the time they'd made their fourth run down the hill, several families with children had arrived, taking turns and racing side by side down the slope. Toboggans, tubes, sleds.

Laughter filled the space, muffled only by the intermittent snowfall that still floated down over the hillside.

How many times had she, Ree, and Amelia played on this same hill as kids? Sledding with the Christiansens was practically legendary around town.

She scanned the sky for a glimpse of blue. The clouds had thinned a bit, a bright gold lining promising better weather.

The promise reverberated deep within, and more of the hymn

niggled in the back of her mind, this time causing her to hum the melody.

Through all the tumult and the strife
I hear the music ringing;
It finds an echo in my soul—
How can I keep from singing?

"Duck!" A snowball flew her way, and she dodged it, slipped, and caught her balance before face-planting into the snow.

"Sorry!" Megan's son, Josh, gave her a shy shrug.

"I'll get him, Vivie!" Tiago Morales chugged across the snow, lobbing a loose snowball at Josh before ducking behind a small snow berm.

"You'd better be careful, boys." Boone stepped up beside her, forming a snowball between his hands. "Vivie's been working on her throw." He handed her the well-formed ball.

She drew in a lungful of cold air. "I can't throw that at the kids!"

He gave her a smile. The one that turned her insides all mushy and made her breath catch.

Three more days.

Then she'd stand before him in the dress she'd designed. Brought from her imagination to the page and then worked so hard with the seamstress to get just right. Four months it'd taken them. And every detail was exactly what she'd dreamed it would be.

The way the lace-covered bodice fitted her curves and spilled out onto the floor with a scalloped hem and chapel train. The ornate appliqué lace and V-neck. A fit-and-flare tulle-and-lace that was modern with a total old-Hollywood twist.

Boone tossed the snowball between his hands, his blue eyes sparking with mischief. "What happened to living a little?"

She held up a finger. "Oh, you can't use my song against me." But she smiled at the reminder of the day they'd met at Fish Pic, when they'd accidentally landed themselves in the middle of the car show parade.

And won.

"Oh? What are you going to do about it?"

She stepped up to him, tugged on his jacket, and drew him close. She was on a small rise, which put her nearly at eye level with him.

A dangerous choice, she realized. His aftershave, warmed by activity, combined with the soapy scent from his morning shower and the smell of his laundry detergent that had grown so familiar. A trifecta that both tantalized her senses and terrified her.

"I'm gonna…"

Don't ever give away your whole heart. You've got to protect yourself.

"I'm gonna…" she started again.

He shook his head, and a crooked smile slid across his face. Before she could try again, he leaned forward and pressed a kiss to her cheek. His cold nose tickled her ear, and she tucked her chin into the scarf with a giggle.

She shoved her mom's words back down and looked around the slope.

Several other families from church and teens from the playhouse had joined the hillside cluster. Ella Bradley and Adrian Vassos had stopped to help several kids build a snow fort.

Couples. Families.

People who stayed together.

"Ready to go again?" Boone leaned down, his eyes on her lips.

"Sure." She trucked up the hill, her body warmed from the physical activity.

She paused halfway to watch a father-daughter pair go howling by, shrieks of glee punctuated by the dad's deep belly laughs. The girl looked to be maybe five or six, with blonde ringlets peeking out from her beanie.

The scene filled Vivien's soul with a lightness.

Yeah, she could totally see it…Boone bringing her and their kids out for a snow day.

Their kids.

I wasn't sure he'd make it to our first child's birth, though… There I was, alone on our bathroom floor, in dire agony…

She shrugged off Emma's words. Stomped them into the snow under her boots.

That was different. They were different. Different people, different priorities.

She paused at the top of the hill while Boone set the sled up again.

"Having fun?" he asked, settling into position.

"I am." She snugged into place in front of him, letting the moment fill her soul.

"Ready?"

She nodded and helped Boone push them off the top.

The sled launched down the hill, and Vivien let out a whoop, throwing her hands in the air. The icy breeze pulled tears from her eyes.

She blinked them away.

Oh no!

They were gaining on another sled, its trajectory slightly angled.

Toward their path. The little blonde girl and her dad.

Boone must have seen it too, at the same time, as she felt his body tighten.

Their speed ate up the distance between the two sleds.

They were going to crash right into them. She closed her eyes, screamed. Felt Boone's weight shift hard, his arms locked around her.

"Hold on!" he shouted above the scraping of snow.

They lurched sideways.

The sled tipped and—they were flying.

They landed hard and fast and kept sliding. Without the sled.

Snow pummeled her.

Up her nose. Down her shirt. In her ears.

The screaming didn't end until she got a mouthful of snow. She coughed.

They finally stopped and she lay broken, rattled, undone, Boone still holding her, his arms and legs tangled in hers.

"Are you okay?" Boone released his armlock, and she felt the weight of him lift away from her.

She rolled onto her back, her breath heaving, the sky a steely gray overhead. She moved her arms, legs.

Everything still worked. At least she wouldn't be on crutches for the ceremony. Hopefully Zuri could cover up any bruises.

What was she thinking, allowing Boone to take her sledding?

"I just—I want to go. Now."

Before any real tragedies happened.

Boone hoped a peppermint mocha IV drip might bring Vivien back to him. He'd take her by Java Cup and maybe ease the tightness in her jaw and the incessant list-checking. He threw the truck into reverse, backed out of the snowy lot, and headed back into town.

She'd hobbled a few steps when they untangled themselves from their snowy crash, and his eardrums hadn't quite recovered from her screaming.

He'd offered her a hand up, dusted the snow off. "You okay?"

She'd given him a little nod and her voice wavered. "I thought we were going to hit that little girl."

But it was something more than that, and it nicked his confidence. Added to his sense that she was holding back. And Vivien wasn't a woman who held back. Right?

He shook it off. Sometimes it was still hard to turn off the investigator in him. Which was utterly silly—this was Vivien. He was ready to marry her. He knew everything he needed to know about her. Didn't he?

He drove around the corner to find a parking spot, glancing over at her. She stared at her list.

The list.

She'd seemed more rattled than he'd expected as the wedding day approached, and no, that wasn't just since the storm. She'd been a little exacting over the past couple months.

And there he went again, thinking like a detective instead of a husband. Well, fiancé.

But everyone said jitters were normal for a bride.

He held open the door of Java Cup, allowing a customer to exit before Vivien entered ahead of him.

A four-foot plushy reindeer greeted guests. The shop's owner, Kathy, was humming "O Holy Night" behind the counter, and the tables were crowded with patrons. Four Dickens carolers were assembling along the far wall.

Not even a snowstorm would keep the inhabitants of the north woods home for long.

When they made it to the front of the line, Kathy paused, her blonde hair pulled back with her signature moose-ear headband. "Well, if it isn't the happy couple." She hummed a few more notes of the carol. "Do you want pumpkin spice? Maybe an eggnog latte?" She nodded toward the Dickens carolers. "They're about to start."

"I think you'd better give us a couple hot peppermint mochas."

Vivien placed both hands on the countertop and leaned in. "Please."

"That bad, huh?" Kathy poured milk and started the steamer. "I'm trying to feel sorry for you, Vivie, but you're all set to marry a handsome man who's head over heels about you." She winked at Boone.

"She has a point," Boone said, giving Vivien a tentative nudge with his shoulder.

The Dickens carolers started singing "God Rest Ye Merry, Gentlemen."

Oh, not even a four-part harmony seemed to settle Vivien's nerves. He studied her, expecting a response to the music. Maybe hoping. She had nary a toe-tap nor a head-bob to spare.

Instead, she looked at Kathy. "This storm has set all our wedding plans into a tailspin. The flowers, the food—I don't even know if the wedding guests are going to make it. And then—I just almost died sledding on the hill."

"Well, I'm sure everything will come together one way or another, and you don't look too worse for the wear. Good thing you've got your own rescuer on hand." Kathy tamped the grounds into the filter basket. "There have been some pretty bad injuries on that hill over the years. In fact—"

Boone sliced his fingertips across his throat in the universal "cut" sign and shook his head. Vivien didn't need any encouragement to add to the saga.

Vivien stood upright and faced Boone. "I saw that." She met his look, a challenge lighting her deep blue eyes.

Man, she was pretty. Not just *pretty* pretty, either. She had the kind of beauty that glowed from the inside out. And in three days, she'd be his wife.

He didn't even know how the outcast who'd always been trying to prove himself was about to marry the most incredible woman he could have ever imagined.

Boone placed his hands on her shoulders and held her gaze. "I'm teasing. Are you okay?"

Her shoulders slumped beneath his fingers. "It's true—I could have broken a bone. Crutches—at my very own wedding. It would've been ruined."

Kathy poured the espresso into the cups and went to work finishing their drinks.

"But you didn't." Boone released his hold and enveloped her in his arms. Felt her soften against him. Let the smells of ground beans and fresh pastries mingle with the jasmine in her hair. "You're okay. Everything's going to come together."

"We need to stick to the list." She tilted her head as she looked up at him, those blue eyes setting him ablaze.

The list. "Okay."

"Here you are." Kathy handed off their drinks, and Boone followed Vivie to a table.

She plopped onto a chair and flattened her list out on the pine table. "I just want to pick up my dress. Get things settled. This snowstorm really threw me off."

They tugged out of their coats. Boone laughed at his ugly sweater. "I forgot about this." He hit the button to activate the lights.

She stared at his sweater, arms crossed. "Boone—"

"It's okay. We'll get your dress as soon as they open. That's super easy." He took a sip of the hot mocha. "And I'll bet then we can quickly tackle the rest of that list."

The door opened with a bell jingle, the cool air swirling in. Peter Dahlquist's big form filled the space, a sprinkle of snowflakes whitening his thick beard. He paused when he spotted them, then walked to their table.

"Hey, Peter," Vivien said.

"Hi, how's it going?" He shook Boone's hand.

They'd had quite a few opportunities to work together, since Peter was fire chief and his fiancée, Ronnie, was a paramedic who split her time between the city and the Crisis Response Team.

"Pretty good." Boone glanced to Vivien, hoped his answer was truthful.

"Wow. Nice sweater." He gave Boone a once-over, a hand covering his smirk.

Boone laughed. "Thanks. Just working our way through Vivie's list." He caught her eye, gave her a smile, hoping it told her the list was important to him because it was important to her. "How's the Living Nativity?"

Peter looked at Vivien. "Actually, I tried to call you earlier. I can't find a few of the costumes."

"My phone isn't working. You'll have to call or text Boone to reach me."

He ran a hand through his hair. "You don't happen to know where the shepherd and angel costumes would be, do you? Could they be at the playhouse?"

Vivien set down her drink. "No, they should be at the church in the storage room with the manger and other set pieces. That's where I put them."

Peter shook his head. "Yeah, for some reason I haven't found them. They might have been moved when the flooring was replaced last summer."

Vivien pressed her lips together. "I'm pretty sure I saw them when we put the Vacation Bible School stuff away."

"I'll look again." He put his hand on Boone's chair. "I'll let you two get back to your list. I'm going to grab a coffee and hustle back to the church. I think my sheep fell through, so I need to make a few calls."

"Your sheep?"

"For the Living Nativity."

"Sure. See you later." Boone lifted his cup.

Vivien waved. "You'd better get baa-ck then," she said, giving a surprisingly good sheep impression.

Peter pointed a finger at her. "Good one."

By the look on Vivien's face, she was proud of that quick quip. And this time, she smiled at Boone across the table.

"That was funny."

She held a straight face for a beat before giggling. "I couldn't resist."

He loved hearing her laugh.

She looked at her watch and then scanned her list. "I'll need to grab my mail while we're in town too."

"Is that on the list?"

She pointed to the well-worn piece of paper. "It is."

"Well then—" His phone buzzed, and he pulled it from his pocket. Read the text. "Great. Jack says the battery chargers aren't with the radios."

"And that can't wait?"

"If they weren't shipped, then I need to follow up before the vendor closes for the holiday. I'll have to check at the house. We need the radios—we can't be sending out the team without communication equipment."

"But do you have to do it right now?"

He couldn't miss the disappointment in her voice and, shoot, he didn't want to have to sidetrack to the house or HQ.

"I'll be gone next week. You know that Caribbean honeymoon we planned?" They should have just planned a destination wedding like Caleb had suggested—or better yet, eloped. Because all this wedding stuff was starting to suffocate him. "Shall we go?" He stood and pulled his coat back on. "We can run by my place and see if I missed a box."

She wrapped her hands around the tall cup and stared at it a moment before looking up at him. "You go ahead. I'll wait here."

"Sure?"

"Yeah. The dry cleaner isn't open yet. Go ahead." She waved him off, her voice quiet and resigned.

But even as he drove through town minutes later, Vivien's disappointment gnawed at him, and he couldn't help but think he'd gone right ahead and made the wrong decision.

CHAPTER 5

*V*ivien had nearly had enough of the merriment and mistletoe. Everyone else seemed wholly unaffected by the calamities at hand—a winter storm, stranded guests, and disrupted flower shipments. Not to mention a catastrophic sled crash that could have resulted in a concussion, cast, or crutches.

And, okay, she hadn't actually almost died while sledding, but still.

A wedding dress with crutches. Oh, that would probably go viral on her Instagram profile.

Everywhere she looked, faces were jolly and bright. And, well, certainly their Christmas would be white.

Kathy walked by, pausing to wipe down the vacated table next to Vivien.

"Where did your groom run off to?"

Good question.

Oh, she didn't want to be jealous of Boone's work. But home, being with family—those were pieces of the family she'd always hoped to have. The pieces she hadn't had as a child herself.

And he'd bailed on her. Yes, she'd told him to go. But deep down, she'd been hoping he'd see it through her eyes. Put her first.

She gave a smile she didn't feel. "He just had to go take care of something."

"Ah. Got it. Can I get you anything else while you wait?" Kathy finished wiping down the table and scooted the chair back in.

"No. I'm good. Thanks."

The carolers started in on another chorus. Everyone was sitting with someone.

Except her. The bride-to-be. No, she was not feeling comfort or joy.

Could she really give her whole heart, knowing this is who he was? Dashing off for this thing or that?

Don't ever give away your whole heart.

Because if there was one place she really wanted to be center stage, it was in his life. And it had been different while they were dating. Separate houses. Time apart.

Plenty of margin to buffer other commitments.

Like his emergency callouts.

Oh, boy. A little self-realization cut into her. Like her community theater events and the crazy amount of time the rehearsals and performances took.

She grabbed her coffee cup and stood from the table, wove her way out the door, and stood on the frozen sidewalk. Shoveled snow mounded along the curbside, and footsteps left wintry prints where passersby had trod.

Her hat slouched forward on her head, and she tilted it back, snugging it into place. The post office wasn't a long walk and, well, maybe the frosty air would cool her nerves.

Maybe.

Minutes later, she grabbed her mail from the post office box and tugged her glove off, the cold air stinging her bare skin. She shuffled through the bills, her fingers landing on a pamphlet for the coming Minneapolis theater season. *My Fair Lady. Carousel. Into the Woods.*

The audition dates were posted next to the summer and fall show listings.

And a little familiar itch rooted itself. She could almost feel the warmth of the makeup table lights. See her reflection in the mirror. Hear the applause when the curtain fell.

I'm glad New York didn't get to keep you. Emma's words bit at her soul.

She ran her hands across the glossy cast headshots for the spring show, already cast, and a sharp blade of what-could-have-been sliced through her tender emotions. The life she'd left behind.

Chasing dreams.

She ambled back toward Java Cup.

Ahead, a door opened on the sidewalk, and the smell of baking bread swallowed Vivien.

"I've been looking all over for you!" Ree stood in the doorway of Flashy Fox Bakery. "What are you doing?"

"Getting the mail?" She waved her stack of envelopes and flyers.

She stepped past the placard with daily specials on it and followed Ree inside. Her mouth watered at the rich blend of aromas filling the small space. The long glass case revealed breads and sweets.

"What's with the Scrooge-y face? We've got food and flowers for your wedding. And from the calls Courtney's made, it seems like most of the guests are still on track to make it."

"Well, that is good news, then. Thank you for helping Megan chase down these loose ends. And I do not have a Scrooge-y face. What is that even?" Vivien wrinkled her nose.

She surveyed the scene. A Christmas tree stood in the corner with shiny balls, colored lights, and popcorn garland. "White Christmas" played over the sound system, and decorative snowflakes hung in the fogged bakery windows.

Christmas cheer oozed from every corner of the place.

Yeah, maybe she was a little bit Scrooge-y.

Ree turned on her, looked her up and down. "So, did you pick up your dress? Where's Boone?"

She recounted her morning, finishing with Boone's dash out the door for something not nearly as important as her dress.

"Oh."

Vivien paused at one of the four tables in the dining area. "Right? I mean, it seems like the priorities are a wee bit out of order. I'm going to need my big foam finger '#1' from cheerleading."

"No. You don't." Ree walked up to the counter, made a purchase, and returned with an oversized cinnamon roll and two plates.

"Marriage takes compromise. You and Boone—you'll figure it out."

Ree teased apart the cinnamon roll, spreading the cream cheese frosting that had stuck to the fork back onto the split roll.

"I'm afraid." Vivien stared at the sweet treat Ree had put onto her plate. She let the quiet settle between them. Ree had known Vivien her whole life. Knew every sordid detail. Even the ones Vivien wanted to forget.

"Because of your dad?" Ree's eyes met hers, a knowing passing between them.

Vivien nodded. "It's…scary. I mean, up until now, it's been this great romance. Sure, we've had our moments of disagreement. Normal things. Letting those moments of growth root us stronger than before. But something started worrying me." She chewed a bite. "Maybe it was reading through my vows these past few months. Really letting them soak in. Asking myself if I really believe in 'till death do us part.'"

Ree set down her fork. "Do you?"

"I want to, but that's when I realize how afraid I am. Like, positively petrified. How I worry he'll disappear. Or maybe just choose his job over me."

"He isn't going to do that."

"Isn't he? I mean—I had this silly fantasy that when we got married, somehow, he'd work this regular shift and then come home to me. Me and maybe our…kids."

"He will. Most days."

"And that's the thing—what about the other days? What about when I'm pregnant and he gets a callout?"

"I'm sure you'll work that out with him when that day comes. He loves you—adores you. I can't imagine you having another man more utterly and completely devoted to you. It's in his DNA."

Except her mom once thought that of her dad too. And then he'd walked out on the marriage. On his family—traded them for a new one.

This was Boone, though, so maybe… Yes. Of course, yes.

Vivien plunged her fork into the gooey roll. "How do I get over being afraid?"

Ree finished chewing her bite. "You're going to have to decide if you're willing to give your whole heart. Because that's what it takes. You'll each have to give your all to the marriage and be humbled by the enormity of that."

Just thinking about it practically gave her hives. Because she finally might have what she'd always wanted, but the fear of losing it—the fear of it being a mirage like her parents' marriage—made it almost unbearable to embrace.

"What if I can't do that?"

"What if you can?"

She imagined Christmas morning. The tree surrounded by gifts. Her. Boone. Their children.

Their children.

Who deserved two parents who were all in.

Was she equipped to play the role of a lifetime?

"If and when God blesses you with children, He'll equip you to parent them too. Don't let fear tear you away from the wonderful plans God has for you."

Ree's words settled over her, awakening a truth she knew to her very marrow.

She loved him. All in, whole-heartedly loved him.

She checked her watch. "I need to call Boone. It's time to pick up my dress."

Yes. Everything was going to be just fine.

WEDNESDAY, 12:05 P.M.

Boone was pretty sure he was failing miserably at the groom-to-be role. The look on Vivien's face when he left had said as much. Between their sledding mishap and having to run to the house to look for radio batteries, something was not great in Vivieland.

Okay, battery chargers.

Which sounded as important as cleaning out the attic right about now.

When had life gotten so complicated?

He made his way through his house, down the hallway to the office where his laptop sat on the broad pine desk and the windows gave a glimpse of Lake Superior's gray expanse. Only a few boxes remained on the floor. He started checking through them, one by one, his mind only half on the task.

No chargers in the first box. Or the second.

He blew out a breath, the dissonance like clashing chords in his soul.

For the past year and a half of dating, things hadn't felt this restricted. Of course they did things together. A lot of things. But Vivien still had her life. He had his.

And all that was about to change.

A new weight he hadn't carried around as a bachelor. Nope. Life as a bachelor was simple.

He stood and looked out at the frothy lake, and the empty house closed in around him. He picked up the framed picture of them sitting on the shoreline last summer. It was a candid selfie after a day spent on the water.

He'd snapped it just as she'd looked at him, smiling, her eyes alight with a look of…adoration?

The thought swelled in his chest. She'd chosen him.

So, yeah. Simpler did not necessarily mean better.

Because he loved how Vivien's joy filled the spaces of his life. There was nothing he wanted more than to return home to her after a rescue. He wanted many days on the lakeshore, just like the photo.

And shoot. He'd be lying if he didn't admit he'd imagined a blue-eyed little girl with brown waves, wrapping her daddy around her finger. Or maybe a son.

Fishing. Campouts. Christmas caroling and birthday parties.

The third box held the chargers and extra batteries.

Great. Except, not great. He looked at his watch. He couldn't leave Vivien waiting.

He hoisted the box from the floor. A knock interrupted the silence, and he carried the box to the living room and set it on the side table.

He opened the door to face Jack Stewart, one of the team's flight nurses. "Hey. I was driving by. Figured you could use some help getting the chargers over to HQ. Looks like you already found them?" He gestured toward the box on the table.

"Thanks. Yeah, I did. I was just starting to wrap things up here."

"No worries. I still have to go through the final financial audit report files you left for me. Thought I'd take a break first." Jack stepped inside, and Boone closed the door behind him. "That's some good snow out there." Jack stomped his boots on the large floor mat.

"Tell me about it. All our wedding plans have been completely disrupted."

"You never struck me as the big-wedding type."

"Have you seen my fiancée? Everything about Vivien is big-wedding type." Even he could hear the haze in his voice. "And her type is my type," he finished, hoping he'd concealed a bit of his planning fatigue.

"You seem less than excited."

Okay, maybe he hadn't quite covered the wedding weariness. "She's stressed about all these plans, and a little of me is starting to feel…" Oh, he wasn't sure he wanted to go there.

"Like?" Jack narrowed his blue eyes.

"I don't know." Except he did. He knew exactly how he was starting to feel.

Jack stood there, watching. Waiting.

Fine. "Like the plans are more important than the marriage."

"I think many a groom has walked in those shiny shoes."

"Yeah. Probably." He ran a hand through his hair.

"You know, on the other side, the future awaits." Jack set his eyes on Boone, wisdom and knowing in them.

Yeah, Jack, a former convict, knew a few things about that. Boone could only imagine what it had felt like to finally get to walk free. To start over. To walk into a new future.

And that's what he and Vivien were doing. Starting fresh as husband and wife. And yeah, there were bound to be some growing pains.

For the first time since the storm had hit, he felt like the sun was truly starting to shine.

CHAPTER 6

*U*nder different circumstances, Vivien might just like the snow. And, to be sure, she should really appreciate the fact that the storm had broken and her wedding was still more go than no-go.

But she was getting tired and impatient—she just really needed to grab her dress and get back to Wilder House. Tackle the rest of her list. Cross every last item off.

She should have spoken up when Boone had to run home to look for—what was it? Batteries?

She'd borrowed Ree's phone to tell him where she was, and when he finally pulled up in front of the bakery, she said goodbye to Ree and climbed into the truck.

She settled into the truck seat and crossed her arms.

"Sorry, it took longer than expected." He reached over and let his fingers brush across hers, then left them there. Waited.

She let the warmth soak into her. Melt a bit of the freeze she'd been feeling. She took a breath. Let her hand weave into his.

Yeah, they could do this.

She squeezed his hand. "We'll need to hustle at this point. I still have seven items on this list to tackle before dinner tonight."

He drove straight to the dry cleaner's, and Vivien didn't even wait for him. As soon as he put the truck into park, she was out the door.

Grab and go.

She pushed through the entrance and waited while Alecia Miller helped another customer, who paid for a stack of dry-cleaned suits, scooped them up, and headed out the door.

Alecia bent over, pen in hand, making careful notes on a pickup tag before taking several dropped-off dress shirts and moving them to a new rack.

Vivien stepped up to the counter, and Boone stepped into the spot just behind her.

"Hi there." Vivien smiled.

Alecia turned from the rack and adjusted her messy auburn bun. "Good afternoon, Vivien. How can I help you?"

"Good afternoon. I stopped by Kate's Alterations earlier today, and she said she'd sent my wedding dress over for steaming."

"Sure." Alecia stepped back and activated the button on the garment conveyor. Paused. Sorted through several shirts with plastic over them. "Did she leave it under her name or yours?"

"I'm not sure."

"Let me check under yours."

Vivien tried not to tap her foot. Tried not to hop up and down. Anticipation hummed through her veins at an impossible volume. "You can't peek," she said to Boone, reaching back to give his hand a squeeze.

"If you say so."

She turned around, still holding his hand. "I do." She planted a quick kiss on his lips. "Thanks for coming with me. I know it's been a crazy morning." In all the busyness and stress of their day, she'd let the joy in those moments slip away from them.

"I don't mind. We'll get your dress stowed at Wilder House and see what's left on that list of yours." He looked over her shoulder. "Is that mani-pedi for me? Maybe a spray tan for St. Thomas?"

Now he was goading her. "Very funny." She gave him a once-over. "Though, you are looking a little winter-white."

His smile faded. "I am not getting a spray tan."

"Says the man in the Christmas sweater." Vivien giggled and turned back to Alecia, who activated the garment conveyor again. Stopped it.

Vivien blew out a breath. "Okay, look away," she instructed Boone. She pointed toward the door, and he complied with a low laugh.

This time Alecia lifted a large dress bag from the rack and hung it on the hook at the end of the counter. "Here you go." She pulled the tag. "No charge for you—Kate prepaid for this."

Vivien stared at the dress through the clear plastic bag. "I'm sorry — You grabbed the wrong one. This isn't my dress." She looked at the tag Alecia had set on the counter.

VIVIEN CALHOUN PREPAID

A tremble started in her gut, a sinking, spinning sensation. She rubbed her palms against her coat pockets.

Boone turned around and looked at the dress, his jaw a little slack. "Oh." It came out somewhere between a gasp of horror and grunt of disbelief.

Exactly. Even *he* could see this was not the right dress. A circa-1980s high-neck nightmare, complete with poufy sleeves and a beaded heart cutout.

Alecia looked at the tag and checked her conveyor again. "I don't understand. This is the dress tagged for you."

"I don't know how or why this tag"—Vivien waved the paper card —"got put on that dress." She pointed at the gown. "But *that* isn't my dress." She drew her hands up and down at the fashion-don't on the counter hook. "I mean, look at it." She lifted the gauzy plastic that had come untied. It even had a *bow.* "This"—she pointed a shaky finger—"is not my dress."

Seriously—a vintage gown was one thing. But that? No. Not her dress.

Boone raised his hands, as if to mediate. "I'm sure this…lovely dress means a great deal to someone, but perhaps you could locate Vivie's actual dress?"

"I see." Alecia gaped at the dress, and her brows drew into a deep line. "Yeah. That doesn't look like it would be the right dress."

"It isn't."

Alecia tucked the gown back into the plastic bag and tied off the end. Set it aside.

"I'm sure it's here, Viv." Boone's hand settled around her waist.

She tried to cling to Boone's voice of reason. It had to be here. Right?

Alecia blinked. Looked at the tag. The dress. The tag. Hit the button on the conveyor. The low buzz of the rotating garment rack filled the space.

She grabbed the next dress she came to and read the tag. "What does it look like?" This time, she held a fabric dress bag. She pulled it from the garment conveyer and hung it from the counter hook.

"An appliqué lace overlay with tulle. A V-neck and V-back." So much for surprising Boone.

"Not this?" She opened the dress bag to reveal a soft pink taffeta.

"No." Vivien grabbed her phone to show a picture. Except not even a defibrillator could save the device now. She shoved it back into her pocket. "White. Tulle. Lace. A chapel train. Elegant." She took another breath. "From this decade." The dress she'd painstakingly designed and had made in Minneapolis—which cost a small fortune. That she'd designed as exactly the right dress.

Alecia pulled the dress bag from the counter hook, returned it to the conveyer, and moved to the next one.

Nope. Not that one. "No."

Vivien shook her head, dress after dress after dress.

The drone of the conveyer stopped. Alecia stepped away from the garment conveyer's button. Raised her hands. Dropped them. "That's all of them," she said.

Vivien blinked. "That's not possible," she whispered.

"Should we call Kate?" Boone offered. "It must be there."

"Of course." Alecia snatched up the landline and ran her finger down the list of phone numbers next to the base before dialing.

Acid pooled in Vivien's stomach, her body electrified. Kate would tell her it was actually at her shop, and then she could find it, grab her dress, and go.

"Hi, Kate. I have Vivien Calhoun here, and she's looking for her wedding dress she thought you sent over?"

A pause.

"Yeah, I have a tag on a bag, but no, it's not her dress." She pulled the tag, looked at the hideous dress again. "No, there's no doubt. It's not right… Yeah, already did that… I see. Got it—no, that's okay… I'll let her know. Thank you."

She hung up and wiped her hands on her shirt hem. "We've been through all the dresses. I'm really sorry—Kate suggested you come back by her shop. She's going to look again. We're both really confused about where it could be."

Vivien slumped against Boone. No. No. No.

WEDNESDAY, 1:15 P.M.

Vivien was coming unraveled right before his eyes, and he had no idea how to stop it. Okay, yes, the dress was weird and gaudy, but what did he care?

They were getting married in three days. It didn't matter what the dress looked like, what the cake tasted like, or what food was or wasn't in the buffet. He'd even wear his ugly sweater if need be.

Still, Vivien was wound tight, and she was looking at him like he was the guy to fix this.

"How about we take Kate's suggestion and head over there. Let her straighten all this out. I'm sure your dress is over there."

Alecia nodded. "These are the only wedding dresses and formals I can find in the shop." She chewed on a fingernail. "I have a newer employee who's covered a few shifts this week on his own due to the storm. Let me give him a call. Maybe he remembers it coming in or knows where it could be." She picked up the phone. Dialed.

Waited.

She looked up and shook her head. "This is Alecia. I'm down at the shop and have a question. Give me a call back." She hung up and turned back to Vivien. "Voicemail. I'm sorry. If I hear anything, I'll let you know."

Boone grabbed a piece of paper and jotted down his number. "Call this one. Vivie's phone is dead."

"Sure."

"Thanks." He turned to Vivien. "Should we head back to Kate's?"

She backed away, her hands strangling the gloves she held. "You think she has it?"

"I think it's our best bet—it isn't here."

Vivien didn't move.

He'd found lost hikers and cross-country skiers. He could find a wedding dress. *Please, Lord.*

"Vivie?"

She blinked. Swallowed. "Okay. Let's go."

"I'm really sorry," Alecia said again. "I'll let you know when...if..." She didn't finish.

If. The big *if*. Because they all knew if it wasn't at Kate's, it wasn't anywhere. They'd already looked through all the dresses hanging from the garment conveyor, and while they'd found the good, the bad, and the extremely ugly, they hadn't found the tulle-and-lace chapel-something-or-other Vivien was looking for.

Vivien wiped tears from her cheeks. Nodded. Let Boone take her hand and lead her back onto the sidewalk.

A few snowflakes landed on the seat when Boone opened the door. He swiped them off and she climbed up.

He leaned close, drew his fingers down her jawline. "You okay?"

Her shoulders heaved with a big breath, big exhale. "I'll feel better when Kate hands my dress to me."

Yeah. Him too. "Well, then, let's go get it."

A short drive later, the grim look on Kate's face said everything they needed to know. She hadn't found it either.

How could he possibly fix this? "What about a trip to Duluth? The highway is plowed."

Vivien shook her head, and if he knew Vivien, she wasn't ready to give up on this one-of-a-kind dress just yet. No matter that finding it was as unlikely as finding a daffodil blooming outside Kate's shop.

"I have some dresses here, Vivie. Why don't you take a look at them? There are probably about twelve different dresses for you to look at that are right around your size. Some are new that I've added beading to. Some are consignment."

Vivien nodded. "Sure, I'd be happy to go through them."

Boone thought she sounded surprisingly agreeable, but grit wound her jaw tight, the muscles flexing.

Oh boy. Boone knew exactly what Vivien was doing the minute she walked over to the racks. She had exactly zero intention of trying one on. She was flipping through the racks like a crazed Black Friday shopper.

"Vivien?"

"It's got to be here." Oh, the quake in her otherwise-determined voice shredded a piece of his heart. It was like their very wedding—maybe even their marriage—hinged on the dress. The details. And he didn't know how to fix it.

"I don't think it's here." He tried to use his calming voice. The one he used on rescues when things looked pretty grim. "Kate would have found it."

"It has to be here, Boone. Dresses don't just disappear. It wasn't at the cleaner. It's got to be here."

For ten more minutes she went through the racks dress by dress, only to go through them again. And again. Like a math problem she hoped to get a different answer for.

She collapsed into the overstuffed chair, her head in her hands.

"Oh, Vivie. Just try on another dress."

"I don't want another dress."

"It's just a dress."

"It's *not* just a dress." Her blue eyes flashed, something of fear and need in them. She flung her arms wide, her voice rising. "I don't know how to explain it to you. I know it sounds silly, but that dress is *the* dress." She dropped her hands to her sides. "It's the dress that felt exactly right for our special day."

Boone's phone buzzed.

He silenced the call. "Please? Can you try another dress?"

His phone buzzed again. Great. He glanced at the caller ID. "It's Jack—I'm sorry, I have to take this."

Vivien didn't move from the chair.

"Hello?"

A beat. "Me again. I hate to bug you."

"I feel like there's a 'but' coming up." Boone met Vivien's gaze. Admittedly, something about it sent a shiver through him.

Oh boy.

"Yeah. I tried to open the drive you gave me, and I can't access the financial reports for the audit. I've tried everything."

Boone groaned. Glanced away from Vivien.

"All right. Give me a few." He couldn't find a dress, but at least he could make sure the CRT passed the financial audit so they didn't lose any federal funds. And that their honeymoon wouldn't be interrupted.

"Sure," Jack answered.

Boone ended the call. "I'm sorry—I have to run by HQ again. Jack can't get my file with all the year-end reports to open."

"Like, right now?" She stood, her hands on her hips.

"It won't take long. Our reports are due back to the auditors, and Jack's working on finalizing it for me." He placed his hands on Vivien's shoulders and gave them a little squeeze. "It won't take long." He lifted a hand toward the dress racks. "Would you please try on these dresses? I can have Ree come meet you here."

"You really aren't staying?" A deep line creased her brow, her jaw tight.

He gave her a half smile. Tried to lighten the mood. "You didn't want me to see the dress."

She stepped away, pacing the carpet. "That was before it went missing."

"This won't take long." He snagged her hand and drew her to him. Pressed a kiss to her cheek. "I'll be back."

Leaving her left an ache in his chest.

They'd be getting married with or without the dress, but heading out on his honeymoon with the required audit response pending? That was a different story altogether. He couldn't risk losing federal funds or the legal ramifications. Not when it jeopardized the team and threatened to cut their honeymoon short.

He couldn't find the dress. But he could make sure their honeymoon didn't fall apart.

She'd see. Everything would work out.

He just had to keep saying it…

CHAPTER 7

Vivien looked around Kate's shop, unsettled, wishing Boone hadn't left her.

...alone on our bathroom floor, in dire agony...

It was already happening.

"Do you want me to call a couple shops in Duluth?" A thread of desperation wove through Kate's words.

"No." Vivien slumped back into the chair.

"Minneapolis?" Kate pressed again. She kneeled on the floor in front of Vivien. "I feel responsible for this, Vivie. Please, let me make it right."

Vivien swiped tears from her eyes. "I just don't understand where it is."

Kate shook her head. "Me neither. I was certain I dropped it off. Completely certain." She stood and began shuffling dresses along the rack as if she, too, thought it might materialize before them. "I know I've been busy, but I thought I was keeping a handle on everything."

Vivien tugged her list from her pocket and unfolded it. The crease lines had deepened, and the edges were growing worn.

Number one: pick up dress.

The door flung open. "Vivien!" Ree swept in. "Boone told me what happened. Have you found it?"

"No."

"We were getting a little worried about you."

"What am I going to do?"

"We'll find you a different dress." Ree walked over to the rack of gowns and began looking at each one. "These are stunning."

Which was true. They were stunning.

They just weren't *her* dress.

"Well, it seems you're not the only one with missing apparel," Ree said. "Peter's been trying to reach you. I think he might have left a message for you on Boone's voicemail."

"What's wrong?"

"He still can't find the shepherd or angel costumes. He called Ingrid Christiansen in Florida, and she said there might be a couple in the basement of Gustav Hagborg's old antique shop. Peter has the key, but he's short on time. He was hoping you could meet him there to help."

This was what happened when she had her hands in all the different costume events in town. Everyone expected her to know where things were.

Vivien wrapped her arms around herself. "Peter will just have to look for them himself."

"Because you're trying on dresses?" Ree gave her a pointed look. Turned to Kate. "Which ones has she already tried on?"

Kate stood, silent, not giving up Vivien's resistance to Ree.

"I knew it!" Ree turned on Vivien. "You haven't even tried a single one on."

"I can't." Vivien pointed to the rack. "I just can't bring myself to..." No, she couldn't. She couldn't admit her dress was actually gone. That item one of her carefully curated to-do list for her perfect wedding would be scribbled out and substituted with *find new dress*.

Ree enveloped Vivien in a hug and gave her a squeeze. "I'm so sorry your dress has gone missing." She released her and shook off her coat, rubbed her hands together. "But we have work to do. We are going to find you a different perfect dress. Because you're still getting married. You still need a dress."

Vivien closed her eyes, took a deep breath, and looked at Ree. "Sure."

Ree clapped her hands, as if she could infuse excitement into the dispirited air. "All right, Kate, show me what you've got."

Kate shifted a few hangers across the rack. "This is one of my favorites. Classic ball gown style with a corset top and beading."

Ree turned to Vivien. "Try it on!"

Vivien's feet rooted her in place.

"Oh, come on. You can do this."

Ree sounded like she was trying to convince one of the preschoolers to go onstage at Vacation Bible School to sing "This Little Light of Mine."

And just like that preschooler, Vivien kind of wanted to sit down on the floor and cry until someone came and made it all better.

But she wasn't a preschooler. She was a woman. A woman who was getting married in three days. And she would dig deep—pretend if she needed to. That was the only way to make this all better.

"Vivie?" Ree stood, holding up the dress. By all accounts, it was beautiful.

She nodded toward the dressing area Kate had screened off from the rest of her shop, and both ladies jumped up to help her try on the dress. Probably before she changed her mind.

"I really think you'll like this one," Kate offered on their way into the dressing room.

And she did like it. She didn't love it. But she did like it. Which was pretty much how she felt about every other dress from the rack that she tried on after it too.

She'd narrowed it down to the first and fourth dresses, the latter more of an A-line with a crystal-encrusted bodice.

"You don't have to choose today," Kate said. "I'll hold both of them for you—honestly, I don't have people knocking down my door right now with the sudden need to buy a gown." She smiled. "That will be next week, when all the women who are surprised with a Christmas ring get the wedding bug."

Vivien nodded. "Thanks."

Kate unlocked the rack's wheels and tugged it toward the back room.

"You okay?" Ree asked.

"I don't know. This is a big deal. We had all these plans for it."

"I know. But we've been making calls with Megan today. Things are shaping up…well."

"That was super convincing."

"Well, I mean, there are a few loose ends we're still chasing down."

Vivien let out a moan. "I probably don't want to know." She rubbed her hands together. "I just wish I felt like Boone was focused on it too."

Ree reached out, threaded her hand into Vivien's. "Would having Boone here right now change anything?"

Vivien lifted her shoulder. "Maybe."

Ree gave her that look. The one that said she was possibly being ridiculous. Potentially overreacting.

"Really?" Ree's brows rose and she squeezed Vivien's hand. "He'll be back." She lifted her arm and forced Vivien into a twirl. "This is good practice for the future. Balance. Sacrifice. Compromise."

Vivien just hoped it wasn't practice for a broken heart.

WEDNESDAY, 1:45 P.M.

If Boone could put out an APB on the wedding dress, he would. He'd enlist the help of every department he had connections with if it would do any good.

Unfortunately, neither he nor his peers were in the dress-locating business.

And that made him feel about as helpful as a rock.

He walked down the headquarters' hallway to the open door of his office. Jack sat hunched over the computer, his eyes on the screen.

"Any luck?"

"No, are you sure this is the drive?" He held up the thumb drive Boone had given him.

"Yeah, that's the one."

"I think it's corrupted." He pushed the drive into the port again.

"There's no way."

Jack moaned. "Oh, look at this." He turned the monitor. "This is a new message."

DRIVE IS NOT ACCESSIBLE. THE FILE OR DIRECTORY IS CORRUPTED AND UNREADABLE.

"Great. Can you fix it?" Boone shrugged out of his coat.

"Not really a tech guy." Jack scrubbed his hands over his face. "I already tried closing it and re-opening it."

"Well, let's start googling." He pulled out his phone and typed in a search. "I have two tickets to St. Thomas that require these reports to be filed."

"If you can't use those tickets, I could probably..." Jack looked up at Boone with a mischievous smirk.

"Right. Not happening," Boone answered and looked back to his phone, scrolling through the search results. "You said you already tried a reboot?"

"Not a system reboot. One sec." Jack clicked on the mouse. "How's the dress thing going?"

"Well, I left Vivien with a rack of dresses and a frown over at Kate's shop."

"Oh, I'm sorry. I had terrible timing, huh? You should have said something—"

"It would be worse if I had to cut our honeymoon short—or miss it altogether. No, let's figure this out, because Vivien and I are getting married, with or without that dress."

Jack nodded and waited for the computer to come back online.

Boone checked the web page on his phone again. "Okay, open the file directory."

Jack pushed the chair back. "I can get out of your way and let you do this. Might be easier."

Boone took the chair, opened the directory, and ran a file check. Clicked to attempt to repair the corrupted files.

No luck.

Jack grabbed his coffee cup from the desk, took a drink. "I hope Vivien can find a backup dress."

Boone tried to open one of the spreadsheets as a Word document.

Nope.

"I hope so too." Boone paused. Clicked. "But that's a good idea. Let's see if we have a good backup file." He removed the thumb drive and opened his file directory again. "If everything was working correctly, I should have a backup copy of these reports on the cloud."

Please. Because something had to go right today.

"Outstanding." Jack leaned forward to watch the monitor.

He clicked on his H drive and scrolled through. Found the backup folder. Clicked.

Bingo.

"Now, if you can just get those spreadsheets to open without another error..." Hope punctuated Jack's words.

And yeah, Boone said a little prayer before he clicked open the file.

The window opened with each of the backup files listed.

"See if one will open," Jack prompted.

Boone opened the first file. "It's good." Tried the second, third, and fourth.

"I'll make copies of these files and use those."

"Good call." Boone stood. "If there's anything else you need, let me know."

Jack put a hand on his shoulder. "You've got your hands full. I'll wrap up the audit response, and I'll cc you when I submit it."

"Thanks. I owe you one. I was getting a little desperate."

"Nope. I'm happy to help. I'll see you later."

All the way to his truck, Boone just hoped Vivien had found a dress. He backed out of his parking spot and drove around the berm of snow. When his phone rang through the truck's Bluetooth, he rolled to a stop in the lot.

Peter.

He answered the call, adjusted the settings on the defrost. "What's up, Peter?"

"Is Vivien with you?"

"No, on my way to her now."

"Would you see if she can meet me at the antique store later? I still haven't found the costumes, and I'm hoping she can help. I'm getting kind of desperate."

Oh, who wasn't today? "Sure. I'll let her know. But she's got a lot going on. Not sure she can make it."

"I get it. I hate to even ask. Just text me if she can meet me over there."

"Will do." He disconnected and turned the truck onto First Avenue, hoping to salvage some part of the day. Hoping even more that Vivien had found a dress she liked.

Before he'd made it past the next stop sign, his phone rang again. What now?

Unknown number.

He considered ignoring it. Except Vivien might have borrowed a phone.

"Hello?"

"It's Alecia—at the dry cleaner. I've got the dress."

And with those four words, Boone smiled.

Yes. Today, he would be Vivien's hero.

CHAPTER 8

*N*othing against Kate, but if Vivien had to spend one more minute in the shop, she just might break. And yeah, the fact that Boone had left her there while he gallivanted off to deal with a crisis at the Crisis Response Team didn't make her feel all warm and fuzzy inside.

Shouldn't the team be able to help themselves?

She took a breath, the words of the hymn still weaving through her mind.

What though my joys and comforts die?

The Lord my Savior liveth...

She shouldn't have sent Ree away, but she just couldn't stand to see the pity in her best friend's eyes. Not when there was nothing anyone could do for her besides try to scrape together the rest of their wedding plans. But she had passed off half her to-do list to Ree, at her insistence.

The jangle of keys caught Vivien's attention. Kate stood with her coat on, purse over her shoulder. "I need to run to pick up my mom for an appointment. She's not feeling well. Can I give you a ride? Or is Boone coming back?"

Vivien looked at her, no answer on her lips. She managed to shake her head before adding, "He said he'd be back."

Kate gave her a hug. "Hey, it's okay. You can wait here. Just lock the door when you go."

"Sure."

The lingering feel of Kate's hug didn't lift Vivien's spirits nearly as much as the sight of Boone walking through the door a couple minutes later.

And he was carrying a box. A gigantic dress box.

And he had a big, silly, super-excited grin plastered across his face.

"Alecia called. She found your dress. Something to do with the new guy misplacing it."

She processed his words. "Found…my dress?"

He stomped the snow off his boots and walked to the large table, set down the box, and lifted the lid.

Embroidered lace. Overlay with tulle. V-neck. Sleeveless. Yes. Yes! Her dress.

"It's my dress!" Vivien covered her mouth with her hands and jumped up and down. "Thank you!" She threw her arms around Boone.

His soft laughter vibrated against the crook of her neck. "Of course."

She lifted the dress from the box, holding the yards bundled in her arms. "It's going to be totally wrinkled." Not that she cared. She had her dress. And that left her positively giddy.

"Do I need to look away?"

"No way. Not after all this. You'll understand all the fuss once you see it." She laughed and hung the dress from one of Kate's racks, then set about unfolding the length of it. "I'm going to have to buy my own steamer, though. I don't want to let it out of my sight again."

She shook out the folds of fabric and smoothed the bodice and skirt.

Oh no. No. No. *No...*

A brown stain darkened the front of the dress, near the hips. Mud? Coffee?

"Oh, honey." Boone's fingers wrapped around her shoulder. "I'm sure we can get that out." But it seemed even he couldn't keep the doubt out of his tone.

"It's ruined."

"It's not—"

"It is!" She'd worked with enough costume fabrics to know. The stain wasn't going to come out.

She shoved the dress back into the bag, hot tears flooding down her face. Everything was wrong. The moment she'd dreamed of yet never thought would ever come.

She drew in a breath. "What if we wait?"

"Wait for what?"

"I can have another dress sewn. The same dress. *My* dress."

"This took *four months* to finish." Boone's jaw had gone slack. "You want to wait four months?" He probably didn't realize he was nearly shouting.

She reached for him. "I just need the dress. I need everything else to work out. I need it to be the perfect wedding we planned."

"Why?"

"Because if it doesn't—" And okay, maybe she sounded like she'd lost her mind. Maybe she had. "I don't want to be lying on our bathroom floor giving birth, scared and alone while you're off saving someone else."

He stepped back, a heavy crease between his brows. "What are you talking about?" He pressed a palm against his chest, his face suddenly pale. "Vivie—you can't be—we haven't—"

She gasped. "No, of course not! I mean in the future." She threw her hands in the air. "I just...need you to choose me."

Again, he gaped, clearly still flummoxed. "I did choose you. I am choosing you—I'm *marrying* you."

She wasn't doing a very good job of explaining herself. "But work —the Crisis Response Team."

"What about it?"

"Maybe I'm afraid it's more important—that it will take priority over me. Us."

"I really don't understand what you're talking about."

"I want to be number one in your life. I don't want to come after anything else."

"God?"

"Okay, fine—God can be first." She palmed her forehead. "That didn't come out right. But I mean, after God. I need to know that I come first."

His shoulders sagged. "Vivien, I'm the same man you started dating a year and a half ago. Back then, I had my job as a detective. Then I moved here—took the CRT coordinator job. You've always known that sometimes that means I have to drop everything and go."

"I know, but I guess I just figured once we were married that we'd…that you'd…stay."

He threw out his arms. "Vivien, if people are in trouble and it's my team's job to save them, then that's what we do. That's what I signed up for."

"But what about me? What about anniversaries? What about birthday parties?"

"I hope to be at every single one."

"But you can't guarantee it."

"How could I? And why have you never brought this up before?"

"Because I thought it would be different once we got married, and I'm starting to realize that it won't be."

"Vivien, I can't walk away from it."

"I'm not asking you to—but can't you say no sometimes? I thought you were all-in on this. On *us*."

But the look on his face said his answer far louder than any words could. He shook his head ever so slightly, as if he couldn't even process her words. Like she'd asked him to let someone die. "What are you saying? Say no when someone needs me? Just walk away?"

"No—of course not."

"Then what, Vivie? I thought we were talking about a dress, and now, somehow, we're talking about the team and my commitments."

"I don't know—The storm. The dress. Maybe this is a bad idea. Or...maybe it's God's way of telling us to wait until the timing is right."

WEDNESDAY, 2:40 P.M.

Maybe it's God's way of telling us to wait...

The words gutted Boone.

He held up his hands. "Wait? For what? For some dress? For everything in the world to be perfect so the team is never activated? Maybe"—he shook his head, the words almost unbearable—"we shouldn't get married."

She stilled. "We'll still get married." She blinked. "What are you saying?"

"You keep talking about the dress. My duties. Maybe I can't live up to what you want, Vivie."

"That isn't true. You know that isn't true."

Oh, his heart wanted to believe that, but how could he marry Vivien knowing he couldn't live up to her expectations? Knowing that the first time duty called him away from a special event, it might unravel the tender fabric of trust in their relationship.

"It sure seems true." He stared at her, willing her to contradict him.

No. Instead, her eyes filled with fresh tears, and she picked up the soiled dress.

He couldn't stand here and watch his life unravel. "I need to go help Peter. He's expecting me. I'll make sure you have a ride."

She said nothing, even then.

So he walked away. Couldn't look back.

Just got into his truck and drove straight to the antique store, numb. He punched out a text to Vivien's mom and chucked his phone into the back seat. No more messages. No more calls.

He needed to clear his brain.

Peter's truck pulled up behind him, and he met Peter on the sidewalk.

"Sorry to pass this off on you. I know you're crazy busy."

"No. It's fine." Except nothing was fine. He hadn't imagined any part of this Christmas that didn't include getting married to Vivien.

In truth, he was still trying to sort out what had just happened.

Peter unlocked the front door, stepped inside. "Man, this place is dusty. I'd love to see it opened up again."

Boone closed the door behind them and followed him through the shop.

"Is Vivien coming? She's the one I figured would know where to look and what to look for." Peter pulled open the door to the basement.

"No. Just me. I'll figure it out." This mystery, at least, he could solve. How hard could it be to find a few shepherd and angel robes?

Peter studied him a beat. Nodded. "Follow me—just watch that stairwell door. It likes to lock on you."

He bent down and used an antique iron to hold the door in place, then flipped the light switch on the opposite wall. It illuminated a single bulb hung in the stairwell and a dull yellow glow from below. Peter proceeded down the steps.

"Okay, it should all be in one of these." He gestured toward an inordinate stack of boxes. "Or one of these." He waved his arm in the opposite direction toward several more boxes. "I've been trying to reorganize them. I apologize they aren't in better order. We'd moved a bunch of stuff over here before Gustav passed away, and it all got put on the back burner after that." He pointed to the two lightbulbs protruding from the low ceiling. "And that's the best light you've got too. Do you need me to scrounge up a flashlight?"

"No, it's fine." Because he really just needed something to keep his mind busy.

"Everything okay? Vivien didn't sign you up for Christmas karaoke, did she?" Peter laughed.

Boone shook his head. "It's fine."

Peter stopped. "Okay, that's the third time you've said that. Everyone knows 'it's fine' is code for 'I'm going to pretend it's okay because I don't want to talk about it.' Spill it."

Boone sized up Peter—Vivien's cousin by marriage—and, well, he'd hear about it sooner or later. "I don't know that we're getting married in three days. Or, well, ever."

Peter choked out a cough. "Excuse me?"

Boone rubbed his temples. "The storm has made a mess of things, and Viv was stressed about that. She kept saying how everything had to be perfect. She has a list. And then her dress was gone—her wedding dress. Then I found it. Except it has a stain on it. And honestly, I don't see what the big deal is. But she went off about us waiting because of the storm and the dress. Then the CRT. I guess I just don't know that she really wants to marry me."

A nod from Peter.

"And she said it had to be perfect because…I don't know. She said something about being in labor—someday in the future, of course— and being in the bathtub or on the floor or something. It didn't make any sense. But being alone and me being with the team."

"Oh."

"What do you mean, 'oh'? You said that like you understood what all that nonsense meant."

"I kind of do. I mean, not exactly about the whole bathtub-floor thing. I got lost there a bit, but this is Vivie we're talking about." He rubbed his hand over his beard. "That sounds like maybe she feels like she's competing with the team for your attention."

"But I love *her*. I'm marrying *her*. The team is my job."

"Yeah, but that's probably where her whole tub-floor-whatever thing comes in. Ronnie and I deal with that too, but since we're both in service positions, we get it. It still hurts sometimes, though, to know that duty supersedes other priorities. Even a spouse or significant other sometimes."

"But we've been dating all this time. This isn't new."

"You know how her dad bailed on them. Wasn't there for those milestones and holidays in her life. And she always felt like she was competing with her half sister for his attention." Peter grimaced. "And her half sister always won out."

"This isn't like that."

"Not to you, but ask her. My guess is she has the expectation that you'll be there for all those things."

"But I'm not going to leave her or pick the team over her."

"In her mind, it's all the same and it's all related. Vivien's been planning this wedding pretty much since she was a tween with acne."

"I highly doubt Vivien ever had acne."

Peter laughed. "Okay. Well, she probably believes the perfect bride becomes the perfect wife. And in the perfect marriage, she's always the priority."

"Of course she's my priority."

"Are you really hearing me though? Her dad walked out on them—had a whole different family, another *daughter*. Vivien wants to feel emotionally safe. And she's going to cling to any sense of control she has because that's her lifeline. That's what's going to tell her you won't stray. You won't leave."

"But I won't. And she'll still be my priority, even when I can't be home."

Peter nodded. "You know that here"—he pointed to his temple—"but she doesn't feel it here." He patted his chest.

"So, what, I'm supposed to leave the team?"

"I don't know what you need to do. But I think you need to talk to her." Peter's phone buzzed and he snagged it off a nearby box. "Oh boy. I'm sorry, but I have to go see about a donkey." He gestured toward the boxes. "I can send someone else to look for the costumes."

Boone waved him off. "No, it's fi—" He caught himself. "It's all right. I got this."

Peter nodded. "Just lock up when you leave."

"Sure."

He patted Boone's shoulder. "It's going to be okay."

Except...it wouldn't be okay.

Vivien's dress was ruined. She'd told him she couldn't marry him without that stupid dress.

And then, somehow, everything had gone sideways.

He grabbed the top box off one of the dusty stacks and eased the lid off. Peter's words hung in the damp air. And he felt like maybe Peter had left the donkey right there in the basement.

CHAPTER 9

The pulse in Vivien's ears blasted like ten thousand drums. What had happened?

Maybe who I am isn't really enough.

Boone's voice just kept echoing in her head.

It sure seems true.

And in that moment, she'd said nothing. *Nothing.*

Because all she could think was…He didn't want to marry her.

And then he'd walked away, and the air had been sucked out of her lungs.

Gone was the comforting low timbre of his voice and the joy that made her heart sing. His absence, instead, carved out a large empty space in her chest.

Don't ever give away your whole heart. You've got to protect yourself.

Well, that had pretty much backfired on her.

She pushed her way out the door of Kate's, locking it behind her. A white rental car sat at the curb, her mom wildly waving her over.

Vivien lifted her hand to give a hello, though it was probably lack-luster at best.

After kicking the snow off her boots, she sank into the front passenger seat.

"Look at that—perfect timing!" Mom exclaimed. Her chestnut hair was tucked into a beanie, and she wore a thick, blue sweater under her coat. "I texted Boone because you didn't answer. He sent a message that you needed a pickup. I'm going to wait to hug you, though, because man, it's cold here! You should have come to Arizona to get married." Her blue eyes beamed. "It's a good thing I still own thermals—and they fit."

"Mm." Vivien acknowledged her with a grunt, buckled her seat belt, and looked out the window.

"Nice to see you too. Where's all the pomp and circumstance? Aren't you excited?" She reached out and squeezed Vivien's arm. Paused. "What's wrong? You look like someone misspelled your name in the paper."

Their old joke fell flat.

Vivien swallowed. Opened her mouth to speak. No words. Tears splashed down her cheeks with relentless force until a sob broke out.

"Honey, what's wrong?" Mom grabbed a packet of tissues from her purse and held it out to Vivien. "Are you stressed about the wedding? It's going to be perfect. This is totally normal. Brides are always on edge."

Vivien pulled one, two, three tissues from the packet. "I don't know what I was thinking—I just didn't want to end up like you and Dad. I thought if I had the perfect wedding, then we'd have the perfect marriage. We'd be together. We'd stay together. And now I've still managed to make a mess of it." The dam broke and her filter was clearly off. "I told him maybe we should wait, and he said—he said maybe we shouldn't...marry at all." Her voice broke in a wrenched cry.

"Whoa—I'm sure he didn't mean that. And you know there aren't perfect anythings. How could you possibly make a mess?"

Vivien blew her nose. Sniffed. "Well, I figured we at least needed to start out as near perfect as possible. I mean, it's only downhill from there, right? I heard you…after Dad left. I heard you one night begging him to tell you what you'd done wrong."

"Sweetheart, you never should have heard that." Her mom dropped her hands to her lap, curling them together. "I was hurt…I was looking to make sense of his betrayal. I had told myself that if I'd been a better wife, he wouldn't have strayed." She reached out, wrapped her warm hands around Vivien's. "But whatever things were imperfect between your dad and me, his choices in how he behaved were his own responsibility. It took me a lot of years and counseling to under-stand that."

"But how do I protect myself? How do I protect our marriage?"

"Communicate. Pray. Don't allow anger and bitterness to fester in your hearts." She reached out and smoothed a lock of Vivien's hair from her face. "Each day, the two of you will have to wake up and make an active choice to love and honor each other."

"I'm afraid if I'm not perfect and if Boone's not totally devoted to me, that someday he'll leave me. And you warned me—I should have listened."

"Warned you about what?"

Vivien blew her nose, not even caring that it honked louder than a Canada goose. "You said not to ever give away my whole heart. That I needed to protect myself."

Her mom recoiled. "When did I say that?"

"After Jacob Platt dumped me for Lillian Reinke."

"For crying out loud, you were sixteen—tell me you haven't been hauling around jaded, bad parenting advice from me all these years."

"You meant it. I *know* you meant it—it makes complete sense. I saw how Dad hurt you—hurt *us*."

"I didn't want to see my girl hurt by some boy who wasn't even good enough for you." Mom tucked a lock of hair behind Vivien's ear. "And I was still deeply wounded." She shook her head, a raw edge to her voice. "I had no business telling you that."

"But you did, and I've lived by that."

Mom bowed her head, wiped her eyes. "Oh, Vivie. I've hurt you with terrible advice."

Vivien let silence fill the space between them. "I'm still afraid."

Her mom nodded. "It's scary. Ultimately, the only person whose choices you can control is you."

"That makes me feel so much better." Vivien stared at her to-do list. Twelve items, even after Ree had taken six. And those were just on today's list.

Number one, her dress, remained unchecked. Not to mention the bridesmaids' gifts, since her order was stranded in Chicago. Something old, something blue.

Not that any of it mattered now.

"I'm so sorry if I messed things up between you and Boone," her mother said quietly.

Vivien reached over and gave her mom a half hug. Great. Now she'd hurt her mom too. "It's okay, Mom. I'm fine." But truthfully, she wasn't sure she could act her way out of this one.

The idea of not marrying Boone?

No. The role of her lifetime was meant to be Mrs. Boone Buckam.

"But it isn't. Sweetheart, it *is* scary to give someone your whole heart and give them the power to decimate you."

"Wow, Mom. Again, not helpful." She pulled out another tissue and blew her nose. "I thought you were trying to be a better parent here."

Her mom snatched a tissue and wiped her own nose. "Hear me out. I've learned a lot over the past few years about the beauty of marriage—the vulnerability and trust in a good marriage. That's what marriage is meant to be. Work. Compromise. Repentance. Forgiveness."

"How can I know that Boone's that man? Especially when he's willing to leave me at a moment's notice to go help someone else? What if I need him too?"

"Those are going to be tough situations. Imagine how he will feel, to be torn between the woman he loves and the work God has placed before him in that moment. Remember, you belong to Christ too. Imagine how difficult it was for Jesus to be separated from His Father.

He did it because that was His purpose. But His heart was still connected to heaven, and His Father carried Him. We can find comfort in our faith and our knowledge that God is bigger than whatever challenges and hardships come before us."

Faith.

The peace of Christ makes fresh my heart,
A fountain ever springing;
All things are mine since I am his—
How can I keep from singing?

The hymn wove itself through her soul.

"What do you love about Boone?"

"His commitment. Loyalty. Humor. Intelligence. The way he's a leader and compassionate. The way he's always ready to jump in and..." Oh.

"Jump in and help?" Mom asked. "His sense of duty?"

"Yes." The word came out a whisper. "I just don't know how to bring those two things to congruence. How do I want him with me, with our family, and then accept him having to be gone?"

"I've never been in your position, loving someone who serves in that capacity. I imagine it stretches people. Can strain relationships. But what if you used it as an opportunity to be *Boone's* safety net? To be the one who holds him when the rescue is a recovery. To be the one he can rely on to be waiting with the light on, no matter how late he comes home. To be the one to keep dinner warm when he gets called away, hungry and tired."

That's exactly who she wanted to be for Boone. Because she *had* given him her whole heart.

"I've seen Boone look at you. I saw it when the two of you visited me in Arizona your first Christmas together, and I saw it last year when I came for vacation. You're his rock, Vivien. You make him laugh. You bring him joy. You've got something really special. Don't let what happened between your dad and me tarnish that."

Vivien watched a snowflake land on the windshield. "It's still scary."

"It is. And ultimately, you have to trust that the God you believe in is big enough to get you through whatever challenges are ahead."

"What do I do now? He doesn't even want to marry me. And even if he does, I don't have a dress."

"Go. Find him. Work it out." She steered the car away from the curb. "In fact, just tell me where he is, and I'll drop you off. And don't worry about the dress. Go get yourself a groom."

WEDNESDAY, 3:20 P.M.

Vivien tried the front door of the antique store. It opened with a groan. Darkness loomed across the shop where small knickknacks still sat askew on display, thick dust settling over them. Larger items stood like phantom sentinels, sheets draped over them.

"Boone?" Vivien called out.

Silence. A musty aroma of dust and old things tingled her nose, and the cold air curled its fingers around her.

She snugged up her coat and walked toward the back of the store, easing around the stacks of odd whatsits, whosits, and thingamajigs.

Shuffling sounds and clunks. The door to the basement stood open, and dim light filtered through the dusty air.

"Boone?" she called down.

"I'm here," he answered. She stepped into the stairwell, squinting against the shadows. She searched the wall for another light switch. Moved the iron propping the door open and patted her hand along the wall.

Nope.

"Vivien?"

Her boots thunked on the staircase, the air colder as she descended. "Kind of dark on the stairs." The sight of him eased the tension on her heart. "Hey."

"Hey." He stood in a sea of boxes, lid in hand. "Yeah."

"It's been a really rotten, terrible, no good, very bad day," she offered.

He blew out a long breath. "I agree." The words were quiet, soft.

They anchored her. "Can we talk?"

"We should." He set down the box lid on the nearby stack. Looked at her with eyes full of questions and…love.

Boone. *Her* Boone.

And the little crooked smile on his face said he was glad she'd come.

He walked toward her, his lean torso covered in gaudy Christmas glee.

She held out her hands and gestured up and down his body, stifling a giggle. "I told you earlier, it's hard for me to take you seriously in that—that—getup."

He clicked the button to activate the music and lights on the sweater. "Oh yeah? Is this serious enough for you?" He reached for her hand and drew her close. "This ugly-sweatered man is sorry."

The rich timbre of his voice, his very presence—they soothed her soul. "I'm the one who's sorry. I panicked. I don't care what I wear. I'll wear that hideous satin pouf-ball thing and tease my bangs. I just want to be your wife. I love you."

"I love you too. I should have understood why you were panicking." He framed her face in his hands. "Vivien, you could wear a burlap sack for all I care. I'll marry you wearing anything at all. The only thing that matters at the end of the day is that we are legally married."

Yeah. Legally married.

She stared at the pile of fabric he'd cast aside. "Maybe I can make a dress out of the curtains." She giggled. "I can even use a curtain rod." She nodded toward the decorative finials sitting on a table.

"Maybe." His fingers danced across her jawline, causing goosebumps to zing down her body. "Or there's some burlap over there." He nodded his head toward another pile.

"Mm…cozy."

"But first, I need to ask you something, and you need to give me your honest answer."

"Okay."

"Do you need me to leave the Crisis Response Team?"

Oh. She searched his face. Right here he stood. Held out his whole heart to her, with all the love and hope in his eyes.

She swallowed, tears welling in her eyes. "I can't tell you that I'll never be frustrated or upset if you're called away—like, you know, if I'm in the middle of labor."

He held up a hand. "To be fair, I've never left you while you've been in labor."

She placed her palm on his cheek, ran her thumb across his jawline. "I don't want you to miss out on those special moments in our lives. But my mom, when she picked me up, she asked me some hard questions…"

He placed his hand over hers, the warmth of it soaking in.

"And I realized some things." She met his eyes. "Boone, we both know that service is part of who you are. And God has called you to use your gifts to lead that team. You find people in their darkest hours. Whenever you can, you make sure your team gets them home to their loved ones or brings the families closure."

"You know it never means they are more important than you."

She nodded.

"And it never means I'll leave you—abandon you."

"You are exactly the man I want to marry. I want to be there for you. Each time you come home. I want to be the arms that welcome you. Comfort you. Hold you." She took his hands, wove her fingers into his. "To answer your question, no. I don't want you to leave the team. Not until a time when that's what God wants you to do. But give me a promise? That we won't ever let bitterness or anger take root in our hearts."

"Never." He released her hands and wrapped his arms around her. Enfolded her against his body and ducked his face to kiss her.

Soft, sweet, tender.

She melted into him. His kiss tasted like peppermint and chocolate and winter snow. She clung to him, molding herself against the hard planes of his body.

She sniffed.

He paused, resting his head against her cheek. "Are you crying?"

She wiped her eyes. "I'm just very, very happy. I don't have a dress; I don't even care. I thought I knew what our marriage might look like, but now I see it will be more. So much more."

He held her tight, and she relaxed against the thrum of his heartbeat.

A squeak and a clunk came from the stairwell. A door closing.

"Did you happen to move the iron that was holding the door open?" he asked, his lips against her hair.

"When I was looking for another light switch."

His laughter rumbled through her. "Well, I'm pretty sure we just got locked in."

CHAPTER 10

"You should probably know that I left my phone in the truck," Boone said, releasing her.

But maybe he didn't care if they were locked in. He wouldn't mind having Vivien all to himself for a while.

Wow, he loved her. Her honesty. Her courage. Her beautiful wide eyes as she stared at him.

"You did not."

He held out his empty hands. "I really don't have it."

She pursed her lips together, as if digesting the information. "What did you do that for?"

"I was a little distracted when I got here. Needed to clear my mind."

"Oh…that. Well, maybe it didn't lock." She scrambled up the steps and tried the doorknob. Rattled it. "Yep. It's locked." She dropped onto the top steps and set her chin in her hands, elbows on her knees. "My phone is dead. Like, *dead* dead. You're going to have to pick it."

Right. "We've had this conversation before. I break down doors, I don't pick locks. Maybe it's just jammed." He reached around her and tried the handle too, putting some shoulder into it. It groaned but didn't budge. "Peter warned me that it likes to lock."

"You could pick locks—you just choose not to." She tromped back down the stairs. "We're going to miss our own wedding. They won't find us until the spring thaw."

"They can't have the wedding without us."

"You tasted the food samples. You don't think they won't just throw a big party anyway? Well, that's if Grace is able to still cater."

"Well, okay—they might eat all the food, but there will definitely not be a wedding until we arrive."

Her stomach rumbled. "I haven't even eaten breakfast. All I had was part of a cinnamon roll with Ree and my peppermint mocha."

Boone fished around in his coat pocket. "Protein bar?" He offered it to her.

She gave it a pensive look. "We should save it. We might need to ration it." Her bright blue eyes caught his. "We could be here for days —weeks, even." She raised a perfectly groomed brow.

He laughed. "I don't think we'll be here *that* long." He set the protein bar on a box. "Peter still needs the costumes. Is your phone working at all?"

She pulled her phone from her pocket and pressed the power button on her phone one more time. "It still isn't speaking to me."

He rubbed the tight spots on his temples. "Well, someone will come looking for us at some point."

She grabbed the protein bar and ripped it open. Looked it over before taking a bite, slowly chewing the bar. "This isn't *too* bad."

He quirked a brow at her. "What happened to rationing?"

"I'm stress eating." She took another bite. "There's no ice cream down here, though it's just about cold enough for it."

"We aren't going to be stuck here forever. What are you stressed about? Certainly not this—" He gestured at the dim, damp basement.

She began pacing. "It's all a mess. The band. The guests. The flowers. The food. We'll probably end up serving corn dogs and Tater Tots."

"What if we do?"

She stopped. Turned at his words. A small curve of her lips softened her face. "Then we'll need ketchup."

He held out his hand to her, and she stepped forward, burrowed against his chest, and he wrapped his arms around her.

He pressed a kiss into her hair. "I love you."

"I love you." She squeezed her arms around him. "We could be waiting hours, though. Only my mom and Peter know where we are. My mom is going to assume we're getting back to wedding arrangements after our big makeup and—"

"How does your mom know we made up?"

Vivien looked up at him. "Really?"

He lifted his shoulder. "I'm just asking."

She rolled her eyes, mischief in them. "Trust me. She knows." She loosened her grip and pulled away. "Hey—I could squeeze through that window and go back around the front to let you out."

Boone turned to see the window. It looked like it hadn't been opened in the past century.

Vivien hummed a melody, every so often singing a few lines.

"'What though the darkness gather round? Songs in the night He giveth....'"

He boosted her up onto the stack of boxes under the window. "Be careful."

"Always." She kneeled on the stack of boxes and worked the lock. "I think it got painted shut." She tugged at the lever, forward and back. "Maybe. Almost—"

A snap. Vivien's hand jerked and her body flew backward, the boxes she'd been standing on tumbling with her.

Boone dove, broke her fall, landing in a heap of broken boxes. "Umph!"

Vivien lay on top of him, her hair a wild mass. "Oops." Her body shook with giggles.

"I'm guessing you're okay?" he asked.

"Yeah. Good save—that's twice today." She held up the window lock lever. "I got the lock open."

"I'm not sure that breaking it is the same as opening it."

"It is if it works." She pointed above them, where a few snowflakes drifted through the angled pane.

She tossed the broken lever aside, rolled off of him, and tucked her hair behind her ears.

The boxes had spilled their contents across the floor. A mass of fabric, lace, and—

"The costumes!" Kneeling in the pile, Vivien held up a handful of long, child-sized robes in browns and white.

"Look at this." He lifted a fur shapka and wrap from the pile. "I think these are real." He set the hat on a nearby pile of clothes and handed her the fur wrap.

"It's beautiful." She set down the robes and examined it. "It's a vintage stole." She flipped a box flap over and looked at the label. "Looks like these were left for consignment." She returned the stole to the box. "Oh…what is this?" Surprise lilted her voice. She worked her hands past the stole and several other garments, then drew a long, white dress from the box. Held it up. "Oh my. It's a vintage gown."

The silky fabric was covered with lace and sparkly things. Even in the dim basement, it glowed, luminous and elegant.

Just like his bride.

"Wow," he said, maybe a little more at the Christmas-morning look on Vivien's face than the actual dress—even if it was a rather nice one.

Vivien's fingers glanced across the dress. "Wow is right. This is exquisite."

An idea took form in his mind. It looked like it could fit her. And it would, if he had anything to say about it. The radiant smile on Vivien's face was the only incentive he needed.

She held the dress up against herself. "Imagine the story this dress could tell." She lifted the hem. "See this?" She pointed to a seam on the inside of the dress. "These are French seams. They were used from the 1900s to the 1940s. They're only used today in very high-end clothing."

"Why does it not surprise me that you know that?"

She winked at him, the gesture leaving him a little weak in the knees. Man, he couldn't wait to be her husband.

"I don't think this dress is that old—the style is newer—but it's very well made. Truly a couture gown. See how this lace overlay sits, with the handsewn beading and crystals throughout?" She laid the dress out across the box. "It's a sheath with a bit of a mermaid train."

Boone looked around the basement, his eyes landing on an empty suit bag. He held out his hands for the dress. "I'll take that. We shouldn't leave it down here." He didn't really know what couture or overlay or mermaid meant exactly, but Kate would.

"It's a shame it was left in this basement. It's musty." Vivien released the dress to him and turned her attention back to the stole. Held it out to inspect it before wrapping it over her shoulders. She looked up, her eyes alight. "Do you think I could borrow this? For the wedding?"

"I'm sure it would be fine. Looks like it's been here for quite some time. I'll ask Peter."

"It can be my 'something old,'" she said. "Then I can cross that off my list." She shot him a teasing grin and picked up the hat. Plopped it on his head. "You could wear this."

The last thing Boone wanted to wear was a Russian shapka at his wedding. "I think I'll pass."

"Too soon?" A broad smile spread across her face, and he felt her fingertips trace his scar—the result of his last run-in with a Russian when he saved Vivien from a maniacal ex-boyfriend.

"Careful. I'll show up wearing this sweater at our wedding."

"Oh, you wouldn't."

An icy breeze chased the snowflakes through the open window. "Shall we get out of here?" He tugged the hat from his head and placed it back in the pile.

"Oh, right." She shoved the fur stole and robes into his hands. "I'll climb through and run around to open the door." She turned toward the window. Paused. Turned back. "And I think we'd better go buy me a new phone after we drop those costumes off."

"Good idea." He gave her another boost up to the window and

watched her wiggle through the narrow opening, her booted feet flailing, laughter filling his chest. Yeah, he was looking forward to a lifetime of adventures with Vivien.

THURSDAY, 5:00 P.M.

Boone led Vivien through the kaleidoscope of twinkle lights he and the guys had hung at Wilder House. The text he'd received from Kate putting an even bigger smile on his face.

Because Vivien was about to get her own wholly unexpected Christmas miracle.

He squeezed her soft fingers threaded through his own. "What is that song you've been humming?"

"It's a hymn. 'How Can I Keep from Singing.' Pieces of the lyrics have been stuck in my head for the past two days." She wrinkled her nose. "Maybe a prompting. A reminder—my peace doesn't come from what I do. What I think I control."

"Sounds like a good reminder for both of us."

"Yeah? Me too." She smiled up at him.

Love poured through him, white-hot and molten.

This—this was the woman he needed in his life.

He tucked her against himself, reveling in the warmth and softness of her curves. "Peter said he got the window boarded up, and yes to using the stole. Edith Draper said there's quite a story behind it, and the next time you see her, I expect you might hear its tale."

Her breath caressed his cheek. "Sounds intriguing."

"Doesn't it?"

"Indeed," she answered.

"Speaking of which—do you really want to go through with this wild and crazy Christmas wedding?" he asked.

"What?" She leaned back, looked up at him, a question in her eyes.

He ran his fingers through her hair. "I just mean…it's not too late to elope somewhere warm. We could head to St. Thomas early."

"I do," she answered, looking up at him with blue eyes, bright and clear. She curled her fingers around his. "I really do want to go through with this wild and crazy wedding."

"I thought you might say that." He paused, waited.

"What aren't you telling me?" The corner of her lip curved.

"I have something for you."

"Oh? A surprise?" A trill of excitement warbled through her words.

"Yes, ma'am. You want it now?"

"Definitely." She rubbed her hands together.

"You have to close *and* cover your eyes."

This time, her big, broad smile spread across her face and she stepped back. Excitement bubbled out in laughter. "Okay…" She placed a hand over her eyes.

"No peeking. I know you like to peek."

"I do not," she protested. "I have them closed."

"I'm going to lead you into another room."

He wrapped an arm around her waist and led her back through the doorway, down the hallway to the library. He set her into the spot facing the vintage dress, the hanger hooked on a shelf to display its full length. "Are you ready?"

"Yes." She stomped her foot. "Don't make me wait!" Anticipation filled her voice.

"Okay. You can look."

She dropped her hand. Gasped. "What?" She stepped closer. "How did you—" She bent forward, inspecting the lace. "This is the dress." She examined the lace with gentle hands. "From the basement. You had it cleaned!" She held up the skirt. "It's like something Audrey Hepburn would have worn."

"It isn't the dress you designed, but—"

"It's perfect. Better than I ever could have planned."

She ran her fingers across the lace, beads, and crystals, her smile worth every call he'd made. Every favor he'd called in to get it to Duluth and back for cleaning to remove the musty odor.

"I can't even imagine how you did this." She took a step back, tapped her finger to her lips. "Oh— What if it doesn't fit me?"

"Oh, it will fit." He laughed. "Kate had all your measurements. It only took a few adjustments, she said—and she found a little surprise inside."

"Another surprise?"

"Can you handle that?" His heart pounded in his chest. Vivien was going to freak, in the most wonderful, delightful way.

He lifted the train, followed the seam up, just like Kate had shown him. "Take a look."

Vivien stared at the label. Looked at Boone. Looked back at the label. Her jaw went slack.

"Is that...real?" She pointed to the handsewn label, the name *Margaret VanEaton* written in cursive appliqué.

"Kate assures me it is."

A shriek. A squeal. A jump in the air. "This is incredible. Thank you." She threw her arms around him, making little sobs as she sucked in air. "You know, I was really ready to go for the burlap."

"And you would have been a beautiful sight in that, as well." He kissed her, inhaling the jasmine, letting his lips linger until he drew way, took a breath. "I told you, all that matters is that we're legally married."

"Two days. Just two more days."

He pointed to the doorway. "Shall we see how everything else is coming along?"

She let out a little sigh. "Do we dare?"

He wove his fingers into hers. "We're up for it. We make a great team."

Vivien smiled and stepped up to him. "We do. All this makes me think everything will be perfect." She nodded her head toward the dress. Laughed. "But that's going home with me. I'm not letting it out of my sight."

"I'm with you on that." And he drew her into a kiss. It tasted distinctly of love, promise, and tomorrows.

Oh yeah. Luckiest man on the planet.

Boone's phone buzzed, and Vivien's lips curved against his in a grin. "Hmmm..." Her voice teased. "Who could it be now? The butcher? The baker? The candlestick maker?"

"I don't have to answer that," he said. "I don't even care who it is." He stole another kiss. "I could turn it off. Maybe *accidently* drop it into an ice fishing hole."

Her laugh warmed his cheek. Rich and musical. "Oh, hon, answer it." She cupped his face in her hands, her eyes lit with delight and mischief when he lifted the phone without even looking at the caller ID. Just drank in the incredible connection between them.

He winked at Vivien before forcing his eyes to his phone.

"It's just a text." Huh. "From Peter."

"Tell him we're not looking for any more costumes." Vivien gave Boone a playful nudge.

He tapped the message.

There's a problem with your Mustang.

We're Happy Tonight

MICHELLE SASS ALECKSON

CHAPTER 1

*D*etective Duke Lowry hated Christmas. What was merry about the season of an uptick in theft, crime, and a pile of work dealing with the darkest parts of humanity? And now out of all 365 days of the year he could pick, his former partner decided to get hitched on Christmas Eve and make Duke the best man.

He thought Boone Buckam had better sense.

Still, he couldn't say no to the man who'd saved his life on an investigation gone wrong. Even if the holiday was a reminder of the worst mistake of his life, Duke would use his PTO, drive over five hundred miles round trip, and do whatever Boone needed for the next five days.

Duffel bag? Check. Extra charger? In the bag. Security alarm set? Yep. Passenger? Not yet—but her flight was due to arrive in the next hour, so he still had time.

He stepped out of his cottage with the keys to the sparkling white F-150 truck already warmed and running in his driveway. If he had to make the five-hour trek to Deep Haven in a snowstorm, at least he and his passenger would be comfortable and safe.

But as he looked up, he clenched his keys tight enough to leave marks on his palm.

Not again.

A big inflatable Santa-in-an-outhouse display lay tipped over in his lawn. A long evergreen garland stretched across the snow from the neighbor's house to his front yard.

Bad enough he had to see the tacky display every time he stepped out the door. Now this? The least his neighbor could do was to stake it down properly.

Still, Mrs. Murphy, at the young age of eighty-two, shouldn't be the one out in the storm staking down the ridiculous thing her grandson insisted on putting out in her yard. Duke grunted as he dragged it back over to her lawn, plucked his hammer from his truck toolbox, and set it back up. As he stood in calf-high drifts pounding in the last stake, falling snowflakes flew in his face and snow soaked through his pants and socks.

He hated wet socks.

He glanced at his watch. Not that he had time to change now. He would be cutting it close, but he could still get to the airport in time.

If Christmas didn't sabotage him again.

He stowed the hammer away, hopped in his truck, and hit the road.

As Boone's best man, he was all for supporting his former partner's upcoming nuptials, but why in the world did he want to get married on Christmas Eve?

It was probably Vivien's idea. And Boone did anything these days to make his fiancée happy. He said he'd finally found the right girl in the right place.

The right girl. What a myth. Or maybe it was only truth for guys like Boone. He deserved all the happiness in the world. Duke, on the other hand, was meant to live this life alone, and he'd come to terms with it.

He sped up onto the I-494 ramp. The next five days weren't about him, though. Duke would stand up for Boone and be there to make sure things went off without a problem. So, as long as everyone kept their Christmas cheer to themselves for the next week, he'd be fine.

And yeah, he liked Vivien, but he'd been blindsided by beauty before. So if Boone needed an escape or a quick getaway, Duke should scope things out and be prepared with an exit plan. That's what partners were for. Even ex-partners.

He had to take his foot off the gas as he traced the long line of bright brake lights at a dead stop in front of him.

Aw, great. Holiday traffic. He let out a deep sigh and used his voice-activated system to call Boone.

He answered after the second ring. "Duke, my man. What's up. Is Zuri there too? Her plane is landing soon, isn't it?"

The guy was way too chipper.

"I'm on my way, but I'm stuck in traffic on 494. I asked Vivien earlier for Zuri's contact info, but I never heard back from her."

"Yeah, she's been a little preoccupied."

Whatever else Boone said was lost as Duke zeroed in on something red moving alongside the cars lined up behind a stoplight on a frontage road parallel to the interstate. "What in the world…"

"What's going on?"

Duke squinted in the dusky light and snowfall. "Some idiot dressed up in a Santa suit is walking down the line of cars."

"Along the interstate? In the storm?"

"No, along the frontage road." Duke watched a few seconds longer. "Looks like he's passing something out."

"Well, what do you know. Someone spreading Christmas cheer in a traffic jam."

"Don't think so." A tingling along Duke's spine kept him on high alert.

Four cars away.

"He's probably just trying to cheer people up during the storm. Where's your Christmas joy?"

Duke peered through the thick falling snow. The guy in the cheap red suit and black combat boots was ho-ho-ho-ing his way along the driver's side and passing out something in a silver wrapper to those who lowered their driver's side windows. But the tingling sensation only intensified. Didn't anyone learn about stranger danger in preschool?

"I'm telling you, Boone, there's something off about this guy. He's got two bags, and the way he keeps his hand in one of them…"

"You've been working too long, taking things way too seriously. Once you get up here—"

Suddenly, Santa pulled out a pistol and pointed it at the driver's side window of a luxury SUV. A teenage girl behind the wheel panicked as he pounded on her door and yelled for her to get out.

"Boone, call the local PD. Skinny, white male in a Santa suit is carjacking a gray Cadillac Escalade on the frontage road by exit three," Duke called out as he threw his truck in park on the shoulder of the interstate, grabbed his own gun from the holster hidden under his coat, and rushed out into the cold. Santa wrenched the girl by the arm and dragged her out of the car. Her cry of terror cut through the wind.

Duke jumped over the median separating the roads and ran up the embankment. "Stop. Police!"

Santa dropped his gun in the snowbank and dashed off on foot, weaving between cars and slipping across the road. Duke took off after him, holstering his gun as he yelled for people to remain in their vehicles. He almost caught up with Santa when the guy bolted over a snowbank and across a hotel parking lot.

No way. Duke burst forward, leaped, and tackled the man. A cloud of freezing snow and the impact stole his breath. Oomph.

That was gonna hurt later.

Duke gritted his teeth and pulled himself and Santa up off the ground. Pretty sure a jolly saint wouldn't be saying anything that was coming out of this guy's dirty mouth. And would it kill some of these onlookers to call 911 or help rather than whipping out their phones and recording the whole fiasco?

And Boone wondered where Duke's Christmas spirit was.

As soon as local PD arrived on the scene and took over, Duke took his cold and aching body back to his own vehicle…only to find another holiday surprise.

You gotta be kidding me!

A dark black-and-red scrape ran across the whole driver's side of his brand-new truck.

Could this day get any worse?

A black Suburban honked as it flew by, and slushy snow flew up and hit Duke's leg.

That's what he got for asking a stupid question. Better get in his truck before he took a cue from Bad Santa and threw out some choice words of his own—or before more damage could be done to him or his truck.

A message from Boone flashed on his dashboard screen when he started the truck.

Zuri knows you're late. She's waiting by D5-T1 MSP. Have fun! Every grinch needs a Cindy Lou Who.

Door 5, Terminal 1 at the Minneapolis/St. Paul Airport. That made sense, but what did the rest of it mean?

Probably just Boone trying to set Duke up again. *Phfft.* Like that would ever happen. The guy falls in love, and the next thing you know he thinks everyone should be subjected to it.

Well, if there was anything Duke hated more than Christmas, it was romance. Not that he had any time to worry about it. He had a responsibility to pick up Zuri, and he was already incredibly late.

Blasted holidays.

He quickly merged into the flow of traffic and soon approached the arrival doors at the airport. As he slowly nudged his way closer to door number five, a large group of people blocked his sight.

Okay, what now? Why was everyone clumped together outside the door instead of lining up along the curb waiting with luggage and minding their own business, like travelers usually did? And was that *singing?*

He cracked the passenger window. A group of strangers, young and old and every race and creed, were all bundled up and singing "Walking in a Winter Wonderland."

How was he supposed to find Zuri Milano in this? By now she was probably ticked. Weren't New Yorkers pretty uptight?

He got out and stepped up to the sidewalk. The singing stopped. The crowd broke, and a curvy woman in a bright red coat, green dress with gold trim, reindeer antlers, and candy cane stockings parted the sea of people and walked up to him.

"It's your lucky day, Duke Lowry. I have one more candy cane left." She winked and held out the striped candy. "I've been saving it for you."

Duke's jaw dropped open as he studied her—from the white puffy pom-pom on her Santa hat down to her shiny black shoes. She had honest-to-goodness jingle bells on her pointy toes. Her silky dark-brown hair must've taken hours to do to look like something from a freaking shampoo commercial. Her face was flawless, almost plastic in appearance, with thick makeup and long lashes that had to be fake, along with her ridiculously long nails painted with some elaborate Christmas design that probably cost more than he made in a month.

Heaven help him, he'd be stuck with her for the next five-plus hours.

His day officially could not get any worse.

TUESDAY, 11:54 P.M.

Her brothers would have a field day with her costume, but there was nothing Zuri Milano wouldn't do for her Minnesota friend. Even travel a thousand miles through a snowstorm to do hair and makeup for her wedding. Or suffer from frostbite as she stood in the freezing cold, passing out the candy canes and leading Christmas carols with strangers outside the Minneapolis airport.

So what if the elf getup was a little over-the-top? That didn't matter.

Vivien's wedding did.

And spreading holiday cheer was all part of the mission. One she hadn't left her family and her favorite season in NYC to fail. She would make sure all of Vivien's Christmas wedding dreams come true. Even if it meant converting a grinch.

Because after Vivie had given her a place to stay when she'd needed to move out, helped her get started in the stage makeup biz, and comforted her through the devastation of "The Breakup," she was family. And you always showed up for family.

So when Vivie had mentioned Boone's best man wasn't keen on the whole Christmas scene, well, that just wasn't going to fly. Zuri couldn't have the best man throwing shade on the occasion. So she'd start with making him laugh. Help him loosen up.

Maybe, at the very least, coax a grin out of the grinch.

But as her ride to Deep Haven pulled up to the crowded curb outside MSP in the big white truck Boone had told her to look for, Zuri realized Vivien had failed to mention one important thing.

Boone's best man, Duke Lowry, was one hunk of a cop.

Wowza. He might act like a grinch, but he certainly didn't look like one. Not with that intense brooding stare, a chiseled jaw, and full lips. His bronze-brown skin looked great even under the horrid fluorescent lights of the airport overhang. She always did have a thing for tall, dark, and handsome with a good skin care regimen.

Zuri gave him her brightest grin and held out the candy cane to him again. "Go ahead. Take it."

He continued to stare, unblinking.

"You *are* Duke Lowry, right? I'm Zuri. Zuri Milano."

"Yes, I'm Duke." He took the candy cane but didn't return the smile. In fact, he glowered. "Is that your luggage?"

"Yeah, that's all of—"

He didn't wait. Just picked up her huge hot-pink suitcase as if it weighed nothing and placed it in his back seat. He came back and reached for the hard-sided makeup case she'd carried on the flight.

She quickly grabbed the handle and held it tight. "Be careful with this, please. It's my life."

His only response was to lift one dark eyebrow.

"It's my makeup and styling products. The tools of my trade."

His espresso eyes locked in on hers, making her cheeks heat. Great. That would do wonders for her scars. But goodness, there was something darkly appealing about a man who could take someone down with a hard stare. Someone who wouldn't be intimidated by a girl with chutzpah.

Even Christmas chutzpah.

Clearly, she'd have to up her game.

"I'll take good care of it."

And somehow, with those words, she knew she could trust him with it. Maybe it was because Vivien and Boone had mentioned multiple times what a good guy Duke was. But something in his direct stare spoke even louder. She peeled her hands off the handle of the case and passed it to Duke.

As soon as he turned around to put it in the truck, Zuri released the breath she'd been holding. Man alive, she was supposed to be the one affecting *him*. Not the other way around.

He opened the passenger side front door for her.

Now that was a positive sign. She loved how her grandfather always held the door for her *nonna*. Duke must have a soft, gooey center in there somewhere beneath his holiday-hating shell. All Zuri had to do was find it.

Duke closed her door, then jumped in the driver's side. He didn't say anything as he maneuvered the car out into traffic. A whiff of his clean, citrusy scent filled the car. Just like the clove oranges her mother used to decorate with.

"So, we have a while to Deep Haven, huh?"

"About five hours on good roads."

Looking out the window, she watched thick snowflakes pelting the windshield. So probably, she shouldn't bank on good roads. "Then I guess we have plenty of time to get to know each other."

Because there had to be a reason Duke hated Christmas. If she could discover that reason, she could find a way to fix it. Like she did when her clients asked her to cover up their flaws and blemishes. When she knew what kind of skin condition it was, she knew what tools worked best in covering them up.

Speaking of flaws... She pulled down the sun visor and checked her cheek in the mirror. She could use a touch-up. She pulled out her compact and dabbed powder on her nose and cheek. Just a gentle pat on the big scar to keep the thick layer of concealer in place.

That was better. Wouldn't want to scare off Duke just yet.

She fluffed up her hair before leaning in toward her driver. "So, is Duke a nickname?"

"Nope."

"Were you named after *The Dukes of Hazzard*? My mom loved that show."

"No." He checked his blind spot.

She waited until he was finished merging onto the freeway, but he didn't elaborate on his answer.

"I'm named after my mom's best friend. I guess that's how an Italian girl like me has a Swahili name. My brothers are named after saints and old ancestors. I mean, after six kids you have to get creative, right?"

Still no response.

"Do you have any siblings?"

Duke shook his head and kept his gaze fixed on the early afternoon sky out of his windshield.

"You're an only child? I often wished I was, growing up. You don't know what it's like squeezing nine of us plus my nonna and Pop into an '80s split-level in the New Jersey suburbs. There was no such thing as privacy in my house." And even then, surrounded by people, sometimes Zuri felt the loneliest there.

Her driver gave a noncommittal hum, acknowledging her words, but offered nothing to continue the conversation.

This was going to be harder than she thought. And there was always the distinct possibility that hunky Duke was keeping his emotional distance because he had a girlfriend.

But Vivie would've mentioned that, right? Especially because Zuri got the distinct impression that Vivien was hoping something would develop between her best makeup gal and the best man.

Which was pretty ridiculous. Sweet, but ridiculous. Vivien just had romance on the brain after finding the man of her dreams.

Zuri had given up on her own happily ever after long ago. She was here for Vivie's. "So, how do you and Boone know each other?"

"We used to work together."

"Where was that?"

"The Kellogg Police Department. Not far from here."

"So you're a cop."

"Detective."

"And how do you like being a detective?"

"It's fine."

"You know we have a long drive. You don't have to be so shy. Tell me more about yourself. Your family. Hobbies."

His gaze slid over to her. "I'm named after my mother's favorite musician, Duke Ellington. You already know I'm an only child. My parents have both passed away. And I don't have time for hobbies."

Oh.

"I'm sorry about your parents." She'd really stepped into that one. But if he thought that would put her off, he was wrong. The idea of poor Duke being all alone in the world only tugged at her heart. No wonder he was a little surly. She couldn't imagine Christmas without her parents and grandparents and all her crazy family. It was crowded, loud, and often by the end of the night, overheated with that many bodies packed into the house. But Zuri wouldn't have it any other way.

Duke had nobody.

She couldn't give him a family, but maybe music would help lighten the mood and bring back good memories. She reached for the screen mounted on his dash. "Do you have any Christmas music radio stations? I love—"

"No."

"Really? That's strange. I would've thought the Midwest would eat up stuff like that. But that's okay. I have a great Christmas playlist we can listen to on my phone. It has all the classics—"

"No thanks." His deep voice practically grumbled.

"You don't like Christmas music?"

"Let's just say I'm not a fan of Christmas *anything*."

"Oh, come on, Duke. There has to be *something* you like about Christmas."

The muscles along his jaw went taut, and his eyes never left the windshield. "Look, it's a long ride, and I need to concentrate on the road. Besides, after this wedding we'll probably never see each other again. So, no need to pretend you want to get to know me. We obviously have nothing in common." He set the station on talk radio, turning up the volume loud enough Zuri couldn't respond even if she wanted to.

So that's how it was going to be.

She blew out a short breath through her nose. It fogged up the window she looked out. If it weren't for Vivien, she'd have nothing to do with this jerk ever again.

But Duke the Grinch didn't know this Jersey Girl. She didn't take "stand down" for an answer. Not when his mood might sour Vivie's happy day.

She had five hours to restrategize.

Her brothers always did say she was stubborn as the day was long and she eventually got her way. This would be no exception.

Duke Lowry had better watch out.

CHAPTER 2

The next day, even in the still-dark morning under the glow of the outdoor light mounted on the garage, Duke could see why Boone had moved to Deep Haven. His new custom log house outside of town, embraced by the surrounding forest, was a far cry from the grind of city life. The crisp pine air and open space helped release the tension in Duke's neck from the long drive last night.

Here, a guy didn't have to deal with his neighbor's Christmas decorations flying into his yard. In fact, Boone's nearest neighbor was at least half a mile away. There were no nosy women—or wannabe elves—butting into Duke's business, trying to mess with his radio presets. And there were no criminals to run down. Just good, honest work clearing snow out of Boone's driveway. If he stayed busy enough, he could forget all about the upcoming holiday.

And yesterday's torturous, silent, five-hour drive.

Wow, that Zuri was a piece of holly-jolly work. He'd never been so glad to get to Evergreen Resort and go their separate ways.

"Thanks again for picking up Zuri yesterday," Boone said, piling another scoop of snow on the mound lining his front yard as they worked a path to his unattached garage.

"Don't get used to it. As soon as you and Vivien say 'I do,' my best man duties are fulfilled." He quirked up his lips to let Boone know he was kidding.

Kinda.

As much as he respected and liked Boone, as soon as it was polite, Duke would duck out of the reception and start back home. Without an added passenger.

"So the ride went okay? Zuri didn't talk your ear off?"

"Nope. I listened to talk radio the whole way up. She did her own thing."

"Talk radio? For real? Some welcome committee you are. And here Vivien thought you two might hit it off." He stopped scooping snow and stared at Duke.

"Me? And Zuri?" Duke almost dropped the shovel. "The makeup and hair princess? That woman has *high maintenance* written all over her."

"High maintenance? What are you talking about?" He picked up his shovel again. "Zuri's hilarious. Yeah, a little talkative and outgoing, but that would be good for you."

Nope, not gonna happen. "Remind me again why you need the car detailed in the middle of winter?" Surely Boone's precious red '65 Mustang convertible they were trying to clear a path to would be the perfect distraction.

"Vivie wants some pictures with the Mustang, since it's how we met."

"And you're okay with me driving it?"

"I've got winter tires for it. And I figured if I trusted you with my life while we were working together, then maybe I can trust you with my second favorite girl." He zoomed in on Duke. "You won't let anything happen to her, right?"

"Of course not."

"Good, because remember, I know where you live." Boone gave him a hard stare.

"I know you mean to look intimidating, but it's difficult to take you seriously in that sweater." Duke nodded to the hideous green pullover Boone wore. It was covered in shiny garland and little plastic Christmas ornaments. And if that wasn't bad enough, the thing had real lights flashing on and off. It was enough to give Duke a headache.

"Wait until you get engaged, and let's see all the crazy things that you'll do for your future wife."

Yeah, he wasn't even going to dignify that with a response. "So, I'm getting the car detailed. What else? I'll do anything to *not* go to this gaudy-sweater and decorating party you've got going on." Tasks that hopefully had nothing to do with Christmas.

"Okay, along with getting the car detailed, you can pick up Vivien's ring at Johnson's Jewelers and our tuxes at Megan and Cole's. When you're done, you can drop the car off at the Evergreen Resort, since you're staying there anyway. They have a big maintenance shed you can park her in until we're ready for those pictures. Vivie has some of the girls scheduled to decorate the car later today."

"I can do that." Duke pitched his shovel into the diminishing pile of snow. "Sure hope she's worth it."

"Oh yeah. Vivien's the one."

Duke scooped and threw a pile over his shoulder. He'd thought that himself once about a woman. Worst mistake of his life.

Boone stuck his shovel in the drift and leaned on the handle. "Nothing to say?"

"I'm…happy for you."

"You know what you need? You need a woman like Zuri."

This again? "No. Way. I'm fine on my own."

Even if Zuri's perfume still lingered in his truck, and this morning, when he'd gotten in to drive to Boone's, it…well, he didn't *hate* it. And her story of growing up with a house full of family had sounded… nice. Maybe a little like heaven. When she'd popped her earbuds in and focused on her phone, it'd surprised him how uncomfortable the silence was in the truck. Like he'd been a jerk or something.

Maybe he had been. And after an hour of listening to some political chitchat, he'd almost wanted her to start talking again about her life. Might have made the ride go faster. But she never opened up after he shot her down on the Christmas music.

Aw, that was probably a good thing. Because what did he have in common with New York City? Or a woman obsessed with Christmas? Relationships led to heartbreak. And his heart couldn't take that again.

"You're not thinking about Nichole, are you?" Boone asked.

"No, bro. Why would you ask that?"

"That scowl on your face. It's always there when she comes up. And I know that was rough, but not every woman is like that."

Maybe not, but Duke had better things to do with his life than to go searching for someone who could handle being married to a cop. Well, married to him. He was better off alone.

All the tenseness in Duke's neck rushed back. "Did you look at the time? You're gonna be late." He scooped the last swath of snow in front of the garage door.

Boone checked his phone. "Fine. I'm going. But we will resume this conversation. Nothing opens in town until eight, so make yourself at home until then." He rushed into the garage and soon left with a salute goodbye.

Once he was out of sight, Duke breathed a little easier. Rather than sit around in the big log house by himself, he spent the time clearing snow off Boone's walkways and the back deck. Before long, it was time to hang the snow shovel up in the garage and hop into the Mustang.

He took it slow on his way to Jared's Detailing on the outskirts of town. Duke drove the Mustang into the open carport where a worker named Steve, who was wearing a Santa hat, directed him. Duke stepped out of the Mustang and was immediately assaulted by paint fumes and the Chipmunks' Christmas song blaring through the speakers of the garage.

In the next car, someone vacuumed the back seats. Against the far wall, the fender of a black muscle car peeked out from behind a curtain of plastic splattered with different shades of paint. Another worker in coveralls, with long, greasy hair, dug through a toolbox while sucking on a candy cane.

Duke left the keys with Steve and escaped as fast as he could.

Once outside, he took his time walking the few blocks over to the small family jewelry store. The breeze off the ice-covered lake might be cold, but it helped clear the smell and awful music from his head.

It didn't last long.

As soon as Duke opened the door, a mechanical toy reindeer on the glass jewelry counter started singing "Grandma Got Run Over by a Reindeer." The overpowering cinnamon air freshener gave him an instant headache. He introduced himself to a middle-aged woman in a festive red sweater.

"Ah, yes. Boone said you were stopping in this morning." The jeweler handed over the velvet box. "We spent a lot of time with the couple finding the right one. We custom ordered the white gold setting for the solitaire. One full carat. Just gorgeous. And now it's soldered to the wedding band."

Like he cared.

The jeweler didn't seem to mind that Duke failed to respond. "Vivien has good taste. I trust you'll take good care of it."

"Of course."

"While you're here, is there anything we can interest you in? A diamond necklace for a special woman in your life, perhaps? It would make a great stocking stuffer."

"No." The last thing he'd bought in a jewelry store for a woman had had to be returned a month later.

Thanks for that lovely reminder.

He quickly stuffed the box with the ring in his inner coat pocket and made a break for fresh air once again.

With time to kill, he found a decent cup of joe at the Java Cup and sat by the window overlooking the frozen bay. Breathing in a welcome aroma of fresh ground coffee, he settled in with a discarded newspaper. After catching up on the local news, he streamed some football bowl game coverage on his phone.

His headache slowly faded.

Sure beat decorating with holly and mistletoe or whatever else a Christmas wedding entailed.

He finally walked back to Jared's and picked up the sparkling clean Mustang. This time the only sounds were the guys working on cars. Thankfully the paint fumes had dispersed. One more errand and he was done.

Duke drove to the Black Spruce. The plain white lights and Christmas tree on the porch wasn't too obnoxious as far as Christmas decorations went. He'd met Megan and Cole Barrett before when he came up for a guys' canoe trip. Seemed like a nice couple. This should be a painless, quick stop.

"Duke, come on in! I just got back from Wilder House, and the sitter had to run." Megan waved him in with one hand while cradling a baby wrapped in a blue blanket in the other. "I heard you picked up the ring. Can I see it?"

He dug into his pocket and opened the box to display the white gold set, a band of smaller diamonds circling the one carat center solitaire. Megan fawned over the cut and clarity, all the while rocking back and forth in a motherly sway while the baby slept.

The little guy sighed in his sleep. Megan responded with a kiss on his dewy head. A mix of bitter memories and broken dreams rushed back.

First the jewelry store and now this. Talk about the tormenting of Christmases past and Christmases that would never be. "So, you have a couple of tuxes I can take off your hands?"

"Oh, yes. In here." She handed him the ring box, which he quickly stuffed in his pocket, and led him to a hall closet. Two black garment bags hung on the bar. "Here you go. With everything Boone has to remember, why don't you hold on to these and just bring them to Wilder House on Saturday."

"Sure." Duke took the hangers. The sound of boys laughing and running down the hall came toward him.

"Josh, Tiago, the baby is sleeping. Not so loud, huh?" Megan said.

Two boys on the cusp of the teenage years swept past, their snow gear leaving a wet trail. "Yes, ma'am."

"Boys, I tell you." She shook her head, but anyone could see she reveled in being a mom. "They've already been sledding and built a snow fort this morning."

The hangers grew heavy in Duke's grip and the air too warm. "I'd better drop these off and get out of your way." After a quick goodbye, he carefully laid the garment bags on the back seat and took off his coat, tossing it on the passenger side of the Mustang. He'd stand longer sucking in cold air and cooling off if it wouldn't look so weird to see a guy standing in the middle of the driveway for that long.

Instead, he got in the driver's seat once more and ran his hands over the smooth steering wheel. "I'll tell you what—if you were mine, you would be the *only* girl in my life. And that would be just fine with me. Now, let's get out of here."

He'd had more than enough Christmas cheer for one day.

WEDNESDAY, 11:51 A.M.

Deep Haven was everything Vivien had said it would be and more. When Zuri arrived yesterday, Evergreen Resort was downright magical with its little log cabins covered in sparkling white snow and guarded by pine trees, the winding paths tying everything together. The wedding venue—cutest little place called Wilder House—was now swathed in twinkle lights, tulle, and evergreen boughs thanks to everyone who'd shown up in crazy Christmas sweaters to decorate. It was better than a cheesy holiday movie.

The only things missing were the grinch and the bride. The two people Zuri was supposed to be helping.

Since neither was anywhere to be found, Zuri took over the upstairs bathroom of the old Victorian, where she instead coached bridesmaid Beth Strauss on the finer points of creating a smoky eye and put the finishing touches on her wedding updo with a spritz of her favorite tropical-scented hair spray.

"How do you like it?" Zuri spun the bridesmaid around to face the large mirror.

The shy woman blushed as she took in the loose braids gathered back into a cascade of curls and the sultry eye makeup. "I love it. I can't believe that's me."

"Of course it's you. I simply emphasized the beautiful features you already had, girlfriend. The silver necklaces and earrings will pull the whole look together when you put on that dress."

The dress that hung on the door of the bathroom for inspiration. Vivien had chosen a sleeveless, slate-blue chiffon gown. The filmy dress with the ruched top and sweetheart neckline was absolutely gorgeous. Not that Zuri would ever wear it. She didn't do sleeveless *anything*.

But all four of Vivien's bridesmaids would be stunning.

And the transformation of sweet, down-to-earth Beth would certainly turn heads. Zuri could see the confidence rising in her new friend already as she studied herself in the mirror. After hearing that Beth had broken up with her own fiancé a few months ago, Zuri had decided the girl deserved a little pampering.

"My pale, Minnesota skin doesn't look so washed out with that bronzer you brushed on." Beth turned her face side to side, checking out Zuri's handiwork. "Now I won't be so worried about standing next to a beautifully tanned Amelia when she gets back from Florida with her family."

"*If* they get back. While decorating, I overheard people mention they were having a hard time finding flights. As it was, I barely made it out of New York City yesterday." Zuri gathered her brushes and clips, sliding them in their case.

"You even covered up that awful zit that popped up on my chin."

The hint of awe in Beth's voice made Zuri chuckle. At least someone appreciated her efforts. "Covering up blemishes happens to be one of my specialties. The green corrector is key."

"You'll have to show me how you did that." Beth leaned in closer to the mirror and studied her chin. "How did you learn all this stuff? Did you have older sisters to show you?"

Zuri busted out laughing. "Oh no. I have brothers. *Six* older brothers. And Mom is a genius with hair but not so much with eye shadow. So when I was twelve and going to be a junior bridesmaid in my brother's wedding, she took me to one of those professional makeup counters and had them do a free makeover. I knew right then that this is what I wanted to do."

The way the older woman behind the counter had made the scar on her cheek disappear had been like a fairy godmother granting her most desired wish. If makeup could do that for her, she wanted to empower others too.

"Well, you're a genius at what you do." Beth checked her phone again. "Still no word from Vivien. I don't know where she is. Maybe we should head to Evergreen to decorate the Mustang now."

"What Mustang?"

"Oh, it's how Vivien and Boone met. They ended up driving his red '65 Mustang convertible in the town festival and winning the car show, all on a fluke. The best man is supposed to be getting the car detailed and leaving it at the resort in the maintenance shed so we can decorate it."

Aha. So that's why Duke had been absent from all the earlier festivities.

If she couldn't find Vivien, she would at least make the car look great and then take another crack at the scrooge in cabin four.

Last night's drive might have been one of the greatest challenges of her life, staying quiet for five long, dark hours. She'd never been so happy to arrive in this winter wonderland, even though Duke had, in his begrudging, stoic chivalry, carried her suitcase to her romantic, one-bedroom cabin in the woods.

He was a mystery, that one.

A mystery she intended to solve.

"Great. Let's go." She tugged at the bathroom door. The loose knob slipped out of her hand, and the door itself stuck tight in its frame. "If

I can get out of here." She wiggled the antique knob until the latch caught and finally jerked the door free.

Beth laughed as they left. "Gotta love old houses and their sticky doors. Remind me to tell one of the guys about that."

They drove from Wilder House to a huge metal shed in the woods on the Evergreen Resort property. A shiny red convertible was parked inside.

Zuri plopped her bag of craft supplies down and carefully set her makeup case on the cement floor. She whistled as she stepped up to the Mustang. "Wow. Now that's what I call a ride!"

"It will make for some really fun pictures. But I don't have a lot of time before I have to be back at the library for children's story hour."

"Let's get to it, then." Zuri carefully wiped the few specks of snow and dirt off her case and set it in the front seat of the still-warm Mustang to keep her liquids from freezing.

Beth pulled out the *Just Married* sign she'd already painted. Together, they wrapped the frame in more evergreen garland with blue juniper berries and set it in the back seat. Vivie could set the prop up wherever they drove to take the pictures. They trailed blue and white ribbons and bows to the back bumper and attached a small wreath to the front grill, circling the running Mustang logo.

By then Zuri was shivering. "Brrr. I think this is about all I can do. I can't feel my hands anymore."

Beth stomped her feet and shook her gloved fingers. "I have to leave for my library program anyway. But this looks amazing. Vivie will love it."

Good. Because that was the point.

Zuri helped load the extra supplies back in Beth's car and waved as she pulled out of the parking lot. As she walked back toward the cabin, fatigue hit hard. Fat, fluffy snowflakes fell lazily from the sky, landing on the pine trees and winding path. Even the thick cloud cover above resembled the white down comforter on her bed at home. Obviously, her all-nighter packing before her trip and the early morning were catching up to her. She should see if Duke was in his cabin, but a nap beckoned her to her own door.

A huge yawn overtook her as she stepped inside her warm and cozy one-room cabin. She peeled off her coat and sweater and stood in front of the mirror in her tank top. She swept her hair off her neck to reveal the puckered skin on the left side of her neck and shoulder. Makeup covered the red scars on her cheek from the cuts, but nothing would make the burn scars smooth again.

Still, she did what she could. With quick, gentle strokes Zuri rubbed her expensive balm over the scar tissue, from cheek to collarbone down over her shoulder and chest. The lavender scent soaked into her skin.

She turned away from the ugly image in the mirror, slipped her boots off, and was soon fast asleep in the queen bed.

A pounding on her door later woke Zuri with a start. She wrapped herself in a blanket and staggered out of bed to answer it.

Duke stood on the porch, his eyes snapping with enough fire to melt all of Lake Superior. "What did you do to the car?"

"What car?" Zuri wiped the sleep out of her eyes and tried to make sense of his words. "You mean Boone's Mustang?"

"Yes, the Mustang. What did you do to it?"

"We decorated it." Was he really that upset by it? "Vivien wanted—"

"It's not in the shed where I left it."

Wind and snow blew in from the open door, slapping her face. It took another second and a good look at the scowl on Duke's face for his words to sink in. "Wait, the Mustang is *gone*?"

"That's what I said. Now where is it?"

"Sheesh, calm down. You're as bad as my brothers. Couldn't find a thing if it was right in front of them." Zuri slipped her feet back into the UGGs she'd left by the door. "Just give me a sec."

With a huff, she threw the blanket on a nearby chair, slipped her arms into her coat, and walked outside.

Duke was right on her heels as she followed the path to the maintenance shed. The big doors were wide open, snow blowing in and piling on the floor.

She stopped, nonplussed.

What—

There was no trace of the red convertible. Just a lone, white ribbon caught on a sawhorse, whipping in the wind. "Someone probably moved it…"

"I already checked the parking lot and all the paths wide enough to drive on." Duke stood, hands on his hips. "It's not here, Zuri. What did you do with it?"

CHAPTER 3

"What did *I* do with it?" Zuri just stared at him, and in that moment, a whiff of her perfume snaked over to him.

He didn't like it. Or the way she glared, throwing his question back at him. Because yes, he sounded like a jerk.

He sighed and studied the empty space on the cement where he had last parked the car. Some best man he was turning out to be. He pinched the bridge of his nose.

"Sorry. I just...where is it?"

"I don't understand. We left it right here." Zuri walked farther in, her brow wrinkled with confusion.

"You're certain you didn't move it somewhere else? If you did, you need to tell me. Now."

She whipped around to face him, hands on her hips. "Believe it or not, Duke Lowry, I might do makeup and hair for a living, but it doesn't mean I'm a ditz. We decorated the car and left it right here."

Whoa. She sounded like his mama, using his whole name like that. He could hear her voice from the past clearly.

Duke Carter Lowry, don't you talk to a lady like that.

No, his mama wouldn't be happy with the way he was treating Zuri right now. He blew out a long breath. "Okay, I deserve that." He bent down to examine the tracks in the sawdust. "I didn't mean to imply that you were forgetful. I'm used to interrogating criminals." He glanced up at her. "Sorry."

She took the icy stare down a notch. "Look, all that matters now is that we find the car for Boone and Vivien. My makeup case is in it too, and I need that for the wedding. The car *has* to be here."

Zuri didn't look like she was hiding anything. Maybe a little tired, but he guessed he'd woken her up. Still, her makeup seemed unsmudged, her hair perfect—silky and shiny. He *had* caught a hint of a scar on her neckline when she opened the door, wrapped in a blanket. It hinted at something traumatic. But he didn't want to know. He just needed to find the car.

"I should call Boone and tell him." He reached for his phone.

She grabbed it out of his hands before he could open the screen. "What kind of best man are you? You'll stress Boone out and even more so Vivie." She paced back and forth. "No. We can handle this. I mean, you're a detective, right?" She spun around to face him again.

"Right. So if anyone will 'handle it,' it will be me." He reached for his phone back. Ultimately, he was the one responsible for the vehicle. "I work alone. You should go back to your cabin and—"

"And what? Kick up my feet and relax? No way. I'm coming with you."

What? No. "Doesn't Vivien need you for...something?"

"I haven't been able to get ahold of her today since she left Wilder House. This is how I can help. So, what should we do first?"

We? Over his cold, dead grinch body.

He drew in a breath. *Duke Carter Lowry...* "I appreciate the offer, but I've got this."

"Nuh-uh. You're not gonna give me the brush-off. Thanks to my brothers, I'm an expert at dealing with bullheaded men who try to ditch me."

He suppressed a growl and found his cop tone. "I'm not trying to ditch you. I'm just saying, you probably have better things to do."

She folded her arms across her chest and narrowed her eyes. "Like it or not, I'm your partner now."

She was determined, all right, and obviously loyal to her friends. He couldn't help but respect that fierceness in her eyes. And the last thing he wanted was a fight with one of Boone's friends.

He closed his eyes. Nichole could never stand being outside in the winter for very long, always worried about it drying out her skin and the wind messing up her hair. Two minutes out there and Zuri would probably have had enough and head back to her cabin.

This would work. He looked at her. "Fine. We'll start by following the tire tracks in the snow."

"Perfect."

Duke waited for Zuri to exit before shutting the shed doors. Outside, he followed the tread marks. The snow fell lightly from the gray afternoon sky. The tracks were easy enough to see, but once they reached the parking lot it was impossible to distinguish one set from another.

"Well, that didn't get us anywhere. Now what?" Zuri stood in the snow, a brightness in her clear, blue gaze showing her eagerness to keep going.

She wasn't sick of the cold yet? Or his—what had Nichole called it?—oh yeah. His stifling presence?

"I'll head to the sheriff's office. Cole Barrett is one of the other groomsmen and a deputy there. Maybe he's heard something."

"Then I'm coming with you." She headed to his truck, which he'd brought back from Boone's that afternoon. Before she reached it, she did a quick spin with her arms wide open, her face toward the sky, and her tongue stretched out.

Duke stopped in his tracks. "What are you doing?"

"Enjoying the moment. You should try it." She caught a snowflake on the tip of her tongue and grinned at him before hopping into the passenger seat.

Intriguing. Nichole would never do that.

He shook the thought right out of his head.

Hello. He had a case to solve.

Walking into the sheriff's office after the quick drive, Duke forgot about everything but the case. No feminine perfume here setting him off or clogging up his logic. This was his world. Everything from the crackly voices over the radios in the background to the smell of coffee on the Bunn burner added to the sense of familiarity. And he could definitely use some right about now.

The deputy looked up from his desk. "Hey, Duke. Zuri. What are you two doing here?"

"We need your help. I…"

Zuri cut in front of him as she walked up to Cole's desk. "We lost Boone's Mustang. We're wondering if you could help us find it."

"How do you lose a Mustang?" Cole asked.

How indeed. But they should call it like it was. "It was stolen."

"Borrowed." She flashed that big smile of hers. It sort of lit up her eyes. How could she be so upbeat about this whole thing?

More importantly, why was he noticing her eyes?

Sheesh. It had to be Boone and all this sappy romance.

Duke pulled his gaze away from her and looked to Cole. "Either way, have you heard anything? Seen it around town? Last we saw it, it was parked in the maintenance shed at the Evergreen Resort."

Cole reached across his desk to grab a notebook and started writing. Finally, someone who got it. "And the keys? Where were they?"

"I left them in the vehicle, in case the girls needed to move it while they were decorating. Beth and Zuri left it in the shed…at what time?" Duke turned to his optimistic counterpart.

"Oh, somewhere around one, I think."

"And what time did you discover it missing?" Cole looked up from his notes.

"Just now."

A gust of cold air at their backs marked the entrance of another person. "What do we have here?"

Cole stopped writing. "Duke, Zuri, this is Kyle Hueston, our sheriff. Sheriff, these two are here for the wedding. Duke is a detective down in the Twin Cities. Boone's former partner. Zuri came to us from New York. I met her this morning at Wilder House."

"Ah. So what brings you in? Is the bride still missing?" The man in the uniform chuckled as he poured himself a cup of coffee.

"Stolen vehicle." Cole and Duke spoke at the same time.

Kyle's smile slid off his face and was replaced with serious concern. Duke's gut clenched. That wasn't good.

But Zuri was oblivious. "No, I'm sure it wasn't stolen. Probably just borrowed. Or a wedding prank. I mean, this is a small town. People do that kind of thing. Right?"

And here he thought New Yorkers were supposed to be cynical.

He hated to burst her happy little bubble, but he was a realist. "Shoot straight with me, Sheriff. Have you had auto theft problems recently here? Should we be worried?"

Kyle and Cole shared a look before the sheriff spoke up. "It's probably nothing, but we have had a few cars taken recently." He pointed at the cork board with BOLOs posted on it. Pictures of vehicles and individuals to be on the lookout for.

One of the cars, also a red convertible, caught Duke's eye. "Are there a lot of vintage cars stolen? This is a '69 Camaro."

Kyle looked at the printout. "That BOLO is from Duluth, in the next county over. Nothing around Deep Haven as valuable as a vintage Mustang has been stolen. And the few that have all happened at night, not the middle of the day. But we'll keep an eye out."

Cole tapped his pen against his thumb. "It's been pretty quiet in town lately, especially since the storm had most people hunkered down. The only call so far today was that poor guy wandering on Highway 61, lost."

"Any of these stolen cars turn up?" Zuri's voice was hopeful.

Kyle stared into his coffee cup a second before making eye contact, not with Zuri but with Duke. "Sort of. We found some parts of one up at Rusty's gravel pit."

Yeah, that's what Duke thought. Even a sleepy little town like Deep Haven had its dark side. He sighed. "Better give me directions."

Cole set his pen down. "You never know. I mean, Zuri is right. People around here are known to borrow cars. Check the parking lots in town first. And did you ask Boone?"

"We were trying to spare him the stress. I called him after I picked up the Mustang, and he and Vivien were tracking down her missing dress."

"Missing dress? That's where she's been all day? Poor Vivie." Zuri's lips puckered in concern.

Sure. *Now* she was worried. Not about the car, of course, but about a dress. Typical.

Kyle nodded. "Sounds like he already has his hands full. We'll keep our eyes and ears open. I'll get the word out to some of the guys around here before we do anything official."

Duke appreciated the effort, but something deep inside told him not to hold out much hope. He'd better prepare himself, and Zuri, for the worst.

WEDNESDAY, 7:51 P.M.

Not that she'd admit it to Duke, but Zuri's optimism was starting to lag.

They'd been driving around Deep Haven for a couple hours, going through each parking lot and checking behind buildings, but nothing. Her gut clenched at the idea of telling the bride and groom they'd lost the Mustang, the thing that'd brought them together in the first place.

And she didn't want to make a big deal about it…but she'd left her makeup case in the car and…well, how was she supposed to do everyone's hair and makeup without it?

Yeah, they needed to find that car now. Not to mention it would be the perfect opportunity to show Duke what the Christmas spirit was all about.

It was a season of hope. Joy.

And the handsome but cranky guy next to her could certainly use some of that. She had yet to see a smile on that dark, brooding face of his.

And she might not be as taken with Duke as Vivie had hoped when she set up transportation from the airport, but she *was* smitten with the town of Deep Haven. Evergreen garland with white lights twined around lamp posts. Many doors sported wreaths with huge, red bows. The thick drifts covering lawns and trees made everything sparkle like the stars above as they drove through the residential blocks. It was enough to bolster her mood and pray for a Christmas miracle of their own.

Duke's deep voice interrupted her thoughts. "All right, we've gone up and down the main streets of this town and haven't seen a thing. Now can we go to the gravel pit?"

"I suppose. But what makes you so sure that the car was stolen and not borrowed by some well-meaning townsperson?"

"You live in New York City and you really have to ask that?"

"But we're not *in* New York City. Vivie was always telling me about this concept of Minnesota-nice, and I didn't really believe her. But since I landed at the airport, people really have been…nice. And helpful." She glanced over at Duke. "Well, most people."

He gave her a look, his mouth pinched, and stared again at the road.

Perfect strangers had helped her get her huge suitcase off the baggage claim belt. Ree Turnquist, Beth, and the other bridesmaids had had a welcome basket all set for Zuri in her cabin when she arrived last night. Everyone helping at Wilder House this morning had been kind and warm and welcoming. So what was it that made Duke Lowry stand out as such a scrooge?

Maybe he wasn't a true native. "Did you move to Minnesota as an adult?"

"Are you implying I'm not nice?"

His glower didn't scare her. Especially with…wait—was that a tone of *amusement* lacing his words? Hold the phone, she might be on the verge of a breakthrough. But she kept her voice even. "Come on. You don't let me listen to Christmas music. You couldn't get rid of me fast enough when you dropped me off at my cabin last night. And it's obvious you didn't really want me to tag along this afternoon. So what's the deal?"

A long pause stretched between them. "Like I told you last night, I'm simply…not a fan of Christmas."

"That's the lamest excuse I've ever heard. Who doesn't like Christmas?"

"Can we just look for the car?"

Touchy, touchy. "Fine." So maybe she'd dreamed that moment of… cheer. Obviously she wasn't going to charm her way into Duke's good graces. But like it or not, she would help find that car. And he wasn't going to dampen *her* holiday spirit. He could put up with her attempt at making her own music. She hummed "Have Yourself a Merry Little Christmas" as he drove to the gravel pit.

They approached the entrance to a wide-open area in the woods. A streetlight guarded it. Everything was covered in two or more feet of snow, from the looks of where it hit the chain-link fence around the perimeter. It was impossible to tell what was under the snowy mounds and hills.

According to the groan coming from the driver's seat, Duke had hoped for something different. "It hasn't snowed enough in the last few hours to completely bury a car, and I don't see any tire tracks. It's not here."

"Are you sure you don't want to poke around? Maybe there's some back entrance to this place. The car could be hiding behind one of these mounds. We owe it to Boone to look. And I really need to get my makeup case back before the wedding."

"Might as well look." Duke drove farther in until the truck came to a halt. "This is too deep."

He shifted the truck to reverse, but it didn't move more than a few inches. Going forward again only resulted in the unmistakable sound of tires spinning.

"That's just great," Duke mumbled through clenched teeth. "Stay here. I'll dig us out."

Yeah, right. She wouldn't mind watching Duke shoveling snow—a little penance for all that attitude—but she wasn't the kind of person to sit around and watch others work.

She looked around the cab and found a long-handled ice scraper with a brush on one end. That would work. Zuri tugged her black mittens on and pushed hard against the snowpack to open the passenger door. When she hopped out of the cab, snow came up over her knees. She trudged through it to the front tire.

"What are you doing?" Duke walked up to her, carrying a small shovel and a container of kitty litter.

"Look at you, Boy Scout. Prepared for anything."

"It's basic winter driving 101. Now get back into the truck. I got us into this mess, I'll get us out."

"Like I said, we're partners now. So I'm going to help you whether you like it or not." And to prove it, she started digging around the front tire with the ice scraper.

Somewhere behind her he sighed. "That will take forever. Just wait in the truck and stay warm."

She stopped digging and turned to face him again. "Duke, you're stuck with me. And I'm not gonna sit on my tuchus when I could be helping."

He stilled and stared at her for a moment. And he must've believed her or come to some sort of conclusion, because he handed her the shovel. "Here. I'll use the scraper."

Together they dug out around the tires and spread kitty litter on the snow behind each one. The wind kept whipping her hair in her face, but she brushed it aside repeatedly and didn't let that stop her.

After they cleared enough of a path, Zuri waited off to the side with the shovel in hand while Duke jumped back in the cab, shifted into reverse, and feathered the gas. He crept back onto the plowed road.

He retrieved the shovel and kitty litter container and stowed them in the back of the truck. As he shut the tailgate, he looked at her.

"Thanks for the help." The tiniest bit of softness in his gaze caught her by surprise and sent her pulse skipping a beat.

Okay, that was weird.

But maybe this meant she'd at least earned his respect. And she had to admit, it was a nice change from the other men in her life, namely her big brothers. She'd heard all their jokes about being a useless hairstylist and makeup girl.

But Duke didn't seem to write her off. Maybe there was hope for him yet.

Now they just had to find the missing car, and the wedding would be back on track.

CHAPTER 4

WEDNESDAY, 8:29 P.M.

*W*ell, that was unexpected. Maybe Zuri wasn't the pampered princess he took her for. Nichole wouldn't even pick up an ice scraper, let alone try to use it to clear huge drifts of snow to help him free the truck. And after hours of searching for the Mustang, Zuri wasn't asking to stop. He had even gotten strangely used to her chatter and humming as they'd searched Deep Haven.

And now she stood beside the truck, staring up at him with, well, impossibly huge blue eyes.

Pretty eyes, if he wanted to be honest.

A dark smudge on her cheek—probably from the tire—caught his gaze.

He stepped closer to her and pointed to her cheek—

"What are you doing?" She froze. Panic flashed in her eyes.

"You have some dirt from the tire on your cheek."

"Oh." She swiped at the last bit of the gray streak and stepped away. She used the sideview mirror on his truck to check her makeup.

Quick as a flash, she was back in the truck cab, pulling something out of her purse.

Duke made his way back over to the driver's side and got in. He watched her as she frantically dabbed some goop on the scar on her cheek.

"Why do you even bother?"

"Excuse me?"

"The makeup. I mean, you don't need it."

"How would you know? You haven't seen me without it." She flipped the visor mirror back up. Looked at him with a smile that felt…off. As if he'd offended her.

And he didn't know why, but suddenly he wanted to, well…maybe fix it.

"Scars are…our history. You don't have to cover it up."

She swallowed hard as she looked at him. "You…you saw the scar?"

"Well, yeah. I'm a detective. I notice details. So you've been through some stuff. Scars mean you're a survivor."

She looked away. "That's one way of looking at it," she whispered.

The cab grew awkwardly silent.

Now he really had made it worse.

Great. See, this was what happened when he tried to be…nice.

But as he started the engine, she turned toward him and offered a cheeky grin. "So have I earned the right to a little Christmas music?"

"So that's how it's going to be."

"Yep." When he looked over at Zuri, she was already messing with his radio, scanning for a Christmas station, bouncing in her seat.

Okay, she was a little cute. In a pretty, Christmas sort of way.

If a guy liked that kind of thing.

He pulled out of the gravel pit.

Zuri found a station playing Bruce Springsteen's "Santa Claus Is Comin' to Town" and started singing.

He quirked an eyebrow as she belted out the chorus.

"What? I can't help it. My brother Tony and I used to sing this one to wake everyone up on Christmas morning."

"You have a lot of good Christmas memories with your family?"

"Yeah. We're a loud bunch. But we have good times."

She pulled out her phone and showed him the screen when he pulled up to the stop sign at the end of the deserted country road. With no one behind him, he put the truck in park and studied the picture.

There had to be over twenty-five people crowded into a small living room with a decorated Christmas tree in the background. Kids sat on laps of many of the adults, and teenagers leaned in toward the camera. One guy had a toddler sitting on his shoulders. And in the middle of it all, an older couple, both with snowy-white hair, sat on the couch kissing.

Duke searched the sea of faces for Zuri. "Where are you?"

"Who do you think took the picture?" She was probably going for a playful quip, but he didn't miss the undertone of longing.

"So this is your family."

"This is them. And it all started with the two lovebirds in the middle. That's my nonna and Pop, my mom's parents." She went on to point out her parents, her six brothers, their significant others, and their children.

"How many nieces and nephews do you have?"

"Sixteen, with one more on the way."

"And what is that guy holding up in the air? Is that a trophy?"

Zuri's laughter filled the darkness of the cab. "Kind of. That's the rotating fruitcake."

"A fruitcake trophy?"

"It's more of a joke. One of the neighbors gave Nonna this fruit-cake, insisting it was so much better than her panettone."

"Is it?"

"Not even close. Now we pass it off as a joke during our gift exchange."

"How old is that cake?"

"It came over on the Mayflower."

He pulled away, onto the highway, and found himself laughing.

Laughing. Huh. "Are you missing that this year? The gift exchange?"

"Oh. Yeah, but that's okay. I want to be here for Vivie. She's done so much for me. She helped me get my start in stage makeup. And as much as I love Christmas and our big loud family, my mom's lasagna Christmas Eve dinner, and the candlelight services at home, I was ready for something different this year."

Was it just him or did Zuri actually sound...lonely? How was that possible coming from such a big family? "I always wanted a big family growing up. Grandparents, siblings, cousins. The whole bunch. But it was just my mother and me. You're lucky." The admission left him feeling a little exposed, but also right. Especially when she smiled at him.

"Not everyone can handle the Milano chaos. You should've seen the Christmas Vivien spent with us. I thought we'd scare her away for sure. But she jumped right in like she was born into the family."

"Better her than me. I'd probably scare *them* all away."

Did he really say that?

She laughed. "I don't know. My nephews would think it's pretty awesome having a real cop there."

Now she was just trying to make him feel better. But his neck grew warm as Zuri studied him intently, like she was looking beyond skin and bone to everything he hid underneath.

"You do remind me a little of my grandfather. He's quiet and serious. He never says a whole lot, but he is protective and would do anything for his family."

It was sweet. She didn't want him to look like a sap. And yes, part of that was true. But when push came to shove, he'd chosen Nichole over his only family. What did that make him?

He didn't want to know.

He couldn't make up for Zuri missing her family, but he could at least buy the woman a hot drink for putting up with this cold trek looking for the lost Mustang and...well, his chilly attitude.

"I can't make lasagna or panettone, but how about some hot cocoa?"

She looked over at him with a coy smile. "That depends. Will it have marshmallows?"

Was it just her or was Duke Lowry actually loosening up a little? Of course, his offer to buy her a hot cocoa was a small friendly gesture, not necessarily a complete conversion on the whole Christmas thing, but she intended to enjoy it and bask in her success a bit.

And maybe she was warming up to him too. It had nothing to do with the surprising admission that the handsome guy wanted a big family.

Or that he saw her scars as…strength. She'd never seen them as anything but something to hide.

With the heaters on full blast, Zuri's feet thawed back to normal, and the cab of the truck stayed pleasant as they drove to the local coffee shop. But the only lights shining at the Java Cup were on the outside of the building.

"Looks like they're closed." She tried to swallow down the disappointment and keep her voice light and merry. "We can just head back to the cabins. It's getting late. Maybe we'll have better luck tomorrow. And I'm sure you're tired of my chatting."

He shrugged, his arm resting casually on the steering wheel. "I've gotten used to it. Besides, I'm a man of my word. I promised you cocoa. You're getting hot cocoa." He gripped the wheel once more with both hands, determination etched across his forehead.

Zuri tried hard to ignore the warm, swirly feeling his words evoked. "All right, but where?"

A quick drive around downtown showed all the businesses locked tight for the night—the whole town asleep.

Duke would not be deterred though. He looked up every cafe on his phone and insisted on driving by them to make sure. The one restaurant he called that was open didn't have hot cocoa on the menu.

Still, he didn't lose that stubborn glint in his eye.

Heaven help the criminal that ever got in Duke Lowry's way. If she peeled back the grumpy exterior, there was a good and honest man there.

He turned toward her. "All right, I didn't say it would be the best hot cocoa ever, but I've got one last resort."

"I'm game."

His only answer was a smirk. And goodness, what a handsome smirk it was.

Stop. This wasn't a holiday romance, despite Vivien's wish.

But oh, it was hard to find a guy in NYC with morals and integrity that wasn't scared away by her family or scars.

He drove back to the highway, and she could only laugh when they pulled into the Holiday gas station right in the middle of town.

"Wait there," he said as he parked. He jogged over and opened her door.

Her heart melted a little more.

Hold it together, girl. He's only being Minnesota nice.

Inside, they grabbed gas station hot cocoa and half-off donuts, all of which Duke insisted on paying for. He even threw a whole bag of marshmallows on the counter.

A man behind them in line eyed their purchases. His hair was long and a little stringy, could use a good cut and some product.

"You can't have cocoa without marshmallows," she explained to the stranger.

He held up stained hands. "No judgment here." He leaned in suggestively. "But if you want anything stronger, I'm sure we can find that too. There's a bar right next to my hotel."

"Oh. Uh, thanks, but—"

"Back off. She's already got plans." Duke wrapped a strong arm around her shoulder.

"Sorry, man. Can't blame a guy for trying."

Duke met the guy's smarmy smile with one of his famous glares. No surprise, the other guy backed off and slapped a twenty on the counter to pay for his chips. His fingers, covered in black paint or ink, and missing teeth gave him a devilish appearance Zuri was grateful to escape.

She quickly stepped back out into the clear night as Duke held the door open for her.

"Well, look at you saving the day, Detective. My own Christmas miracle."

"Christmas miracle?"

"You fought off that creep and found me cocoa. So maybe there's hope for you yet," she said as they walked toward his truck.

He rolled his eyes, but one corner of his full lips tilted up. The hint of a smile. "I'm no hero. And I'd hardly call gas-station hot cocoa and day-old donuts a Christmas miracle."

"Come on, let's walk a little, look at the lights. I'll bet we can find some of that Christmas spirit you're missing." They crossed the quiet, dark street at the stoplight and followed the sidewalk toward the lake.

"I'll walk around since I could use some exercise after all the driving. But I doubt that will rekindle a long-extinguished love of Christmas."

"Aha! So at one point, you *did* like Christmas! What happened?"

He stared down at his cup and stuffed a quick bite of donut in his mouth. They moved toward the bay, their steps crunching on the layer of snow that had fallen earlier. Zuri forgot she'd even asked the question as she got lost in the lights and sounds of the town. "Silent Night" played through her mind as she looked up at the stars blinking in the night sky. They walked awhile before Duke spoke again, his deep timbre breaking the quiet between them.

"Christmas was my mom's favorite time of year." He pointed to the twinkle lights swinging from the eaves of a tiny red building with the sign *World's Best Donuts*. "She would've loved all this."

Tears sprang to Zuri's eyes. Her mom loved Christmas too. She couldn't imagine how hard this time of year would be if she wasn't around to celebrate it.

So maybe Scrooge McDuke just missed his mother. Mystery solved.

She didn't say anything. But, crazily, she reached out and slipped a gloved hand in his and squeezed.

And he squeezed back.

Rightfully, there should be angels appearing in the sky to sing hallelujah, such was the joy that stirred inside her.

"So, now that I've bared my soul, tell me, why is this makeup case so important?" Duke asked.

"What are you talking about?"

"Like it didn't kill you to let me put it in the truck yesterday? I practically had to pry it out of your hands. And I know you're worried about it now."

"Do you realize how much it would cost for me to replace everything in that case?"

He stared her down and plowed right through her poor excuse. "Really?"

She sighed. "The whole reason I'm here is to help Vivien have the wedding of her dreams. They'll be taking pictures of this moment, pictures they'll hang up in their home and have for the rest of their lives. I just want everything to be as beautiful as it possibly can be."

He looked over at her, and they stopped in the middle of the sidewalk. A rhythmic sound of rocking waves and ice dancing on the shore carried over. Her own heart thumped a little faster as Duke turned to her, his stare so intense she couldn't turn away.

Yes, the man had special powers.

"I'll say it again. You really don't need the makeup. And maybe what some consider flaws are really the things that make someone unique. A different kind of beauty."

The soft, solid stillness in his voice made her believe it. But really, what did he know?

"You don't believe me."

She sipped her cocoa and looked away from his too observant gaze. "I know you're talking about my scars, but let me tell ya, there's nothing beautiful about them. They're ugly. And most people can't handle the ugly. Certainly not any of the men I know."

Especially since Duke Lowry had only seen a glimpse of them, not the whole package.

"I see the ugliness of society every day in my job. So I'm kind of an expert at it. And I can tell you this, Zuri. Real ugliness can't be covered up. You can't make a dump heap not stink no matter how much you try to make it look nice on the outside."

"Are you really comparing me to a dump?" Please, change the subject. "How romantic."

But he didn't smile. "All I'm saying is, the scars on your skin can't deter from the true woman you are inside. And even though we just met, I haven't seen anything ugly about you yet. Annoyingly chipper, maybe. But not ugly."

She laughed, probably too loud, because oh, how something inside leaped at Duke's words. This wasn't fair. Even though she'd set out to burrow past his icy shell, he was turning the tables on her.

Which only smacked of another broken heart for her when he discovered the truth.

CHAPTER 5

*I*t was official. Duke was the worst best man ever.

He'd lost the ring.

The weak sun streaming in the window shone a spotlight on the clothes strewn all over the cabin while he searched. When Duke checked the pockets of the pants he'd worn yesterday and came up empty once again, dread pooled in his middle.

How were Vivie and Boone supposed to get married without the ring?

He'd had it when he grabbed the tuxes and when he picked up the Mustang yesterday. He'd double-checked after showing Megan and putting the velvet box back in his inner coat pocket.

He sank down to the bed. It had to have fallen out of his coat when he threw it in the passenger seat of the Mustang on his way back to Evergreen. It was the only place it could be. Probably sitting on the newly vacuumed floor mats under that front seat.

Duke texted Cole. *Any word on the Mustang?*

Sorry. Not a thing. But we're all keeping an eye out.

But it wasn't their job. It was his. He tossed his phone on the bed and scrubbed his hands down his face. How had he messed this up so badly? Boone was going to kill him.

For some reason Zuri's hopeful face came to mind. But now was not the time to think about how she'd slipped past his defenses. How he actually enjoyed walking around town with her.

Now was the time to start asking around the resort and see what kinds of clues he could kick up. But that meant talking to people. And for that, he needed coffee. He grabbed his coat and keys and drove to the Java Cup. Hopefully it would be open this time.

It was open, all right. Apparently, everyone else in Deep Haven wanted coffee too, because the line wound around the coffee shop.

Duke sighed as he stood behind an older man in a green parka, who reminded him a little of Harrison Ford. He turned around and offered a sympathetic smile. "Long line," he said with a shrug.

The way everything was going, Duke should be used to it. "Yeah, I really don't have time for this, but if I don't get some caffeine, I'll never make it through this day."

The man nodded like he got it. "You can go in front of me if you want." He stepped to the side, letting Duke take his spot.

Wow. People did that? "Thanks. I appreciate it." Now that he took a closer look at the man's build and coat, he looked familiar. "Do I know you from somewhere?"

"Probably not. I'm here on vacation. Staying with my family at Evergreen Resort a little ways out of town."

What do ya know? Something finally going his way. "I'm staying at Evergreen too." Duke shook the man's hand and introduced himself. And no better time to start canvasing the resort guests.

"Bob Brown."

"Say, you didn't happen to see someone around the resort driving a red vintage Mustang yesterday afternoon, did you?"

Bob shook his head. "No. I would've remembered seeing a classic like that. Is your car missing?"

"Something like that." Not that Bob needed to know the logistics of it. "It's not my car. It belongs to a friend and went missing from the resort garage yesterday." Duke studied the man for a reaction. No flicker of panic or recognition flashed across Bob's features. He didn't know anything.

Instead, both men moved forward in line. Duke ordered his triple shot latte and waited at the other end of the counter for his drink.

So much for that.

He went to the small counter and was doctoring his coffee with a couple packs of sugar when Bob approached again.

"Have a little faith. Christmas is the time of miracles. One might show up where you least expect it."

Oh good, another optimist. Duke kept his mouth shut and looked around for an open table.

But the older man must've sensed his skepticism. "It couldn't hurt to ask for guidance. If you're a believing man, send up a prayer. God is, after all, in the business of finding lost things."

Yeah, right. The last time he prayed for a miracle, God was silent.

His mama had believed until the very end, though.

One way or another, I will be healed, Duke. Don't stop believing just because I'll be in glory. Goodness knows, with the life I've lived, that itself is a miracle.

But it wasn't the miracle Duke had wanted.

Bob said it couldn't hurt to pray. But he was wrong. It hurt to *hope.* To believe despite the odds. And it was downright agonizing to have hope extinguished when reality crashed in and those prayers went unanswered.

But walking around with Zuri last night, thinking of how his mother would've loved all the lights around town...well, he was tempted to try again. And he obviously needed all the help he could get. Maybe if God wouldn't do it for him, He'd listen for Boone's and Vivien's sakes.

So he stared out the big window to the lake—angry and frothing on shore—the sounds of the coffee grinders whirring, the people in conversation, and...

Lord, remember me, the guy whose mom bit the dust on Your watch? I know I screwed up, but I need Your help. I'd be grateful if You could lead us to that Mustang. And the ring. And maybe help get me through this whole wedding without ruining it. Boone doesn't deserve that.

A pretty girl laughed at the next table, her hair pulled back into a messy bun, and he thought of Zuri and her perfect hair...

And God, I suppose Zuri needs her makeup box thing too.

He sat down and listened to the conversation hub in the shop. Nothing about a found Mustang.

Bob lifted his coffee to him as Duke left and headed back to the resort. He'd promised Zuri he would check with her in the morning, but when he knocked on her door, she didn't answer.

He couldn't wait around to start canvasing, so when he spotted a young couple wearing matching puffy coats and walking a big curly-haired dog out on the trail to the lake, he stopped them.

Duke slapped on what he hoped was a friendly smile and introduced himself as a fellow guest. "Say, did you see someone driving a classic red Mustang yesterday afternoon? I heard there was one around, and I'm a bit of a gearhead. I was hoping to talk to the guy who owns that beaut."

The woman's face lit. "You know, I did see an older gentleman yesterday driving a red car. I don't know what kind it was though. I remember thinking how sweet it was that it had a Christmas wreath on the front of it."

That had to be the Mustang. Duke schooled his features to show only a mild interest. "An older guy? Have you seen him before? Do you think he's staying here?"

"I don't know. But I did hear someone calling 'Grandpa' around the cabins last night when I took Penny out. That would probably be an older guy, right?"

The man next to her nodded. "I heard that too. Down by the cabins that way." He pointed deeper into the woods. Cabins closer to the shed.

Finally, something helpful. It was the first promising lead in the whole case. Maybe praying wasn't such a bad idea after all.

※

THURSDAY, 9:41 A.M.

Zuri bit into a World's Best glazed cake donut as she sat in a bright red booth in the little donut shop and listened to Vivien explain her adventures of yesterday in tracking down her runaway gown. The last thing this bride needed after all she'd been through looking for that dress was to worry about the missing Mustang. And since there wasn't really a good way to explain where her makeup and hair tools were without divulging that, Zuri suggested pushing off their hair and makeup run-through another day.

But this time would not be wasted. Zuri needed more ammo.

Duke had let down that steel guard a tiny bit yesterday. In fact, it was really sweet how he'd gone out of his way to find her hot cocoa. But there was still a lot of hidden scar tissue around the man's heart.

Before, she'd wanted to make sure Vivie's Christmas wedding went without any bah-humbugs from the best man. Now she wanted more. Because somehow, in a little over twenty-four hours, her own guard had slipped. She wanted Duke to find healing for his wounded heart. She wanted him to enjoy the Christmas season again like his mother used to.

"Vivie, what is the deal with Duke Lowry? And don't deny it, but you were totally trying to set us up, weren't you?"

"Whatever do you mean?" Her mock innocent expression didn't fool Zuri for a second.

"Oh, come on now. Why in the world would you think Duke and I would hit it off? He's handsome, no doubt. But he couldn't be more rigid and dry if he tried."

"So he's more like a hearty pasta, and you are a bold marinara. It's a match made in heaven."

Zuri set down her coffee mug. "He hates Christmas."

"But he didn't always. I think it has something to do with his ex."

"Ex...wife?" He had an ex?

"No, ex-girlfriend. Boone said she was a model or something. Apparently Duke was head over heels for her."

"What happened?"

"She really wanted to go to a fancy ski resort out in Colorado. Duke took her over the holidays and was going to propose, but she met up with her ex-boyfriend and left with him instead."

"That's horrible. Poor Duke." But it explained a lot.

"It gets worse. Soon after he got back, his mom was diagnosed with pancreatic cancer. She was gone within a matter of weeks."

The donut Zuri swallowed hit her gut hard. No wonder he hated Christmas. Duke's heart was broken, and he was all alone. And here she was shoving pictures of her big family on him, sharing all about their Christmas traditions, trying to warm him up.

All she'd done was rub in his face what he had lost.

"I've only met him a few times, but Boone was his partner for years. We both hate seeing him so caught up in work. He has no life. No family and few friends. This is the one time since the guys' summer canoe trip we've been able to get him to take a day off work. I was just hoping you could show him a good time—make him laugh, maybe get him to smile. Besides, it wouldn't hurt you to spend some time with a hot guy and remember what dating is all about."

"What are you implying?"

"Zuri, you haven't gone out with anyone since Damien. It's been years. You're gonna have to get back out there at some point."

It was all hitting too close. Zuri cleared her throat. "It's sweet you wanna help, Viv, but look. Duke and I are as different as night and day, and we live, like, a thousand miles apart. Besides, I'm here for *you*. This is your wedding. Don't worry about me."

"Well, I do. But speaking of my wedding, I do have a big favor to ask."

"Shoot."

"Amelia, one of my matrons of honor, called. The entire family is stuck in the Keys. There's no way they'll make it by Saturday. I need you to fill in as a bridesmaid."

A bridesmaid?

But a bridesmaid wore a bridesmaid's dress.

A *sleeveless* bridesmaid's dress. Zuri would be standing in front of a crowd with all her scars completely exposed. The stares. The pitying looks. The grimaces. And pictures would capture it all. The images in her head made her lungs squeeze tight.

"Oh, uh, I don't know, Vivie. I mean, I'm honored, of course. But isn't there anyone else who could do it? You know everyone around here."

"But I want you. You brought me into your family back when I was in New York and couldn't get home for holidays."

And Zuri wanted to help. That was her sole motivation for coming. She just wasn't sure she could do it without passing out in front of the church and ruining the whole wedding.

"But I've seen pictures of Amelia. No way I'd fit into her dress."

"All the dresses ran too big. I'd bet we'll have to take it in for you. I got good at adjusting my costumes, so I know I can make this dress work for you. The color will look amazing with your eyes."

Yeah, but what about her scars?

She opened her mouth to decline, but Vivien cut her off. "Don't decide now. Just promise me you'll consider it. Although, don't wait too long—I need time to alter the dress."

Consider it? She was kidding, right? Zuri slipped her hand beneath her scarf and felt the bumpy scar tissue on her neck.

Duke's words trickled through the panic.

So you've been through some stuff. Scars mean you're a survivor.

He made them seem like badges of honor or something.

Zuri looked over at Vivien's beautiful face. Beyond the surface beauty lay a loyal friend and the whole reason Zuri had even come to Minnesota.

She couldn't promise her anything yet, but she deserved something. "Okay, I'll think about it."

But it wouldn't matter if they didn't find that Mustang. Because there was no way she could face the world without her makeup.

CHAPTER 6

*D*uke turned a blind eye to the frozen lake surrounded by evergreen trees and birch. And while he was at it, he'd ignore the sweat seeping through his long-sleeved shirt as he marched through the snow to the cabin farthest down the trail. Whoever this older guy was, he better have some answers.

Duke's phone rang before he approached.

Boone.

Maybe he should let it go to voicemail.

Nah, it would only raise suspicion. And Boone would call again.

He punched the green icon on the screen and cleared his throat. "Hey. Did you and Vivien find the dress?"

"Long story, but I'm working on something. A surprise for Vivien. So, sorry I was MIA most of yesterday. Did everything go okay with the car detail?"

Duke cupped a hand around his neck and paced. "I picked up the ring and the tuxes, got the car detailed, and then it was decorated." All true statements.

"Great. I really appreciate that. So, for today I was thinking—"

"I actually have a case I need to do some research on. I'm hoping to tie it up by tonight. Then I'll be back to being at your beck and call."

"You sure? Do you need help?"

"No, man. It's all good. Just something that came up last minute I need to deal with."

Boone hesitated. "All right. So, I'll talk to you later?"

"Yup. Later." Duke ended the call and released a long breath.

He hated lying. Okay, so technically nothing he'd said was a lie. But still. He was close to fixing this. He just needed time. He would give himself one more day to track down that Mustang and the ring. If he didn't find it by tonight, he'd have to break the news to Boone.

Which meant he needed answers now.

He strode forward to the log-sided cabin with sharp icicles hanging from the eaves. An elderly man in a brown cardigan answered his knock. "Good morning."

"Morning, sir. I'm Detective Lowry. Have you seen a red '65 Mustang around the campgrounds?"

"A '65 Mustang you say? She's a beauty. I used to have a Mustang." He smiled, something faraway suddenly in his eyes.

"Did you see one yesterday? Here at the resort? Did you drive it?"

The man stared over Duke's shoulder, still lost in thought.

"Sir? This is very important. Did you see anyone driving a red convertible Mustang yesterday?"

He looked back at Duke. "I took my Phyllis for ice cream like always. We were supposed to share a banana split with two cherries. But she was late." He frowned. "I don't know why she was late." He blinked, then looked away, shaking his head, and shut the door in Duke's face.

"Wait!" Duke knocked again on the door. "Sir?"

He knocked harder, but the elderly man didn't answer. Duke was ready to break the door down when a much younger man in a blue coat and worried look marched up with a box of donuts.

"Excuse me. Why are you disturbing my grandfather? He's supposed to be resting."

Now he could get somewhere. "I'm Detective Duke Lowry. I have reason to believe your grandfather knows something about a car that was stolen yesterday afternoon from the maintenance shed on the premises. A '65 Mustang."

The man sighed and hung his head. "So *that's* how he ended up lost on the highway while his car was still here." He looked back at Duke with a guilty expression. "I'm sorry. For the past sixty-something years, my grandparents spent the week before Christmas here. My grandma died last year, so we canceled, but Grandpa was so upset… well, we brought him. But he's having some memory issues."

"Memory issues?"

"Yesterday he went missing—threw us all in a panic until a deputy picked him up on the highway. He didn't know where he was or how he got there. But it makes sense. He used to have a red Mustang. He must have wandered to the shed and taken it."

"But where did he leave it?"

"No idea. Like I said, he was very confused when they found him."

"I need to speak with him now." Duke wouldn't take no for an answer.

The man shrugged. "I'm not sure how far you'll get. Half the time he's in a different decade in his mind. And if you try correcting him, he gets mad and upset." He unlocked the cabin door. "But we can try."

In the cabin, the younger man introduced himself as Tom Karlson and his grandfather as Gerald. The elder was sitting near the window of the cabin, sipping coffee.

His grandson approached him. "Grandpa, I've got some donuts to go with your coffee. And this detective here is wondering about a car. Did you take a drive yesterday? Is that how you got to town?"

"Town?"

Duke stepped up. "Yes, sir. The '65 Mustang you drove yesterday afternoon. Where did you leave the car?"

"A Mustang? I used to have a Mustang. Great car. Phyllis loved going on drives with the top down." He grinned as he picked through the donuts for one covered in cinnamon and sugar.

"Okay, but, sir, where did you drive it yesterday? What time did you take the Mustang?"

Gerald's smile fell. "I don't have the convertible anymore. I drive a sedan." He looked out the window at the snow drifts and trees, then back at Duke. "It's not a great time of year for driving a convertible, young man."

"But you drove a red vintage Mustang yesterday to Deep Haven. Where is it?" Duke asked.

Gerald bit into his donut and chewed. "Phyllis and I always split the banana split." He smiled at the memory, oblivious to anyone else for the moment.

Banana split? "Mr. Karlson, I need to know where you left that car. You could be charged with auto theft."

Gerald dropped the donut, startled. "Theft? I've never stolen anything in my life!"

Tom rushed over. "Now wait a minute. He hasn't admitted to anything. Do you even have proof? He's a confused man."

"I have an eyewitness who saw him in the Mustang yesterday. I can bring this witness by to confirm, if that's what you want."

"Mike, what is he talking about?" Gerald asked, his breathing fast, his eyes wide.

Tom laid a protective hand on his grandfather's shoulder. "We're done here. I'm calling my lawyer. If you want to come back and charge him, you'd better have a warrant. Otherwise, get out." He pointed to the door.

Duke stared for another beat. Gerald Karlson had taken that Mustang. And left it who knew where. He blew out a breath.

The elderly man stood abruptly and spilled his coffee on the side table. "Mike? Where's—"

"Shhh, it's okay, Grandpa." Tom moved to help calm his grandfather. He glared back at Duke. "Look what you've done now—he's getting agitated. He doesn't even know who I am. So unless you want me to call this in for harassment, leave now."

The last thing he needed was a harassment suit in a place that wasn't even his jurisdiction. Duke yanked the door open and left. That man knew where the car was. But how would Duke get those answers out of him?

Zuri's face came to mind.

Somehow, she'd convinced a bunch of strangers to sing Christmas carols at the airport. She had a way of sneaking past one's defenses and making them feel comfortable. She could probably draw a confession out of this guy too.

And maybe it wouldn't be so bad spending a little time with her. Last night as they'd walked through the town, her presence had filled up the empty spaces he'd grown used to. Even the Christmas music she listened too wasn't so bad. It reminded him of his mother singing along to Bing Crosby.

And he liked it.

So there. He could admit it.

And if Zuri Milano had gotten past his own walls, she could certainly charm some answers out of Gerald Karlson.

THURSDAY, 11:14 A.M.

Zuri stood in her cabin, staring at the dress Vivien had insisted on leaving with her. It was only a dress. A gorgeous, blue chiffon dress.

So why did the thought of putting it on make her break out in hives?

A sharp knock sounded. She'd take whatever it was over this stupid gown.

Zuri grabbed her scarf and wrapped it around her, then opened her door to find Duke standing there in his typical handsome glower. But she knew better now. That hard-clenched, chiseled jaw did not scare her. He was the same guy who'd searched all over town to find her hot cocoa. And marshmallows.

"I was coming to find you. Looks like you beat me to it," Zuri said.

The corner of his lips quirked up, almost like he was happy to see her. "Hi." His gaze locked on hers, and his brown eyes warmed.

For some silly reason, heat flushed her neck. "So...what's next on our case? I just had breakfast with Vivien, and so far, she doesn't know anything about the Mustang. But I put the word out to all the others in the wedding party. Everyone has their eyes open."

"We might not need them. I have a lead, but I need your help."

"Of course." Duke needing her? Her curiosity was stoked. "Why don't you come in out of the cold."

He stepped in, bringing with him the crisp evergreen scent of the woods and that hint of citrus and clove he wore so well.

"So, what's the lead you found?"

"I asked other guests here about the Mustang, and a woman said she saw an elderly man driving a red car yesterday afternoon."

"That's great! We have an eyewitness. Now we just have to find the man."

"I found him. But the problem is he doesn't remember anything."

"What do you mean?"

"Gerald Karlson and his grandson are staying in cabin seven. Yesterday, I believe Gerald took the car and drove it around, but he doesn't remember where. He's the guy the deputies talked about finding wandering Highway 61. The grandson says his memory comes and goes. When I tried talking to him, he spouted out some nonsense about banana splits and his dead wife. And then he got upset."

"Let me guess. You went in there and demanded answers, didn't you?"

His mouth tightened. "Maybe. But he obviously stole the car. He's got the answers we need."

She could see it all in her head—Duke's glower and a sweet old man. Duke didn't know his own power. No wonder he didn't get far.

"He might've taken the car, but you can't interrogate a confused elderly man like he's a common thug on the street. You need to make him feel comfortable. Like it's a friendly chat."

"Yeah, I figured that out. I was hoping you would talk to him." A hint of vulnerability in his rock-solid demeanor sent a fluttery feeling through her whole body.

He trusted her with this, and it felt…nice. Really nice.

"Come on. Let's go talk to Gerald and find our car. And my makeup case. Then we'll have this wedding back on track."

Duke grimaced.

"What? What was that look?" Zuri stopped in the middle of putting on her coat.

He closed his eyes and pinched his nose. "I…uh…I also might have lost the ring." He winced as if the admission gave him physical pain.

"You didn't!" Without thinking, Zuri reached out and laid her hand on his chest. His well-honed, muscular chest.

"I know, I know. But I'm pretty sure it's in the Mustang. It was in my coat pocket yesterday when I drove here. I think it fell out on the floor of the car when I tossed my coat on the passenger seat."

He probably didn't realize it, but he'd covered her hand with his own during his earnest plea and squeezed. The warmth of it made Zuri's knees go weak.

What in the world was happening to her? Duke Lowry just might be the last man she should fall for—and not just because of his loathing of Christmas. But…well, she could start with about a thousand miles between here and New York City.

And then there was, well, Damien. And the wounds he'd left.

No. She didn't care what Vivien said. She didn't need a date.

She just wanted a friend.

With reluctance, she slipped her hand out from under his.

The ring. The wedding. She needed to focus. "Well, then we'd better go find that Mustang." She led the way outside.

When they knocked on the door of cabin seven, a guy probably in his thirties with dark hair and a slender build, wearing a red-and-green flannel shirt, opened the door. He immediately scowled at Duke. "I thought I told you to leave."

This must be the grandson. And boy did Zuri have some smoothing over to do. She gave him the brightest grin she could manage. "I'm Zuri. It's so nice to meet you."

"I'm…Tom." His focus swung from Duke to Zuri.

She placed her hands over her heart and gushed. "Tom, I have to say, Duke told me all about how you're spending your holiday here taking care of your grandfather, and I think that is so sweet."

Tom actually blushed. "Thanks. I try."

"No, really. How many people would do that? And I know you're just looking out for him, but we really need to find that missing Mustang. Could we please talk to your grandpa again?"

"He tried and it didn't go so well." He glared at Duke, who thankfully kept his mouth shut. Though that flare of his nostrils said it was taking a lot of effort.

"What if I talk to him? I promise to be gentle." Zuri stopped just short of batting her eyelashes at him.

Tom considered for a moment and eventually opened up the door farther. "Fine. But the second he gets upset, you leave."

"We will." Zuri followed Tom inside. "I promise."

She made her way over to Gerald and introduced herself. She waved Duke back, signaling him to stay by the door. She didn't want his presence to intimidate the sweet man in the brown sweater sitting by the window.

"It's nice to meet you, Mr. Karlson." Zuri took the seat across from him at the small table.

"Call me Gerald. So, are you dating my grandson?"

Tom sputtered. "Grandpa!"

"Well, you should if you're not. I don't know why you're still single. You should ask this beautiful woman out instead of sitting around with me." Gerald sent Zuri a wink.

She liked this guy already. But she should probably put Tom out of his misery. "Actually, the man I came to see was you, Gerald."

"What did you have in mind? I'm not as young as I once was, but I still have some moves if you get me out on the dance floor."

Zuri laughed. "As great as that sounds, I was wondering about going for a ride. If you were going to drive me around, where would you take me?"

Gerald's smile grew sad. "My Phyllis loved going for rides."

That's right. Keep talkin'. "In your Mustang?"

"Yes. With the top down."

"Did you go for a ride yesterday in the Mustang?" Zuri gently pressed.

He stared out the window again, confused. "I…I stopped to get ice cream. Phyllis and I always split the banana split."

Duke turned to Tom. "Where would he go for ice cream?"

"There's an ice-cream shop right in town. Licks and Stuff. He must've gone there."

"That's right. I remember driving by it yesterday," Zuri said. "But we didn't see the car in the parking lot. We checked."

Tom sat next to his grandfather by the window. "Where did you drive the Mustang after Licks and Stuff, Grandpa?"

He didn't respond. They were losing him.

Zuri laid her hand on Gerald's. "It sounds like you really miss your wife. She must've been quite the lady, huh?"

"Yes, my Phyllis was a looker. Fell for her the first time we met at the high school winter formal. We both came with friends and left with each other."

"And you took Phyllis for a ride?"

He nodded. "She liked to go fast."

"Did you take her for ice cream in the Mustang yesterday? Do you remember?"

"Maybe." The older man's raspy voice grew strong, confident. "Wait. I did. But we liked to eat our ice cream by the water. I drove to Artist Point and…" He frowned. "But she wasn't there. So I drove to our favorite lookout on the highway. It's where I proposed."

"A lookout?"

Tom pulled out his phone. "I can show you on the map here. It's a small parking lot on the side of Highway 61 where you can pull over and see the lake. He must've left the car there, because the deputy found him not too far from that spot."

"Wouldn't we have seen it on our way into town?" Zuri asked Duke.

Duke looked at the map. "No, it was in the opposite direction." He came over to Gerald. "Thank you, Mr. Karlson. You were a big help."

"Did I take your car?" His countenance fell. "I'm sorry."

"The important thing is you remembered and are helping us find it." Duke shook Gerald's and Tom's hands.

Well, look at Duke Lowry making friends with the criminal. He was definitely coming around. Zuri's heart swelled.

"Sometimes...I get lost in the memories. She was the love of my life. I miss her." Gerald's voice shook.

"She was one lucky woman to have you, sir." Zuri bent over and kissed his wrinkled cheek. "I hope you can still have a merry Christmas with your grandson here."

Gerald's eyes cleared and he looked up at Tom. "I think we will. What do you say, Tom? Are you up to some ice cream? I'm in the mood and I'm buying."

"Sure, Grandpa. Let me see these two out, and we'll go get that banana split."

Duke and Zuri assured Tom they weren't going to press charges and left.

And by the spring in his step, Duke had caught the scent of the trail once more and was on a mission.

When they got in his truck, he nodded toward the dashboard screen. "Go ahead. I know you want to."

Zuri laughed as she found a Christmas song on the radio and cranked the volume up. Yes, Duke Lowry was thawing, and that was something worth celebrating.

CHAPTER 7

*D*uke glanced over at Zuri snapping her fingers and singing "Jingle Bell Rock" in his truck. He had to admit, after watching her with Gerald, that she wasn't the pretentious, shallow woman he'd first taken her for.

And yes, she needed that makeup case, but he could read people. Zuri really *cared* about that old guy. A guy she'd probably never see again. Her gentleness and compassion with Gerald had gotten them a lot further than his intimidation tactics.

And she'd certainly handled his admission about losing the ring with more grace than he'd given himself.

Duke had trusted Boone when they were partners. Maybe Zuri was worth trusting too. It wasn't so bad working with someone again.

They soon hit the highway and turned left. Not too far down, Duke slowed the truck. "It's near here."

He strained to see anything among all the white snow. The lake was white, the trees were white, even the road before them had another layer of snow from last night, making it hard to tell where it ended.

"Look!" Zuri pointed to a flash of something red glinting in the sunlight up ahead.

Sure enough, there was a small pullover spot by the lake. A car buried in snow—probably from the plow truck clearing the highway —with a corner of red showing through on the hood was the only thing in the tiny lot.

Duke grabbed his trusty ice scraper with the long-handled brush. "You can wait here in the truck and stay warm. I don't want to use the shovel on this and risk scratching the car."

"Stay here and let you get all the glory? No way. Didn't you learn your lesson with the tires?"

"Right. You don't want to sit on your…what did you call it? Some New York City slang."

"Tuchus." She grinned at him and held his gaze, a quiet passing between them. "We did it."

Yeah. They'd done it. The pinch in his neck started to ease. They'd found the car. Now they just had to dig it out.

They both hopped out of the warm cab into the frigid breeze.

Duke used the ice scraper to clear the thick coating of snow off the hood of the car.

Wait. This wasn't a convertible. He brushed more snow off. "This isn't right. It's not a Mustang."

"What? It has to be." Zuri started clearing the snow on the window with her mittened hand.

Duke cleared the roof and then moved to the back. A Toyota logo on the trunk was chipped, and the bumper had more than a few dings. This wasn't the meticulously restored Mustang. Just an old red Corolla.

His heart sank.

"Would Gerald have taken this car accidentally?" Zuri asked.

Duke shook his head. "The man knew cars. He said he drove the Mustang here. And this car doesn't look like it would get very far."

"There were other places to pull over, though. Maybe this is the wrong place."

"If his mind was in the past, he wouldn't have pulled over in the wrong place. This is the one Tom said." Defeat sagged his shoulders. The tension in his neck was back.

"I was so certain this was it. What are we going to tell Vivie and Boone?"

He still had time. He wasn't going to give up now. But clearly, his optimistic, holly-jolly Zuri was losing heart. He lifted a shoulder, finding his inner grinch.

"See, I told you this whole Christmas miracle thing was a sham. Even *you* are ready to give up."

His reverse psychology worked. "It is not a sham!" She lifted her chin and marched over to him. "And I'm not giving up. I'm simply asking what to do next. Don't accuse me of losing my Christmas spirit."

And she was back. He released a smile. "Glad we got that straight."

"Wait a sec. Were you teasing me?"

"Maybe."

She slugged him in the arm and smirked. "All right, Sherlock, what's next?"

The light inside her brightened her whole face. He was close enough to see rays of green in her blue eyes, sparkling like the frosty evergreens against the clear sky. He leaned a little closer. Her full lips and—

Whoa, now, Duke.

This was *not* on the agenda. He couldn't be thinking about her lips! His spine snapped back to attention, and he took a step away.

"I'll...uh...call the sheriff's office. Maybe Cole can run the plates to find the owners. Then we can track them down and see if they know anything."

Zuri beamed. "I like that plan. See, there's still hope."

There was. Because somehow with Zuri by his side, impossible things seemed possible. She didn't give up easily. She was loyal to her friends. She'd proven she wasn't the type of girl to bail out on a guy.

And it didn't hurt that she was gorgeous.

But a partner, even a friendship, was one thing. Anything more than that was asking for heartache.

THURSDAY, 1:37 P.M.

Zuri sat in the cab of the truck, watching Duke pace outside as he called Cole.

For a second it'd looked like Duke wanted to kiss her. The way his gaze had heated and then dropped to her lips smacked of attraction and chemistry. But that was crazy, right? This was straightlaced, uptight Detective Duke Lowry. They'd known each other less than forty-eight hours.

But crazier still, she'd *wanted* him to kiss her.

Heaven help her. He was dreamy, no doubt. But it was that peek into his heart, his broken and lonely heart, that drew her in. The way he would do anything for Boone and Vivie's wedding, even though he obviously was not into the Christmas theme. His integrity and insistence on keeping his word, even if it was a silly little promise like finding her hot chocolate with marshmallows. He'd trusted her to talk to Gerald.

And her scars didn't scare him away.

So yes, she was attracted to him.

But it had to end there.

Her stage makeup career in NYC was just taking off and, well, her family could drive her absolutely nuts, but she couldn't imagine being hundreds of miles away from them. So what point was there in falling for Duke? There was no future there.

None.

She'd simply keep it friendly, and after the wedding they would go their separate ways.

And yet a quote from her sophomore-year paper on Emily Dickinson whispered doubt into her resolve. *The Heart wants what it wants —or else it does not care.*

Yeah, not helpful, Emily.

Duke opened his door and hopped in behind the steering wheel.

Back to the real world. They had a wedding to save. "Well, what did Cole say?"

"Not a whole lot. Right as I asked about the plates, they got called out. He said he'll look them up after they get back from the call."

"I hope it wasn't something serious."

"Domestic disturbance."

"You must see a lot in your line of work. How do you do it?"

"I don't know. I guess there's so much wrong in the world, and I want to do what I can to set things right where possible." He faced her. "Did you always want to work in makeup and beauty stuff?"

"Beauty stuff?" She laughed. "Yeah, I guess so. I want to showcase the beauty in people. When people feel confident about themselves, they're more likely to go out and do good."

"Did your...scars have something to do with your career choice?" He gave her a soft smile, as if hoping to soften the question.

She drew in a breath. "Probably." She picked a piece of lint off her red wool coat.

"Do you mind me asking what caused your scarring?"

Wow. He wanted to go there? She studied his face. His brown eyes were sincere, curious, like he really wanted to know.

Okay. Fine. After all, they were partners. And she'd never see him again after this weekend.

"Being the baby of the family and the only girl, I was a tad spoiled. My brothers always called me Daddy's little princess and said I didn't do much for myself. But one afternoon I was hungry, and Mom was gone. My brothers Joey and Tony were watching the Yankees with Dad. When I whined about wanting lunch, they told me to warm up some soup and leave them alone. So I did. I heated up a ceramic bowl of broccoli cheese soup for eleven minutes in the microwave."

"Eleven minutes?"

"Yeah. I know. I didn't even know how to properly warm up soup at ten years old. And when it was done, I reached for the bowl in the microwave above the stove and—"

"You spilled it and burned yourself."

"Yeah." Her throat grew tight. "I dropped the bowl, which broke and cut my cheek. The soup spilled on my neck, chest, and shoulder. I just started screaming, and my dad didn't really know what to do. They started wiping it off…" She could still remember her father's face—the panic, the horror.

"I can't imagine how much pain you must've been in."

"It was bad. Excruciating. I was admitted to a burn unit where they kept me sedated. But whenever I woke, my mom or Nonna would be by my side. They never left me."

"What about your dad?"

"He, uh, he never visited me in the hospital. My mom tried to make excuses, but I overheard Nonna telling her men weren't equipped to deal with the ugliness in life. I guess she was right, because after that incident he never looked at me the same. Never called me his princess. In fact, he rarely touched me."

Duke just looked at her. "Maybe he couldn't handle it."

"Clearly. And my brothers weren't much better." Lost in the memories, she looked out her window to the cold white world. "When I went back to school, kids—mostly boys—called me Scar Face, Freddy Krueger, or other horrible things. And the last time I wore something without sleeves, at my boyfriend's insistence, he covered me right up and broke up with me soon after."

"You're kidding."

The angry edge to his voice had her turning. She blinked at him.

"I'm sorry, Zuri. Guys can be jerks."

She swallowed, her mouth suddenly dry, her eyes burning. "Yeah."

"And your dad—maybe he wasn't horrified at your skin as much as his failure to protect you."

She had nothing for that, so she turned away again, blinking hard against the wetness in her eyes. "And now Vivie wants me to stand up in front of a whole church full of people in a sleeveless gown where everyone can gawk at me."

Duke said nothing. Silence, of course. Oh, how had she gotten to this point of exposing her wounds before a man she'd just met?

Duke's warm finger lifted her chin, drawing her attention back to his bold stare. His deep brown eyes spoke for him. He was fierce and intense and angry.

But not at her. He was angry *for* her. There was a sharpness to his quiet voice when he spoke. "Don't you believe a word of what those others have said. You are exquisite."

She held her breath as his gaze roamed her face.

"I mean it, Zuri." Then he moved closer and—

His lips gently caressed her cheek. Tears pricked her eyes as another feather soft kiss landed right on her scar.

What? She pulled away, but only far enough to look into his eyes. Yeah, he was real, all right. And it wasn't disgust or shame or anything else she'd always associated with her scar tissue that she saw staring back at her.

It was admiration. Respect. And a hefty dose of...*desire?*

His citrus-clove scent surrounded them. Their breaths mingled in what little space was between them, fogging the windows and veiling them from the outside world.

Well then.

Zuri curled her fingers into his coat and tugged him closer. Their lips met in an explosion of senses. She'd come to Minnesota to change a cold-hearted scrooge, but there was nothing cold about Duke Lowry now.

Hot and passionate, gentle and firm, and a heady combination of sweet and spice. The man could kiss.

And for the first time in years, Zuri didn't feel like hiding.

CHAPTER 8

*D*uke could hardly catch his breath. There was no way he deserved this taste of paradise. He'd held back the desire to kiss her before, knowing she was way out of his league. What did a grumpy cop have to offer a woman like her? But in hearing her story, he'd only wanted to show her that her scars did nothing to detract from her beauty. He hadn't thought she would dive in quite so…enthusiastically.

Which was stupid of him, really. She was all passion and heart. When had she *not* thrown herself wholeheartedly into anything since the first moment he saw her?

Maybe what was more surprising was that she wasn't repulsed by him. Her touch opened up long forgotten dreams. Dreams of a family. Of coming home to share the hardships and victories of the day with a loved one. Of passing along traditions his mother had shared with him with his own children. Dreams he'd lost along the way and lost all hope of ever coming to fruition.

Until now.

And for a long, sweet moment, he lost himself in the what-ifs and basked in Zuri's kisses.

He finally pulled away, his finger tracing the contour of her face from brow to cheek to her neck, where the scarring started. She watched him intently, waiting for his reaction. Almost like it was some sort of test.

"This doesn't define you, Zuri."

"Easy for you to say. You haven't seen it all."

"Then show me."

Her head reared back. "Excuse me? What kind of woman do you take me for?"

"No! Not that." Oh, he was messing this up big time. "I meant the dress. You have the bridesmaid's dress, right?"

"Oh." She looked sheepish. "Well, yeah, but—"

"Try it on. You think these scars are so bad—let me be the judge of that."

"We have to find the car. And the ring, and—"

"We have to wait for Cole to run the plates anyway. Let's check the next few lookouts, just in case, and go back to the Evergreen. You can try this dress on and see that you have nothing to be ashamed of. You came all this way to help Vivien in the wedding, right?"

He could see the conflict in her eyes but stayed silent. He'd said his piece. Now it was up to her.

After a beat, she gave him a firm nod. "Okay. I'll try it on."

"I knew you had it in you."

He didn't know why he felt like he'd solved a case, but that warm, satisfied feeling sank in as he drove farther up the highway and checked the other lookout spots and hiking trail parking lots.

Everything was empty.

Still, he refused to lose hope.

Back at the resort, he waited in his cabin while Zuri changed into her dress.

Was he really falling for a woman he'd just met? A woman who lived—he checked his phone—one thousand, one hundred and ninety-six miles away from him, give or take a few.

More, was she standing in her own cabin thinking what an idiot she was for kissing him? Or maybe it hadn't shaken her up as it had him. Maybe it wasn't as significant or—

His phone chimed. She was ready. Before he could talk himself out of it, he walked over to Zuri's cabin and knocked. She opened the door, hiding behind it. But she couldn't hide the nervous tell as she crinkled her nose and fiddled with a strand of her shiny brown hair.

Sheesh, she was completely endearing.

He waited on her front porch. "Do you want me stay out here? I mean, it's a little chilly, but I'll stand here as long as it takes."

"No, come in." She opened the door wider and shut it behind him when he came into the cabin. She blew out a quick breath, threw her shoulders back, and spun around to face him. She looked like she was ready to face the firing squad. But she lifted her chin and met his eyes.

And took his breath away.

Yes, her face was gorgeous and the dress pretty as it hugged her curves and flowed down to little pink toes peeking out from the hem that pooled around her on the floor. Her wavy locks framed her cheeks and cascaded down her back, exposing a graceful neck and delicate collarbones. But it was the scarred shoulder and neck show-casing her perseverance and courage that amazed him. It was her bravery to stand there under his scrutiny as she waited for the verdict. She swallowed hard.

"Well?" she whispered.

He stepped closer and reached for her hands. "You, Zuri Milano, are one of the most beautiful women I've ever met. And if you don't already have a date, I'd be honored if you would accompany me to this wedding I have to go to on Saturday. If you don't mind attending with a grinch, that is."

Her smile bloomed full and bright. "I'll have to check my calendar, but I bet I can save you a dance or two." She gave him a sassy smirk.

He was such a goner.

And it felt...good. To believe again in some goodness in this dark world. To have something hopeful as he looked into the future.

The ringing cell phone in his pocket broke the spell of the moment. He checked the screen. "It's Cole."

"Maybe they found the car. I'll change so we're ready to go." Zuri rushed to the bathroom while Duke stepped outside and answered the call.

"Hey, Cole, did you find the owners of that Corolla?"

"That car is registered to a Josiah and Maria Branson who live on Hollow Rock Road near Grand Portage."

"Did you call them?"

"Yeah. No answer. But listen. That's not why I called you."

Duke knew this tone of voice, had used it many times himself when delivering bad news to victims or their loved ones. The same voice the oncologist had used when delivering his mother's diagnosis. "What is it?"

"There's a car on fire up at Rusty's gravel pit, and we think it's Boone's."

THURSDAY, 5:16 P.M.

Zuri quickly changed back into her jeans and sweater. Leaving the dress on the hanger, she ran her hand down the silky fabric and smiled. Duke was right. She was here for Vivien. She should push past her own insecurities and stand up for her friend. Even if the thought of all those eyes on her still made her want to pass out.

But the way Duke had looked at her? It definitely gave a girl a boost of confidence.

And who knew? It was early in the game, but maybe she and Duke could figure out a long-distance relationship. It wasn't unheard of. And they still had a few days together before she left.

She pulled her hair back in a low ponytail and walked into the empty main room of the cabin. Duke must've gone outside to take the call from Cole. She stepped into her boots and bundled up in her red coat and black scarf to go out to look for him.

Outside, the sun had set, the outdoor lights casting long shadows on the snowy resort. Duke paced between her cabin and a cluster of pine trees.

"Hey, what did Cole say?" Zuri asked as she approached him.

He looked up and her heart fell. The look on his face said it wasn't good news. "They think they found the car."

"That's great, right?"

"It's not great, Zuri. The car is on *fire*." His glower was back in full force with a bit of an angry glare thrown in for good measure. "I'm going there now."

The car was on fire?

Before the words could sink in, Duke turned and marched toward the parking lot.

Zuri rushed to keep up. "Hold up. I'm coming with you."

As soon as he started the engine of his truck, Nat King Cole's voice sang about chestnuts roasting on an open fire. Zuri jabbed at the music icon on the screen to shut the radio off.

"Wow, talk about bad timing, huh?" She forced a bit of humor into her voice and glanced at Duke.

His jaw clenched tight and his vise grip on the steering wheel were the only hints of emotion she could see. Obviously humor wasn't helping.

"C'mon, Duke. Don't lose hope. Maybe they have the wrong car. Or—"

"Let's just get there and see what we're dealing with."

The hopelessness in his grumbly voice tore at her.

The short drive was rife with a silence that was anything but peaceful. Not too different from their first ride together. But they'd gotten over that obstacle. They could handle this too.

Whatever this was.

She spotted the fire as soon as they pulled up to the gravel pit. The fire had totally engulfed the vehicle and the area around it, making it impossible to get near the car or even see it. Flames reaching high above their heads crackled and spat sparks into the bleak night sky. Two burly guys from the Deep Haven fire department aimed the hose at the fire, creating plumes of steam. It didn't diminish the flames a bit, and the fire volunteers scrambled to get the monster under control.

Duke stood with arms crossed and jaw clenched tight. He toed Boone's collector license plate, bent and covered in soot, at his feet.

Sheriff Hueston approached and picked up the plate with gloved hands. "We'll run this for prints and see if we can find who's responsible."

Duke only nodded. The warmth in his brown eyes had gone cold.

Zuri reached for his hand. "We can't even see the car. There's still a chance—"

"Just stop."

"But you can't give up—"

Familiar voices cut through the smoky night air.

Boone.

Uh oh.

"Is that my Mustang?" He and Vivien skidded to a stop at the edge of the clearing.

Vivie's hand flew to her mouth. She hooked her arm through Boone's as they watched in horror as the fire consumed what was left of the car.

Duke closed his eyes for a second, then swallowed. "I need to go talk to them."

"I'll go with you. You don't have to do this alone. And maybe there's still hope—"

"No, Zuri. You've done enough." He practically growled at her. His hand sliced through the air. "It's over."

"What's that supposed to mean?"

"I need to stop playing make-believe with you and go tell the groom that not only did I lose his car but also the wedding ring."

"Wait a minute. You said they *think* it's Boone's car. There's still a chance—"

"For Pete's sake, stop!" His eyes darkened, even as his voice lowered—lethal, brutal. Angry. "You can't slap a bow on this and make it pretty. This is the *real* world. There's no miracle coming. This isn't some fairy tale with a genie granting me three wishes or a superhero to save the day. The sooner you realize that, the better off you'll be. Now if you'll excuse me, I have a job to finish." He turned away.

"Duke. Wait—" She grabbed his jacket. "I thought we were in this together. Partners." Zuri fought to keep her voice even. Was he really dismissing her that easily?

Duke jammed his hands into gloves he dug out of his pocket. "Like I told you yesterday, I work alone. It's better that way."

"Better for who?"

"Better for everyone." He jerked out of her touch.

"So you've gone back to grinch-mode, huh? Push everyone away and act like you don't care. Is that really what you think your mother would want?"

He took a breath, his eyes wide. "Keep my mother out of this!"

Oh, she'd done it now. Duke stood against the black silhouette of the trees, the reflection of the fire heating his face and his breath puffing around him like a dragon.

Yeah, well, he probably meant to intimidate her, but she was from Jersey.

She didn't intimidate easily. Besides, she knew the truth. "You already do a great job at that. You're so busy trying to forget her, forget what your ex did to you, that you've forgotten how to live. You've forgotten that there's still a lot of good in this world and people who care."

He blinked at her. "What do you know about my ex? Are you going behind my back now?"

Her voice cut low. "I know you were going to propose but she left you for someone else. And no, I'm not going behind your back. I only asked Vivien why you hated Christmas so much. I was trying to understand you better."

"Yeah, and did Vivien tell you that Nichole planned the whole thing? Had been texting the guy behind my back for months?"

Oh, Duke.

Zuri shook her head. Even in her anger she could hear the pain of betrayal in his voice.

Duke's stare went cold. "What kind of detective doesn't know when his own girlfriend is cheating on him? But like an idiot, I turned my back on my mom, thinking all my dreams would be coming true and I'd have this magical holiday proposal. Instead, Nichole left me for another man, and I came home to find my mother had a cancer diagnosis. So forgive me if I don't share your Christmas cheer. I don't have your knack at making ugly things look pretty." He pointed to the burning car. "This is my reality."

He spun on his heel and left her alone with the wind whipping up the loose snow around her. And another man she'd thought she could trust walking out on her.

Guess that's what she got for falling hard for a grinch.

CHAPTER 9

*D*uke braced himself as he walked over to Boone. Vivien left her fiancé's side and chased down Zuri, but not before giving Duke a long glare of disapproval.

He deserved it. And more. But it was better for Zuri in the long run that he stop any of the romantic nonsense before things got worse.

Now to face his other failure.

Boone was talking to one of the firefighters. He turned back toward the fire as Duke approached. They stood side by side. "What happened?"

"I left the car in the Evergreen shed yesterday as planned. I should've kept the keys, but I didn't. This is my fault."

"And the rest of the story?" Boone crossed his arms.

"Near as we can tell, an older guy with memory issues also staying at the resort took the car for joy ride. Drove it to town and left it at a lookout on the highway. I haven't been able to track it from there."

"Any suspects?"

"There's a broken-down Corolla at the lookout now. Trying to find the owners, but nothing so far."

Boone finally turned his dark stare on Duke. "And why in the world would you not tell me about this as soon as it went missing?"

"I thought I could handle this on my own and not have to worry you." Obviously not. Duke braced himself for what was coming. "It won't be the same, but I'll pay you back for the car and the ring."

"The ring? What about the ring?" Boone's voice roared over the fire.

Oh yeah. He didn't know about that part. "I...uh...the ring was in the car."

If ever Duke deserved a cussing out by his former partner, it was now. Instead, Boone walked away a few paces, muttering into the night. He spun back around and got right in Duke's face. "You've got some nerve, you know."

"I know. You trusted me and I failed. I'll head out tonight and contact you as soon as I have the—"

"You're gonna bail on me now? Leave me an even bigger mess?"

"I'm trying to make things right. What more do you want?"

"I want you to *be* the best man. That means you don't leave me hanging high and dry. I want to get through that thick skull of yours that your Lone Ranger act isn't getting you anywhere."

What?

"But...the car. And ring. I completely screwed up. Surely you don't want that kind of guy standing up for you at your wedding."

"The car and ring are insured. I can replace those. Am I angry about them right now? Oh yeah. But I'm baffled by *you*. Why in the world would you leave me in the dark? I could've helped."

"You shouldn't have to. You have Vivien now. She's your priority."

"But that doesn't mean I don't need my friends too. Or that I won't be there when they need me. Seriously, Duke, I thought you'd know that by now." Boone shook his head. "Ever since Nichole left you and your mom died, I've watched you push everyone else away. But I still thought we were good. Until this year. Now you've shoved me off too."

"That's not—"

"It *is* true. How many times have I asked to get together over the last year and you've turned me down?"

"You know how crazy work is—"

"And I also know how much PTO you have saved up. Face it. You've checked out of our friendship. I thought we were more than work buddies. Guess I was wrong."

Wait a minute. Boone wasn't kicking him out of his wedding or out of his life? And yeah, maybe Duke had pulled away a bit since his partner moved away.

Or more than a bit.

Because the office wasn't the same without Boone behind the desk across from him. And Duke had gotten used to going at it alone. No girlfriend. No mother. No partner. God had left him alone, and there must be a reason.

Or maybe Duke chose to be alone because it was easier than being eviscerated when the next person he cared about walked out of his life. Even God.

Boone's tightened lips eased a bit. "Zuri was right. You've forgotten all the things your mom loved about Christmas. It's not the lights and gifts and tacky sweaters. It's about Emmanuel. God with us. That is the miracle of Christmas. That God the Son came down in the flesh to be with us. And I think your mom would want you to remember that."

It was true. Duke had never had much for family, but Gladys Lowry had brought the joy of Christmas wherever she'd gone. She'd collected people around their dinner table and made them feel loved. Remembered. Cherished. And until now, he'd thought all of that died with her.

But Boone and Zuri were two big in-his-face manifestations of good still left in the world. Evidence of God's presence.

A friend that forgave and invited him to be a part of the biggest day of his life.

A stranger who sang songs, handed out candy and made people smile, and went out of her way to cheer up grumpy scrooges like him.

Yeah, there was a lot Duke had pushed away. Maybe it was time to engage again.

Shouts interrupted Duke's thoughts. The fire crew was finally getting the upper hand on the beast. Through the dying flames, Duke could see the shape of the car.

Something wasn't right.

"Wait. That's not a Mustang. Look at the grill, and that ridge down the middle of the hood."

Boone peered into the fire. "You're right. It's not. But Kyle had my license plate."

"That's a *Camaro*. Someone must've stolen the plates off the Mustang and replaced them. Which means your car is still out there."

Boone blew into his bare hands, something lighting his eyes. "What do you say, partner? Back on the case?"

"I did say I was at your disposal this week. But there's someone else I want to bring in on this one. And I might've messed that up bigtime too. Maybe you can help?"

"It's about time you asked."

THURSDAY, 6:09 P.M.

Thank goodness Vivien had offered to take Zuri back to the Evergreen and didn't press her for anything. She was just glad to get away from the fire, the shouting of the crew, the rush of hose water, and the acrid smell of smoke and gasoline that was probably embedded deep in her pores at this point.

But even in the silence of Vivien's car, she couldn't get Duke's words out of her head.

I need to stop playing make-believe with you.

I don't have your knack at making ugly things look pretty.

Right. Because underneath all the decorations and bows, despite the cosmetics and hair products she used to help others, overwhelming ugliness remained.

Like her scars.

She could cover them with clothes and concealer, but they were still there. The only thing she was really good at was hiding them for a little while.

Pretty stupid of her to think Duke was the kind of guy that could see beyond them. In the end, he wasn't any better than her father.

Vivien opened her cabin door and ushered her inside. Her brow was puckered with concern. "Are you okay? What's going on with you and Duke?"

"Nothing." Zuri sniffed. What she wouldn't do for a big serving of her nonna's panna cotta.

She shrugged out of her coat, sank down into the wingback chair by the window, and wrapped herself up in a throw blanket. "He's just doing what guys do. Acting like you're the most beautiful, amazing person in the world, and then the minute things get ugly, walking away."

"That doesn't sound like Duke. I mean, pushing people away in general, yeah. But he's not the kind of guy to put on a show. I would know. He can't act at all." Vivie dug through her purse and found a little container of Tylenol, which she passed over.

"Maybe that was just my interpretation." Zuri swallowed three pills down past the big lump lodged in her throat. "But he was right. I'm not some hero to save the day. I thought I could help find that car. Do more than make everyone look pretty for a little while. But—"

"But what?"

"Face it, Vivie. How does doing hair and makeup help anyone?"

"Hello! You see the beauty and light in the dark places. You see people and draw out their best qualities where others would write them off, cast them aside. Stop listening to your dumb brothers."

"I'm not. I just… Sometimes I wonder if I'm still that helpless girl who can't even warm up soup."

Vivie leaned forward. "I saw Beth today and hardly recognized her. And it wasn't just the hair or eyeliner techniques you taught her that made the difference. She was more confident than I've seen her in a long time, because you took an afternoon and listened to her."

"That was one person."

"You did it for me too. When I moved to New York, a small-town girl from Minnesota, discouraged from the rejections, you offered to do my hair and makeup for auditions so I felt good onstage. But mostly it was your belief in me that got me through. And I've seen you do this for others too. When so many out there criticize and put down, you find a way to hope and encourage. Why else would I ask you to come all the way from the East Coast to do hair and makeup and now be my bridesmaid for this wedding?"

True. Vivie could've asked any number of people here in Deep Haven.

So maybe her skills went beyond the brushes and bronzers to seeing the potential in others. That wasn't exactly useless. "I can do a mean smoky eye."

"And you're still the only one who can do the sideswept bangs I love."

But she'd still failed. "I'm sorry I couldn't bring Duke around. I really hoped to help him find the Christmas spirit. But I think that's impossible."

"Forget about Duke for a second and tell me what you decided. Will you be my bridesmaid?"

Zuri glanced at the gray-blue dress hanging from the top of the bathroom door.

Maybe she hadn't changed Scrooge McDuke, but ultimately, she'd come to support Vivien. She could still do that. "Of course."

Vivie hugged her around the neck. "I knew I could count on—"

Pounding on the door cut off Vivien's words. "Zuri!"

Duke? Zuri marched over and whipped open the door to see Duke bent over, sucking in air.

"What do you want? A haircut? Clothing advice? You've already made it clear I'm not good for much more than that." She folded her arms and gave him a good dose of his own medicine—a hard stare down.

And he just...smiled?

"Zuri. I just want...you."

CHAPTER 10

Zuri's jaw dropped. Surely she'd misheard the man on her porch declaring he wanted her while Boone watched in the background. But Vivie's shocked expression said she'd heard it too.

Duke stood up to his full height and leaned against the doorframe. "I want my partner to help me find a lost Mustang convertible."

"I thought it was on fire at the gravel pit."

"Turns out you were right to hope. It was the wrong car. What do you say? Will you help me?"

"You don't really need my help. And like you said, we have nothing in common. We should just go our separate ways."

She started to close the door, but Duke's hand stopped it.

"I'm an idiot, okay? You...scared me. And you were right. I've pushed everyone away."

She stood a little taller and lifted her chin. "Yes. You have."

"And I'm sorry for that. I'm sorry for pushing *you* away most of all. Because...with you I find myself hoping for things that I haven't wished for in a long time. I don't want to go separate ways, Zuri. I want to be with you."

His words shot straight to her heart. Her eyes misted.

Scared? She could understand that. Duke scared her a little too. It scared her how fast she was falling for him. And as much as she accused him of shutting everyone else out, she had hidden parts of herself away as well.

Duke held out a hand. "What do you say, partner?"

If there was any chance of finding Boone's car, she was there. But the question went deeper. Was she willing to step out of her own shadows and see what she and Duke could share?

Would she forgive him?

"Well, I was going to head to the bar and see if the guy from the gas station would be my date for this wedding, but I suppose you will do."

Duke's worried look faded away, and he stepped forward.

He wrapped her in his arms and kissed her softly on the lips. Thank goodness he held her, because she was melting faster than Frosty the Snowman under a Paragon hood hair dryer.

She twined her fingers around his neck and pulled him closer. Breathing in his spicy-citrus scent, she kissed him back.

He suddenly pulled away. "Wait. The guy from the gas station!"

Huh? "The creepy guy with black-stained hands and rotting teeth? Duke, I was joking."

"No. It was bugging me when he was hitting on you, like I've seen him before. I remember now. He was greasy-hair guy at the car detailing shop."

Boone came inside and stood by Vivien. "You think he has something to do with the Mustang?"

"Someone at that shop could've easily changed the license plates on the car. Zuri, didn't he say something about staying at a hotel to you?"

"That's right. He said there was a bar right next to his hotel."

"And he probably walked to the gas station since there were no other cars in the parking lot. The hotel has to be in Deep Haven."

Vivien whipped out her phone. "He must be staying at the Mad

Moose Hotel in town. Ree's family owns it and were upset when a new bar went in next door." She made a call.

"There's still that car at the lookout too. Did Cole ever track down the owners?" Zuri asked.

Duke shook his head. "No. Boone and I talked with Cole and Kyle. They had someone drive up to the address listed for them, but no one was home."

Boone moved over to Vivie's chair. "Why don't we split up. Vivien and I can check out the Corolla. It's been towed to the impound lot. Maybe we'll find a clue about the owners."

"Then Zuri and I will track down the guy at the hotel and see what he knows." Duke turned to her. "That is, if she's willing."

"Well, I'm not gonna sit on my—"

"Tuchus. Right." He grinned.

Whoa. His smoldering gaze was one thing. His bright, full smile was downright devastating.

Vivie looked up from her phone. "Ree is calling the front desk now. She'll text you the room number."

The two couples split up and headed to town.

Duke didn't even bat an eyelash when Zuri cranked up the Christmas tunes. "So, what makes you think this guy knows something?"

"There was another muscle car when I dropped off the Mustang to get detailed. I didn't see the whole thing, but it was freshly painted black, like our guy's hands, and I have a hunch it was the Camaro that was set on fire at the gravel pit. I bet our friend here switched the license plates with Boone's Mustang."

"Why would he do that?"

"Remember that BOLO the sheriff said was from Duluth? Could be our friend stole that Camaro and was lying low here. Maybe he decided to paint the car black and switched the license plates to throw us off his scent."

"And then he burned the car? That doesn't make sense."

"He painted it before everyone around town started looking for Boone's Mustang. If he heard and got worried people would find the

Camaro, he could've done something drastic to get rid of the evidence."

"How will we know?"

"We'll see what he has to say first. Once I get a name, we can run it and see if he has a record. If nothing else, maybe he saw something in the shop go down."

A text came through on Zuri's phone. "Ree said there's a guy who matches our description staying in room nine."

Duke drove to the Mad Moose Hotel and parked. "You could wait here if you don't want to see him again."

"Oh, but we had such a connection in the gas station. Maybe he'll make it easy on us and confess to everything."

Duke chuckled. "Still the eternal optimist. And a bit of a smart aleck, huh?"

"It runs in the family. Better get used to it."

"I can do that." He kissed her again. "Let's find that Mustang, partner."

They walked across the parking lot to room nine and knocked. No answer.

"Maybe we try the bar—"

"Hey, did you come back for that drink?" The man they were looking for walked toward them with bloodshot eyes and reeking of cigarette smoke. He sent her the same smarmy smile he'd tried using on her at the gas station.

Zuri gladly let Duke take the lead.

"We wanted to talk to you about a Camaro. I saw you at Jared's Detail—"

The guy zipped past Duke's white truck and took off.

Duke bolted after him. The man didn't get far before Duke jumped and tackled him to the ground. The two men rolled in the snowy parking lot. The guy got off one punch to Duke's face, but Duke rolled him over and shoved a knee into his back.

"I didn't do nuthin'. Let me go."

"Really? Then why'd ya run?" Blood dripped down Duke's cheek. He pulled the guy up to his feet.

"I don't have to talk to you."

"It would be in your best interest to, since you've already assaulted an officer."

The guy blanched. "You're a cop."

"Detective Duke Lowry. I might not press charges if you tell me what I want to know about the Mustang I dropped off yesterday to get detailed. But if you prefer to do this at the Cook County Sheriff's Office, we can do that."

"But...I don't know anything about that Mustang!" he sputtered. "Yeah, I work at Jared's. M-m-maybe I took the license plate—I'm not saying I did—but I didn't touch the car."

"You didn't take the Mustang?"

"No, man, I'm telling the truth. I switched the plates, but that's it. I switched them out for the collector plates on the Camaro."

Before Duke could say anything else, flashing lights from a deputy cruiser flooded the parking lot.

Cole, in his tan deputy uniform, got out and approached. He took one look at the situation and took over for Duke, cuffing the man. "William Bittner, you're under arrest."

"I didn't do—"

"Save it." Cole read him his rights.

After escorting William to the back seat of the cruiser, Cole turned to them. "Rusty finally got surveillance out at the gravel pit. Guess who set the Camaro on fire and left their fingerprints on the license plate?"

"That'll make the prosecutor's job easier," Duke said.

"Any sign of Boone's car?" Zuri asked.

Cole shook his head. "Sorry. I'd better get this guy processed. But if we find out anything else when I question him, we'll let you know."

Duke leaned against the back of his truck and gingerly touched his cheek. "Guess it's up to Boone and Vivien now. Hopefully they'll find something to track down the Corolla owners."

"You're bleeding quite a bit there." Zuri pulled a tissue out of her purse and gently pressed it on his wound. "Does it hurt?"

"He had a ring on. Cut me good, but I've been through worse."

"We should probably get this checked out." Zuri lifted the tissue. Blood oozed out of the deep cut. "I think you need stitches."

Duke checked in his truck mirror and grimaced. "Stitches and a tux. Vivie is gonna kill me."

Zuri laughed. "I don't know. Scars show that you're a survivor. But we really should get it looked at. Last thing you need is an infection."

"You think it's that bad, huh?"

"Come on, tough guy. I'll hold your hand while the doctor sews you up."

"Promise?"

His dark gaze probed.

She kissed his cheek. "A good partner sticks with you. And as I said before, like it or not, I'm your partner now."

And the way he kissed her back said he liked that. A lot.

THURSDAY, 7:48 P.M.

Duke drove them to the hospital. His cheek burned. Not that he would tell Zuri that. It burned even more that they hadn't found Boone's car yet. But he wasn't hopeless. They still had a couple days before the wedding.

Zuri's optimism must be rubbing off.

He parked and went to open Zuri's door for her. But she was already out of the truck, staring off into the distance, a strange expression on her face.

"What's wrong?"

"Look." She pointed behind him. He turned to see—parked around the corner of the hospital, under a bright streetlight—a shiny red '65 Mustang convertible.

A little wreath circled the logo on the front grill, and ribbons trailed behind the fender.

Boone's car? Intact?

Zuri ran up to it, then cleared a small circle from the frost on the window and peeked in. "My case is there! It's just the way I left it yesterday."

They tried the doors, but they were locked.

Duke walked around the car. Not a scratch or dent or anything. The car was perfect. He even spied a corner of the ring box under the passenger seat.

Duke blinked. "How did this happen?"

Zuri squeezed his arm. "It's our own Christmas miracle."

"Someone must've taken the car from the lookout by the lake and driven it here."

"That doesn't make it any less miraculous."

"True." Duke ran a finger along the body of the Mustang. It wasn't a figment of his imagination. It was real. Then Zuri's sweet fragrance drew his eyes back to her. "But I think the real miracle is something even better."

"What's that?" she said, her gaze sweet and shiny on him.

"You. You looking beyond *my* scars, reminding me of joy and hope and faith...all the things I thought I lost with my mom's death. You helped me discover them again."

"I guess I was stubborn enough you couldn't scare me away."

"That's one word for it." He tucked her close and kissed the tip of her nose. "Let's get out of this cold."

"And find out who drove the car here. They're probably still inside with the keys."

Zuri walked up to the woman in reindeer scrubs behind the desk. "Do you know who drove that Mustang that's parked outside?"

"The Christmas Mustang?" The woman smiled. "I do. One moment."

Christmas Mustang?

She left the desk and a few minutes later came back.

A man walked into the lobby holding a baby swaddled tight in a white hospital baby blanket with blue and pink stripes. "Are you the owners of the Mustang?"

"No, but we know who is. I'm Detective Duke Lowry. Did you take that vehicle?"

Zuri looked at him with a *down, boy* look.

Whoops. He offered a smile.

"I'm so sorry, Detective. Yes, I took it, but it was an emergency. Our car broke down on the highway. And I was going to call the police and explain, but when we got here, I was so worried about my wife—"

Suddenly, it clicked. "Are you Josiah Branson?"

"Yeah. I'm Joe Branson."

"And your wife is Maria?"

"Yes, sir."

"And who is this?" Duke softened his voice and peeked into the blanket. "Your emergency?"

Joe's shoulders relaxed, and he beamed down at the baby. "This is my son. Joshua. He's a few weeks early, which worried us, but doctors say he's doing great."

Zuri stepped over and cooed. "He is beautiful." Her blue eyes shimmered. "Another Christmas miracle."

Joe nodded. "One of many miracles. Maria wasn't due for a few weeks, but her water broke. Neither one of us knew what to do. This little guy is our first after multiple miscarriages. Then our car started acting up as we drove in, and I didn't know how we would get to the hospital. All I could do was pray."

"What happened?" Zuri asked.

"The car died right as we approached that lookout. We pulled over by the Mustang. It was sitting there, keys in the ignition and no one around. I knew it was an answer to that prayer. We left a note on the windshield of our car and drove straight here. We arrived just in time."

The note would've been buried under snow. No wonder they hadn't seen it.

"So everything is okay?" Duke asked.

"Joshua here is doing great and already discharged, but Maria had some complications. Doc says we might've lost her if she'd had the baby in the car or anywhere else. Thankfully, they've stopped her bleeding and she's recovering."

And thank goodness she hadn't delivered in Boone's Mustang. But Duke kept that thought to himself.

The baby let out a little squeak as he yawned.

"Looks like he'll be waking soon. I should get him back to Maria. But first"—Joe started to reach for his pocket with his free hand—"we'll pay for using the car."

Duke stopped him. "No need. I know the owner of the Mustang. He'll be happy to have helped."

"Are you sure? I'd feel better if you let me pay something."

"Save the money for diapers. You'll need them." And maybe he could pool some resources together to help with the old Corolla stuck in the impound lot. Keep the Christmas spirit going.

Joe nodded, his voice a little choked up. "Thank you." He handed the keys to Duke. "And Merry Christmas."

Duke took the keys and shook his hand. "Merry Christmas." And for once, it didn't hurt to say.

He turned to Zuri. "Let's get this Mustang back to the garage before anything else happens."

She slipped her hand into his. "I think the tragedies are over. It's all Merry Christmas and happy endings from here."

"We're back to that?"

"Never left it. By the way, if you want, I have an extra pair of antlers."

He grinned. Looking into the eyes of the woman next to him, he saw beautiful possibilities for many happy Christmases to come. "We'll see."

The Snow is Glistening

SUSAN MAY WARREN

Soli Deo Gloria

CHAPTER 1

MONDAY, 5:00 P.M.

*R*omeo hated it when Owen was right.

And it wasn't that Owen had turned into some kind of bossy older brother. After all, he was the boss, and Romeo got that.

It was that Owen and the rest of the Christiansen clan were down in Florida, lying on a beach, not freezing their backsides off while Romeo fought his way out of bed at zero-dark-thirty to plow not only the Christiansen resort parking lot but also the narrow drive to Wilder House in the resort pickup. And it was that after a barrage of panicked calls from Sammy Johnson, the current road services chief, Romeo had headed down to the city garage.

It was also that he'd nearly slid into the ditch, twice, while driving into Deep Haven, narrowly missing that embarrassing moment when he would have had to call the local sheriff to drag him out.

He would have never heard the end of that debacle.

And then at the garage, where Sammy Johnson held court assigning plowing duty to the local road crew, only the coffee dregs remained, along with one sad, plain cake donut.

His only sustenance since four a.m.

Worse, the snow just kept coming, icing his windshield despite the full-blast heat trying to keep up. Flurries had turned into a near whiteout, just the ghostly shapes of trees reaching into the gunmetal sky. The wind howled, shaking the cab of his tandem-axel commercial truck, and the snow had so packed the roads that a touch of his brakes too fast would careen him the length of a football field, completely at the mercy of fate.

But most of all, it was the crazy drivers deciding that a guy on a two-ton snowplow, kicking up a plume of grime onto the side of the road and going, say, twenty miles an hour, was somehow a road nuisance.

They passed him going fifty, laying on their horns.

He hoped they all landed in the ditch—no, that wasn't right.

He hoped that Kyle Hueston and his fellow road warriors pulled the idiots over to contribute to the road service general fund.

"How you doin', Romeo?" The radio above him crackled with the voice of Birdie. She sounded tired too, despite her chipper tone. And the night was just starting.

Romeo picked up the radio. "Still heading west toward the Cascade River. I'll turn around there and head back." He paused, wanting to ask just how long Sammy expected him to keep scraping the roads. Because he also had a business to run, and if he remembered correctly, he had a reservation coming in tonight. He couldn't remember who, but at some point, he should probably be at the front desk to check them in. Show them some Minnesota-nice hospitality.

If Owen were here, he'd have his pretty wife, Scotty, to fill in for him at the desk, probably four-month-old Paxten on her hip. Or maybe his brother Casper would come over, although Casper had his own plowing contracts in and around town. In a pinch, Grace Sharpe, their sister, might come down, especially now that Max was back from Mayo Clinic, recovering from his latest Huntington's trial.

But no, the entire family had abandoned Romeo without a glance behind.

"How are you doing on gas?" Sammy's voice came through the radio.

Right. Gas. Romeo had barely looked at the tank, having filled up at the garage before the day started. He'd also done a walk around the plow, checking the lug nuts on the tires, the brakes, the plow blade, and even the windshield wiper fluid. Reminded him a little of his days as a smokejumper, watching the pilots do a preflight check.

"Less than a quarter tank."

"Swing back in and fill up. Colleen and Jack brought in some chili. It's going to be a long night."

Romeo confirmed, trying to keep the groan out of his voice, and hung up the radio. He picked up his travel mug.

The coffee had turned to ice. He drained it anyway.

Outside, the late afternoon had turned to shades of deep gray, the whiteout still brutal—maybe thirty feet of visibility, just headlights cutting through the fog of snow. It didn't help that the plow made its own storm, kicking up the powder both from the tires and the massive wave of snow that he dumped into the ditch. After ten hours of plowing, he could barely hear his own thoughts, the roar of the truck finding his bones. The wipers could lull him to sleep, and save for the heat blowing in his face, cold had turned his entire body numb.

He should have worn the padded coveralls, but he'd only pulled on a parka, a hat, gloves, his jeans, and boots this morning. He knew better, frankly, after living in Alaska the past two winters.

He tried not to think of Owen by the poolside. Instead, he was searching through his brain for one, just one, good reason why he'd said yes to Uncle John's pleading missive to return to Deep—

Lights flashed in his side mirror, and he jerked at the sight of a car coming up alongside him, trying to pass.

What. An. Idiot.

He didn't touch his brakes—sure, the blade might slow him down, but it also might spin him. Better to stay steady and let this joker pass—

Lights ahead cut through the fog.

An oncoming car.

He glanced at the passer, and his breath caught.

This was going to be ugly. And maybe even fatal.

The car seemed to slow, and Romeo pressed on the gas, hoping to give the guy room to slide back in.

The lights ahead grew bigger, the passing car still in their lane.

Oh—

And for a second, just one second, he was back in Alaska, watching through the smoke and ash as Disco's chute refused to deploy, the recruit screaming as he drifted down on his own round, Romeo helpless as his recruit plunged to earth.

Then he was back, riding on instinct.

He touched his brakes and jerked the truck over, hoping the car might find room beside him.

The truck started to slide.

The oncoming driver also hit his brakes. The car skidded, took a brutal turn, then jerked back.

The car in the middle held course.

As Romeo sucked in his breath, the passing car sailed right between them, escaping the swing of the truck's back end.

The other car somehow skated into the ditch. It bumped along the snowbank, sending up a plume of debris into the thick air.

Romeo dropped his blade, and it dug into the snow, slowing him. The truck shuddered, then jerked to a stop.

For a second, he just sat there, tasting his heartbeat.

The red lights of the passing car disappeared into the whiteout.

Romeo unhooked his belt, opened the door, checked the highway for lights, then jumped out, running across the highway to where the car—an older model Honda CR-V—sat against the snow. It didn't look like they were badly stuck—probably a good push would dislodge them.

But honestly, he was shaking, his breaths thin as the driver rolled down his window.

"You okay, son?" Early sixties maybe, salt-and-pepper hair, concern in his eyes.

Romeo drew in a breath, still trying to find his voice, when the back, passenger window rolled down.

A woman, mid-twenties maybe, sat in the back seat, her blonde hair streaming out under a pom-pom cap, her eyes alight. "What was that? You trying to get us killed?"

Romeo stared at her, and maybe it was the cold, or the hunger, or the hours, or just the fact that he'd been dealing with road crazies all day, but he simply couldn't help it.

"Yeah. That's *exactly* what I was trying to do. Because anyone out in this storm is already tempting fate, and I thought I'd give them a little push over the edge. Welcome to Deep Haven!"

Then he turned, looked both ways, and jogged back to his truck.

He was about to get in when he heard it—the unmistakable sound of tires spinning.

Shoot.

Turning, he spotted the old guy trying to back up, spitting out road slime from his tires.

Perfect.

He jogged back over and simply headed to the front of the car, got down and put his weight against the bumper. "Put her in reverse!"

The man waved out the window and gunned it.

Snow and dirt spat out from the front tires, coating Romeo's jacket, wetting his jeans. But the car moved out of the snowbank and onto the shoulder, free.

He stood up, brushing himself off as the driver got out.

"Thanks."

"No problem."

"Sorry about my daughter. She was just scared."

"I get it."

Snow fell on his hat, his eyelashes, and he shivered.

"Do you know how the roads are north of town? We're staying at the Evergreen Resort tonight, but I'm afraid the road in won't be plowed."

He wanted to groan. "I plowed it this morning, but I'll head up there and make sure the road in is clear."

"Really?"

"I'm the... I'm with the resort. You're Reverend Brown, Pastor Dan's friend?"

"I am." He held out a gloved hand for Romeo to shake.

"I'd like to be at the desk when you arrive, but I have a long night ahead of me, so—"

"No worries, son. We can check ourselves in. Where do you want us?"

Romeo's brain simply went blank. He knew he had reserved one of the cabins for them, but— "I think cabin six is yours." Yes, that sounded right.

"Perfect. Thank you." He stuck his hands in his pockets. "I'll bet this place is gorgeous when the sun is shining."

Romeo nodded. "It's worth the trip, I promise. You'll never want to leave." He smiled his best Christiansen-family smile.

"Can't wait." Reverend Brown got back into his car as Romeo ran across the road again.

He looked back to see the girl watching him as they pulled away. Yikes. He'd make sure to stay out of her way.

Then he got back in the truck, put it in gear, and tried to believe his own words.

Woman dies while derailing her parents' second honeymoon.

Okay, Stella was probably overreacting to the fifteen seconds of sheer terror, but it felt true, given the silence between her parents over the past two hours, and especially since she'd overheard their fight.

About her.

About inviting her on this romantic getaway to some tucked-away town in northern Minnesota.

She probably shouldn't have told them she wasn't leaving for Vienna, or at least the part where she wasn't hopping on a plane in the near future. She didn't have the courage to tell them the rest, aka, the results of her audition for the Fritz Kreisler Institute in Vienna.

Lackluster. Dispassionate. Try again next semester. The words had sat in her brain throughout last night's recital, so much that she'd missed a couple crucial notes in the oh-so-familiar "Ave Maria," part of her Schubert concert, and reqs for her masters in chamber music for the violoncello.

The other part being, of course, her one now-defunct year of study in Vienna.

But if they didn't want her, she didn't want them either.

"You okay, honey?" Her mother turned in her seat as they started back out into the night, her dark hair poking out of her white knit hat. The heater in her father's ancient Honda CR-V barely kept ahead of the storm, and frankly, they should have stayed another night in Duluth. But Mom seemed particularly excited to escape to their vacation, despite her words this morning, the ones she thought Stella hadn't heard—*You invited her on our trip? Really, Bob? I thought we were going to spend some time alone.*

Stella got it, really. Their first real vacation in years, and never at Christmastime. Most of all, she hadn't been blind to the look of excitement on her mother's face last night at the concert when she told Stella about the getaway. Or the embarrassing lingerie she'd seen in her mother's suitcase this morning while her father folded up the pull-out sofa in Stella's cramped apartment.

So Stella probably should have kept quiet about her shattered plans. Even if she had to spend Christmas alone.

But maybe this getaway would be good for her—spend some time figuring out, well, *what next?* Because she had no backup plan.

Just a sense that she wanted...more. More life. More...anything.

She just didn't know what more meant. It certainly didn't mean that she was going to throw in her bow and quit the instrument she'd spent her entire life playing, right? Especially after her parents had put everything into the dream of her being a concert cellist.

Because if not that, then what? Wait tables down at the local diner in her hometown of Big Lake, Minnesota?

"Yeah, I'm fine," she said now to her mother. "I was just freaked out."

"You were a little hard on the snowplow driver."

She cocked her head at her mother. "Seriously?"

"He did push us out of the ditch."

"He nearly killed us."

"No, that was the *other* driver," her father said now as he slowed. They were descending a hill, the roads deeply salted. Through the loosening whiteout, she made out the tiny village of Deep Haven, the shops and houses huddled against a storming lake, the waves thrashing themselves onto the shore.

"Where is this place you're staying?"

"Where *we're* staying," her father said. "I'm glad you agreed to come with us."

Her mother glanced back, her lips smiling, her jaw tight.

Yeah, they were.

"The Evergreen Resort and Outfitters. According to my friend Dan Matthews, who pastors here, it's a beautiful family-owned resort back in the woods."

"I still can't believe you're taking a vacation at Christmas."

Her father drew in a breath. Her mother glanced at him, then sighed and looked away.

For sure, there was trouble in Brownsville, and it sent a tremor through her.

Her parents were a rock, a sure foundation. But their best friends had just gotten divorced after thirty years, so…

No. That was not this. She was just putting her own troubles onto them.

Everything was… Just. Fine. Still, "I'll try and stay out of your way."

"What?" Her father glanced at her in the mirror. "No, you won't. We'll play games and do puzzles—"

"I'm sure there are plenty of things to do here at Christmastime," her mother said.

Oh brother.

They pulled into the only coffee shop in town and piled out. She could admit that Deep Haven seemed like a quaint place to spend the holidays. Laurel entwined the lampposts along the snowy main street, the lamplights shedding an ethereal glow upon the street. She even spotted a tall evergreen in the middle of the park.

The wind, however, bit at her face as they hustled to the coffee shop. A bell jangled on the door as they entered.

People sat around a small metal fireplace in the corner, the place humming with conversation. Old thermoses from bygone years lined a bookcase stocked with sweatshirts and local fudge as well as tattered, used books.

Stella grabbed a small table while her parents ordered coffees. She shed her gloves but kept on her hat, like the locals.

For a moment, the image of the man who'd nearly killed them flashed in her mind. Sort of the kind of guy she expected here—grizzled beard, furry hat, parka, sturdy boots. What'd surprised her was the eyes that had sort of narrowed at her a second before he'd turned away.

Like he'd wanted to respond but had bitten it back.

Yes, she shouldn't have been such a jerk to him. She'd just been scared.

"One vanilla latte," her father said as he sat down and set her coffee in front of her. Her mother sat down with a cup of hot cocoa.

"I like this place," her father said. "I'm going to have to make this a regular hangout this week."

"They might have coffee at the cabin," her mother said.

He turned to Stella. "So, what did you mean last night when you said you weren't going to Vienna?"

Perfect. Cutting right to the core of the matter. She opened her mouth, trying to figure out how to form the words that would crush him. After all, they'd done everything, spent everything to give her the best instruction, sent her to music camps, then the best private music schools, and finally, driven to all her out-of-town recitals and listened to endless, mind-numbing hours of practice.

Frankly, they might be as tired of it all as she was. As desperate to escape the expectedness of life. After all, her father had been a pastor of his small-town church for nearly twenty years.

"I—"

The doors opened and a couple of burly lumberjacks barreled in. "Kathy! We need a dozen coffees for the CRT," said one of them, a tall blond man with snow on his eyelashes. "We have a three-car pileup just north of town. No injuries, just a mess." The man peeled off his gloves and set them on the counter.

The other man, however, had stopped and now turned to them. "Bob?"

He had brown hair, was solidly built, and came over, his hand out as her father rose. "Dan. How are you?"

"You made it to town. Excellent." Dan shook his hand, and she correctly guessed him as her father's pastor friend when he introduced him. "You'll love the Evergreen Resort. I think the family is stuck in Florida. But they left Romeo in charge. He's fantastic—"

"I think we met him," her father said. "He pulled us out of the ditch."

Oh no. The snowplow driver also ran the resort? Maybe she could successfully avoid him. Especially if he spent his entire time snowplowing the highway.

"Can't believe he's alone for the week of Christmas at the resort. It's their biggest week of events. With Casper out of town, Romeo will probably have to oversee Wilder House too. And Boone here is getting married there on Saturday night."

The big blond turned, holding a tray of coffee. "I'm sure Romeo will pull it together. Between my bride and her to-do list, I'm sure everything will be perfect. But he definitely has his hands full." He turned to the Browns. "Nice to meet you. Have a great vacation."

"Plan to," her father said. "Thanks."

They left, and her mother turned to her. "Maybe you can help."

Stella looked at her, a little nonplussed. "Help? With what?"

"You know. With Christmas at the resort. The wedding." She drained her cocoa. "After all, you organized your senior prom."

"That's because I was class president!"

"And a good one too," her father said. "Ready to go?" He stood up.

She looked at her mother, who was gathering the cups.

What on earth?

She followed her parents out into the storm, sliding into the dark, cold back seat.

Definitely a third wheel.

She leaned her head against the window as they headed out of town and into the whiteout.

CHAPTER 2

Under the blue-skied day, powered by four cups of java and six hours of dead-to-the-world sleep, maybe Romeo would make a comeback. He'd risen with the sun, still making a run for the morning, ground some of Aunt Ingrid's favorite beans from the local Java Cup, and woken up his bones with a workout of chopping a cord of wood for his newest guests.

Today, two more guests were due to arrive, so he cleaned out the parking lot, again, then delivered wood to the bin of cabin six.

Clearly, the Browns had settled in okay, their little Honda CR-V parked in the drive and footsteps stamped into the snow of their deck.

He retrieved the shovel and went to work on the deck, clearing it and the steps. Then he cleaned off the decks of the other cabins and the path back to the house.

The snow had turned the resort into a winter wonderland, the frosting heavy on the evergreens and icing the lake. He walked out to the dock and cleared the platform that remained on shore. He and Owen had taken the rest of the dock out of the water last fall.

Back then, he'd felt a part of the team, busy caring for the guests who'd arrived to enjoy the fall colors. They'd built bonfires in the evenings, helped kids roast marshmallows, and he'd even taken a few guests out in the canoe to enjoy the moonlight.

For a while, it had silenced the what-ifs, stopped the mental pull to check in on the Jude County Firefighters and their whereabouts. His old jump boss, Tucker, had texted him once, asking him how his old hometown was, and they'd had a short conversation. Tucker and his wife, Stevie, had headed up to Alaska for Christmas, and it'd only stirred in Romeo an old longing.

But those days were over, destroyed after Disco died, and probably Uncle John's request to return to Deep Haven had actually been a rescue mission.

Romeo put away the shovel, then took the resort truck into town to plow Casper's route. Which necessitated a trip into Java Cup for another cup of coffee, this time a caramel macchiato.

"Thanks, Kathy," he said as he retrieved his order.

"Your cronies are in the back room," she said.

His cronies? He didn't have any cronies…but he stuck his head into the back area and spotted Sammy sitting on a chair, leaning back on the legs. With him sat Sheriff Kyle Hueston, Cole Barrett, director of the Deep Haven Crisis Response Team, along with Boone Buckam, also with the team, and Jack Stewart, CRT flight nurse, and fire chief Pete Dahlquist. By the sound of the conversation, they were chewing over last night's accidents.

"Hey, Romeo," Kyle said. "Good work yesterday. Sammy said you worked fourteen hours."

"Way past regulation, but we were short-staffed." Sammy lowered his chair. "Take the day off."

"I wish," Romeo said. "I have guests due to arrive and Wilder House to plow, not to mention Casper texted and needs me to do his plowing route."

"The Christiansens still 'stuck' in Florida?" Kyle finger quoted *stuck*, and everyone laughed.

"Apparently." Romeo laughed too. Probably he should just let it go. It wasn't like Owen had tried to abandon him.

And now he was just acting like a child. Sheesh. "I hope they're having a great time."

"I hope they're all sunburned," Kyle said, grinning. "Jerks. Casper and Owen should be freezing with the rest of us." More laughter.

"Could be worse," Sammy said. "Romeo could be freezing his backside off in Alaska." He turned to him. "Didn't you winter in a one-room cabin without electricity?"

"Or plumbing," Romeo said. "We had an outhouse."

"That's a cold trip in the middle of the night," Cole said.

Romeo smiled, but the words turned to acid inside him. Yeah, it had been cozy, but he'd been holed up with two of his teammates.

Somehow, suffering together felt better than suffering alone.

Stop. He didn't know why this was bothering him so much. It wasn't like he was a kid, spending Christmas shivering in the back seat of his mother's car. He had a roof over his head, a job, and, like Kathy said, cronies.

"Gotta get back." He lifted his macchiato.

"My best man and Vivie's makeup girl are coming in tonight," Boone said.

"I'm on it."

Romeo headed back outside and got in the truck.

The lake had calmed since the storm last night, the clouds blown away, and Deep Haven had turned downright magical with the decorated main street, wreaths on all the shop doors, a Salvation Army ringer near the Blue Moose Cafe.

Maybe he needed a little more cheer up at the resort. Lights on the evergreen. A skating rink with lights.

He put the cup in the holder between the seats, then started on Casper's list, plowing out the community church parking lot, Pastor Dan's house, the Deckers' places, and even the CRT lot, although much of that snow had been already cleared by their four-wheeler.

An hour later, he headed out of town, the radio turned to a local station now spilling out a jazzy rendition of "Jingle Bells"—"Dashing through the snow…"

His phone rang, and he sent it through the truck's speakers. "Tell me you're on a flight."

"Sorry." Owen's voice. "There's another storm front headed across the Midwest. It might miss Deep Haven, but the flights are all messed up. We're thinking of driving."

"Driving? For three days? Ten of you in a van? I thought you ruled that out."

"Casper is worried about the wedding—"

"I got this, Owen. Really. I'll swing by the place and make sure everything's fine. The guests are all tucked in, the wood is cut, the place is plowed—calm down. I might even try and throw some lights on the big tree."

A sigh on the other end suggested that maybe Owen was more worried than he let on.

"Seriously, boss. Nothing is going to burn down. No guest will perish. I promise, everything will be fine."

"Okay. Just keep the guests warm and happy. We'll be back as soon as we can. I knew I could count on you, Romeo."

He didn't know why those words heated him to his core as he hung up.

Maybe because it wasn't easy being the outsider, wannabe, tagalong of the Christiansen clan.

And maybe that's why it had hurt, being left behind. Because no matter how much he wanted it, how much he tried, he'd never really belong.

He had climbed the hill out of Deep Haven and was coming around the curve when the sun hit his mirror, cutting into his eyes. Shoot— he'd forgotten his sunglasses and now squinted, touching his brakes.

Wrong, wrong—the truck started to skid on the veneer of snow. He turned the wheel the opposite direction, and it spun the other way.

Shoot!

Then he spotted the other car, also careening his direction. He winced, bracing himself, everything moving in slow motion on the skating rink of the highway.

His truck landed with a *poof* into the ditch, a pillow landing, really, for such a big vehicle.

The other car, a mid-sized SUV that should have been able to grab the road, landed frontside in a snowdrift on the opposite side of the road.

Oops.

He got out, not quite as rattled as last night, but still buzzing. Probably the coffee. The lack of sleep. The—*oh no*. He knew this car. And the woman getting out of the driver's seat, with the pom-pom hat and the angry set to her mouth.

Oh goody.

"Seriously?" she said as she came toward him.

He took a breath, schooled his voice. "Are you okay?"

She stared at him, her mouth opening, and in that moment, he noticed her pale-blue eyes, her blonde hair spilling out of her hat, and most of all, the way, suddenly, she looked terribly, even beautifully fragile.

And then, right there on the side of the road, she burst into tears.

Oh no, no— *No.* She *wasn't* unraveling here, now, in the middle of nowhere, in front of a stranger who'd nearly killed her, again.

Except it hadn't been his fault, not really. Stella had probably been driving too fast for the curve, and his truck had just sort of come out of nowhere, and the sun had hit her eyes, and— "I'm sorry—I'm so sorry."

"Are you hurt?"

Yes. No. Yes—oh, what a complete mess she'd made of things.

So she put her hands over her face, trying to push the tears back, but, well, apparently her heart didn't want to listen to her brain—as usual—and there she went.

Turning soggy on the side of the highway.

"I don't know…what to…um…" The man came up to her, his hands out as if wanting to touch her but also not, and so he just stood there, worry on his face.

A handsome face, if she were looking. Same handsome face as last night, although she hadn't really gotten a good look at it, what with the snow and darkness and—

"And I'm sorry for last night," she said through her mittens. Wow, she was pitiful.

He took a breath. "It's okay."

"No, it's not. I'm a jerk. And a disaster and…I'm fine. Really." She wiped her nose with her mitten. "Just leave me here in the ditch."

He laughed, something bold and thick against the morning. "Right. For one, yes, I see that you're completely fine. And two, I regularly leave people in the ditch. Especially when they're wearing the wrong footwear."

She glanced at her feet. High top Cons. Her travel shoes of choice. Apparently, she hadn't been thinking yesterday when she'd grabbed a few things from her packed bags and headed out the door for her unscheduled getaway in the woods. "I was supposed to be on a plane for Vienna."

He made a face. "I'd cry too if I ended up in the ditch instead of Vienna."

She looked at him. He'd sort of nailed the story of her life.

Then he smiled. Oh, he was cute. Sunshine and heat through her barren soul. She couldn't help but laugh. "Right." She wiped her face. "Truth is, it's just…been a really bad couple of days. And now I'm sabotaging my parents' second honeymoon."

"Yikes." He walked to the front of her car. "No dents in the car. I think you can just back up."

"Sorry I fell apart."

"I get it. Adrenaline. Going into the ditch is scary. Especially twice in twenty-four hours. Let's get you back on the road."

For some reason, she let out a laugh, and even to her ears it felt a little feral and crazy, and he looked at her, his green eyes wide.

"Sorry. It's just…it'll take more than a push to get me back on the road—"

"I don't think it's that bad."

"Oh, it's that bad. I promise." She walked over to survey the damage. He was right—she'd barely bumped the sidewalls of snow. But she might need some traction to get the front wheel out.

But that wasn't the real problem, was it? She turned, staring at the view—the glorious blue lake, the clear sky, the towering evergreens frosted with snow. Okay, she still wanted to cry, but she drew from her stage persona and exhaled. "Ever feel like you're exactly where you're not supposed to be?"

He said nothing, and she finally glanced at him. He was looking at her, his mouth a small bud of consideration. Then, "More than you know."

"Right? I mean, one minute you're driving along, the next you're spinning, and snow is flying everywhere—"

"And you end up in Deep Haven instead of Vienna?"

She looked over at him. "Something like that." She took a breath. "Stella."

"Romeo." He shook her hand. "My mother had a sense of humor." He grinned again, and for a moment, she simply stared. His dark blond hair curled out under his wool hat, and he wore a green canvas jacket with an evergreen tree on the breast pocket and a pair of work boots. He hadn't shaved either, and the sun picked up the hint of gold in his beard, and hello, his mother had probably known *exactly* what she was doing. But the last thing she should be thinking about was some random guy when, when—

Well, she just might be the worst judge of character—and currently of decisions—in the world. "It's a great name." She walked up to the driver's door, opened it, and popped the trunk. He backed up, giving her room.

"It's taught me a few things. Why do you think you're sabotaging your parents' second honeymoon?"

A bag of kitty litter sat unopened in the trunk. She made to pull it out, but he grabbed it, clearly familiar with the trick.

"There's no door on the bedroom."

He stared at her. "Oh no. Cabin six is a one bedroom. I'm sorry—I didn't even think."

"That's fine. I slept on the sofa. But they barely spoke on the way up, and last night Dad actually offered to take the sofa."

"I can move you."

"No. My dad loves it—says it has the best view. And it's not the cabin. Something isn't right—Mom practically pushed me out of the door today. Told me to get coffee."

"We have bags of beans in the lodge." He had opened the cat litter and now poured some behind the front wheel. "I should have stocked it for you. I was out late—"

"You have to be exhausted."

"Naw." He smoothed out the litter with his boot, kicking it behind the wheel, then did the same with the other wheel, on the ice.

"A true Minnesotan."

He looked at her, and she lifted a shoulder. "No, really. I get it. I grew up in a small town in Minnesota too. I learned to keep my troubles to myself. It's the Minnesota way. And especially, the Brown family way."

He wore a frown, his green eyes in hers. "Really, I can move you. We're not that full."

"No. I just need to do something to stay out of the way so they can figure this out." She got in the car.

He bent down, put his shoulder against the car's bumper. "Slowly."

She gave it gas, and he eased the car out of the ditch, back onto the pavement. Just like last night.

Yeah, she'd been completely wrong about him. Of course.

She got out of the car. "Thanks. Can I do anything for you? Buy you some hot cocoa maybe?"

"I have coffee in the truck. Just…stay on the road. And let me know if I can make your stay any better." He grinned, winked. "Like not running you off the road again."

"That would get you five stars on Trip Advisor."

He laughed, lighting that little stupid fire in her again, then headed off toward his truck, got in, and pulled away.

And just like that, the conversation from last night was in her head. *But he definitely has his hands full. Maybe you can help.*

Whatever.

Or…

She got in the car and pulled out toward town.

CHAPTER 3

*R*omeo had finished the Millers' half-mile drive when he spotted the low oil pressure light on in the truck. How long it had been flashing at him on the dash, Romeo couldn't guess.

His mind had been replaying the conversation on the side of the road with Stella.

Who should be in Vienna.

Who had said she liked his crazy name and apologized for last night, and, well, *cried*. And that had simply undone him.

He didn't handle women falling apart well. *Thanks, Mom.*

But Stella had pulled herself together, and frankly, he'd ended up liking her. Sorta wished he'd said yes to her offer to buy him cocoa. But then what? She was a guest.

Hello, awkward.

But he couldn't get those blue eyes and the way she'd looked at him through the windshield as he pushed her out of the ditch—like he might be a hero or something—out of his brain.

And right then, the check engine light pinged on.

Perfect.

He got out and climbed under the Ford F-350 and spotted the trouble right off—a hole in his oil pan, courtesy of some rock in the ditch, probably.

Which meant he'd be pulling the oil pan and replacing it before he could do any more plowing. He didn't want to take a look at his growing to-do list.

Miraculously, he made it home without the engine seizing, but by the time he pulled into the parking lot of the resort, the truck had started to ping. He got out, unhooked the plow, then drove the truck into the garage.

He'd noticed that the Browns' car wasn't back. Hopefully Stella wasn't in a ditch somewhere.

Romeo wasn't the best mechanic, but he'd learned a few things from Uncle John over the years, and if he got into a pinch, he could retrieve the extra keys to Casper's truck and use that until the crew returned.

But he'd rather get the truck back on its feet before the Christiansens could stand around and critique his work.

Uncle John had left his very impressive toolbox, the one on wheels and a tow hitch, behind when he moved to the boat. And now Romeo dug through the tools for a ratchet and socket kit.

He probably wouldn't need to drop out the engine, but he'd probably have to remove the steering linkage. Then it would just be the bell housing shroud and oil pan bolts.

Four hours to get it out, drain the pan, patch the hole with a nut and bolt—for now—and he'd have it back in and running.

In theory.

In reality, he stood staring at the truck, painfully aware that he could get this thing apart and end up with pieces that he had no idea what to do with.

"I brought you that hot cocoa."

He turned, and for a moment, just blinked at the voice.

Stella. She stood at the garage door, and something about her simply made him stop. Breathe.

Maybe it was her smile, something gentle and yet inviting, the look in her blue eyes so absent of last night's ire. But mostly, the sense that she had come looking for him, holding two cups of cocoa from the Java Cup in her hands.

"I know you said you already had coffee, but that was over an hour ago, and I figured that everybody has room for hot cocoa— Is everything okay?" She gestured with one of the cups. "That doesn't bode well."

He followed her gesture to the ratchet in his hand, then put it down on the counter. "I blew a hole in the oil pan. And I'm trying to figure out how to change it without destroying the company vehicle."

"Then you definitely need chocolate." She advanced into the garage and handed him the cup. "I wish I were handy, but the best I can do is restring a cello."

He took the cup. "I can't do that. I can pack a parachute, though."

"Wow. I can make a mean batch of chocolate chip cookies."

"I can tie a fishing lure onto a line in less than thirty seconds."

"I can do a skating toe loop." She grinned and took a drink of her cocoa.

"I can parallel park in Minneapolis."

She raised an eyebrow. "Now that's impressive."

He laughed. Took a sip of hot cocoa. It was still warm. Creamy. "Thanks."

"No, thank *you*." She drew in a breath. "Actually, I was hoping that maybe you'd let me help you out a little this week."

He frowned. "Help me out?"

She made a face. "I overheard someone mentioning that you were working the resort alone this week."

Thank you very much, Deep Haven gossip crowd. Kathy and whoever else was holed up at Java Cup. He could imagine the conversation—

Did you hear that the Christiansens brought in that foster kid again? To run the place? What were they thinking—

"I can handle it."

Her smile fell, and shoot, he didn't mean it quite like it sounded.

Or, frankly, at all. Because he could admit that with the truck kaput, he might be a little in over his head. And then there was, *Just keep the guests warm and happy.*

But most of all, *I just need to do something to stay out of the way so they can figure this out.*

Right. "Are you sure?" he asked, just in case.

She nodded, her eyes brightening.

And it cost him nothing at all to say, "What do you know about stringing Christmas lights?"

She might have gotten in over her head.

Stella stood at the apex of the ladder, some forty feet in the air, reaching out to place the massive star topper on the evergreen that towered over the roof of the resort.

Trying not to kill herself.

"Are you sure you're okay?"

Romeo stood at the bottom, holding the ladder that leaned against the tree. Shaggy branches poked through the rungs, and the whole thing had shaken on her way up.

Why, why, *why*—but apparently, this was her MO of late. Impulsive, risky decisions.

"I'm fine!"

Liar. But she'd gotten off to such a great start when he'd asked her what she knew about putting up Christmas lights. Like it might be hard or something. *Lots of lights, wound around every branch?*

You'll do. He'd smiled then, approving, and in that moment, she'd simply lost her common sense. He'd rolled out four massive coils of lights wrapped in wooden spools, then set up the ladder. "We string four strands, starting at the top, down to the bottom, each one covering a quarter of the tree."

Made sense. She'd grabbed one end of the strand and climbed up.

"What—wait, what are you doing?" Romeo had run to steady the ladder. "I can't let you go up there."

"You can't *let* me?" She'd looked down at him, nearly missing a rung. Okay, maybe—

"No, I mean—I don't want you to get hurt." He had dug his feet around the base of the ladder, deep into the snow, his worn leather gloves holding on to the sides of the ladder. Seeing him down there, braced, protecting her from a fall…

She wouldn't fall. But it didn't mean she couldn't wish for a Superman landing.

Stop. Her brilliant idea didn't include a holiday romance with a local snowplow driver-slash-woodsman of the north. She just needed to occupy her time and stay away from cabin number six.

So she'd climbed to the top, then secured the lights and started to wind them down the tree.

"Not bad, Elf Brown," Romeo had said as he unwound the next spool.

Right about then, her parents had emerged from their cabin, on the way into town.

Interesting.

When she'd dropped off the groceries, her dad had already hunkered down with a puzzle, her mother heading in for a nap. But not before quizzing her on her whereabouts and getting the lowdown about the second skid into the ditch. "Romeo helped dig me out," Stella had said.

"The snowplow driver?" Her mother wore a funny smile, and Stella rolled her eyes.

"Look, I'm sorry for worrying you. Forgive me?"

"Of course we forgive you." Her dad had stepped between them and put an arm around each of his girls.

"Absolutely." Her mother had smiled then, and maybe Stella had simply dreamed up the tension. Especially when her father had waved to her on their way to the car.

Still, it didn't hurt to give them room. And Romeo didn't seem to mind, despite his words when she'd offered—*I can handle it.*

Yes, he could. And she'd been a little presumptuous to think she could just barge into his life and—

"Be sure and get the star on there well. The wind can take it off."

After she'd strung the first light, she'd held the ladder for him and he'd strung the second and third sets, but she'd already grabbed the end for the last. When she'd made it back to the bottom, she'd reached for the star topper.

"You do this every year?" She'd untangled the cord from the star. It was a good three feet tall, two feet wide, but made of plastic and wire, so not terribly heavy. It came with extra clips on the back to secure it to the tree.

"This is only my second season here, really." He'd shown her how to clip the light on. "Just hang it over your shoulder as you climb up. You sure you don't want me to do this?"

"I got it. Only your second season?" She'd put the light over her shoulder, the cord hanging down, secured it with the long extension cord that ran to the bottom, then started up.

"Uncle John wrote to me last year and asked me to move back and help Owen. But before that, I'd only spent one Christmas here."

"You didn't grow up on the resort?" Okay, this was harder than she thought. At the top, she had to grip the edge of the ladder, then lean in with the star, one handed…no, no, this was a terrible idea—

"No. Mom and I traveled a lot. Usually we were on the road for Christmas."

Something vacant rang in his voice. But at the moment, she was trying not to fall to her death.

"You sure you're okay up there?"

She looked down. Swallowed.

"I'm coming up."

"No, I can—"

"Resort rules. No guest dies on my watch." The ladder shook as he ascended.

"What are you doing? Isn't there a rule against two people on a ladder?"

"Tell that to any firefighter." He kept coming, his eyes on her. "Just stay still."

She wasn't going anywhere, thank you, her hand like cement on the roofline, her feet jammed against the edges of the ladder, her other hand gripping the light, trying not to drop it. How anyone managed to put this up without help—

And then he was there. Behind her, his feet between hers, grabbing on to the roof to tug himself in. His body secured her to the ladder while his other hand lifted the light. "I'll hold it against the tree, you snap it on. You can use two hands—I got you."

Three sexier words had never been spoken, at least to her, and she suddenly couldn't ignore the strength of him, keeping her safe as she reached out to latch the light to the apex of the tree.

Oh boy.

He even smelled good—woodsy, chocolaty, a hint of soap lifting from his beard, his face so close to hers.

She snapped the light into place. "Got it."

"Good job. Stay put until I get to the bottom." He started down the ladder, so sure of every step.

"Are you a fireman?" She didn't know why that question popped into her head, just—

"Was. A smokejumper. But we learned some urban skills." He hopped down to the bottom, then braced the ladder again. "C'mon down."

She should have guessed he'd been a firefighter. Because suddenly she was in a Hallmark Christmas romance. Next thing that happened —she'd accidentally end up on a sleigh ride with him through the woods.

She was halfway down when he pulled his phone from his pocket. Frowned.

"What?"

He made a face. "Nothing."

She landed in the snow next to him, and he walked over to the house, where the extension cord end was plugged into a timer.

He turned on the light.

Despite the daylight hours, the tree shone, tiny sparkles against the sunlight. She couldn't wait to see it in the twilight. Preferably with—

Oh, good grief.

His phone beeped again. Another frown.

"Is it serious?"

He sighed. "I don't know. Maybe. The heat seems to be falling at Wilder House. I need to get over there." He pocketed his phone. "I guess I'll take the four-wheeler."

She didn't know why the words emerged from her, why suddenly she thought this might be a great idea, why, apparently, she assumed he might want her tagging along, but just like that, the question simply erupted out of her. "Can I go with you?"

Her request hung there, bright and raw, and oh, she just wanted to pull it back—

"Really?"

And again, she didn't know what possessed her. Simply, yes. Yes, she wanted...well, she didn't know, really, what she wanted. But maybe she was tired of living by the plan, the rules, the sheet music.

She wanted to improvise. "Sounds fun."

He considered her long enough for her to open her mouth to take it back when, "Okay then. But on one condition."

Probably that she'd stop prying into his life.

"You're going to have to wear boots."

CHAPTER 4

TUESDAY, 4:00 P.M.

This was probably a bad idea. At least, that's what Owen's voice in Romeo's head was shouting.

A bad idea to bring a guest along to fix whatever disaster awaited him at Wilder House.

Romeo's phone kept buzzing, despite turning off the internet-connected thermometer that alerted him to problems with the heating system. But according to his app, the temperature in the wedding venue had dropped to less than fifty-five degrees and was headed quickly into pipe-freezing temps.

So, who knew what he was walking into, and yes, he probably should have told Stella no when she asked to go with him. But she'd looked so...well, if not hopeful, then eager.

Like she wanted to spend time with him.

And he wasn't unaware of his own forbidden, surprising reaction to the look of fear on her face when she'd looked down at him from her perch on the ladder.

Yeah, he hadn't been listening to Owen when she'd grabbed the star and headed up the ladder. But maybe he'd chalk up his response—to barrel up the ladder—to resort responsibility rather than the crazy urge to protect her.

He didn't have such an excuse now. Simply that somehow, the urge to say yes to her had swept over him. And suddenly, dangerously, a pretty girl had ended up on his four-wheeler as he trekked through the snow to Wilder House.

"What is this place?" she said, leaning in, her voice in his ear. She wasn't exactly tucked up against him—instead, she held onto the seat handles. But he was very, very aware of her presence, the tiny gasps or even laughs she gave when he skidded or went over a bump.

As if she were enjoying herself? So maybe, mission accomplished?

"It's an old Victorian home that my cousin Casper restored and turned into a wedding venue. There's a wedding here this weekend."

Even as he said it, he turned off the gravel road and down the long drive toward the house. As they drew nearer, the five acres of cleared land opened a glorious view of Lake Superior, blue and smoky today as fog lifted from it, the water warmer than the crisp air.

The house, with its tall tower turret, wraparound front porch, dormer windows, and a Christmas-red barn, wasn't a large venue, but it was the top of its game in Deep Haven, booked every weekend since it opened last February.

"Wow, it's gorgeous."

"Yeah. And inside, there's an industrial kitchen, bride and groom's suites upstairs, a room for a small reception or dinner, and another grand room for the ceremony."

He pulled up to the house and she got off.

"It's magical." She spread her arms wide, leaning back. "And it smells amazing here."

"It's the lake effect. That, and the white pine that surround the place. The Evergreen used to be surrounded by them too, but they were taken out by a fire years ago and are still growing back."

"A forest fire?"

He stepped up to the porch—he'd have to shovel—unlocked the door, and went inside, checking for anything amiss. "Yeah. I wasn't around, but I heard about it from Darek Christiansen. He's the oldest brother and used to run the resort. He used to be a hotshot with the Jude County Firefighters, same outfit that I worked for."

She followed him in. The air carried the sharp edge of chill. He stopped by the thermometer, and sure enough, the head had dropped to fifty.

"Something has cut out the heat."

She tried the lights. "Electricity is out."

"Hmm." He headed outside. And discovered, on the backside of the house, a birch tree had fallen, hanging on a line. "That's the culprit. I'll have to take down the tree and call the electric company."

"Need help?"

"I'm pretty good with a chain saw."

"Of course you are."

He smiled at her, then headed to the barn and found a chain saw. Then he called the electric company and got an update on the restoration of power.

When he came out, he spotted her on the deck, shovel in hand. He walked over to her. "You don't have to do that."

She gave him a look. "I promise I won't tell anyone. But this place needs a little wedding magic."

It did, and he had nothing in argument. So he headed to the tree and attacked it, taking it down, then cut up the tree into manageable chunks to be chopped into firewood later.

The porch was mostly clean when he returned, and he took the shovel from her to finish the job. The snow drifted into the wind like fairy dust. She leaned against the railing.

"Why did you say yes?"

He looked at her.

"When your uncle John asked you to come here. Sounds like you enjoyed firefighting."

"I did. But..." He finished the last swipe, then headed toward the steps. "About a year and a half ago, we had an accident. One of our team members died when his chute didn't open."

"Oh, Romeo. I'm so sorry."

"Thanks." His mouth tightened as he cleared the step. Sighed. "He was my trainee."

She said nothing as he finished the next step.

He looked up at her. She met his eyes. Something about her expression made him continue. "I blamed myself. It was an accident, but...I had spent the last winter with a bunch of guys at a cabin in Alaska, but...I just couldn't..."

"You couldn't face their disappointment every day."

He made a sound, deep inside. "Uncle John heard about it through...well, my jump boss, Tucker, is also from Deep Haven, so maybe that's how. Anyway, he called, and I said yes and..."

"And now you're here, trying to entertain a guest who is also running from disappointing the people she loves."

He looked at her, and she wrinkled her nose. "Just saying, I get it."

He didn't know why, but her words sank in with an almost unbearable heat.

Oh.

"Let's see if the furnace is on." He went inside. "Sounds like it got reset. Just needed to take the tension off the line." He toed off his boots and walked to the kitchen. Turned on the faucet just to make sure that the water was running. "I think we're in the clear. Ready to go?"

She made a noise behind him.

He turned. And for the second time in the day, she looked like she might cry. "Stella?"

"I'm fine. I'm fine, I'm just..." She closed her eyes, looked away. "A freakin' disaster."

He came over to her. "What's going on?"

She looked away. "I would really love to stay here and hide in this winter wonderland forever, if that is okay."

He didn't know why he fought the sudden urge to reach out and... what? Hug her?

"How about if we start with a little lunch? I'll see if I can rustle up some grub."

She looked at him with such a look of gratefulness he could almost believe he was a hero.

"I don't know what's wrong with me. I just knew, in that moment, I wasn't going to Vienna."

Stella sat on one of the tall stools in the magnificent Wilder House kitchen with the massive granite countertop and forked another piece of white, strawberry-filled cake.

Romeo sat next to her, eating off the same hunk of leftover wedding cake they'd found in the freezer. They'd thawed it and added ice cream as if this might be a perfectly acceptable version of lunch.

Maybe it was. Maybe she had to stop trying so hard to live by the rules. Except rules kept her from doing crazy things.

Like giving her heart away to a stranger she'd met a mere eighteen hours ago.

Or, conversely, her artistic director.

Whatever. In this moment, Romeo was just a really nice guy who hadn't blinked when she'd reached over and scooped the flower from the top of the next piece and plopped it on her plate.

"Just because you botched the audition?"

She'd already told him about the debacle at the conservatory in New York City, where she'd played for the Fritz Kreisler Institute admissions committee, messing up not only her premier piece but two technical pieces assigned to her, and most of all, her improv. That had been absolutely disastrous.

As if she might be a first-year cellist.

"It wasn't like I forgot some notes. It was…well, it's incredibly difficult to improvise on the cello. The scales and arpeggios don't match up on the fingerboard like they do on a piano. You have to really think about it, and I…I just blanked. I oversimplified. They said my performance was lackluster. It probably was—I was angry and tired and…and Harry was there, in my head, the whole time, critiquing me."

"Harry?"

Oh, she'd forgotten herself for a moment and now looked over at Romeo. He sat in a flannel shirt, open at the neck to reveal a white thermal shirt. Both were pushed up his forearms—the flannel shirt rolled—and he rested his elbows on the granite, his hands folded, listening. With his entire body. Green eyes fixed on her, a frown on his handsome face, his lips pursed under that dark-blond beard. He still wore his stocking cap, but it was somehow terribly sexy in a lumberjack sort of way, his hair curling out the bottom.

And he smelled like the woods, a little untamed, sawdust from the downed birch flecking the collar of his shirt. She couldn't help watching him as she shoveled. He'd shed his jacket after a few minutes, and he'd handled the chain saw with a precision and strength that outlined his shoulders, his arms, his firefighter physique, and good grief, no wonder she found herself caught in his silent, mesmerizing gaze.

For Pete's sake, she'd practically thrown herself at him.

"Sorry. I didn't mean to spill out all my problems onto you."

"That's what cake is for." He picked up his fork, took a bite of his piece. "It's good too. Now, who's Harry and why is he in your head?"

Harry?

Oh. "He was my director. And…we had a—"

"Fling?"

"I guess that's the word. I thought he liked me, but…anyway, it turned out that he was actually a petty thief."

Romeo's fork stopped mid-bite. "What?"

"Yeah. I was part of an international chamber orchestra last summer, and we traveled around the world. What I didn't know is that Harry—Joseph Harrington Amherst the Third"—she said it with the appropriate accent—"was actually breaking into hotel rooms and stealing from guests. And the worst part is that he'd hide his goods in our instruments after we dropped them off to our luggage carrier. I was nearly arrested in Brussels."

"Terrifying."

She glanced at him. "Exactly. I trusted him and was completely duped."

"Which is why he was in your head at the audition."

She nodded. "Worse, he'd made me first chair. I thought it was because I had talent."

"You can't spend your entire life doing something and stink at it."

She cocked her head. "I think you can. But even if I don't stink, what if the institute is right? What if my heart isn't in it? What if I don't want this?"

"Then you do something else?"

"My parents have invested everything into this life. What else am I going to do? Make cake?" She scooped up the flower and stuck it in her mouth.

"Maybe, right now, you don't think about it. Just…let the tension go a little. Enjoy the week. You'll figure it out."

Not with him looking at her that way. Like she was interesting, and he had nothing else in the world to do but listen to her.

Yeah, she was a disaster, because too easily she could believe he actually…well, that he was *interested* in her.

Clearly her instincts were all off. "It didn't help that Harry was my first real—not real—boyfriend. My entire life, I've followed the rules. And then I broke them by falling for my director. Which turned out to be a colossal mistake."

"A colossal mistake that led you here, eating cake." He lifted a shoulder. "Doesn't seem so off the rails."

She considered him. "You're pretty good at this 'keep the guests happy' thing."

He laughed. "Actually, I'm in way over my head. I'm supposed to create a 'holiday experience' for our guests"—he finger quoted the words—"and I don't have the first idea how to do that. I chop wood. And I drive the snowplow."

"I think we can work with that," she said.

His eyes were in hers with a frown.

"Let me help. I planned my senior prom. And countless events after that—it was sort of my thing. I'll help you pull together a fabulous week, and in the meantime, it'll help me forget Harry. And stay out of my parents' second honeymoon. And maybe by the time I leave, I'll have some idea of what I'm doing next."

He smiled. "Unless you end up staying."

Her mouth opened.

"I was kidding." But a blush had weirdly, suddenly, burned his face. "Just…what you said before, about staying…"

"Yeah. I know." She looked away. Dug into her cake.

His phone buzzed on the table, and he picked it up. "Evergreen Resort."

Oh no. He winced and bracketed his forehead. "Right. Sorry. I'll be right there."

He nodded, listening, then, "Thanks. Sorry, again." Hanging up, he looked at her. "Guests from Minneapolis. They're waiting to be checked in."

"Let's go," she said, picking up her paper plate and debris. "We have a resort to run."

He smiled as he got up. "You sure?"

"You've met me, right? Not in the least."

He laughed. "I can work with that."

But as they left, closing up and climbing back on the four-wheeler, as she put her hands on his waist to hold on and lost herself in the exhilaration of speeding over the snow, she felt, for the first time since leaving Duluth, that coming here had been the right decision.

CHAPTER 5

The early morning call could only mean trouble.

Romeo chased the phone around the floor of the A-frame—Darek's old place—after hitting it off his nightstand. He finally got hands around it, caught the name, and swiped it on. "What?"

"What if I'd been a guest?" Casper said.

"You're not. And all my guests are still happily asleep. Which I should be." Romeo walked into the great room, the dawn still a simmer over the lake, splashing golden light through the trees along the shoreline. It glistened on the snow, and for a moment, Stella was in his head. *I would really love to stay here and hide in this winter wonderland forever, if that is okay.*

He hung his head into his hand, listening to his stupid words, a few hours later. *Unless you end up staying.*

Good grief, she was a *guest*.

"I got an alarm on my phone about the house," Casper said. "Heat is low."

Romeo put the phone on speaker and opened the app. A toasty seventy degrees. "That was yesterday. A birch tree fell on the power line—I took care of it."

A pause, then, "Right. I put my phone away while we went diving and just turned it on. You're right—sorry. How are you doing?"

He liked Casper—not nearly as bossy as Owen. "Fine. I decorated the big tree yesterday." Sorta.

"I'm impressed. That usually took four of us just to hang the lights."

Huh. "Any idea when you'll be back?"

"Not in time for Boone and Vivie's wedding, I'm afraid. But if you let Megan in, she'll take care of the decorations. Just make sure they open the flue all the way if they want to light a fire. It's a little finicky, so they'll have to jiggle it."

"Yep."

"Thanks, Romeo. I'll tell Owen to calm down—you got this."

Romeo didn't know why those words irked him as he hung up. Owen sort of reminded him of Jed Ransom, the fire chief of the Jude County Firefighters—hotshots and smokejumpers. He'd been relentless in their training.

Probably a good thing—maybe if Romeo had been tougher on Disco…

He shook away the memory and got dressed, made himself coffee, and by the time the sun was up, had chopped a cord of wood and plowed the driveway of the skim of snow that had accumulated last night. He managed to glance at cabin six only a couple of times, a wisp of smoke that curled out of the chimney evidence that they were using the firewood he'd left in their crib.

Yesterday, after he'd gotten back to the resort, he'd checked in two arrivals—Duke Lowry from Minneapolis and Zuri Milano from New York City, here for Boone's wedding. Then he'd gone into the garage and spent the rest of the afternoon wrestling with the oil pan, nearly dumping oil on himself, googling over and over the disassembly of the steering drag link, and finally, as twilight set in, he'd managed to fire the truck back up. He'd gone inside, answered a few emails and checked on a couple reservations and returned to his A-frame late, thawing some soup that Scotty had left in his freezer.

Stella had checked in on him once while he was working in the garage, but her parents had returned, so she'd gone back to the cabin.

He sort of missed her.

Sorta.

Let's not get crazy. She was fun and pretty, and sure, if she wanted to help him inject some cheer into the resort, he wasn't going to turn her down. After all, like she said, it might help her forget the jerk who'd lied to her and broken her heart, made her doubt herself.

Yeah, he wouldn't mind getting in a room with that guy.

He blew out a breath, headed inside the lodge, and checked his emails for any new reservations. He answered and booked a couple cabins for the week of New Year's and then emerged into the kitchen and whipped himself up a couple scrambled eggs.

He hoped Casper did talk to Owen because, yeah, he *did* have this.

No problem.

The bell over the door rang, and he got up and went to the lodge office. A man, maybe in his late thirties, early forties stood in the lobby, an elderly man with him, dressed in a parka and a black-and-red checked shapka.

"I'm Tom Karlson, checking in with my grandfather, Gerald."

Romeo logged on to the computer, then opened the reservation. "Right. I've got you in cabin seven. Two bedrooms. It's ready for you." He reached for a key—the resort still used a key on a wooden fob.

"No, that's not right," Tom said. "We're supposed to be in cabin six. At least, my grandpa is. You can put me wherever you have room."

"Where's the skating rink?" This from the elderly man, who'd been looking out the window toward the lake.

Cabin six? Shoot—he'd put the Browns in cabin six. But even now, an echo of a conversation he'd had with Owen returned to him. "Sorry. I...cabin six is booked."

Tom sighed. "Fine. Seven will work."

"And the candles, in bags," said Gerald. He turned to Romeo. "We need the candles if we want to skate under the stars."

Right. Skating under the stars. He remembered Uncle John clearing a rink when he'd lived here so many years ago. "The rink will be cleared tonight, and we'll have the candles out. I promise." He handed Tom the key to cabin seven. "I just stocked it with firewood. Let me know if you need anything."

Tom nodded, his mouth pinched, and headed outside, Romeo right behind him.

Romeo walked over to the maintenance shed and opened it, grabbed the snowblower.

Now he just needed to figure out how to get candles.

He plowed a path down to the lake, then headed out onto the ice. If he remembered correctly, it wasn't just about plowing it, but he'd have to flood it also, making it a smooth, skateable surface.

He'd cleared the ice and had found the hose, again in the maintenance shed, when he bumped into Duke Lowry from last night. The guy reminded him a little of a parole officer.

"Can I help you?"

"I'm going to pick up my buddy's car for his wedding—he's having it detailed. When it's done, can I store it in the maintenance shed?"

Romeo glanced inside. There seemed to be enough room. "Sure."

He walked back out to the ice and turned on the hose.

"You don't think there's enough water out there?" Stella wore a fluffy white sweater, her blonde hair up, a warm headband over her ears, and a blue vest that brought out the pale blue of her eyes.

And when she smiled at him, shoot, everything inside him sort of exploded.

"Morning," he said, and his voice sounded weird.

"Morning, boss."

"Boss?"

"I expect my pay in cake, by the way."

He smiled. "I'll see what I can do."

"I spent all night thinking up how to turn this place into a holiday party, and it starts with a sleigh ride."

"A what?"

"A sleigh ride. You know—dashing through the snow? One horse open sleigh?"

Right. "I...we don't have a sleigh. And I don't know the first thing about horses."

"I called around and found a stable. And a sleigh. And don't worry —a driver for tomorrow. It'll be fun, and I promise you won't have to do anything."

He looked at her.

"It'll be perfect. Now, tell me why you're watering the lake."

"Ice-skating rink. I need candles in bags, I guess, and a bonfire."

She looked at him, and a slow smile crept up her face. "Oh, we can do better than that, boss."

Guest. Just a *guest*.

"What's with the sigh?"

He looked at her, grinning into the sunlight, and shook his head. "I'm just wondering how in over my head I am here."

She winked. "Very."

Stella hadn't been as crazy proud about something since she nailed the entirety of Prokofiev's Sinfonia Concertante in E minor for cello and orchestra, op. 125, without a glitch.

And that had taken her months, the better part of a year to get right. This feat—creating a winter wonderland skating arena—had only gobbled out most of her day.

But it seemed, with the stringing of the twinkle lights around the four corners of the rink, then across the middle, creating a festive glow to the late afternoon gray, it had also sent the shadows of the past month into hiding.

"It's pretty magical, I'll give you that," Romeo said, standing in front of a growing fire.

She grinned at him. Nope, she wasn't a complete failure. She'd added battery-operated candles in paper bags along the edges of the snowbank and had connected her phone to a pair of Bluetooth speakers now playing "Joy to the World" into the crisp air.

"I'm just hoping people show up," she said, sitting down on a bench topped with a blanket.

"I put flyers under the door of every guest cabin," Romeo said. He tossed a log onto the fire, and it showered sparks into the brisk air. Somehow, being around him felt easy. As if her heart didn't have to try so hard to relax.

Shoot, she really liked him, and maybe she should be sprinting the opposite direction, but really, what did she expect? Happily ever after didn't happen in a week, and it wasn't like, really, she was going to give up her plan of finishing her education, right?

Nope. Not thinking about that. She pulled on one of the skates she'd dug up in the pile Romeo had brought out from the maintenance shed. She glanced at Romeo. "Are you going to join me?"

He stared at her, wide-eyed, for a moment. "I...um...I'm not very good—"

"C'mon. No judgment."

His mouth lifted on one side, and something sweet sparked in his eyes. "Promise?"

She crossed her heart, and he came down to the ice.

"Last time I went skating was the year I stayed with Uncle John and Aunt Ingrid. I'd never learned to skate, but you can't be around this family without getting on the ice. My cousin Owen—he runs the place—is a former hockey star. And my cousin Grace is married to Max Sharpe." He was pulling on a pair of hockey skates as he spoke.

"Max Sharpe? He used to play for the Blue Ox. I heard he retired. Illness?"

"Huntington's disease."

"That's terrible."

"It is. He's in a study, and it seems to be helping. But he's a fighter, and his faith seems to keep him going."

Faith. For some reason, the word pinged inside her as she got up and circled the rink. The ice had frozen into a sleek, smooth layer.

Maybe that was what she was missing. Faith that at the end of the journey, she didn't make the wrong decision.

She almost ran into Romeo.

"Sorry!" He grabbed her, trying to keep them from falling. "I told you I'm not very good."

She took his hand. "Stop thinking and just glide over the ice."

He pushed out beside her. "That's my problem—too many scenarios playing out in my head."

"I get that." They rounded the end of the rink and turned. "I lie in bed replaying songs, trying to get the fingering right."

"How long have you been playing the cello?"

He nearly fell, and she righted him. "For as long as I can remember. My parents were given a hand-me-down cello when I was about four, and I got free lessons from our choir director at church. I guess I took to it, because they sprang for private lessons when he retired and moved away. That led to private schools, recitals and travel, and… well, they've sacrificed so much for me, I can't imagine giving it up."

She turned, skating backward, still holding his hand. His gaze found hers. "And yet, you're not in Vienna—look out!" He yanked her away just before she plowed into the snowbank. The force turned them, and in a second, they'd landed on the ice.

Romeo grimaced. "Now I remember why I don't skate."

She made a face. "Story of my life. I get too focused on something and completely miss the disaster ahead."

He lay back on the ice, looking at the sky. "And now we're talking about the international smuggler?"

She lay beside him. The sky had turned a deep gray, the sun barely fracturing it. "Maybe. I don't know. I was so humiliated in Brussels, sitting in customs, wondering how I was so easy to fool. It was so… stupid to fall for him. I know better."

"It's hard to see the truth when your heart is in the way."

She glanced at him. Frowned.

He met her eyes, then looked away. "I told myself for years that the world was simply unfair to my mom, to me. That we were homeless because people were cruel or did us wrong, that my mother was just trying to do her best." He sighed. "But she was simply selfish." He drew in a breath. "And I was in the way."

His words stripped any from her. What?

"When I was ten years old, we found an old van that we decided to call home while Mom tried to find work. We'd been kicked out of our apartment—everything I owned was in this shopping bag from a department store. A big red one, like you get at Christmastime. One night, she left me in the van to…I don't know. It's not important. But I was afraid, so I went out searching for her. Some cops found me and took me to a shelter, and later I ended up in foster care. Everything sort of changed after that—my mom really went downhill, and I was in and out of foster homes. I can't help but think that…"

She tried to imagine him at ten—cold, alone, scared. Sheesh. And here she'd been, whining about her life—

"Well, anyway, the thing was, I'd left the bag behind. Mom came to the shelter—I don't know how she found it, but when they opened the door, I just—I just ran to her. My brother had joined the army, so he wasn't around, and I thought—she'd come to get me. And maybe that old van wasn't a warm bed, but at least I was with someone who…" He swallowed. "Anyway. She hugged me, then she pushed me away and said 'Merry Christmas.' Then she handed me that red bag and walked away."

Stella wanted to reach out, hold his hand, but he wasn't ten anymore.

Except, maybe the gesture was for her.

"That's when I realized that no one was coming for me. That I was in this alone. She got an apartment a few weeks later, and they returned me to her, but…things changed after that."

"You stopped trusting her." She didn't know why she said that, just a gasp, really, under her breath, but he nodded, shrugged.

Silence fell in the deepening twilight.

Then he rolled over, looked at her. "Joseph Harrington Amherst the Third is a jerk, and he doesn't get one more second of your brain. Or your regret. You're not a fool. You just believed in someone who didn't deserve it. Don't let him steal your dreams from you."

His eyes were so impossibly green in hers that she almost couldn't hear him. She took a breath.

Then who did she deserve?

He swallowed, and his gaze roamed her face.

Oh, what was her problem that she wanted him to kiss her? The thought rose, like steam from the ice into the sky.

She even leaned toward him, her breath caught—

"Romeo!"

His gaze jerked from her, and he sat up, as if they'd been caught in a romantic clutch.

Okay, nearly—

"What's going on, Mr. Karlson?"

A man stood at the edge of the shoveled path, his jacket open, blowing out a breath, hand behind his neck. "It's my grandpa. He's gone missing."

Romeo was scrambling to his feet—not easy in hockey skates. She used her toe pick to get up and reached out a hand.

But he ignored it, found his edge, and skated over to the side. "Don't worry, Tom. We'll find him."

Then he yanked off the skates and left her standing there, alone under the twinkly lights.

CHAPTER 6

THURSDAY, 9:00 A.M.

By the grace of God, the old man hadn't been killed. But the image of Gerald walking along the highway chased Romeo into the night, and by dawn he was up, chopping wood, trying to scatter the voices.

His voice. *Nothing is going to burn down. No guest will perish. I promise, everything will be fine.*

Right. As long as he kept his head in the game and didn't do stupid things like go skating and daydream his day away with the guests.

One guest.

One very pretty guest that he'd almost kissed.

What. Was. He *thinking*?

Romeo slammed his axe into another log, and chips flew as it separated and fell off the block. He'd shed his jacket, but the early morning air held a snap to it that burned his nose. Still, sweat trickled down his back.

He'd just finish chopping this cord, then...

Well, then he'd have to ask the Browns to move out of cabin six.

Perfect.

But according to Tom, his father's dementia had worsened in the unfamiliar surroundings of cabin seven. He needed to be back in his old cabin, the one embedded with memories.

Which meant that Romeo would need to move the Browns to cabin five, clean cabin six before Gerald moved in, then check the schedule to make sure that he wasn't overlapping guests. A couple had arrived last night with their dog, and thankfully, he'd put them in cabin two.

Breathe.

He picked up the fallen logs and tossed them onto the wheelbarrow. His conversation with Stella crept into his head, her words about his mother at the end. *You stopped trusting her.*

Yeah. Stopped trusting anyone, really. Until that Christmas with the Christiansens when he'd felt like he belonged.

But he'd been a kid, and since then, had grown up and remembered the very important lesson that he had no one to depend on but himself.

He split another log, then gathered up the pieces. The sun had risen, gilding the ice with gold.

It's pretty magical, I'll give you that.

Oh, for Pete's sake. So what Stella was easy to talk to. And that she'd helped him search the resort for Gerald. And that, when she'd returned to her cabin for dinner with her family, he'd stayed on the ice, watching the lights twinkle against the snow.

She was a guest. Hel-lo. And in truth, sooner or later he'd screw up. And she'd plummet from the sky. Or something akin to that.

He delivered the fresh supply of wood to the decks of the cabins, then drew a breath and knocked on the Browns' door.

Pastor Brown answered, wearing jeans and a flannel shirt. Kind eyes. "Romeo. How can I help you?"

He made a face. "I was…wondering if you guys would be interested in a bigger cabin? I've got one available, and I can help you shift your stuff into it whenever you want."

The man sighed, glanced inside. The smell of scrambled eggs spilled out, and Romeo's traitorous stomach growled.

"That's okay. You don't have to put yourself out for us. We're fine here."

His wife came to the door. Pretty, her dark hair pulled back. She touched her husband's arm. "What's all this?"

Bob repeated their conversation about moving, ending with, "I don't think we need to. We're all unpacked and settled in."

Oh. Well. "Actually—" Romeo started.

"I think we should move, Bob," his wife said, and behind her, Stella appeared, smiling. She mouthed a *thank you* as her mother also thanked him. "That's very thoughtful," she said, while her husband turned to her to argue.

Oops. Maybe Stella was right—there seemed to be trouble as the two tussled over the move, the hassle, and the need for Stella to have her own bed.

Poor Stella even got pulled in when her father suggested she was fine on the couch. He couldn't believe the lie that came out of her. "I don't mind."

What was she saying? But worse, an expression of panic washed over her face.

Oh, Stella.

"Actually, you'd be doing *me* a favor," he said. "I want to move one of my other guests. He's used to having this cabin, but I accidentally gave him the wrong one and he needs to be in this one for personal reasons. I'll move you to cabin five."

Stella glanced at him, her eyes wide. But the tiniest of smiles emerged.

Pastor Brown turned to him. "In that case, we'll be happy to switch."

Huh. Okay, then.

"Would you like some breakfast, son?" Pastor Brown said. "We have plenty and it sounds like something is alive inside of you."

Oh. And what was he going to say when Stella grinned at him and pulled out a chair? "Sure."

And suddenly, he found himself at the table, enjoying eggs, bacon, and Flashy Fox cinnamon rolls reheated in the microwave. Bob was asking him about his plowing job—he'd have to check on Casper's route after last night's dusting—and Stella mentioned he'd been a smokejumper, so there were a few stories there. He left out the story of Disco, but Stella's eyes were on him, knowing.

It felt strangely intimate to share that between them only.

"Sounds like you're a guy who likes adventure," the pastor said.

"It was a job, not a calling."

The man made a sound, nodding, staring into his coffee. Bob and Marilyn—they'd switched him to first names after a couple formal tries—seemed like a couple foster parents he'd lived with when he was twelve. Solid. Sweet. No wonder Stella turned out so...

Good.

Romeo sort of lost his appetite then, seeing her between her parents, their golden child. So terribly pretty with that blonde hair, those beautiful blue eyes. She wore a blue denim shirt and a pair of yoga pants and laughed when he told them about the crazy Nativity scene fire so many years ago.

"We chased sheep for blocks," he said.

"Gotta love small towns," Bob said.

"Or seeing the world," Marilyn said, patting Stella's hand. Stella gave her a thin smile.

Glanced at Romeo.

Oh. Clearly she hadn't told them she hadn't gotten into the school in Vienna.

He raised an eyebrow.

"We should pack," she said suddenly, and got up.

He washed dishes while they packed, and then he helped them carry their belongings to cabin five. At cabin seven, Gerald was already packed, and Tom was waiting, so he hustled back to cabin six to start cleaning.

"Hey!"

He turned and spotted Stella running along the path between cabins. "What's up?"

She fell into step. "Thanks for not…you know."

"Outing your great escape from Vienna?"

"Shh." She glanced back. "But yes."

"You need to tell them."

"I will. I just have to figure out…well, maybe I *will* go to Vienna."

He didn't know why, weirdly, those words shook him. What, did he think she was staying?

Hello—guest!

"Or not. I don't know…maybe I'll stay."

For some reason, that idea settled inside him, took root.

Turned his entire body warm.

No, oh no. He took a breath. *Calm down.*

"I was thinking about what you said about Harry. You're right. He's been in my head too long. But then I was thinking—what if I purposely messed up the audition?"

He had reached the cabin. "Why would you do that?"

She stood on the step. "I dunno. Maybe I'm tired of the cello."

"No, you're not." He started up the steps. "You're just afraid."

"Of what?"

He turned. "You dared to give your heart to something, and it crashed and burned. And now you're afraid to do it again."

She stared at him. And rightly so, because he hadn't a clue where those words came from.

Silence moved between them, and in it, the world quieted, narrowed.

"I'm not afraid," she said quietly and moved up a step.

He stilled, terribly aware of the smell of her—fresh from a shower, the wind tossing her hair.

She might not be afraid, but his heart had turned to thunder in his chest and—

Behind them, in the parking lot, a pickup pulled up towing a trailer.

"The horse is here," she said quietly.

The— "What?"

"The guy with the horse. For the sleigh ride."

Right.

"Don't worry, I got this." She stepped onto the path. "But for your information, this conversation isn't over."

Then she headed down the path toward the parking lot.

And as he went inside cabin six to clean, crazily, he hoped it wasn't.

Clearly Stella was starting to make a fool out of herself, because even her mother had said something about her being in charge when she signed up for the sleigh ride.

"I thought we were here for a break, not for work. Or maybe you're just making music with that pair of green eyes."

Her mother had glanced at Romeo, who was talking to Jesse, the local wrangler who had brought in the beautiful black-and-white gelding and the sleigh. So far, she had four people signed up, including her parents.

Which meant she wouldn't tag along, thank you very much. She didn't know why she hadn't put up more of a fight about sleeping on the sofa—it just felt like suddenly she'd become a burden.

She'd never wanted to run away more in her life.

And probably that was why, after he'd moved them in, she'd sprinted after Romeo, who had a job of his own that didn't include babysitting. Sure, he'd been polite, if not a bit, well, almost annoyed at her for not telling her parents the truth about Vienna.

Had even accused her of being afraid.

What*ever*. He'd never taken the stage as a solo performer and played for two hours without stopping to an audience of thousands.

But maybe she'd been a little too...*helpful*. It had been a little strange to sit with him at breakfast at her parents' table, like he might really be in her life.

It suddenly felt real and possible and...

No longer a distraction or just a way to avoid her parents.

So maybe, just— *Calm down, Stella*. It wasn't like she and Romeo had a future together. He was some lumberjacky, plow-driving woodsman, and she...

Oh, who cared? Because right now, he was running his hand down Domino's blaze, speaking softly to the animal, and everything inside her simply turned liquid.

Wow, he was handsome, with that blondish hair twining out from under his stocking cap. He hadn't shaved, smelled a little of fresh wood, some chips still on his green canvas jacket, and when he laughed, the wind picked it up and turned the air sweet and magical.

Oh boy.

Then he turned and looked at her, nodding, and Jesse also smiled at her, and it seemed she was the subject of their conversation. Maybe a good conversation, because Romeo winked before he turned away.

Her body turned to fire. *What—?*

He patted the horse again, then came over to her. "Jesse told me that you helped him unload Domino."

"A couple summers at horse camp. The only other thing I wanted to do besides play the cello—be a cowgirl."

"I could see it."

Oh, she didn't stand a chance.

"Everything set with the sleigh ride?"

"I think so."

"Good. I was thinking..." He glanced away, as if suddenly—what? —shy? "I need to plow Casper's route, and I thought you might...aw, it'll be boring—"

"Yes." She put down the clipboard and pen she was holding. "I'll spring for the hot cocoa."

She practically sprinted to the truck. Not throwing herself at him in the least.

He turned the radio to Christmas music as they worked their way through Deep Haven, cleaning parking lots. They sang to carols, drank cocoa, and he cleared the driveways of a number of local houses tucked away in woodsy neighborhoods. They finally ended up in a small lot overlooking the town. "This one is technically a city park, but it often gets missed in the craziness of keeping the highway clear, so Casper swings by on his way back to town."

It wasn't a big lot, and overlooked the village of Deep Haven, snug along the harbor. Smoke rose from the surface of the water.

"It's called sea smoke," Romeo said. "It happens when cold air meets warmer water and makes the water steam like a pot on a stove."

"It's cool."

He put the truck into park. "Want to see something even cooler?" He hopped out and she came around to find him tugging a couple pairs of snowshoes from behind his seat. "Do you know how to use these?"

"I did grow up in Minnesota." Except, despite her words, it felt like she walked like a duck as they ventured into the forest that surrounded the parking lot. Romeo led them onto a trail, the snow crunching beneath her. A stillness settled around her the farther they walked. Towering evergreens decorated with snow shivered now and again in the wind, shaking off snow like powder.

He reached a narrow trail, uncut by footsteps, turned and reached out his hand.

"Where—"

"Shh."

She took his hand and he led her through a passageway until they emerged under a canopy of frosted, heavy branches that made a sort of archway. Here the snow was deep, heavy, and sparkling with the late afternoon sun.

She stepped under the canopy and stared out.

"Don't go any farther—the cliff drops off in about five feet." He still had ahold of her hand though.

No worries. She couldn't move with the beauty of it. The land had risen, and from here, the forest fell and spread out, then stopped again at another cliff, this one broken by a frozen river, the falls miraculously suspended in ice. The sun glinted off them, turning the ice to gold as it dropped into the gorge below.

In the distance, the lake spread out in frothy, icy glory as waves hit the shoreline, frozen chunks floating in the water.

The brutal magnificence took her breath away. "It's so glorious."

"I know. Makes you feel a little small."

It made her feel quiet. Still. "The town looks so peaceful." She pointed to the hamlet, smoke rising from the houses. "So safe."

He laughed. "Oh, hardly. I spent a summer here, and the entire town nearly caught fire!"

"Really?"

"Yeah. The pizza place burned to the ground. And they recently started a Crisis Response Team for all the accidents. Everything, even Deep Haven, has an element of danger to it. Nowhere is totally safe, Stella."

She turned to him. He stood close, his green eyes in hers.

"No one," he added.

You just believed in someone who didn't deserve it.

Maybe it wasn't about being afraid but picking the right person to trust.

She stepped closer to him, searched his face. "Maybe it's safe enough."

He took a breath. "This is probably a bad idea."

Then he lowered his head and kissed her. Soft at first, almost a question.

Yes. She wrapped her hands into his jacket lapels. His arm went around her, and he pulled her closer, deepened his kiss.

He tasted like hot cocoa, smelled like the forest, and she turned to sea smoke under his touch.

This was nothing like Harry, who'd made her feel a little tawdry and even naive when he kissed her, pushing her too fast.

No, Romeo was gentle, sure, safe, but exciting, and when he lifted his head and met her eyes, for the first time in months—maybe her entire life—she felt…

Well, the way she'd felt when she played her first solo cello concerto.

Alive.

"It's getting dark," Romeo said softly. But his gaze suggested he wanted to linger.

Instead, he took her hand and led her back through the forest—it was getting darker, the shadows longer, the way difficult to follow. And snow had started to tumble from the sky.

But in his steps, her hand in his, she knew exactly where she was going.

Or rather, staying.

CHAPTER 7

"You're real cute, Owen. No, I haven't burned down anything yet."

"I was kidding, take a breath there, cuz," Owen said on the other end of Romeo's speaker phone.

Romeo gave a thin laugh as he tossed another log into the stove of his A-frame. The wind howled outside as the storm pressed in. Good thing he'd returned to the lodge before the snow thickened, although he'd nearly taken out a guest—not, not just a guest, but Stella's mother—on his drive into the parking lot. Of course, she'd been walking in the darkness, head down, as if angry. And then there was that terrible moment when his headlights had illuminated her, his brakes hadn't gripped the icy driveway...and if it hadn't been for Stella's dad pushing her out of the—

Yes, he might not be so flippant in his call with Owen.

Thankfully, though, no one was hurt, and Stella had hopped out and given him a smile—something warm and definitely dangerous—as she went with her family to their cabin.

But still, so far so good. No fires. No catastrophes and all the guests were alive.

"Actually, I was calling to say thanks," Owen said. "My dad got a call from Tom Karlson. Tom was pretty grateful for your work in getting Gerald settled. Apparently, yesterday wasn't the first time he's run off. Said he really appreciated the winter cactus you put in the cabin—it was his grandmother's favorite."

"I know. It was in the guest notes your mom left." Romeo went to the stove and turned down the heat on his pot of soup, one of the frozen packets Scotty had left for him.

"My mom has guest notes?"

"They're in the old registers, next to their names. Details, preferences. I was looking back to see how many years the Karlsons had been coming here. Did you know they've rented cabin six since their honeymoon in 1956? They'd been married for sixty-six years."

"Seriously. No wonder he's having a hard time. A piece of him is lost."

"And he keeps looking for it."

"Good job. By the way, no go on the car rentals. Everything here is booked for the holidays."

"No problem." Romeo tasted the soup. Creamy clam chowder. Reminded him of his aunt Ingrid's Christmas soup. "That storm you predicted is here, so you're probably not getting any flights anytime soon either."

"Yeah. Oh, and with the wedding rehearsal tomorrow, Casper's hoping you can run by the house and make sure everything is all set."

"I'm on it."

"Thanks, Romeo. You're a hero. Remind us to leave you in charge every Christmas."

He didn't know why the remark turned bitter in his chest. "Yeah." A knock sounded at his door. "Wear sunscreen," he said and hung up.

He slipped the phone into his pocket as he opened the door.

Stella stood on the steps, wrapped in an unzipped jacket, her borrowed UGGs, a pair of yoga pants, her hair covered in snow, shivering. What—

"Are you okay?" He opened the door to let her in.

Honestly, after coming home, and after he'd shaken off the near death of his guest, he'd spent an hour shoveling the ice rink and the paths trying to sort himself out.

He experienced a sort of out-of-body view of this afternoon's events, seeing himself inviting her along on his route, then taking her for a walk into the forest, like some cheesy Hallmark movie, complete with hot cocoa and sing-alongs.

The man who looked upon this crazy version of himself wanted to give him a good smack upside the head because, hello, Stella was *still a guest.*

A guest who had turned into a friend.

A guest who didn't see him as damaged but as a hero.

A guest who wanted to be with him.

Who trusted him.

And despite the sirens roaring in his head, she made him feel… well, a whole lot less like having been abandoned in a cold van. Or by his family.

Whatever. He liked it. He liked her, and like she'd said…

Safe enough.

Or not, with her standing at the door in the soft glow of the light, snowflakes on her lashes. "What's going on?"

"Can I come in?"

"Of course!" He stepped back and grabbed a blanket off his sofa, wrapped it around her. She was still shivering, and shoot, he couldn't stop himself.

He pulled her into his embrace.

And that's when, oh no, she started crying. *Again.*

"Stella?"

"It was terrible. My mom wanted to do an early gift exchange, but the tags got lost and…" She leaned back, her hands over her eyes. "The gift to my father was supposed to be private, but it got opened in front of me by mistake."

"So, what? You saw his Christmas elf tie?"

"No. It was—" She lowered her hands. "Never mind. It was the aftermath that matters. It's not pretty over there, and I'm horrified and…wow, that smells good."

"It's soup. Want some?"

"Mm-hmm."

He fixed her a bowl while she hung up her jacket, rewrapped the blanket over her shoulders, then slid into a chair at the table. He brought the bowl over, along with one for himself. "It's getting nasty out there."

She looked up at him. "What if they're getting a divorce?"

Oh. He'd meant the weather. But, "I dunno. I guess you'll just…adapt?"

She nodded, her eyes filling again. "I'm not great at that. Musician. We follow the rules."

He dipped his spoon in, stirred. Heat rose from the surface. "Adapting is the one thing I'm good at. Improvising." He took a bite. Made a humming sound. "I never knew where we'd be, really—what school, what apartment. I was in and out of foster care for a lot of my life."

"That's terrible."

"I don't know. I met some great people. Sure, there were a few homes that were too noisy, too unsafe, but mostly, the people tried to minister to me. I started to realize that maybe I didn't have to worry about where I would land. And then the Christiansens took me in. My mother went to treatment over Christmas, and it was while I was here that I sort of realized that God had me in His hand, even when life felt out of control. I might not be able to trust anyone else, but I knew that somehow, I could trust God. And with Him, I was safe."

He'd never really told anyone that before, and now felt a little naked as Stella looked at him. Then she smiled, nodded. "You're amazing, Romeo."

Aw. Now he couldn't look at her.

"Maybe that's my problem. All my life, my faith has been in my plan. And now, I'm not sure what the plan is," Stella said softly

"Maybe you don't have to figure it out. Maybe God does the figuring out for you."

She stared at him, nodding.

In his back pocket, his phone buzzed. He fished it out. "It's a text from Sammy. I gotta go down to the city garage."

"Can I go?"

Oh, how he wanted to say yes, but…technically, "I don't think so. There's insurance issues and…and I think maybe it's not…"

He could see himself driving off the snowy road, and suddenly Disco was back in his head. "You can stay here if you want. I'll be back in the morning." He grabbed his jacket, sliding into his thick, warm Sorels by the door. "Keep an eye on the fire, okay?"

"I promise not to burn the house down." Then she got up and walked him to the door. "Be safe."

He pulled on his hat, his jacket, held his gloves and—

Okay, fine. He leaned in and kissed her. She tasted of the soup, and in her touch, the way she wove her hand behind his neck, a little of homecoming.

As if this was right. Easy. And that coming home to her was right where he belonged.

He broke away, the taste of her on his lips. Oh, he wanted more. Instead, "See ya."

"Don't run anyone into the ditch."

He laughed as he left, dangerously close to happy as the snow sifted from the sky.

FRIDAY, 7:00 A.M.

She probably shouldn't have slept so hard, but frankly, being wrapped in Romeo's blanket felt so…perfect. Cozy. And here, she didn't have to make any decisions, let anyone down, face her non-existent life plans.

Call it denial. Call it a holiday.

Call it a mad holiday romance.

Although, it felt just a little out-of-bounds to have spent the night in Romeo's cabin, even though he wasn't here. She'd meant to return home, but the wind had simply kept howling, and she'd been so tired and…

She just couldn't face the idea that her news about Vienna might actually make whatever was going down in the cabin worse.

She couldn't be the reason her parents split up.

Which sounded crazy, because they were in the ministry. Except it happened all the time.

Maybe Romeo was right. Nothing, and no one, was safe. *I might not be able to trust anyone else, but I knew that somehow, I could trust God. And with Him, I was safe.*

Okay, no one but God.

And maybe Romeo. How crazy could it be that she'd found a man of honor, of faith—a good-looking man, at that—here in her wonderland getaway?

But maybe that's why God brought her here. A light in the midnight of her soul.

Okay, she was being dramatic.

Stella pushed up, aware of the sun just barely pressing against the windows. Poor Romeo—he was probably still out in that.

Or not. She found a note on the counter, along with fresh coffee in the pot—how had she slept through that? He was out chopping wood.

She opened the fridge and found a dozen eggs and some bacon, dug out a pan and made breakfast. Then she poured coffee and carried it outside.

The dawn had cleared the tree line, rose-gold icing the lake, and the sound of wood cracking split the air. She stopped for a moment, admiring Romeo's form—burly shoulders, strong legs, his feet set as he brought down the ax. She could see the fireman in him.

He looked up. Smiled.

Yes, little fires everywhere.

"Hey," he said.

"You know, there are machines that will chop your wood for you."

He took the coffee she offered. "It helps me think."

She shivered as the wind skimmed snow from the trees. "About what?"

He considered her a long moment, then sipped his coffee. "I have to go to Wilder House and check on it for the rehearsal dinner—"

"Yes. I'll go change. Breakfast is ready."

He gave her a strange smile as she darted off to her cabin.

The place was quiet, the door to her parents' room closed. She changed, brushed her teeth, pulled her hair back, shrugged away any idea of makeup, and was out before she heard noises.

Romeo was finishing his breakfast when she knocked.

"I saved you some eggs."

Sweet. She took the proffered plate and sat at the table to eat. "I'll bet you're tired."

"I slept a bit at the garage before getting up again for an early morning sweep." He drained his coffee and set it, along with her finished plate, on the board.

It felt easy. Like they were a team.

A couple.

She climbed into his truck, and he turned the heater on full blast, along with the radio. A local weatherman predicted sunny skies along with a cold snap. Then the radio turned to Christmas classics, and they sang along to "White Christmas."

He told her about the night, the roads, the traffic—no, he hadn't sent anyone into a snowbank—and they arrived at the white, snow-glistening, peaceful wedding venue on the hill.

This time, a light glimmered on the porch, so no electricity out.

"I need to clean the driveway. Can you just check to make sure the heat is on?"

She slid out of the truck and marched up the steps as he turned up the radio. "Jingle Bells."

She let herself inside. The house had been made over for the wedding, a garland wound up the banister to the second floor, twined with silver, white, and slate-blue ribbon. Birch trees in planters lined the aisle, lit with twinkle lights.

A small grouping of chairs sat in uniform rows in the front room, facing the fireplace. White candles sat on the mantel. A plaque in the middle of the mantel read, *Glad Tidings. Great Joy. A Christmas Cele-bration.*

A table stood in the middle of the parlor, probably for the cake.

A chill sifted through her. The heat clearly couldn't keep up. She could solve this.

In the fireplace, she opened the flue, stacked the logs, then shoved in paper and kindling. She found a long fireplace match and lit the kindling in several places.

Then she replaced the screen and headed to the kitchen. The caterer had left a stack of dishes, table linens, and silverware on the counter. And inside the fridge sat the pieces of the glorious cake, adorned with silver, white, and blue stars, ready to be assembled.

She couldn't help it—she wanted to glimpse the dress, so she headed upstairs. Three rooms—one for the groom, the other two labeled bridal chambers. She headed inside one and spied a collection of slate-blue gowns. Bridesmaid's dresses.

The wedding dress was probably in the next room, but when she entered, she discovered it empty save a makeup vanity and a trifold, full-length mirror. And a bathroom. She went inside and heard a rustle as she closed the door.

A lace-edged, cathedral-length veil hung in plastic from the back of the door. It looked hand-stitched, almost an heirloom, as if someone had taken the time to think out every stitch.

A noise outside made her turn. She looked out the window. Romeo had his window down, his elbow hanging out, cleaning the driveway, his lips moving to a Christmas song. The view beyond the farm stretched out miles, to the lake and the horizon beyond. Cloud-less, blue, and breathtaking.

Yes.

She turned to go downstairs, but although the doorknob turned, the latch wouldn't move. Flipping the lock, she tried it again. Nothing.

Two hands.

The doorknob simply spun.

Of course

She crouched and tried to pry back the latch with her finger. Useless.

And that's when she noticed the smell. Smoke. It was coming from under the door.

And through the vent in the floor.

What?

She reached for the window to open it, but a thousand years of dried paint sealed it shut.

"Romeo!" She banged on the window.

But he just drove out of sight, singing along to the radio.

CHAPTER 8

Could you fall in love in two days? The thought so consumed Romeo as he shoveled the porch that he didn't hear the crunch of footprints on the snow until a board squealed in frozen protest.

He whirled around.

"Hey, shovel down, it's just me."

Seth Turnquist, fellow former smokejumper, stood on the porch holding a package wrapped in plastic over his arm. Looked like a dress.

Romeo lowered the shovel. He hadn't realized he'd brandished it like an axe. "Sorry. Didn't hear you."

"Clearly. You okay?"

"Yeah. Great." He rested on the shovel. More than great, really, and maybe he wore a goofy smile, because Seth raised an eyebrow.

"I'm glad to hear it. I was a little worried about you after talking to Tucker."

Tucker. Newman. His former jump boss, the guy spilling all his secrets.

"He told me about Disco."

Romeo looked away, toward the horizon. A few clouds hovered in the blue sky, and giant icebergs rolled in the undulating surf of the lake.

"Terrible accident. Tucker said Disco panicked when his first chute didn't open. Didn't get the second out in time."

Romeo took a breath. "Maybe he wasn't ready."

Seth nodded. "You don't know until you're there. It wasn't your fault."

Romeo lifted a shoulder.

"Tucker said they missed you last summer. There's a place for you, if you want it." He hung the dress over his shoulder, holding on by the hanger.

Huh. Romeo hadn't expected that.

"Tucker said you left without saying goodbye."

Romeo lifted a shoulder.

"You're the only one telling yourself that you're to blame. And that you don't belong."

Crazy how the guy could read his mind. But they had spent three summers fighting fire together. Watching each other's backs.

He considered Seth. "I do miss it—the guys, the hard work. The sense of accomplishment. Around here, all I do is chop wood and shovel. And I'm not great at the resort part. The little things, the welcome gifts, or showing guests a good time. If it hadn't been for…"

He didn't know why he stopped, but it was enough for Seth to cock his head.

"There's been this girl—woman—here this week who's sorta…helped me."

Seth's grin grew.

"Stop. She's a guest."

"She's more than a guest, by that look on your face."

He chopped at a bit of ice on the deck with his shovel. "I don't know. Maybe. It's only been a couple days, and she's probably leaving."

"Probably?"

"She mentioned staying—but really, she's just a little lost right now. It's not like I'm her happy ending. I mean, I don't even know if I'm staying. I might be just as lost as she is."

"You're not lost, Romeo. You're in God's hands. Always. Wherever you are. Which means that God could totally bring you both to Deep Haven for this moment, to give you more than you ever dreamed."

He looked at Seth. "More than I ever dreamed? You been reading romance novels?"

"Hallmark Christmas channel, but listen—two years ago, I came home to tell my grandfather that I wanted nothing to do with his business. I was going to sell the log home that I'd hand made for a woman who didn't love me and return to Alaska to fight fires for the rest of my life. But I had no idea what God had waiting for me—a woman who loved me, who waited for me, a future all set up for me, if I was willing to trust God. I married that woman just over a year ago, and you know what she told me last night?" He lowered his voice. "We're going to have a baby."

Seth's grin was infectious.

"Congrats, man." He met Seth's fist with a bump.

Behind them, a SUV pulled up. Seth turned to watch with Romeo as Pastor Dan stepped out. "Hello!" He wore a suit.

Probably here for the rehearsal. Romeo raised his hand.

Seth cut his voice low. "Don't tell anyone—it's still a secret. But the fact is, I had to stop being my own worst enemy, running away from people before they hurt me. You trusted God with your life when you were fighting fires—maybe you trust Him with your heart. Stop looking at me that way."

Romeo grinned. "I'm just trying to picture you changing diapers."

"Just you wait. But that's the thing, right? Five years ago, I would have never pictured this life. But God is in the business of miracles. Taking on the impossible."

"Yeah, I dunno. I don't think God is going to do anything miraculous here. In fact, I can't help but think sooner or later, something tragic is going to happen."

"Tragic?"

"Like a guest getting hurt, even killed." He raised an eyebrow. "We had an elderly guest wander off the premises because I put him in the wrong cabin."

"Wow."

"They found him, but yeah, eventually, I screw up and something bad happens."

"Like Disco."

"Mm-hmm. Or Bud, my dog."

"You have a dog?"

"Did. I got him as a puppy the Christmas I spent with the Christiansens. I brought him with me after Mom got out of treatment. She found a house in Duluth, a job cleaning the hospital, and was doing really well. Since she worked the second shift, I usually got up and went to school alone. I'd always let Bud out before I went, and one morning I was in a hurry, and I didn't shut the gate. When I got home from school, he was gone. Never saw him again."

"I'm sorry, man."

"But you get my point. I'm really not someone people should depend on. Even a dog."

Seth looked at him. "Romeo. Trust me when I say that the things that happen to us don't define us. It's how we react to them. How we keep going. You forget I know you. I fought fires with you. I'd trust you with my life."

Heat pressed a hand into him.

"And apparently, so do the Christiansens. After all, they left you with their livelihoods."

Oh. He hadn't thought of it like that. Just looked at the abandonment.

Not the trust.

Romeo drew in a breath. "Maybe you're right. I need to stop believing that every time something good happens, it's only going to turn to ash—"

"Do you smell smoke?" Pastor Dan had come up on the porch.

Seth draped the dress over the railing. Stepped down the stairs.

Romeo set the shovel down. "Maybe it's someone's chimney." But yeah, smoke tainted the air.

He peered into the window. "The house—something's on fire!"

Seth beat them to the front door. He touched it. "It's not hot. Stand back."

He pushed it open.

No backdraft flames shot from the room, but smoke billowed out, more gray than black. Romeo pulled his jacket up around his mouth and followed them in.

The smoke was so thick he barely made out Seth. Pastor Dan disappeared into the gray.

"Fireplace!" Romeo shouted.

A fire raged in the hearth, contained but pouring smoke into the room.

"Pastor!" Seth shouted.

"In here!"

Romeo went to a window and opened it.

Seth headed for the kitchen.

Romeo followed him. "Stella!"

Pastor Dan was running water into a pitcher, his phone pressed to his ear. "I'm calling 911!"

"Did you see Stella?"

"Who?"

Romeo glanced through the back door but didn't see her on the porch. "Stella!" Where—

Pounding. A distant shout.

"Upstairs," Seth said, but grabbed the pitcher from Pastor Dan and carried the water to the hearth where he splashed it onto the flames.

Romeo held his breath as he ran upstairs. The smoke saturated the upper floors, and he fell to his hands and knees and crawled toward the pounding. "Stella!" He coughed, held his breath again.

"In here!" She was coughing too. "The smoke went through the vent! I can't breathe!"

He found the door, tried the doorknob. Stuck. "Open the window!"

"It's…stuck…I can't get it…open." More coughing.

"Break it!" Sorry, Casper.

"There's nothing—I don't…" Coughing. Then—

"Stella?"

More silence.

"Stella!"

As Romeo stood up and threw his weight against the door, he knew.

The answer was yes—you could fall in love with someone in two days.

"*Stella!*"

Romeo! She wanted to form words. Want to shout out to him, but she couldn't breathe, which meant she couldn't talk and—

She was going to die. Right here on the bathroom floor. Having never actually lived. Never fallen in love—not really, because she couldn't call what she'd had with Harry love. Just infatuation.

Her feelings for Romeo could be closer, maybe, but really, she was in love with the possibility, the what-if—

She could love Romeo, was already on her way, if she were honest, and now, even that future—

"Stella!"

She put her fingers on the floor, sliding them under the door, searching for any wisp of air. She was tired—so, very—

"I'm coming!"

And then he was gone. No more banging on the door, no more calling her name.

So maybe she'd imagined it. Maybe she'd imagined this entire week—the laughter, the way he made her feel brave and wanted and…

Shoot. She had way too many feelings for a guy she barely knew.

How did she know he wasn't some kind of criminal? Like Harry.

A crash sounded at the window, then a crack, and suddenly, just like that, Romeo was in the room.

She opened her eyes, but they'd started to run with the smoke, and she sensed—more than saw—Romeo crouch beside her and pull her into his amazing arms. "I got you."

Then he was up and at the window, her body slumped against him, and he was passing her out to someone. More arms, another strong body, but all she cared about was *air*.

Beautiful, crisp, cold air sluicing down her throat, into her lungs.

In the distance, sirens whined, but she closed her burning eyes, listening to Romeo. "Give her to me. I've got you, Stella."

She opened her eyes.

She lay on the snow-covered porch roof, the open sky above her.

Then Romeo. His face covered in soot, his eyes bloodshot, tearing. "Are you okay?"

She pushed herself up. "Yeah, I—" Another cough consumed her, so much her eyes teared. She finally caught her breath, her chest aching.

"I built a fire. I don't know what—"

"You built a fire?"

"The place was cold, so—"

"Are you kidding me?" He stood up even as a fire truck pulled into the freshly shoveled lot. She looked past him to see firemen pile off the truck. Romeo ran to the side of the roof. "There's no fire—just smoke. Everyone's out!"

But a team of two firemen came up the steps in turnout gear, holding axes, and another crew was attaching a hose to the truck.

"Shoot!" Then just like that, Romeo jumped down into the snow, disappearing.

She stood up, her legs shaky.

"I'll help you down," said a voice, and she turned to see another man—probably the one who'd helped get her out of the house.

"I'm Seth," he said. "You gave him a pretty big scare."

"Clearly. By the way he left me on the roof."

"I think he doesn't want them to destroy the place. Although, with this amount of smoke, I think we can cross Wilder House off the list of wedding venues."

She stared at him, her entire body still.

What had she done?

"Hey! Can we get a ladder over here?" He turned to her. "Romeo climbed the porch trellis."

Terribly romantic, under different circumstances.

A couple firefighters brought over a ladder and set it against the house. Seth gave her a hand as she climbed down, and then he led her away from the house, over to a medical van and the care of a pretty Hispanic woman.

"Ronnie, I think she has some smoke inhalation."

"Let's check you out." Ronnie gestured for her to sit on the back bumper.

"I'm fine—" But the cough that ended the words had Ronnie scanning her throat with a light.

"Red, but no swelling. Let's get you some oxygen."

"Really, I'm fine."

The woman ignored her and produced a tank and a mask, pressing it over her mouth and nose. "Just sit here and breathe."

For some reason her words shuddered through Stella.

Sit. And breathe.

She wasn't great at that, just doing nothing, admittedly. But she held the mask on and watched as the firefighters opened the windows, searching the outside—and probably the inside—of the house for fire.

"I was just trying to help."

Ronnie, standing nearby, glanced at her. "Nobody got hurt. That's the important part."

Was it? Because it seemed the destruction of the wedding might be a big deal.

Romeo emerged from the house, his face sooty.

He marched down the stairs and then, as she watched, stepped away from the house, turned back to look at it, his hands held to his head as if in disbelief.

Oh.

She'd done this.

Stupid girl.

Stupid and impulsive. Again.

She pulled off the mask. "I'm fine." Then she headed toward Romeo.

"Romeo?"

He turned, his eyes bloodshot, his chest rising and falling. Quietly, "Are you okay?"

She nodded. "But…I wrecked everything."

She thought maybe, foolishly, that he'd tell her it was okay. That they could clean it up, that everything would be fine.

He just stared at her. Swallowed. Then, "I'm sorry, Stella. This is all my fault."

What? "How—"

"I should have never let you get involved."

Oh.

"C'mon. I'll take you back to the resort."

She just blinked at him. Didn't move. Then, "No."

He drew in a breath and then closed his eyes, so much pain on his face it could break her.

"I want to help. I…want—"

His eyes opened. "How? I'm not your next great adventure, Stella. This is my life. And my mess."

"It's not your mess—"

"It is! I knew better, and I…"

"Followed your heart?"

His mouth made a tight line, his jaw pulsing. "Let's go."

"Romeo—"

"Let's go!" His voice cut low, even as he glanced at Seth standing on the porch. "Before this becomes even more of a disaster and I really do get a guest killed."

She gasped, and with it, her lungs seized. The coughing bent her over, and suddenly Ronnie was back with the portable oxygen.

Stella sucked it in, cool and soothing, even as her eyes burned.

Ronnie turned to Romeo. "I'm taking her to the hospital. Just to get checked out."

Romeo nodded. He glanced at Stella, and she longed to be able to read whatever churned in those green eyes. He opened his mouth as if to say something. Then he looked at Ronnie. "Thanks."

When he turned around, his back to her, his hands in his pockets, she couldn't help but hear…*Thanks for taking her off my hands.*

CHAPTER 9

$\mathcal{I}$t felt a little like getting picked up from the principal's office.

Stella sat on the end of the examination table in the Deep Haven ER, her legs dangling off the end like she might be six years old, listening to the doc give her mother a rundown of her condition.

Stella had given her permission—it wasn't like she could hide the smoky redolence on her clothing, embedded in her hair, her skin, or in the cough that occasionally shook her.

But she was fine. Just fine.

Except, oh, what a fool she'd been. *You just believed in someone who didn't deserve it.*

Yep, that one.

No, that wasn't fair. Romeo hadn't been the one to make a fire without checking to make sure the flue was actually open.

Fireplace 101.

Sheesh.

But his words still stung. *I'm not your next great adventure, Stella.*

He was probably relieved that she'd been carted off to the hospital.

Now, her mother turned to her. She looked tired, as if she'd had a spectacular evening too. She wore her parka, a pair of jeans, her boots. Her eyes seemed reddened. Fighting again? Shoot.

"Where's Dad?"

"He's not feeling well. Something he ate. How are *you*?"

"Ready to go home."

And she didn't exactly mean the resort, but home. To Big Lake.

To hide.

Or whatever.

She slid off the table. "I should have never come on this trip."

Her mother gathered up her coat, her hat. Sighed. "And I know I didn't make you feel very welcome. I should have never pressured you to spend time with…what's his name?"

"Romeo, and you didn't pressure me. I mean…I just wanted to stay out of your way." She put on her hat, then slipped into her coat. "It seems you and Dad—"

"Never mind that—"

"No!" She stopped at the doorway. "We have to stop keeping secrets in this family!"

Her mother stared at her, as if nonplussed. "I'm not keeping a secret—are you?"

Stella blinked at her. Looked away. "Okay, yes. I…I didn't get accepted to the Fritz Kreisler Institute in Vienna."

Her mother's mouth opened. "Oh."

"It's my own stupid fault. I was completely distracted during the audition, or maybe I was just angry—"

"Angry?"

Stella sighed. "It's a long story. But it starts with a guy named Joseph Harrington Amherst the Third." She pushed out into the night.

To her credit, her mother listened without recrimination the entire drive home. Just kept her eyes on the road, nodding now and again, and finally, as they pulled up into the resort lot—Romeo's truck wasn't there—turned off the car and turned to her. "Sounds like God saved you from a disaster by detaining you in Brussels."

She hadn't considered her near arrest God's intervention. Just her stupidity. But, "Yes, I guess so. Only for me to create a disaster here."

"Oh, honey. Nothing is a disaster with the Lord. Life is never going to work out like you think…" Her mother swallowed as if realizing her own words. "But that doesn't mean God isn't in control and that your life is derailed. It just means you didn't know the route." She gave her a soft smile. "Fact is, that is what Christmas is about—we made a disaster of our lives, but God had a plan to save us. And it was nothing like people thought. The Jews thought they'd get a mighty warrior. And we did—of our souls. And our lives, if we trust the Lord completely. But our Savior is not what anyone planned."

She drew in a breath, smiled at her daughter. "So, tell me about Romeo."

"No. It's…over. I mean, it never really began—"

"That's not true. I saw how you looked at him yesterday. And how he looked at you." She sighed. "Reminded me of your father and me, so long ago."

"He still looks at you that way…and, really?"

Her mother smiled. "I am sure you mean something to him."

Stella looked away, toward the lights shining on the smooth surface of the lake. "Probably, but it doesn't matter."

"It does matter. God puts people into our lives for a reason. Briefly, or for years. We learn, grow, and become better people because of them."

"Even Joseph Harrington Amherst the Third?"

Her mother gave her a look.

"Fine. Yes, I like Romeo."

Another look.

"More than like. He's one of the good ones—he's honest and hardworking and charming and…and doesn't want me in his life." Her eyes filled. "And I don't know what I was thinking. I mean, what—am I going to stick around here? Help him drive the snowplow?"

Her mother laughed. "So what if you did? I met your father while I was in college, a music major just like you. He swept me off my feet, took me away to a small town, and we've...we've had many happy years."

Her mother blinked, and a tear fell.

"Mom?"

She turned to Stella, a hand to her cheek. "Here's what I know. God isn't in the business of giving us a dream only to yank it away. Only, often we don't know what our real dreams are until God reveals them to us. I'm not a fan of the saying 'trust your heart,' but I do like the idea of trusting God's peace." She cleared her throat. "'But this I call to mind, and therefore I have hope. The steadfast love of the Lord never ceases;...'The Lord is my portion,' says my soul, 'therefore I will hope in Him.' The Lord is good to those who wait for Him, to the soul who seeks Him.'"

"Lamentations."

"Yes. And a good reminder that we don't have the answers, but God does."

"I wish I knew what they were."

"I do know one. God has given you a great gift. One that blesses others and soothes the soul. You might ask Him what He wants you to do with it." She kissed her daughter. "I need to check on your father."

She reached for the door handle.

"Mom?"

She turned back.

"Thanks."

Her mother patted her cheek. "I do expect you to sleep in your own bed tonight."

She laughed. "Right."

Her mother got out, and Stella followed. But as her mother headed down the path, Stella's gaze went back to the skating rink. To the full moon casting down upon it.

"I'll be in soon." She veered away, toward the lake.

The moon was out, shining hard onto the white lake, glistening, a magical reflection of the sun. Yes, her music was soothing, a blessing. She loved getting swept up in a piece, feeling the music through her fingers and reverberating through her body. It felt almost like...joy.

But lately, playing had become a chore, even a noose.

Maybe that's what she was afraid of—losing the joy.

What if that's what she'd been seeking? With Harry. Even, maybe, with Romeo.

Joy.

We don't know what our real dreams are until God reveals them to us.

Nothing is a disaster with the Lord.

Ask Him...

She stared up at the moon, the gleam of it on the ice and snow. Closed her eyes. And in the quietness, it felt right to hear her voice. "Lord, I don't know what I'm supposed to do. Forgive me for trying to find joy in anything but You. You are my portion, and I trust in Your steadfast love."

God puts people into our lives for a reason. Briefly, or for years...

The snow crunched behind her, and she opened her eyes. Turned.

Romeo stood in the path, illuminated by the moonlight.

"How am I going to tell Vivien the wedding is off?"

The words issued from Boone Buckam, the director of the Crisis Response Team and the very sad, white-faced, would-have-been groom, as he stood in the driveway of the Wilder wedding venue.

Night had descended, and with the lights of the firetrucks on the house, it turned the place into a sort of haunted manor, complete with eerie fog.

Nothing of the cheery, romantic venue from before.

Romeo had no words for Boone, just a hollow in his gut and a burr in his throat as he watched fire chief Peter Dahlquist and other members of the Deep Haven fire department—including Seth—carry out the chairs to the porch.

"I called Megan—her place is booked, and there's no other venue in town." This from Cole Barrett.

Boone sat down on the porch, his head in his hands, and Romeo wanted to just get in his truck and keep driving.

Anywhere but here.

Unfortunately, his gaze traveled over to the firetruck where Pastor Dan was being treated with oxygen, his lungs struggling against the smoke he'd inhaled.

"How'd it happen?" Boone said, lifting his head. "When I left here yesterday, everything was perfect."

"Someone lit a fire—" Cole started.

"It's my fault," Romeo said. "My…friend wanted to warm up the place and decided to light a fire."

"And she didn't know the flue was stuck," Boone said, his fingers pinching the bridge of his nose. "I did notice a nip in the air when we were here decorating."

"The furnace turned off a few days ago. Maybe there's a problem with it," Romeo said. "I should have checked back—"

"This is not your fault." Boone stood up. "Accidents happen, and at least it wasn't a real fire." He looked at the house. "The only significant casualty is our wedding." He pressed his lips together, looked at Cole. "Let me know if Megan comes up with anything. In the meantime, I have a bride to comfort."

He'd left, and Romeo stood there, a little flummoxed. But Seth's words filtered back to him. *Trust me when I say that the things that happen to us don't define us. It's how we react to them.*

He couldn't help but see Stella's face then. The shocked, hurt expression just before he'd turned his back to her. *I'm not your next great adventure, Stella.*

Really, he'd turned away to keep her from seeing his own broken expression. Because as he'd hauled her out of the house, held her in his arms—okay, yeah, he'd *wanted* to be her next great adventure. Wanted to be her hero. Just like a sappy Hallmark Christmas movie.

"So, you going to go after her?"

He glanced over to Seth, who had come down the porch stairs.

"Who?"

"Please. I was there when you were so panicked to get to Stella that you scaled the house like a parkour champ. And then you just let her walk away?"

Romeo's mouth tightened at the edges.

"I get it. Truth was, I was afraid of getting hurt too. So I walked away first. Of course, I was only hurting myself."

"There's nothing—"

"There's something and you know it."

"She's a guest."

"Am I missing a code of conduct here? I don't think that's a breach of ethics."

"She's leaving."

"You've heard of texting, email, and video chat, right?"

Romeo looked away.

"What will hurt more—your broken heart or...well, your broken heart? Either way, you end up alone. It's just your pride that says you want to do the rejecting instead of being rejected."

"Ouch."

"Truth. Listen, try this. Christmas is about God loving us even when we were unlovable. That's what is called perfect love. It's complete—you can't destroy it. But that also means you don't need to fear rejection. Perfect love means we're in the hands of a God who will guard our hearts."

Romeo narrowed his eyes.

"He will keep in perfect peace him whose mind is set on Him, because he trusts in Him."

"Fine. Stop. Sheesh, I get more Bible from you than I do at church."

But Seth's words hung inside Romeo the entire drive back to the resort. He'd check on the place, then head to the hospital.

He didn't expect to see the Browns' SUV in the lot as he pulled up.

Or Stella standing down by the lake, her outline illuminated by the hanging lights.

Perfect love... He got out of the car, shoved his hands into his pockets, and headed down to the lake.

Her voice lifted to him before he reached her. "You are my portion, and I trust in Your steadfast love..."

He stilled. So maybe he wasn't the only one struggling with fear. With hurt.

He opened his mouth just as she turned.

"Stella?"

Oh, she was pretty, her blonde hair spilling out from under her stocking cap, those blue eyes shiny in the lights.

"Is everything…how's the house?"

"It's a wreck."

Her mouth turned into a fine line, her eyes glistening.

"But it's okay—" He stepped toward her. "It's really okay. It was an accident and—" He closed his eyes. *Please*— He opened his eyes. "I'm sorry for what I said."

Her eyes widened.

He drew in a breath. "Okay, here's the thing. I am not great at relationships. Or maybe I don't even try—I don't know. But I do know that…" *Perfect. Love.* "I do know that being with you the last few days has felt pretty amazing. You make me laugh, and somehow with you, things don't seem so overwhelming, and…I really like you, Stella. I don't…" He blew out a breath. "I don't want you to leave."

"You like me?"

He stepped closer. "Maybe more than that." He was so close he could probably wrap his hand around the back of her neck, pull her to himself, but suddenly, he couldn't seem to move.

"I really didn't mean to—" she started.

"Stop. Of course not." He did touch her face then, cupping her cheek. "In fact, I think God brought you here this week to show me that maybe I should stop doubting and start believing."

"In what?" She stepped closer, her hands landing on his chest.

"Happy endings?" Then he took a breath and kissed her. Her lips were soft, yielding, and when a sigh escaped, it shuddered all the way through him.

No, miracles. Because he got it. He was *exactly* where he belonged.

In the Lord's hands.

No matter if he was alone, brokenhearted, or…well, whatever happened next.

He deepened his kiss, losing himself for a long, delicious moment in the taste, the sweetness of Stella's touch, then he lifted his head.

Her eyes were in his, shining.

"Does this mean I can stay?"

He smiled, everything inside him sort of exploding. Merry Happy Christmas to him. "I'll have to check the books to see if I can extend your reservation—"

She laughed, pushed away from him.

He caught up to her, wrapped his arms around her waist, and pulled her into the snow. They lay back, staring at the stars, their breaths caught in the velvety night.

"It's so magical out here. A real winter wonderland," she said quietly.

He looked at her. Sat up. Stared at the ice rink with the sparkly lights glittering against the snow, turning it to diamonds.

"Stella, you're brilliant." He stood up and held out his hand, pulling her to her feet. "Maybe we can save this wedding after all."

SATURDAY, 8:00 A.M.

The dawn made the wedding chapel sparkle with an ethereal glow, tiny golden lights shining against the ice like diamonds and gold.

"It's like a fairy tale," Stella said, sitting on the bench. Sweat lined the back of her jacket, and by all rights, she should be exhausted.

After all, they'd spent the night constructing an ice palace straight out of *Frozen*, the movie.

But under the night glow, the snow falling like fairy dust as Romeo shoveled, then built and sprayed the snow with water, it just seemed...

Perfect.

One chiseled, placed block at a time.

She'd seen it with him when he'd stood at the edge of the rink and drawn a picture with his words of his vision.

"Imagine a cathedral of sorts, with an altar at the front and hanging lights inside, with the sky open—"

"And benches covered with blankets, and we could put a runner down on the ice..."

He'd turned to her then, something in his eyes she hadn't seen before.

Hope. Or maybe…joy?

"Let's do it."

He'd carved out the snow around the fortress, like a moat, using the snow to form the icy blocks in a large wood bin. They'd then moved the blocks into place, creating a rounded apse, like the high altar in a cathedral. While she'd covered the altar in an icy, watery mist, he'd constructed walls that stepped down until they reached the narthex of the building. Here, he'd built an arch, made out of two-by-fours. Then he'd cut evergreen boughs and attached them to the arch to create a door.

All they needed was some ribbon, maybe flowers.

They'd strung twinkle lights across the nave, and then she'd helped him carry some hewn logs, propped on end, near the altar to hold flowers.

He'd then hauled in benches from the snow-covered fire pit and set them up on either side and created an aisle. "We have blankets in the lodge for campfires."

They'd warmed up in the lodge house in the early hours with a cup of hot cocoa and some cookies he found in the freezer.

"This place could use some Christmas cheer," she said.

He told her then about his first Christmas here, how his aunt Ingrid had made him a stocking of his own. "It was the first time I really felt like I belonged in a family."

Only, this time, ache didn't embed his voice. And she didn't stop herself from stepping close and pulling him into her arms and kissing him.

"I think it has plenty of cheer," he said after a bit, his voice a little ragged. He gripped her arms and set her away. "We'd better get back outside before we get into trouble."

Probably. She grinned at him.

"Don't look at me that way. I'm trying very hard to be in charge here."

"Okay, boss."

He grabbed a basket full of blankets, then took another one from the lodge storage closet, and they carried them out right about the time the sun started to glide through the treetops, gold glistening on the snow.

"It's so romantic," she said.

His hand slipped into hers. "I hope it's romantic enough for Vivien."

She looked over at him, and his suddenly worried expression turned a knot inside her. "Call her," she said softly. "Invite her here. Don't tell her why."

Then she leaned up and kissed him. "And trust me."

He gave her a look, but she winked and took off for her cabin.

Her parents' door was closed, so she went into her room. She changed, slicked her hair back, pulled on a pair of black yoga pants, boots, a white fluffy sweater, and her earmuffs.

Then she grabbed her cello and headed back outside.

She moved a log over to the side and pulled her cello out. The cold would affect the sound, but the acoustics of the ice should mask any sluggishness.

She warmed up by drawing her bow along the open strings, inhaling on the up bow, exhaling on the down, letting her shoulders relax, balancing herself with her instrument.

The voice of the cello, as she expected, reverberated out, shaky at first, then deepening, resounding, finding her bones, her cells, and saturating the air.

She started with Bach, Cello Suite no. 1 in G Major, the low draws accentuating the higher notes, the sound soft, the scales almost whispering into the morning sky.

A fine layer of warmth burned into her arm, her shoulder, her stomach—a week without practice. But soon it washed away, and she settled into a groove.

Then, because she was in a chapel, she played the cello portion of Pachelbel's Canon in D. Simple. Elegant. Beautiful, and she lost herself in the romance.

In the hope.

The song faded and she closed her eyes and dove into "A Thousand Years," another wedding favorite. The song had an almost lilting, haunting tone to it, and she hummed as she played, swaying, folding herself into it.

She followed with a little Elvis—"Can't Help Falling in Love."

And then, with the final notes, her eyes closed, and she simply started to play. A mix, maybe, of all her favorites, but as she played, she found herself pulling melodies, launching into new cadenzas, affecting a glissando, then gliding into a variation of the harmony. She found herself in an arpeggio, cascading into the tones of "Silent Night," and then did a string crossing ricochet, picking up melodies of "Joy to the World" and adding an upbow staccato.

She could hear the music before she even played it, her thoughts vibrating down to the strings, playing almost on instinct.

A couple of fingered octave trills helped her catch her breath, then she dove into a quick third run from "Carol of the Bells," the sounds high, strong, vibrant. The sunlight streamed down, pouring into the chapel, heating her face, and she leaned into the song, coaxing, almost willing the music free.

She slowed, plucked out the melody, letting it strike the cold air, then dove into deep chords, reverberant against the icy walls.

The woods felt alive—no, *she* felt alive. Whole. Pulsing with her music, with the—the *joy* of the music.

Wow, she loved this. The feeling of so much beauty, life, passion vibrating through her.

She ended hard, abruptly, the sound lifting into the air, away.

Sweat ran down her back, her heart thundering.

And then she bent over the instrument and drew her bow slowly along the strings in an easy, gentle vibrato of her favorite hymn. The sound filled the chapel, a wave of lush, resplendent beauty. She played it out, the words finding her heart. *Fear not, I am with thee, O be not dismayed, For I am thy God, and will still give thee aid; I'll strengthen thee, help thee, and cause thee to stand, upheld by My righteous, omnipotent hand.*

Yes. She held onto the last note, hearing her heartbeat.

And then, quietly, applause.

She looked up.

In the aisle stood a beautiful woman dressed in a parka, sable hair down, her mittened hands over her mouth, her cheeks wet.

Stella recognized the man behind her—tall, blond—the guy she'd met at the coffee shop so many nights ago. Boone?

Another couple sat on a bench, their hands entwined.

And behind them, Gerald and his grandson. Gerald was smiling, something at peace on his face.

Then her gaze stopped on the only one who mattered, the man who'd created this magical place.

The man who'd helped her find *her* music.

Romeo stood, clapping, grinning, so much in his green eyes as he smiled at her, shaking his head.

She bowed her head, then looked at the couple in the aisle. "Vivien?"

"Yes."

"This is for you."

Stella closed her eyes and slowly drew out the notes to Ed Sheeran's "Perfect." Not quite Wagner's "Bridal Chorus," but it seemed fitting.

As she looked up, Boone had taken Vivien's hand and pulled her into a dance hold.

Sweet.

The other couple got up and joined them.

Romeo stepped away, folded his arms. And grinned like a man who'd won a war.

She took her time, then finished, the notes fading away into the morning.

Silence fell as she looked at the bride.

"It's...well, not to be corny, but...perfect. Isn't it?" She turned to her groom. "Right?"

"Perfect." He kissed her. "Now, please, will you marry me?"

Stella looked over at Romeo. He winked at her.

And no matter what the next step was, where, or how, she wasn't afraid. Because she'd picked the right person to trust.

Thank You, Lord.

And that's how it was done. Romeo sorta wanted to take a picture of the wedding palace and text it to Owen.

Look who'd saved the day. Okay, not him, and not Stella, although —wow—her talent could strip him of words. He'd walked into a piece of magic when he'd led Vivien and Boone down to the chapel, the music at once bold, inspired, and glorious.

He'd watched her and knew—with everything inside him—that she belonged in Austria.

But also here, because no, he didn't want to let her go.

Email, texting, video chatting…and he could get on a plane.

Because maybe she was *his* next adventure.

Which included helping him pull off a winter wonderland wedding.

No, not him. God, who was somehow at the helm of all of this. Romeo could almost feel it, the touch of the miraculous, in his bones.

Maybe that's how it felt to be in the hands of the Lord.

While Stella talked with Vivien about her wedding music, Boone called Cole, and it wasn't long before Megan showed up with her compatriots. Boone left with Duke to fetch his Mustang, and the groomsmen went to Wilder House to salvage decorations, and Megan called in Claire Atwood to deliver the flowers, and…

And three hours later, the chapel was adorned with white and blue roses at the altar and on the evergreen arch, and the guys had brought over the birch trees from the house, creating a semicircle at the front. Megan had added lanterns along the aisle and dug up a piece of faux fur as a runner.

She was arranging candles in the front as Romeo dug out the tall outdoor heaters and set them up around the chapel.

"This is amazing, Romeo."

The voice lifted from the back of the chapel. Stella stood under the evergreen arch, clutching a cup of cocoa. "I can't believe you pulled this off."

"We," he said and came over to her. "I couldn't have done this without you."

She smiled up at him. "We make a good team."

"Yeah," he said, no regret in his voice. He wouldn't make this awkward. But he wasn't going to push her away, either. "That was so...amazing. You are a rare and beautiful talent, Stella. Your music is breathtaking. And I think..."

"Yeah. I'm going to reapply to the institute in the fall."

He nodded. "Please."

"But maybe, until then, you could use a little help around here? Event coordinator?"

"Sleigh ride registrar?"

"Fire builder?"

"Nope." He took the cocoa out of her hands and set it on a bench. Then he wrapped his arms around her and pulled her close.

She lifted her face to his. "I guess I need to brush up on my winter driving skills."

"Why? Then I can never rescue you."

He lowered his head.

"Technically, you were the reason I ended up in the ditch."

"I'm not sorry." Then he kissed her.

No, not sorry in the least.

She was soft, perfect, sweet, passionate, and...his.

For now. Maybe forever. And definitely worth the risk.

It occurred to him then that if he hadn't been abandoned for Christmas...

"Hey! Not before the wedding!"

He lifted his head and spotted Boone coming down the walk. He was swinging a pair of car keys around his finger. He grinned at Romeo. "I need a favor. Can you hang onto these? I don't want them getting lost." He leaned in. "Or stolen."

Romeo took the keys. "You sure?"

"They're in safe hands." He winked.

Romeo closed his hand around them. "Yes, they are."

"Oh no."

The tone, the intake of breath made him turn.

Megan stood at the altar, looking at her phone, then up at them. She sighed and made a face.

"What?" Boone said, his voice a little hollow.

"That was Ellie Matthews, Pastor Dan's wife. The smoke inhalation from last night has swollen his throat. He can't speak."

Silence. A beat.

"Then who is going to marry us?"

Sleigh Bells Ring

Ring

ANDREA CHRISTENSON

Dedicated to ministry couples everywhere.
You are loved.

CHAPTER 1

At least one person in this family was thriving.

Pastor Bob Brown looked around the University of Minnesota, Duluth, Weber Music Hall. Padded panels hung on the walls, and the vaulted ceiling was shaped to allow music to reverberate just so.

At the front of the room on a raised platform, his daughter, Stella, had her eyes closed as she played the final bars of Bach's cello Suite no. 1 in G major on her violoncello. Pride swelled in his throat, causing him to gasp. She was beautiful up there, lost in her music. He knew her graduate program at the Fritz Kreisler Institute in Vienna would be key in launching her career. He could hardly believe she would be leaving Minnesota tomorrow to begin her next adventure.

Tonight, she was finishing up some requirements for her master's degree. She'd put together a magnificent Bach concert, her last big hurrah. Yep. She was truly on her way.

If only he knew what he was doing with his life.

"Her signature piece, and she's doing so well," Marilyn, his wife of forty-one years, leaned over and whispered in his ear. Her breath tickled his neck, raising goosebumps along his arms. "She's making the family proud."

He couldn't agree more. But proud as he was of his daughter, he couldn't escape the feeling that he himself had never done anything spectacular.

He was starting to think he never would.

He glanced at Marilyn. Her dark curls were pulled back in a loose French knot, red sweater giving color to her cheeks. The pearls he'd given her on their thirtieth anniversary dangled from her ears. Only a year younger than his sixty-two, her face was unlined except for a few laugh lines at the corner of each blue eye. A bouquet of roses for their daughter nestled in her lap. She was beautiful as always, of course, but lately he'd felt a certain restlessness in her. Or maybe he was projecting.

Because the truth was, he wasn't feeling like himself.

He wanted to run and keep running until the itchy feeling in his belly went away and the fog in his mind cleared.

Thankfully, he was going to do just that in the morning. After almost forty years as a pastor, Bob was skipping Christmas.

He'd been talking on the phone to his friend Pastor Dan Matthews a few weeks ago and mentioned that he'd never had a Christmas off. He'd always been at the church leading services and doing the thousand other things required of a pastor in the weeks of Advent. Dan must have heard a bit of desperation in his voice, because he'd called back a few days later.

"Remember when you filled in for me that Sunday up here in Deep Haven?" Dan had asked.

Bob remembered. Dan had needed a Sunday off on short notice, and Bob had been between churches. He'd offered to fill the pulpit for Dan. "Yeah. Great little town you have there."

"There's a family in church who owns a resort. I think you met them, the Christiansens?"

Bob grunted an assent. He remembered John and his wife Ingrid.

The couple were about his and Marilyn's ages. They'd invited Bob and Marilyn home for lunch after church. There had been a few grown kids too.

"I've arranged for you and Marilyn to stay at their resort, Evergreen, for the week of Christmas," Dan said.

"Nonsense. I can't go up there for Christmas. I have responsibilities here." But oh, the thought of running away tugged at his heart.

"This is my Christmas gift to you and Marilyn," his friend said. "John's son, Owen Christiansen, will have a cabin made up for you. I've even called your church council president and asked him to help with the surprise. He will be taking over your church duties for the week."

"Are you serious? A whole week off?" Was he hallucinating? Surely Dan didn't mean that he wouldn't have to work on Christmas. Sudden tears sprang to his eyes. He squeezed them shut, kneading his thumb and forefinger into the lids. "Dan, I don't know what to say."

"You don't need to say anything. You and Marilyn deserve to have some time to yourselves over the holiday. Will Stella need a place to stay? We can probably get a cabin for her too."

"No, she's not spending Christmas with us this year." A brief pang passed quickly. Stella deserved to be making her own life.

"Okay! A cabin for two, then. It should be pretty quiet up there on Christmas week."

"What will we do?"

Dan laughed. "Do? How about nothing? You'll have a snug cabin, a fireplace, and the great frozen north. Don't *do* anything."

Do nothing? That sounded like heaven on earth. No council meetings, no sermon to prepare and give? No pressure on the biggest night of the church calendar? Yeah, he could probably do that.

It wasn't like he had any of his Christmas spark anymore anyway.

Over the years, Christmas had gone from being a time to celebrate the birth of Jesus to weeks of worrying about special music and original content for the Christmas play and whether they had enough candles for the candlelight service. This year, as he looked at the date circled on the calendar, he didn't have a clue what he would stand up and say in front of the congregation on Christmas Day.

In fact, he wondered if he should give up the ministry.

These past few months, he'd struggled to stay engaged with the church. Nothing big was happening. Just the ordinariness of ministry. And it was starting to wear on him.

Not to mention the phone call he'd had a few months ago. He'd answered the phone and heard the voice of LeRoy Olson, a friend who had been a few years ahead of him in seminary.

"Bob! How is Wisconsin treating you?"

They'd chatted for a few minutes about inconsequential things before LeRoy dropped a bombshell. Well, two bombshells really.

"Did you hear about the Wilsons? They're getting a divorce."

"Jeff and Wendy? No. That can't be right." Jeff had graduated from seminary in the same class as Bob, and they'd served churches near each other for the first five years of ministry. "They always seemed so solid." His brain refused to assimilate the information.

"I guess Jeff just left Wendy and the church one day and moved to Boca Raton. He burned out and quit everything."

Bob tried to latch on to one of the thoughts buzzing through his mind. "I'll have to give him a call."

"Give him my best. I'm concerned about him." LeRoy cleared his throat. "But listen, that's not the only reason why I'm calling. I have a favor to ask of you. You know I'm on the board for Planting Hope."

As Bob recovered from the news about his friend, he almost missed LeRoy's next words. And he'd definitely missed some in between.

"You would only have to live in Botswana for a year. I know even asking that much is a big commitment, and I know that running a sustainable farming operation isn't exactly like being in the pastorate. We just need someone to fill in while the workers we have stationed there come stateside for medical treatment."

"Wait, back up a minute. You want me to take a job in Botswana?"

LeRoy chuckled. "Yes. I think your time spent in farming country makes you uniquely suited to this job. Plus, you understand the mission. You wouldn't be preaching or holding Bible studies, but you would be helping people with their needs."

"Thanks for thinking of me, but I'm just not interested."

As much as Bob had wanted to hear his friend out, he still couldn't shake the feeling that leaving the pastoral ministry was giving up somehow. He could be all in, or he could be... What? A failure? Plus, Marilyn would never go for it. All she'd ever wanted to be was a pastor's wife. How could he take that from her?

On the stage, Stella stood, bowed, and then swept her bow to the side to acknowledge the group accompanying her.

Beside him, Marilyn wiped a tear from her eye. He'd been so lost in his thoughts he'd missed some of the recital.

He hoped it didn't make him a bad father to also be dreaming about dropping Stella off at the airport and then driving as fast as possible north to Deep Haven.

This was going to be his year skipping Christmas, and he couldn't wait to get started. And then maybe he'd have the energy to figure out what to do with the rest of his life.

A Christmas all to themselves.

Marilyn couldn't remember ever feeling so indulgent. She knew she should concentrate on Stella's performance. After all, it had been ages since she'd heard her daughter play. But she couldn't keep her mind from daydreaming about the trip she and Bob were taking to Deep Haven. A cozy cabin for two at a woodsy lake resort over Christmas.

This would be just the thing to add the spark back into their marriage.

She was pretty sure Bob still loved her. Probably. But lately he'd been so distant. And yeah, she'd been busy too. It wasn't easy being the pastor's wife. Everyone seemed to want a piece of her time. She filled in for the nursery attendant, taught Sunday school, led a

Wednesday women's Bible study, and tried to stay neutral in the debates about what color to paint the church library.

When she and Bob had moved to Sunset Falls, Wisconsin, a few years before, they'd been welcomed into their new church home with open arms. The congregation there quickly felt like family.

So she didn't mind the ways the church made demands on her time. She kind of loved it, actually. But, she admitted, it didn't leave much time to focus on her marriage.

That ended now.

Six days in Deep Haven, just the two of them...well, anything could happen. She'd even left her flannel pajamas at home. It would be like a second honeymoon.

She glanced around the auditorium of Weber Music Hall. Its distinctive domed roofline captured and enhanced the music soaring through the space. The golden wood paneling warmed the room. Overhead, she glimpsed the night sky through a slim skylight, the twinkle of stars echoing back the anticipation in her heart.

The three hundred and fifty auditorium seats around her were nearly full. Stella would be happy with the turnout. She'd fretted that no one would attend a recital in the week leading up to Christmas. When Marilyn had called to confirm the details last week, Stella had even tried to dissuade them from coming.

"Don't bother, Mom." Her daughter's voice on the other end of the phone had tugged at a place in Marilyn's heart. It had always been that way. After nearly fourteen years of infertility, Marilyn and Bob had almost given up on having children when Stella, their miracle baby, had come along. Now her baby, at almost twenty-six, had blossomed into a beautiful and talented musician. All those years spent watering down the soup to pay for Stella's music lessons were bearing fruit. "There probably won't be enough people there to justify having the recital, but my teacher is insisting."

"I'm sure it will be beautiful. You have such talent—your teacher just wants other people to recognize that."

"Seriously, Mom. You don't have to feel obligated to come."

She sensed something else might be bothering Stella but didn't want to push it. She always walked a fine line with her independent daughter. "Nonsense. We'll be there just like we've been to all of your other recitals. Besides, this will be the last time we get to hear you play before you leave for Vienna."

When Stella didn't answer, Marilyn continued. "Plus, it works out perfectly. Dad and I will come to your recital, then head to Deep Haven the next morning. Are you sure you're fine with us staying the night at your apartment? We can still get a hotel."

"No, that's fine. My roommates are gone for the week anyway. If you don't mind the pullout couch, I'd love for you to stay."

"If you're sure. I know you will be leaving for Fritz Kreisler the next day."

"Yes, I'm sure, Mom," she'd said, but Marilyn heard something in her voice she couldn't place. She hadn't chased it.

Now Marilyn watched her daughter as she closed her eyes through the final measures of her favorite Bach piece. That tugging in her heart pulled her back to the present.

Stella was doing a fabulous job. She had first learned this piece in a simpler form as a high schooler. Marilyn herself could probably play it by now, for as often as she'd heard Stella practice it. She'd added difficulty and depth to the score as her training had progressed, until it had become her own.

Except Marilyn wondered if her heart was in it.

She missed a note.

And then, there. Another one.

But Stella pulled herself back together and finished with a flourish.

"Isn't she amazing?" she whispered to Bob. "Even when she isn't quite at her best, she's a natural onstage. She's making us proud."

Instead of leaning in to her comment, however, he sighed and pulled away. "She sure is something else."

She knew he still loved her. Really. Maybe she just needed to apologize for neglecting him lately. The truth was, they both were to blame for the cooling off in their relationship. But this week she planned to show him how much they were both missing. She'd even done something crazy and purchased a little satin-and-lace bedtime number she'd ordered online, blushing the whole time.

She glanced again at Bob. His salt-and-pepper hair was mostly salt these days, but she liked it that way. It suited his complexion. She always teased him that he looked like Harrison Ford and that's why she had fallen in love with him. He would tease back that he should call her Marion instead of Marilyn. She wasn't so sure that she looked like the iconic character from Indiana Jones, but she loved the teasing.

The Wilsons are getting a divorce. Bob's words from two months ago whispered through her mind. *I guess Jeff burned out on ministry and life in general and just left Wendy and the kids behind.* A spark of fear caused her heart to skip a beat, and she had to remind herself to breathe.

Ever since that conversation, Bob had been distant, almost cold. She thought maybe… But, no. Bob wouldn't be thinking of following the Wilsons' footsteps…would he?

She put the thought firmly out of her head. That's what this vacation was for. A time for the two of them to reconnect.

The music ended with a crescendo, and the audience stood to their feet with applause. Marilyn stood with them, clutching Stella's roses to her chest. She reached to take Bob's arm, but he was still in his seat, looking dazed. What was with him lately? He blinked then stood.

Marilyn tugged him to the left and out to the aisle. "I want to get down to the stage before Stella is overwhelmed by admirers."

"Lead the way," Bob said, closing his hand over hers. She threaded them through the crowd until they stood before the musicians, who had moved to the floor in front of the stage.

The crowd cleared and Marilyn handed Stella the roses, then reached to embrace her over the blossoms. An aroma of roses and raspberries filled the air between them. "You were wonderful, honey."

"Thanks, Mom." Stella's voice was muffled against her shoulder. Marilyn pulled back and allowed Bob to give Stella a one-armed hug.

Marilyn gave her daughter a searching look. Her smile didn't quite meet her eyes. "What's going on? Is everything okay?"

"Actually, there is something I wanted to talk to you about."

"Are you upset that we won't be spending Christmas together?"

Whatever else the ministry had required, they'd always managed to spend part of the Christmas holiday together.

Until this year.

Marilyn felt a pang of guilt but shoved it aside. She would not apologize for wanting to spend one holiday with her husband alone. Even if it meant not spending time with their only daughter. Besides, Stella had her own plans.

"No, I'm not upset about that. At least, that's not what I wanted to talk about."

"Oh? What is it, then?" Was Bob even going to clue in to this conversation? He looked like his body was here, but his mind was somewhere else entirely. He stared at the drape lining the stage, and she knew it wasn't *that* interesting.

"I've made up my mind. I'm not going to Vienna. At least...not now."

"What do you mean? Did your flight get canceled?" Surely there would be a new flight in the morning. This storm couldn't last forever.

"Yes, it got canceled. But..." Stella sighed and tucked a wayward hair behind her ear. She wouldn't look her mother in the eyes.

"What? Why?" This sudden change of plans made no sense.

"Mom." Stella's voice held a note of warning. "I..." She trailed off and shrugged.

"Yes, what is it?"

"I just—" But Stella broke off as Bob swiveled his head toward their conversation.

He stepped between them and gave Stella a hug. "Don't worry, honey. We'll figure it out. You should come to Deep Haven with us."

Oh, sure. *Now* he wanted to join the conversation?

"Are you sure?" Stella sounded almost relieved.

"Of course!" Bob tightened his arm around Stella's shoulder. "We can't let you spend Christmas in your apartment all on your own. We'll do puzzles, and maybe take a walk in the winter wonderland where snow is glistening." He winked at their daughter.

"What!" Marilyn couldn't help the exclamation that escaped her. A rushing filled her ears. "But—"

"Thanks, Daddy. I really didn't want to spend Christmas alone." Stella wrapped an arm around her father's waist.

Bob and Stella talked a few moments more about the details while Marilyn pasted a smile on her face. But she could only think about one thing.

What was she going to wear to bed now?

CHAPTER 2

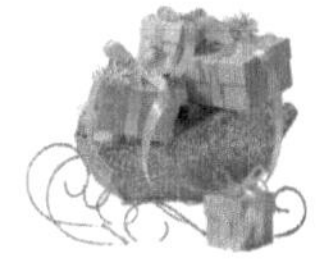

MONDAY, 7:00 P.M.

This was not a great start to his peaceful vacation.

First, they'd waited way too long to get started on their drive, and a three-hour trip from Duluth had stretched to seven with the advent of a winter storm. The weather had kept him concentrating on the road, not making small talk, which only lengthened a strange silence between his daughter and his wife. Worse, his hands ached from clutching the steering wheel.

Then they'd nearly gotten run off the road by some guy crazy enough to try to pass a plow truck. The plow truck driver had gotten out and helped push him from the ditch, only to have his daughter snap at him.

Which was weird.

Then they'd gotten to a coffee shop in town, and his wife had suggested that Stella might spend their vacation away from the cabin, helping the resort owner run the place.

What?

When they'd arrived at the resort, things had only gotten colder.

Bob didn't know why the two women in his life were so quiet, but he was determined to not let it ruin his trip. He couldn't dodge the idea that he'd said something wrong this morning, right before they left Stella's apartment. Stella had had an overnight bag packed already from her canceled trip, so he'd just had to fit it in the trunk with his and Marilyn's things. He'd also wedged in her cello. It'd been a tight fit —he almost hadn't gotten everything in—but he suspected Stella wouldn't have minded sharing her seat with the instrument she'd been playing for years.

When he'd gone back up to the apartment, Stella was grabbing a quick shower. Marilyn sat on the couch with her arms folded.

"What's wrong?" He sat next to her, the springs on the couch bending them toward each other.

"Nothing."

But he knew that look. There definitely was something.

"Are you mad at me?"

"Why would I be mad?" Her left shoulder went up in a shrug. "Everything's fine."

"You've been speaking to me in monosyllables since last night." Oh. Wait. "Is this about Stella coming with us?"

In the bathroom, the water shut off.

Marilyn tightened her arms. "You didn't even ask if it would be okay if she came along."

"Our daughter was going to be alone for Christmas. Is that what you wanted?"

"Keep your voice down," Marilyn hissed. "Of course that's not what I wanted." She turned to him. "I wanted to be consulted before you made drastic changes to our plans."

The bathroom door opened. He heard footsteps, and then Stella's bedroom door clicked shut.

He kept his voice low. "What was I supposed to do? Ignore her?"

"I don't know, okay? I just— Never mind."

"I'm sorry. You're right. I should have checked with you first."

Her arms fell to her sides. "Thank you. And you did the right thing, it's just that—"

In front of them, the TV popped on. Stella walked into the room with the remote, dressed in jeans and a chunky blue sweater. She rubbed at her long blonde hair with a towel. "I thought we should catch a little weather and traffic before we leave." She plopped into an armchair and threw her leg over the arm. "That was quite the storm yesterday, and it doesn't look like it's letting up."

The channel six weatherman had excitedly told them that more snow was coming, and fast. "We should get on the road," Bob had said. "I want to beat the next round, if possible."

Now, several hours later, Bob wished he could go back to that moment, ask Marilyn "Just what?" But the time had passed, and now they were making their silent way onto the Evergreen Resort property, the night heavy and laden with snow.

He just hoped he could find it.

And, he hoped the apology had smoothed things over enough for them to enjoy their trip. But if not—he mentally shrugged—he'd deal with that later.

He drank the last swallow of the vanilla coffee he'd picked up on their way through Deep Haven. Cold.

Running into Dan and the other guys at the coffee shop in town had been a nice surprise. Bob had embraced his solidly built, dark-haired friend. "Dan. How are you?"

"You made it to town. Excellent. You'll love the Evergreen Resort. I think the family is stuck in Florida. But they left Romeo in charge. He's fantastic—"

"I think we met him. He pulled us out of the ditch."

"Can't believe he's alone for the week of Christmas at the resort. It's their biggest week of events. With Casper out of town, Romeo will probably have to oversee the Wilder House, too. And Boone here is getting married there on Saturday night." Dan gestured to a blond man at the counter.

The man turned around, holding a tray of coffee. "I'm sure Romeo will pull it together. Between my bride and her to-do list, I'm sure everything will be perfect. But he definitely has his hands full." He turned to the Browns. "Nice to meet you. Have a great vacation."

"Plan to," her father said. "Thanks."

Now, as Bob pulled up to the drive of Evergreen Resort, the quietness of the snow drifting down around him, he just wanted to revel in the feeling of not needing to think about the candles for the lighting service on Christmas Eve and whether or not there was enough space between the Christmas tree and the altar for the children's nativity. This was his first Christmas off in forty years, and he'd be darned if anything slipped in to ruin it. He was not going to think about the ministry for six glorious days.

Dan had told him that the big blond guy, Boone he thought the name was, was getting married on Christmas Eve. Bob felt a little sorry for his friend, having to officiate a wedding on a holiday, but Dan seemed excited about it. And, Bob admitted to himself, he wasn't so far gone that he couldn't see the appeal of a wedding full of twinkle lights, snow gently falling, and the strains of Christmas music in the air.

Just because he was skipping Christmas didn't mean the rest of the world had to.

Bob slowed as he pulled into a driveway, and the Evergreen Resort spread out ahead of them. Several small cabins ringed a lake covered with snow, evergreens growing in the distance. Smoke curled from one of the chimneys.

The perfect hideaway.

"Ladies, it looks like cabin six will be our retreat from the world for the next six days."

Beside him, Marilyn grunted, and in the back seat, Stella uncrossed her arms and sat up straighter.

Gravel crunched under their tires as he drove the short distance to their accommodations.

Getting out of the car again, Bob stood by the trunk for a moment and took a deep breath. Hints of pine and wood smoke and the clean, fresh scent of new-fallen snow filled his lungs.

Pristine. Peaceful. Perfect.

He couldn't wait to get started.

Okay. Marilyn was determined to lose the bad attitude.

She and Stella sat in the car, engine ticking as it cooled down. Bob had jumped out to find their cabin. A few inches of freshly fallen snow covered the path that led around a smattering of small, cute cabins settled against the lakeshore.

In fact, freshly fallen snow lay over everything, smoothing out the harsh lines of the Evergreen cabins and blanketing the area in a winter wonderland. The still-falling snow made a gentle shush as it dropped to the ground.

Marilyn took a deep breath and let go of the negative feelings she'd been holding on to during the drive up here to Deep Haven. It wasn't Bob's fault that Stella's trip got canceled, and of course he'd done the right thing to invite her along.

What were they going to do? Leave their daughter alone on Christmas?

Of course not.

She could still reconnect with Bob, even with Stella along. She'd just have to be more creative with her plans. She could still recreate some aspects of their honeymoon, even if it wouldn't be as romantic. She just needed to get Bob talking to her again.

Plus, she hadn't missed the strange reaction Stella had had to the guy who had helped them out of the ditch. An overreaction that seemed born of some other deep emotion.

Probably, she'd gone overboard at the coffee shop, suggesting Stella help him add some Christmas cheer around the resort, but frankly, her daughter seemed unusually void of any cheer, and she'd just been trying to, well, fix things as usual.

She watched Bob as he came back from the cabin, crunching through the snow, his head down into the collar of his jacket.

He was still a handsome man. She remembered that feeling the first time she'd seen Bob at the Bible college they'd both attended, and a fire lit in her belly. She didn't believe in love at first sight, but what she and Bob had was certainly close.

Or at least, it had been.

She just needed to capture some of that old fire and fan it back into flame. They weren't going to be like the Wilsons, divorced after forty years of marriage.

And probably, she should also smooth things over with Stella.

She turned in her seat. Her daughter sat with her hands clenched between her knees. Her blonde hair was pulled up. Pale blue eyes were clouded with some distant thought. A dimple in her cheek always reminded Marilyn of Bob. Sometimes she looked so like her father. "I'm glad you are with us."

Stella rolled her eyes. "Come on, Mom. My apartment isn't that big. I heard you and Dad when I got out of the shower. Plus, you guys barely spoke on our way up here."

"I'm sorry about that. I needed to have an attitude adjustment. But really, I want to spend Christmas with you." And it was true. She'd spent a few days mourning when Stella had first told them she'd be in Vienna for the holiday. The main reason she'd come to grips with it had been the promise of this trip with Bob. "It wouldn't have seemed quite right for us to be apart."

Stella looked out the car window. "I would've missed you too."

"The Christiansens sure have good-looking relatives. That man who pulled us out of the ditch…" She paused, waiting for Stella to look at her. When she did, Marilyn quirked an eyebrow.

"Mom!"

"What? I have eyes." She waggled her brows at Stella. Who crossed her arms and looked away.

"I'm not looking for anything like that. Besides, it was *his* fault we were in the ditch to begin with!"

So much for trying to connect.

She hadn't missed the way Stella was silent most of the ride, staring out the window or fiddling with her phone. When her vivacious girl refused to be engaged in conversation, Marilyn knew something was up.

She mentally added another item to her vacation to-do list: figure out what was going on with Stella.

A blast of cold air hit her as Bob opened his door to pop the trunk. "You'll like it. Cute place. Has a stove and plenty of puzzles."

She smiled, hoping her eyes communicated that all was forgiven and that she was ready for their time together. She would tell him with words the first chance she got. For now, she allowed peace to reign between them in the car.

Looking toward the cabins, under the high lights, she saw several snug, adorable buildings, perfect for two. Images of her and Bob cuddled up in front of the fire, mugs of hot cocoa in their hands, filled her mind. Perhaps in such a quiet, romantic spot, Bob would open up to her. Tell her what was really going on.

And if Stella went to bed early one of those nights, they could see what they could stoke up in front of the fire.

Surely they could have a family trip *and* a romantic one. She'd just make it work. That was her superpower, after all. Making the best of an awkward situation came in handy as a pastor's wife.

She stepped out of the car and stretched. Several hours in the car felt different at sixty-one years old than it had at twenty-one. Snow still drifted from the gunmetal-gray sky.

She joined Bob at the back of the car. "I'm sorry for my attitude." She kept her voice low. No need to pull Stella into this conversation again. "This is going to be a great week."

Bob gave her a brief smile. "All is forgiven. Let's get this stuff inside the cabin. I want to get out of my clothes and into some sweatpants."

He didn't even want to explore the resort? What had happened to the adventurous man she'd married? Bob was becoming less like Indiana Jones and more like a stodgy librarian.

Unless.

She put a hand to her heart, restrained a gasp.

What if he just didn't want to spend time with her?

No. That was ridiculous. She put the thought out of her mind.

She tugged her small bag out of the trunk and trailed up the path after her husband.

"Mom, wait up."

Marilyn waited for Stella to catch up to her on the walk. They walked in tandem the few remaining steps to the cabin. Bob had disappeared through the door and was stomping the snow off his feet. A layer of snow covered a firewood box on the porch.

"Reminds me of that cabin we spent our honeymoon in," she said, but he didn't seem to hear her, maybe because he'd toed off his boots and carried the suitcase into the back bedroom.

She thought back to their honeymoon. They'd gotten married just before Bob started seminary. Money had been tight and they couldn't afford anything fancy. A friend offered them the use of their cabin in Bemidji up in northern Minnesota, and they thought they'd won the lottery.

Until they got there.

It turned out to be that friend's rustic hunting cabin. And by rustic, she meant no running water. And by hunting, she meant deer heads covering every wall. But their week in that spot had turned out to be the most romantic week of her life.

"I don't need to be a hunter. I have the catch of my life right here," Bob had said on that long ago day. Corny, yes. But when he'd swept her up into his arms and over the threshold, she'd known she'd love him forever.

She remembered their long walks in the woods, crafting special meals on the tiny stove, and even a few four-wheeler rides, clinging to Bob as they drove over the bumpy trail. Sitting under the stars and dreaming about their future. Their love had transformed the space into a love nest fit for the love birds they were.

She looked forward to repeating it.

She caught herself humming "Can't Buy Me Love" as she entered the cabin.

Inside, a tiny kitchen was tucked into the left-hand corner. Straight ahead was the dining table and a small sitting area with the fireplace roaring. To her right were two doorways.

She could see a toilet and sink in one. So the other must be the bedroom.

Wait.

There was only *one* bedroom in this place? She could hear Bob rustling around in the bedroom. She could see the queen-size bed and—

No. Her breath grew shallow. There was no door to the bedroom.

No. Door.

She *did* have something to wear to bed, right? She tried to remember what she'd packed, but so much had happened since she'd filled a bag, intending to have a romantic getaway for two.

Wait! The pjs she'd worn at Stella's would be appropriate, thank goodness.

And if she wanted privacy to have long talks with Bob, she'd just coax him out to take a walk through the woods.

"Looks like I get the couch." Stella's voice was overly bright. Bob came out of the bedroom carrying a small stack of clothing.

"I thought I could take the couch," he said. "Let you girls have the more comfortable space."

He didn't want to sleep in the room with her? She put her hand to her chest.

Stella walked over to the couch. "Don't be silly. You and Mom take the bedroom. This will be fine for me." She insisted until Bob finally carried his clothes back into the bedroom.

Marilyn sighed. Time to make the best of the situation. Surely this could be salvaged somehow. She would just have to reconnect with Bob another way.

She followed him into the bedroom to unpack. Looked at the suitcase on the bed. "Bob, where is the overnight bag I used at Stella's?"

He carried his shirts to the bureau. "Oh, I left those bags at Stella's. We needed room in the trunk for her cello. I figured we could pick them up again when we drop her off." Bob gave a shrug. "Why, was there something important in it?"

She forced a smile at him, trying not to wince.

No big deal.

Nothing that important in the bag.

Only her intimate-cabin-for-three-appropriate pajamas.

She gave herself a mental shake. Her nighttime attire wasn't what was important here. After all, neither one of her family members was exactly speaking to her. She needed to repair her relationship with Stella, find out the mystery behind her daughter's canceled trip, *and* save her marriage.

Standing there in the silent bedroom, she realized what she really needed was a Christmas miracle.

CHAPTER 3

*A*s it turned out, the small cabin wasn't too small after all.

Bob rubbed his chin as he placed another piece into the puzzle in front of him. Marilyn was napping in their bedroom, and Stella had been gone most of the day. After a quick breakfast, their daughter had practically run out the door. Maybe she was still embarrassed about burying the car in that snowbank yesterday.

She'd gotten home from grocery shopping wearing a sheepish look. "We were about to call the police," Marilyn had said. "You were gone for hours."

"It was no big deal, Mom. I just got delayed because the car got… sort of…buried in a snowbank." Stella had placed two bulging plastic bags on the table and shot her dad a look full of pleading.

Bob had taken the hint and retrieved the rest from the car. He'd given the car a once-over, and everything looked intact. He'd come into the cabin to hear Stella again.

"Romeo helped dig me out."

"The snowplow driver?" Marilyn didn't have her hands on her hips, but she might as well have.

Stella rolled her eyes at her mother, then softened. "Look, I'm sorry for worrying you. Forgive me?"

"Of course we forgive you." Bob stepped between them and put an arm around each of his girls.

"Absolutely." Marilyn smiled at Stella and all seemed well.

Stella had then left to thank Romeo…and still hadn't returned.

Now the small space echoed with silence. He considered putting some music on from his cell phone, but he didn't want to bother Marilyn. She'd invited him to join her in her nap, but he'd declined. He didn't feel sleepy—more like restless.

This puzzle was fun, though. Challenging. A field of hot air balloons against a blue sky, hovering over a field of flowers.

Idyllic. He didn't begrudge Marilyn her nap. She worked so hard, sometimes harder than him. She deserved to have a break. This trip away would be just as good a rest for her as for him. They both needed time away from the church.

He remembered the last time they'd taken a vacation. Two days in, they'd gotten a call that the chairman of their church council had been killed in a farming accident. Of course, they were on the road back home as quickly as they could pack up their bags.

Things like that were part of the job as a pastor, and he didn't resent it. In fact, he felt privileged to be part of people's lives in this way.

No, he wasn't resentful. He was tired.

Maybe even the kind of tired that meant he should quit.

A rustle from the bedroom indicated that Marilyn would be out soon. A moment later, she appeared in the doorway. She tugged at the hem of her shirt, smoothing out the sleep wrinkles.

"Have a good nap?"

"Yeah. It was good."

"Do you want to take a drive into town?"

Her smile cleared the rest of the sleepiness out of her countenance. "I'd love that. Just let me grab my coat and shoes."

A few minutes later they were tooling down the road.

"Do you think there is something wrong with Stella?" Marilyn asked.

"Not really, why?"

"I don't know. Maybe I'm imagining things. But she canceled her trip, and she was off her game at the recital. And she hasn't wanted to spend any time with us up here. After we unloaded the car, she practically jumped at the chance to go to town."

"Let's not read too much into the trip being canceled. Plenty of people had their flights canceled and their trips changed. And going into town probably felt more interesting than sitting around with us reading books and putting together puzzles."

"True enough."

They settled into a gentle silence as he piloted the CR-V into town.

Deep Haven was an interesting little town. Several art shops, some touristy places, a few restaurants, and of course, a great view of Lake Superior. As they drove along the main street and passed by the library, Marilyn grabbed his bicep.

"Did you see that?"

"See what?" His heart rate picked up.

She gripped him tighter. "Turn around."

At the next corner, he pulled a U-turn—the streets were deserted —and headed back the way they'd come.

"What's wrong? What am I looking for?"

"Nothing's wrong. There!" Marilyn pointed at a sign hanging outside the library. "Look! They're having a candlelit snowshoe event tonight."

That was what she'd nearly given him a heart attack for?

He looked over at her, hot words on his tongue. The expression on her face pulled him up short.

Her eyes shone.

It had been a long time since he'd seen that light. Or maybe he hadn't been looking.

Sure, he wanted nothing more than to go back to the cabin, climb back into his sweatpants, and fit a few more pieces into his puzzle.

But.

He didn't want to be responsible for putting out that light. And really, a moonlit stroll through the woods sounded fun. A break from his regular routine, for sure. "Let's do it."

The light in her eyes spread to her whole face.

"Let me just get directions." She punched at her phone a minute. "Okay, it looks like the Wild Harbor Trading Post is only five minutes away. We have a little time to kill before we need to go get signed up."

"How about we find a bite to eat?"

"It's like you read my mind."

They found a little bistro called Trailside and ordered a Reuben sandwich to split. On the walls, Bob spotted several newspaper clippings featuring a local hero. Looked like some sort of dogsled racer.

The waiter caught him staring at one of the clippings. "That's Nick Dahlquist. He's the son of the owners. He ran the Iditarod last year."

"They must be proud of him." Bob indicated another clipping. "His photo is everywhere."

"Yep. He's their shining star." The waiter refilled their water cups and left.

Soon the waiter came back with their order. "Are you new in town?" He slid a plate in front of each of them.

"We're just visiting." Marilyn smiled at the kid.

"We get that a lot. From somewhere nearby?"

Marilyn laughed. "We're from a tiny town in Wisconsin that no one has ever heard of."

"Try me."

Boy, this kid was really working for his tip.

Marilyn was only too happy to fill him in. "It's called Sunset Falls. We moved there five years ago when—"

Bob had had enough. "Honey, he doesn't need to know our whole story."

Marilyn smiled at the waiter again. "Anyway. That's where we're from."

Bob breathed a deep sigh when the kid finally made his way to the next table. "I'd prefer we don't talk about the church this week."

Across from him, Marilyn's brow creased. "O-kay." She drew the word out. "I guess we're on vacation from all that."

"Exactly." He took a bite of the Reuben, and the conversation died off.

Yeah. Maybe he could've handled that better. But somehow, having Marilyn tell the waiter he was a pastor made him feel trapped in a way he didn't understand, let alone have a clue how to explain. Add it to the list of things he needed to talk to Marilyn about. If he could ever find the words.

He laid a twenty on the table for their bill and held Marilyn's coat as she slipped her arms into the sleeves, then they made their silent way to the car.

The sky had darkened to a velvet blue by the time they arrived at the Wild Harbor Trading Post. Bob parked his CR-V next to a passenger van emblazoned with the Wild Harbor logo in the parking lot. A small crowd, around a dozen people, had gathered near the front door. A young man in a heavy coat came out of the building and stood on the stoop.

"I'm Darren. I'll be your guide tonight. In just a few minutes, we'll get in the van. The trailhead is only a couple of miles from here. There will be others who meet us there as well." Darren ran through a demonstration of how to use the simplified snowshoes. "You're all going to have a great time."

As promised, a few minutes later they all climbed into the Wild Harbor van. Darren got behind the wheel. "When we get there, we don't need to stay together as a group. Everyone can proceed at their own pace. Wild Harbor will be sending a van out every hour or so for pickups. The trail is well marked, and a few area businesses have sponsored break stations along the way. Please don't go off the path. You will be on a trail that winds back around to where you start."

They drove into a parking lot and piled out of the van. Darren fitted them with snowshoes and sent them off with a wave.

Soon the group had fanned out along the trail. Next to him, Marilyn giggled as she took wide, waddling steps. The snowshoes were strange on Bob's feet until he fell into a rhythm. It was simply a matter of keeping his legs slightly wider apart than normal and picking his feet up a little higher.

After a while he even stopped concentrating on his feet.

They moved along the trail in silence. Around them, the tree branches brushed together in a gentle whoosh, filling the air with their own kind of music. The candles flickered in their ice domes. Ahead, he saw more lights blinking in and out among the trees. As they grew nearer, they discovered the source.

In a clearing directly off the path, a small, outdoor chapel had been set up. A discreet sign indicated the Catholic church in town was sponsoring this area.

"How beautiful," Marilyn breathed. She tugged his arm, nearly knocking him off his snowshoes. "Let's go in."

He broke out in a cold sweat. Nope. There was no way he was stepping foot in that place. Or waddling a foot, he supposed, given his current foot gear.

Entering the open-air chapel felt too much like going into a church. And going into a church was only a small step from participating. He knew he was overreacting, but his heart was clawing its way out his throat, and around him, the world spun.

A recent conversation with a parishioner unspooled in his mind. *Great sermon, Pastor. I especially liked when you referred to the Trinity as the Father, Son, and Holy Goat.* The man had laughed and clapped him on the shoulder to show he was only kidding, but Bob knew that he'd been slipping, and his latest faux pas was only a symptom of that loss of passion.

Irrational or not, going into that small chapel ignited his fear that he had changed forever. Even participating in something as benign as a moonlit prayer felt like stepping back into the pulpit.

And the last thing he was planning to do was to be part of any religious ceremony.

But with the thought came the realization.

He wasn't just skipping Christmas. He was losing a part of himself he'd never thought would die.

His calling.

So much for optimism. This outing was becoming a disaster.

Marilyn moved into the clearing alone. She still couldn't figure out what was up with Bob lately. First at the restaurant and now here. Was this connected to the distance she'd been feeling between them?

Thank goodness she'd found a sweatshirt and leggings in her bag to wear for pjs last night, but she hoped she'd find a chance to try out her other, um, outfit.

Sure, she wanted to rekindle their spark, but more than that, she longed to connect with Bob. He kept pushing her away. Was it too much to hope that a scrap of fabric could bridge a gap?

Coming out of her nap earlier that day, her heart had twisted to see Bob slaving away at the puzzle. Not that he didn't deserve a break —he just seemed so set on ignoring the problem between them. When he'd suggested this outing, she'd taken a full breath for the first time in days.

Now, under the moonlight and stars playing hide and seek with the clouds scattered above, she believed anything could happen. If she could only get her husband to talk to her.

But first, a word with the Lord wouldn't hurt.

A few plank-and-stump benches were set in front of a rough cross. Candles shone around the edges of the clearing. Somewhere, a speaker played Christmas hymns. Overhead, the clouds blocked most of the stars, and the moon struggled to peek through the obstruction. Picking a bench near the front, she sat. The cold soaked through her jeans.

Keeping her eyes on the cross, she mouthed a few words from the Lord's Prayer. "Thine is the kingdom and the glory," she recited. "Lord, it's easy to see Your glory out here where everything is beautiful. Give me grace to see the glory everywhere else."

A peace stole over her. Maybe this trip wouldn't be a disaster after all.

Humming "God Rest You Merry, Gentlemen," she waddled on her snowshoes back out to where Bob waited.

"Ready?" he asked.

"You betcha." She looped her arm through his.

They took a few steps, but then her shoe got tangled in his and down she went.

"Marilyn!" Bob reached for her hand, but it slipped out of his grasp. She felt her ankle twist under her as she landed in the soft snow.

"Oh!" She lay where she'd fallen for a moment, catching her breath, the snow encasing her.

"Are you okay?" Bob reached out his hand again.

"I'm not sure. Help me up."

He grabbed both of her hands. She untangled her legs and, with a mighty tug, almost stood up. Bob shifted his stance and stepped on his own shoes.

"Whoops!" He landed *splat* beside her. They lay side by side, dazed. "How are we going to get up?"

"Maybe we live here now." She laughed.

"Need some help?" A tall man with longish, wavy dark hair towered over them, a blonde in a ponytail on his arm.

"We were just contemplating building an igloo down here," Marilyn said.

"Not a bad plan," the blonde said.

Beside her, Bob sat up. "I think if you give me a steady base, I can heft myself up." The man helped him to stand, then did the same for Marilyn.

"Let us know if you decide to build that igloo," he said as he snow-shoed away. "I may know someone in the resort business who can help."

Marilyn had snow everywhere—down her collar, up her sleeves. She gave herself a little shake.

Bob chuckled. "You remind me of a wet dog."

"Excuse me?"

"No, I just mean shaking yourself like that."

Okay, she had to admit it probably did look a little funny.

"Are you okay to walk?" Bob's brow furrowed as he spoke.

She took a few steps out onto the trail, moving like an eighty year old. Her ankle gave a twinge, but after a few steps, it felt normal again. "Nothing's broken. I'll probably be sore in the morning, though."

"Do you want to take off the snowshoes?" Bob caught up with her. "Should we turn around?"

"No. Let's finish. I'm having fun."

Overhead, the night deepened, a purple blanket filled with stars. Marilyn took a breath. Now was the time. "Bob, we should talk."

Beside her, Bob stiffened. "Let's not disturb the peace of the night."

"I'm just wondering what is on your mind. You seem so preoccupied." She stopped and put her hand on his arm.

"Is this about me not going into that outdoor chapel?"

"Yes. Well, not just that. You've been distant for a while now."

He opened his mouth. Closed it. She held her breath. Then he took a few steps down the trail. "It's no big deal. I just wasn't feeling it tonight."

He walked out ahead of her.

"Feeling what?" Feeling like being married? She tried to catch up, but her ankle slowed her down.

But with the cold that had slipped under the neck of her jacket, her heart shivered.

She bit back a sharp retort. She wouldn't gain anything by starting an argument.

They moved down the path, stopped for a cup of hot cocoa at the station sponsored by the bank, passed by a group of carolers, and were passed in turn by a clump of teenagers pushing and shoving each other in jest.

"Stop it, Tiago! You're making me nervous," one of the kids called. The laugh in his voice belied his words.

Then they came to a table covered in Christmas cookies. The red-and-gold sign read *Flashy Fox Bakery*. Marilyn chose a star-shaped cookie and bit it in half.

"These cookies are amazing!" Hints of almond and orange ran through the sweet sugar confection.

"If you think these are good, you should try our cinnamon rolls," the man behind the table said. "I'm Jim Fox and this is my wife, Elaine. Flashy Fox is our bakery."

"I think we definitely need to try out your claim," Bob said. "What days are you open this week?"

"We'll be open every day except Christmas." Elaine handed them each a business card. "Here's the address."

Marilyn tucked the card into her pocket. "Won't you want to be with your family during the holiday?"

Jim and Elaine shared a sad smile. Elaine clasped her hands together. "Not this year. Our granddaughter is living in Paris, and we haven't seen our grandsons in several years. It will be just Jim and me."

A pang shot through Marilyn. As much as she'd looked forward to a Christmas alone with Bob, she would have missed seeing Stella. Who knew where their daughter would end up after her program in Vienna ended? She might even decide to stay in Europe indefinitely. The sweet bite in Marilyn's mouth became as dry as sawdust.

"Thank you for the cookies," she said.

"See you at the bakery, maybe." Elaine smiled.

"Yeah, maybe." She wasn't promising anything. Best not to press her luck on getting Bob out of the cabin again.

She had to focus on her family. Getting Bob to open up to her was turning out to be like walking in snowshoes through mud.

CHAPTER 4

So far, this vacation had been just what Bob needed. Peace, quiet, and a total absence of responsibility. Sure, the snow-shoe adventure a couple nights ago had been fun, but he hadn't felt great about his reaction to the chapel and probably Marilyn deserved to know about that.

Not yet.

And how to tell her? He didn't have the first idea.

So, mostly, he'd hunkered down in his cabin for the last twenty-four hours finishing the one thousand-piece puzzle. He could even admit that it was probably time to talk to Marilyn about the things which were bothering him.

Maybe after breakfast.

He sat with Stella and Marilyn in the tiny cabin kitchen sharing a skillet of scrambled eggs. Hot coffee with a dash of cream filled the cup he lifted to his lips, the nutty aroma awakening his senses. Yep. He could get used to the peace of this place.

A knock at the cabin door interrupted their meal. "Romeo. How can I help you?"

Romeo was standing on the stoop. "I was…wondering if you guys would be interested in a bigger cabin. I've got one available, and I can help you shift your stuff into it whenever you want."

Bob glanced inside their cozy space and at the half-finished puzzle on the table. "That's okay. You don't have to put yourself out for us. We're fine here."

He heard Marilyn get up from the table and move to stand behind him. She put her hand on his arm. "What's all this?"

"Romeo said we can move to a bigger cabin, but I don't think we need to. We're already unpacked and settled in." He gave the kid a big smile.

Romeo shifted his weight. "Actually—"

"I think we should move, Bob." Marilyn moved into the doorway. "Thank you, Romeo. That's very thoughtful."

"Honey." Bob didn't know why his wife was acting this way. Normally she would never be one to put someone else out. "This cabin is fine for us. Why make Romeo go to all the trouble of moving things around?"

"Don't you think Stella would like a bed of her own?"

"She's fine on the couch. Aren't you, Stella?"

Stella joined them at the door. "I don't mind."

Romeo shoved his hands into his pockets. He started to say something, but Marilyn cut him off.

"I would like a bigger cabin. Let's take him up on it."

What had gotten into his normally laid-back wife? "Honey, we're fine. Romeo doesn't need to do us this favor."

"Actually, you'd be doing *me* a favor," he said. "I want to move one of my other guests. He's used to having this cabin, but I accidentally gave him the wrong one and he needs to be in this one for personal reasons. I'll move you to cabin five."

Oh. That explained the kid's nervousness. Bob hadn't missed the way he was almost dancing, shuffling his feet so much. "In that case, we'll be happy to switch." Romeo's face lost some of its stiffness. But, important things came first. "Would you like some breakfast, son? We have plenty and it sounds like something is alive inside of you."

At the table, Stella prompted Romeo to tell them a few stories about his smokejumping career. Seemed the kid—no, man—was a hero. Not that he'd say as much, but Bob could read between the lines of the stories he told.

"Sounds like you're a guy who likes adventure." Bob took a drink of his coffee, studying the man.

"It was a job, not a calling." Romeo looked him in the eye.

And yeah, Bob knew that sentiment too. In fact, lately his church work had seemed more like a job than a calling.

Romeo offered to wash the dishes while they gathered their clothes.

The three of them made quick work of packing their things. Romeo helped Stella carry her suitcase. Bob carried Marilyn's items, and she hefted a bag of groceries from the fridge. Their new cabin was similar to the first, except this one had two bedrooms. With doors.

As the girls settled their things into the bedrooms, Bob walked over to the bookshelf. What luck. They had puzzles here too. He selected one and set it out at the table.

A few minutes later, he already had several edge pieces fitted together. He heard the cabin door open and close but didn't turn to look.

He felt rather than saw Marilyn sit next to him. Must have been Stella who left, then. She reached across him and tucked a piece into place.

He began thinking about his church, and his own restlessness kicked in. He imagined the words he would say to Marilyn. Imagined opening up his mouth and confessing his doubts about his abilities.

Marilyn cleared her throat, and he looked up at her. She opened her mouth to speak. "Bob…"

Suddenly, the air seemed to empty from the room, and with the look in her eyes, his chest tightened.

Nope. He wasn't ready to talk to her.

He set down the puzzle piece he held, damp with perspiration he hadn't noticed before. "Now that we have the car back, I think I'll run into town to try that coffee shop we stopped at on our way here. Coffee Moose or whatever?"

"Oh," Marilyn said quietly.

"I know you'll probably want a nap, so I thought I'd get out of your hair for a while."

"That's…thoughtful. Maybe I will lie down for a rest."

And she must have been tired, because she headed straight for the bedroom, her back straight, shoulders high.

"I love you," he said, but the door had already swung shut.

Light snowflakes peppered his windshield on the drive down to Deep Haven. A quick flick of the wipers whisked them away. His mind twisted with thoughts not so easily brushed off.

This break from ministry duties was a welcome one, but it also highlighted the fact that he simply did not want to go back to it. How could he tell Marilyn that he didn't want to be a pastor anymore? Or, well, maybe that wasn't quite it. He just didn't know if he fit the position anymore. He wasn't old enough to retire yet—what would he even do with himself? He wasn't skilled in anything else. The pulpit was all he'd known.

The conversation he'd had with LeRoy Olson those months ago came back to mind.

I think you could be uniquely gifted to help us out, LeRoy had responded to Bob's "Why me?" *Think of it as a sponsored vacation. You and Marilyn always wanted to travel, right?*

True. They'd never found the time or money to travel like they'd always dreamed, but Bob couldn't imagine asking Marilyn to uproot their lives for a year abroad. Taking a week or two to jaunt around a country was a whole lot different than moving their entire lives to someplace they'd never been before.

Plus, it felt a little too close to just running away. Shouldn't he stay and try to figure out where this ambivalence—okay, maybe more like burnout—toward the ministry was coming from?

Some days he wondered if he was just fading away.

The trouble was, fading away sounded perfect to him.

He thought of last week's sermon, mortified once again by the way he had stumbled through it. And the one a few weeks before that, when he couldn't remember the words to the Lord's Prayer. And the week before, when the order of service had eluded him. Thank goodness Mary Ann, the church organist, had put an extra bulletin in the pulpit. He'd referenced it frequently.

Initially he'd been concerned about a medical problem, but he knew that it was more than that. It was a sort of indifference to the whole thing. An indifference he'd never felt before.

His breath came quicker, and he felt sweat pop out on his forehead. He pried a hand off the steering wheel and flipped on the car's air, letting a cool blast calm his racing heart.

Spotting a small gas station, he pulled into the parking lot and shifted into park.

Maybe it was time to admit he needed help.

He grabbed his cell phone from the center console in the dash and punched in LeRoy's number. It wouldn't hurt to hear the man's job offer again.

"Bob! It's good to hear from you!"

Bob's throat tightened at his friend's warm tone. "It's good to talk to you too." He gripped the steering wheel in front of him. "Have you found anyone for that position at Planting Hope yet?"

"I'm glad you called. No. We haven't found anyone yet. Any chance you're reconsidering?"

Suddenly Bob couldn't hold back any longer. The words he'd thought about telling Marilyn were spilling out of him. "I don't think I can cut it as a pastor anymore." He outlined all the mistakes he'd been making in the pulpit, his general indifference to people and their problems.

An indifference he was now realizing was just burnout in a mask.

Outside, the sky roiled with storm clouds. Bob flipped the car's heater back on. "I just want to give it all up, but then what will I do? This job is all I know."

He listened to the thrum of the engine for a moment, waiting for LeRoy's judgment. His condemnation.

"Sounds pretty normal to me."

Wait. What?

His friend's concern resonated over the line. "All pastors have rough patches. Every single one. Pastors are people too, you know." He gave a slight chuckle. "I think what you're going through is not unusual. I'm glad you're at least admitting it."

Bob blew out a long breath. "So you don't think I'm crazy?"

"Not crazy. Human." The sound of pages flipping came across the line. "I know you don't need a Bible bullet just now, but something you said reminded me of these verses in Psalm 94. 'If the Lord had not been my help, my soul would soon have lived in the land of silence. When I thought, "My foot slips," Your steadfast love, O Lord, held me up. When the cares of my heart are many, Your consolations cheer my soul.'" LeRoy paused. When he spoke again, his words were arrows. "You need the Lord's consolation right now. When was the last time someone told you that God loves you?"

Bob could only grunt a reply.

"Well, it's true, my friend. I know you tell it to others often enough, but you need to hear it too. God's love is for you. That's what Christmas is all about, after all."

"I came up to Deep Haven to escape Christmas."

"The trappings of Christmas, sure. But you can't escape the reason for Christmas, no matter how hard you try."

LeRoy's words were punching against the wall Bob had carefully constructed. "I should go. Thanks for the chat."

"Bob, I don't want you to be Jonah, with the job in Botswana as your own personal Nineveh, but the offer stands if you think you need a break. Just remember, God is for you."

Bob's vision went swimmy for a moment. "Thanks again." He cut the call and got back onto the road.

Turning onto Deep Haven's main drag, he spotted the sign for the Java Cup. Soon he parked and was walking in. Twinkle lights were strung from every surface, and "Silver Bells" rang through the room.

The line to the counter was long. It looked like the whole town had the same idea as him.

A man queued up behind him. Chiseled jaw. Tall. Dark. Muscular. Bob felt dwarfed by his frame. The man sighed and pulled a hat from his close-cropped hair. Bob gave a sympathetic look. "Long line."

"Yeah, I really don't have time for this, but if I don't get some caffeine, I'll never make it through this day."

"You can go ahead of me if you want." Bob moved to the side and let the man take his place.

"Thanks, I appreciate it." The man peered closer at him. "Do I know you from somewhere?"

"Probably not. I'm here on vacation. Staying with my family at the Evergreen Resort a little ways out of town."

"I'm staying at Evergreen too. Duke Lowry." He thrust out his hand and Bob shook it.

"Bob Brown."

The line moved forward two paces. A strong smell of caramel and hot milk filled the air.

"Say, you didn't happen to see someone around the resort driving a red vintage Mustang yesterday afternoon, did you?" Duke asked.

He fished back in his memories for images of the vehicles he'd noticed. None were sports cars. "No. I would've remembered seeing a classic like that. Is your car missing?"

"Something like that. It's not my car. It belongs to a friend and went missing from the resort garage yesterday."

They'd finally reached the front of the line. Duke gave his order to the barista, then Bob ordered a large Americano. They stepped aside to wait for their drinks.

Part of him longed to sit with Duke and hear his story, to encourage him. As much as Duke was passing this off, Bob wondered if there was more going on. Something deeper. But he wasn't here to pastor this random guy in line. He wasn't even going to admit to *being* a pastor. He certainly wasn't going to get involved.

But LeRoy's words were ringing in his ears, even as the barista put his order on the counter. He picked up the cup, then walked up to

Duke. "Have a little faith. Christmas is the time of miracles. One might show up where you least expect it."

The big man looked skeptical. Bob shrugged. "It couldn't hurt to ask for guidance. If you're a believing man, send up a prayer. God is, after all, in the business of finding lost things."

Duke gave him a thin-lipped nod.

Huh. Maybe he should take his own advice.

Because it would take a miracle to find his lost passion for ministry.

Marilyn sat at the table and stared into the fire. Maybe their marriage was further gone than she thought. Bob had fairly bolted out of the chair rather than talk to her.

Had he really not noticed her advances? Or hadn't he wanted to reciprocate? It might take more than sexy lingerie to fix what was broken between them. She brushed at the wetness on her cheeks.

Sitting around here wasn't going to fix the problem.

She glanced at the clock. Ten thirty in the morning was definitely too early for a nap.

Stella was still gone. She'd left earlier, saying something about catching up with Romeo. What exactly was going on with those two? Another mystery Marilyn would have to clear up.

Maybe a stroll around the grounds would bring some clarity. She'd have a chance to walk and pray. Some of her best connections with her Savior happened under the sky. It seemed like moving her feet also moved her heart.

Outside, a light snow was falling. She walked toward the lake, the snow crunching under her boots.

"Lord," she whispered, her breath coming in white puffs. "How can I reach him? Is my husband lost to me?"

A jingling noise caught her ear. She searched for the source. There. Up near the main house, a huge black-and-white horse stood, stamping its hooves on the frozen ground. She caught a glimpse of

Stella's blue hat beyond. A well-built man in a cowboy hat was hitching the horse to what looked like an honest-to-goodness sleigh.

Her feet moved toward the little tableau as though they had minds of their own.

She could clap her hands in joy.

A sleigh ride?

God sure had a way of answering prayers. She couldn't imagine anything more romantic than snuggling under a blanket while a sleigh whooshed over the ground, snow amongst the pines making everything look perfect like a snow globe.

She walked up to the horse. Oh my. This horse was even bigger up close, its shoulder nearly reaching the top of her head. She stood near its head and tentatively reached up a hand. A white stripe ran down the horse's dark face. His right ear twitched, and he snorted. She backed up a step.

"It's okay, he won't bite." The man in the cowboy hat walked over from the back of the sleigh.

Slipping off her glove, Marilyn stroked the velvety nose. "What's his name?"

"His name is Domino Effect. But we usually just call him Domino."

"Domino. That suits him. Pardon me for asking the obvious, but are you giving sleigh rides?"

"How'd you guess?" The good-natured wink he gave her told her he was teasing. "Stella called"—he gestured to where Romeo was hefting something out of the bed of the truck, Stella hovering nearby —"and suggested it for the Evergreen guests and a few others in town. Seemed like a good idea to us over at the Trinity Horse Camp, and Domino here could use the practice. We're thinking of starting this up as a regular thing in the winter, but we're not up to snuff yet."

"Well, it sounds marvelous. How do I get signed up?"

"I think Romeo, or that pretty Stella girl over there, is keeping some kind of list."

"Stella is my daughter."

He dipped his chin, acknowledging her. "I'm sure she can help you."

She gave Domino one last pat and then walked over to her daughter. "I hear you're the one to talk to about taking a sleigh ride."

Stella was holding a clipboard against her chest. "That's right."

"I thought we were here for a break, not for work. Or maybe you're just making music with that pair of blue eyes." She lifted her chin toward Romeo, who was now talking with the horse wrangler, his animated arms moving in time to his words.

"Mom!"

"Calm down. Listen, I want to sign me and Dad up for a ride. Do you have an opening?"

Stella loosened her stranglehold on the clipboard and held it out in front of herself. She ran a finger down the paper. "Yep, I have a couple of openings this afternoon." She wrote something down. "I'm heading out with Romeo in a few minutes, but Jesse, the guy who is doing the rides, will be here. He'll tell you what to do."

Perfect. Operation Sleigh Ride was a go.

Now she just needed her husband to get home. She sent him a quick text in what she hoped was a casual tone, asking about his ETA, before heading back to their cabin.

She'd read two chapters of her Agatha Christie novel when she heard the car with its signature engine tick pull up outside. Soon a door slammed, and she waited for Bob to come through the door. She giggled as she thought about what he would say to their sleigh ride adventure.

Instead of the cabin door opening, she heard voices. Peeking through the front window, she saw Bob conversing with an older man who wasn't wearing a jacket. Bob clapped him on the shoulder and steered him toward their cabin.

What in the...

"Marilyn?" Bob's face crinkled in a smile as he led the older man through the door. "This is my new friend, Gerald. I thought he'd like to come in for a little lunch."

She stared at him a moment. Even in the middle of nowhere, Bob couldn't let a stranger stay a stranger. Would it kill him to ask her before inviting someone in for lunch? Then again, his gregarious nature was one of the things that had attracted her in the first place.

"Of course." She gritted her teeth. "I can whip up a few sandwiches for us."

"Oh, no, I can do it. I didn't mean you had to serve us. Sit down. I'll make the sandwiches. Besides, I think you'll like hearing Gerald's story." Bob went to the tiny fridge and began pulling meat and cheese out.

Marilyn looked at him in wonder. It wasn't often Bob was the one making food. Nothing sexist about it—just the way it worked in their marriage. She turned to their, uh, guest. "Want to sit at the table, Gerald? It looks like our waiter will be serving roast beef on rye any minute." She poured their guest a cup of coffee and took a seat opposite him.

From the counter, Bob said, "Gerald was telling me about his wife Phyllis. They used to come here every year around this time."

The old man, who looked to be pushing ninety, nodded. "Phyllis and I came here for many years. I don't remember why she couldn't come this year." His face clouded and he stared into nothingness for a heartbeat. His next words came slower. "Maybe her mother needed her. She always goes to help her mother with her baby brother. That boy is so fussy. Her mama needs all the help she can get this time of year."

Oh.

Bob gave her a look over his shoulder. She tilted her chin slightly. Yes. She understood what this was about now.

"Tell me about your wife." For the next few minutes, Gerald told her stories about his Phyllis and the red car they used to own. She laughed at the antics the couple had gotten into, like the time Gerald had taken Phyllis out in the field to check on the crops but the car battery died.

"I swear I wasn't trying to make a move on her or anything!" he said, eyes twinkling. "The car had an old battery and it just died. My brother had to rescue us in the tractor. We never did live that one down."

A knock sounded at the door. Bob opened it to find a young man, maybe in his late thirties or early forties, standing there. "Have you seen— Grandpa! What are you doing here?"

"Hi, Tom. I met some friends." Gerald waved.

Tom's face relaxed. "Thank goodness. I thought I'd lost him."

"I hope you don't mind," Bob said. "I found him outside without a coat on. We were going to feed him lunch and then contact the authorities."

"It's fine. I'm glad he's all right." Tom rubbed the back of his neck. "I've already lost him once on this trip. Took five years off my life."

"Let's step outside a minute." Bob took the younger man by the arm and moved out the door, shutting it behind himself.

Marilyn focused back on Gerald. "It's so nice that your grandson could be here with you."

"Yes, he's a good boy."

Bob came back in, shutting the door behind him. "Good news, Gerald. Tom said you could have lunch with us. I'll walk you back home a little later."

They ate their sandwiches, their conversation seasoned with stories.

Marilyn looked at the clock. Fifteen minutes until their scheduled sleigh ride. "Um, Bob, can you join me in the bedroom for a minute?"

"I'll clear the table." Gerald began stacking plates.

"I can do that later," Bob said.

"Least I can do," the old man said.

She shut the door behind them and took Bob's hand. "I've signed us up for an adventure." He quirked an eyebrow, but she was determined. "We're going on a sleigh ride!" She held her breath. Would he refuse? Could he hear how much she wanted to do this with him?

"Sounds like fun."

"Really?"

"Sure. Let's do it."

"Okay! It starts in fifteen minutes though, so we need to hustle." She felt like clapping her hands together in glee.

Bob grinned back at her. His crooked smile, hidden for so long lately, and the twinkle in his eye lit a spark in her heart. Oh, the man was handsome. Much better looking than Harrison Ford could ever be. He'd grown dearer to her with every year.

He pulled open the door. "Gerald? How would you like to go on a sleigh ride?"

Wait. What? She reached out to pull him back through the bedroom door, but he was already fully in the kitchen area.

"My lovely wife has signed us up for a ride. We'd love for you to come."

She was sure her mouth stood open. As Gerald turned her way, she quickly schooled her features into what she hoped was a warm smile. "Yes, we'd love for you to come." If she'd stumbled on the words, she prayed the men hadn't noticed.

Great.

CHAPTER 5

Okay, maybe she had been a little dramatic before.

Standing in the crisp December air had a way of cooling her off, bringing clarity. Who cared if Gerald rode along? It wasn't like they were on a private sleigh ride; the driver would be there, after all.

She could still bring some romance to this outing.

The light snow from earlier had cleared, and now the sky was a brilliant sapphire. The anxiety of the general scramble for hats, gloves, and jackets just a few moments ago in the cabin fell away as they walked toward the sleigh waiting near the edge of the woods ringing the property.

The sleigh had two seats facing each other. A heavy blanket was laid across each seat. After the driver checked their names off the list, Marilyn climbed in and scooted over for Bob to sit next to her. Gerald clambered in opposite. A hanging rope of sleigh bells on the horse's harness tinkled a melody.

Their driver introduced himself as Jesse Schmidt. He looked the part of a winter cowboy in his fur-lined suede jacket, flannel-lined jeans turned up at the cuff, and well-worn Stetson. But the stereotype of the taciturn cowboy didn't fit this guy. He kept going on and on about local history, the habits of horses, the average snowfall of the area, and several other things Marilyn didn't give a hoot about. When he started to explain that Domino was a Gypsy Vanner cross, she just tuned him out altogether.

She was trying hard to shake her bad attitude, she really was, but even the beautiful trail through the pines, air crisp with the smell of new-fallen snow, couldn't cheer her up.

Beside her, Bob leaned forward. "I can see that you love this area."

Jesse shot a glance back at them. His teeth gleamed white in his wide smile. "I sure do. People don't usually associate horses with northern Minnesota, but it's the perfect life for me."

"Maybe you're built a little like that animal, Domino, there," Bob said. "Tough, strong, and filled with high spirits."

"True enough." Jesse nodded once.

"My Phyllis was like that," Gerald said. "She was a tough gal, but underneath it all she could be a softy." He wiped at his eyes. "She would have loved this sleigh ride. She had a real nose for adventure."

Marilyn's irritation melted, then evaporated into the cold winter air. How could she hold on to it after that? She shifted in her seat, relaxed her shoulders. Bob covered her hand with his own, their gloves blocking any real contact.

Something moved in the corner of her eye, and then suddenly a rabbit ran straight between the horse's legs. The horse reared, then leaped forward, jerking the sleigh down the trail.

"Whoa!"

Jesse tried to rein in the horse, but the animal took off. Marilyn grabbed the side of the sleigh with one hand and Bob's arm with the other and muffled a scream.

The sleigh bells rang in a cacophony of noise.

They hit a bump and the sleigh launched into the air.

Tilted.

Marilyn caught a view of the snowbank across the sleigh on the left, and she slid until she was practically sitting in Bob's lap. Bob threw his arm out in front of her, stopping her slide.

Across from them, Gerald wore a look of horror, hands clutching both sides of the sleigh.

They landed back in their seats with a thump, the sleigh upright but the horse still spooked. He ran them off the trail until he knocked the sleigh into a pine tree.

It shuddered to a standstill.

In the silence, the thunder of her heartbeat, they all stared at each other.

"Well, that could have been much worse," Gerald finally said. He let go of the edge of the sleigh.

Next to her, Bob rubbed at his arm. "Everyone okay? That's going to leave a bruise."

Marilyn took a long breath. Up front, Jesse clambered down from the driver's box. The sleigh rubbed against the tree with a screech.

"What is that swishing noise?" Marilyn looked up just as—

The pine tree above them dumped all its snow onto their heads.

Marilyn shrieked as snow fell down her open collar and icy fingers ran down her back.

Her face full of snow, Marilyn looked at the men. Snow clumped on their heads and shoulders and clung to their eyelashes like they were some sort of abominable snowmen.

Ridiculous.

And just like that, she started to laugh. Bob joined in, then Gerald, and suddenly they were all hooting in laughter.

"Everybody all right back there?" Jesse said as he came around the sleigh.

She couldn't stop laughing.

"Okay. Good. Everybody out so I can assess the damage."

They climbed out and shook the snow from their clothes. Gerald wandered over to the trail and stood looking down the track.

Bob reached up and brushed the snow from her hair, catching her gaze for a moment. She blinked and turned away. For a moment there, the relief and release of fear had felt almost like…romance. Too many emotions in one short breath.

Bob put his arm around her waist and spun her to face him. She met his eyes again, a thrill racing down her spine. He wound his other arm around her back and leaned in. "Remember when we got dumped off that four-wheeler on our honeymoon?"

"We?" She put her hands on his chest. "As I recall, I was the only one who fell off. You were halfway across the county before you noticed." But then he'd circled back around, face white with fear. He'd cut the engine and dropped to the ground next to her. Scooping her into his arms, he'd asked if she was all right, then covered her face with kisses. She'd gripped his collar and pulled him to her, his taste that of sweet cinnamon gum. His lips had gentled as their breathing quickened. Fire had shot through her as he laced his fingers through her hair.

Remembering, she closed her eyes, tipping her mouth up.

"One flesh, right?" he teased softly. "If you fall, we fall."

She opened her eyes. His were in hers, brown, holding on.

Her throat tightened, something deeper than romance moving inside her.

"I'm gonna need some help pushing over here." Jesse's voice cut through the air and straight between them.

Didn't the man have any sense of timing? Read the room, driver.

Marilyn stood to the side as Bob and Jesse pushed against the sleigh until it moved far enough away from the tree that the horse could pull it back onto the trail. Jesse gave the side panel of the sleigh a shake, then knelt on the ground to inspect the runners.

"The paint job is a little banged up, but the rest of her seems sound." Jesse clapped his hands together, brushing the snow from his gloves. "We'd better get you back before we run into another rabbit."

They rode home in silence. But snuggling closer to Bob, Marilyn let herself believe that maybe they weren't goners after all.

Getting out of the sleigh at Evergreen felt something like the end of a race. Bob couldn't help the sigh of relief he let go as the sleigh came to a stop.

"We should get you back to your grandson," he said to Gerald.

"Oh? Did my grandson come along?" Gerald asked, clearly confused again. Marilyn walked on his right side and Bob on his left as they made their way down the trail to the old guy's cabin.

"I'm sure Phyllis will be glad to see me. We don't usually spend time apart."

Bob grabbed Gerald's upper arm as the older man slipped a little on the snow. "Steady there."

"Thank you. You're doing the Lord's work, helping an old man like me." Gerald patted the hand gripping his arm.

"Walking with you is just a small thing."

Gerald stopped and looked at Bob. His eyes cleared for a moment. "Even small things can make a big difference."

He tried not to snort out a laugh. "Like what?"

"The baby Jesus was a small thing, but He made a big impact. I think God loves to use the small things."

Well, Gerald had him there. They began walking again toward cabin six.

Bob knocked on the cabin door. Tom answered. Bob pulled him aside as Marilyn walked Gerald into the warmth inside. "He may be a little shook up." He explained about the minor accident on the trail.

Tom's eyes widened. "Oh no! Should I take him to the ER?"

"No need for that." Bob held up a hand. "No one was hurt, but Gerald may be more stiff than normal. I wanted you to know about it in case he brings it up."

"Thank you for spending time with him today. He misses Grandma. Ever since she passed away his dementia has gotten worse." Tom rubbed his hand across the back of his neck. "We thought this trip would bring some normalcy. It's good for him to spend time with other people."

"It was our pleasure. He's fun to be around. And he has some great stories. You should consider writing some of them down, for posterity if nothing else."

Tom's quick smile came like a flash of sunlight. "Not a bad thought. I'll see what Grandpa thinks of it."

Marilyn came back to the door. They said goodbye to Tom and Gerald and walked away.

"Let's take a walk by the lake," Marilyn said. "I need to work out a few of these kinks. I don't think I can bear going back to the cabin and sitting down just yet."

Maybe now was the time to tell her about LeRoy's job offer in Botswana. Now, in the peace of the afternoon with the winter sun glinting on the freshly fallen snow. Right now, before he chickened out.

Except.

Telling her about Botswana meant telling her that he didn't think he wanted to do pastoral ministry anymore. A year running away to Botswana wasn't what he needed. This break, this absence of work pressure and any need to be the spiritual one in any conversation, was what he needed. He just wished it could last for longer.

Maybe what he should be telling Marilyn about was the fatigue that crept over him when he thought of standing in front of a congregation again.

No.

He wasn't going to burden her with any of that. It was his problem, and he needed to deal with it. She was always so supportive of him—he could spare her this heartache and worry.

Besides, he didn't want to hear her confirm that she was disappointed in him for even thinking of leaving the ministry.

Most of all, he couldn't risk that Marilyn would think it was a good idea. Couldn't imagine hearing her confirm that his fear was coming true—that he *was* losing it.

"Can we slow down?" Marilyn's breath came in short puffs.

He pulled up short, and she stumbled to a stop beside him. "Sorry. I didn't realize how fast I was going."

"You are like a locomotive. Is there something on your mind?"

Her gentle invitation stopped him for a moment. But. Picturing her saying the words "I can't believe you'd quit the ministry" shut down any thought of sharing. Until he figured things out, he wanted to keep this close. "Nope."

Her face closed. She started walking again. Her next comment was oh so casual. "I brought a couple of strings of lights. I thought we could hang them over the fireplace today. You know, make the cabin a little more festive."

She'd done what?

What part of skipping Christmas didn't she understand? Okay, even to himself that was harsh. But, "I don't want any of that."

"I know you don't want a big Christmas thing, but I thought a few twinkle lights would be fine. Just to add some atmosphere and romance."

"I don't want any of that." And yeah, he was repeating himself, but he couldn't help it. Even thinking of stringing up lights was causing an itch to develop along the top of his shoulders.

She stopped, moved in front of him, and stared at him until he met her gaze. "What. Is. Up. With. You?"

"I'm fine." Liar. "I just don't want any of the trappings of Christmas this year." He resisted the urge to rub at the itch spreading to his chest. "We talked about this."

"I thought maybe it would be different now that Stella is here. Maybe we'd want it to be more like normal." She finally broke her intense gaze. "I threw the lights in the trunk when I put the gifts in there. It wouldn't take much to hang them up."

"It's not the work, it's the principle of the thing."

She considered him a long moment, as if trying to read his mind. He finally looked away.

She sighed. "Fine. You're right. We agreed not to do traditional Christmas this year. Forget I said anything." She turned and walked away.

The sight of her walking away from him, back stiff, hands clenched, jostled something loose in his heart.

He'd hurt her.

"Marilyn, wait!" He jogged after her, nearly to the driveway. "Marilyn!"

Her head was down, and maybe she was crying, because that could be the only reason she didn't step out of the way as a truck came barreling into the lot.

It hit the brakes and slid, and Bob reached her just in time to yank her into a snowbank.

Romeo barreled out of the truck. "Are you okay? I'm so sorry—I didn't see you." He walked over to them, panic in his eyes.

"We're fine. But maybe you need to slow down, son." He helped Marilyn up.

"Mom!" Stella came around the truck. "Are you hurt?"

Marilyn glanced at Bob, then back to Stella. "I'm fine."

Stella stuck her arm through hers. "Good." She glanced at Romeo. Smiled.

Something shifted inside Bob. Wait—was something going on between the resort manager and his daughter?

Romeo lifted a hand. Turned to Bob. "Sorry, again. The last thing I want is to run over your wife!"

Bob gave him a thin smile. Yeah, well him too.

But it seemed that he'd already done that.

CHAPTER 6

He'd almost lost his wife. The thought kept pounding through Bob's mind as he followed his wife down the path to the cabin.

Stella and her friend Romeo had pulled up shortly after, but Marilyn hadn't said anything to her about the near accident as they walked together. So, yeah, maybe it hadn't been that close, but for a moment there, the close call had left Bob breathless.

He might walk away from his ministry, but he couldn't imagine a life without his wife.

Tonight. He would tell her everything tonight.

They reached the cabin, and Marilyn pushed ahead to brush some snow off the steps. She turned back and gave them a tiny smile as she pushed open the door.

With so much to be thankful for, why did he always want more?

Stella went into her bedroom, and Bob met Marilyn by the kitchen table. "I have an idea."

Marilyn gazed steadily at him. "Oh? What's that?" She tugged her jacket off and reached for his.

"Let's give Stella her gift now."

Marilyn blinked. "Stella's gift?"

"Yeah, let's give it to her now." He handed his jacket over. "She just seems a little lost and could use some cheering up. We're not doing the traditional Christmas thing this year, so why not?"

Marilyn folded the jackets over her arm. "Okay, I guess. I don't see the harm. Go and get it and I'll hang these up."

In three steps he was in the bedroom and shuffling through the luggage. Three packages were tucked into Marilyn's bag. Shoot! The tags had fallen off of them. How many did Marilyn say she'd brought for Stella?

Picking up all three, he figured Marilyn could sort them out.

His girls were already sitting by the fire. He set the packages on an end table and grabbed the fire poker. He gave the burning log a turn before adding another one.

"Hot chocolate!" Marilyn punctuated her declaration by standing. She swiped a package off the stack and headed to the kitchenette.

"Did you have a good day?" Bob asked Stella. Honestly, she looked a little dazed. Not for the first time, he wished he could peer straight into her thoughts.

"Yes. It was good." Stella's knees must be really interesting for as much as she was studying them. Also, maybe she should move farther from the fire, because her cheeks were flushed.

"Do anything interesting?"

She jumped at the question. "Oh. I went with Romeo into town. He had to do some snow removal."

"Is everything okay?" His daughter's face was shuttered. Unreadable. "You look deep in thought."

"I'm fine." And yeah, her lips curved up into the semblance of a smile, a hint of a sparkle in her eyes. "Just thinking about the day."

"You've sure been spending a lot of time with Romeo. Are you sure that's a good idea? We're only here for a short time, and I know your mom encouraged you to help, but—" He broke off as her head came up, and she looked him straight in the eye.

"Spending time with Romeo is not a problem. He's a great guy." Now the sparkle in her eye turned brilliant. Bright spots appeared on her cheeks. "I just don't want to talk about it."

Just then, Marilyn came back with three steaming cups. He relaxed against the couch back. The rich aroma of the hot cocoa filled the gaps between them.

Maybe he was imagining all of it—Marilyn's coolness, Stella's strange silence. But it seemed this Christmas everyone in the family was tangled in their own personal conundrum.

And he didn't know how to get himself untangled, let alone help someone else. "Girls," he started, but then Marilyn grabbed the stack of remaining gifts and plopped them in Stella's lap.

"These are for you," Marilyn said, and the moment passed.

Stella set her cup on the table nested between the chairs. "I'm sorry I didn't bring your gifts. I actually mailed them to your house last week. I didn't want to forget to give them to you in the recital rush."

"That's okay, honey. We just wanted you to have your present. No need to worry about us. Marilyn, is that the right one for Stella? I'm sorry, the tags fell off." He pointed at the gift on top.

"Actually, they both are for Stella," Marilyn said. She gestured to the presents. "We were going to give them to you in Duluth, but when you decided to come with us, I thought it would be more fun to open them here."

"What about the other one?" Bob asked.

Marilyn looked at him with wide, innocent eyes. "What other one?"

"The one you stashed in the kitchen." Was he going crazy or was she?

Stella jumped up and set her gifts on her chair. "I'll get it." She handed him the last gift.

Marilyn started to say something. Stopped.

Stella sat down again and put her presents back in her lap.

The silence stretched long. What was she waiting for? "Go ahead, open them."

"Dad, aren't you forgetting something?" Stella's eyes clouded in confusion.

"I don't think so. Did you think this one was yours too?" He looked to Marilyn. "Is this one hers?"

Marilyn made a small choking sound and shook her head. "It's yours. For later." Her cheeks flamed as she whispered the words.

Oh. He didn't know what to say. Especially since he hadn't bought her a gift. Panic sluiced through him. "I didn't...we said..."

"It's okay." Marilyn turned to Stella.

"Okay, then. Go ahead, Stella."

"Shouldn't we read the Christmas story first? We always do that."

Shoot.

He swallowed the last of his hot chocolate. He wished the cup had been bigger—it would have been a handy stalling tactic. "I'm not going to read the Christmas story this year. I'm, um, skipping it."

He could hear the clock on the wall ticking the seconds past.

Stella just stared at him.

Even to his own ears, his words sounded foreign. Not reading the Christmas story? But for some reason, the thought of sinking into the miracle, the love of God, felt...

Well, he just couldn't face God in light of the questions in his soul.

Next to him, Marilyn pasted on a huge smile. "That's right. Since Dad doesn't have to work this Christmas, we're skipping some of our normal Christmas traditions this year. Go ahead, open your gifts."

Stella looked at Marilyn and then at him. He gave her a smile and nod. Nothing was wrong. They'd be okay. Really.

Stella exchanged another look with her mother, then began to turn her gift over.

A weight pulled at Bob, and his head dropped. "Wait."

Both women looked at him.

"Stella, why don't you read Luke 2. I might be skipping the trappings of Christmas, but we should still honor the One we are celebrating."

There. He felt better. He wasn't dodging God. Just…

Oh, whatever.

While Stella opened a Bible reading app on her phone, Bob busied himself with cleaning up the hot chocolate cups. Soon, Stella's clear voice rang out the familiar words. "'In those days Caesar Augustus issued a decree…'" Bob sank back in his chair and closed his eyes. For some reason, Stella's soothing cadence calmed him. He even found himself whispering along to the memorized words of the angels. "'Glory to God in the highest heaven, and on earth peace to those on whom His favor rests.'"

After Stella finished, the family sat in silence for a heartbeat.

"That was beautiful, honey. Thank you." Marilyn patted Stella's hand. "Now it's gift time."

Stella opened her first gift. Inside the first small box lay a copy of a Fodor's guide to travel in Vienna along with a foodies book about Viennese restaurants.

"Uh, thanks, guys." Stella set the package next to her chair without leafing through the books. She opened the second package. It was a travel mug, red-and-white striped like the flag of Austria.

"We knew you couldn't pack much, so I kept your gifts simple this year." Marilyn reached for the coffee mug and pulled off the lid. "You might like what is filling this mug better than coffee." She handed the lidless cup back to Stella, who tipped it over and dumped a roll of cash onto her lap. "We thought you might like a little 'mad money' as my mom used to say. Use it for something fun."

Stella smiled, but her eyes were dull. "Thanks. These are great. Dad, you should open yours."

Marilyn jumped. "No!"

"C'mon, Mom. It isn't fair that I'm the only one with a present."

Bob held the shirt-box-style gift in his hand. It was tied with a red ribbon and very light. He reached for the ribbon. Marilyn grabbed at it, but he lifted it over his head.

"Bob, give it back to me," Marilyn said, reaching again. Somehow, one of her fingers got caught in the ribbon. She yanked it, and suddenly, the box flew out of his hands. The ribbon ended up in Marilyn's hand, and the box popped open.

Something red and glittery spilled out onto the floor.

Stella picked it up and it unfurled, silky and red and lacy, and everything in his body simply stopped.

Was that…a *nightie*?

Marilyn sat in the living room of the cottage but wished she could melt straight through the floor.

She just might be the stupidest person on earth. First, thinking that a sleigh ride would reignite some long-dead spark. Then this silly gift exchange.

Watching that nightie dangle from Stella's fingers caused her brain to stop functioning. She knew she should do something but couldn't make herself move.

Her cheeks—no, her entire body—turned to flames.

Stella's eyebrows rose, and she looked at her mom in a sort of wide-eyed confusion. "Mom?"

Stella's single word unlocked Marilyn's muscles, and she stood, her head swimming a little. "Give me that." Marilyn tugged the satin from her daughter's hand, turned, and headed straight for the bedroom.

Shut the door.

Throwing herself on the bed in her room, she buried her hot face into the cool relief of the pillow.

She heard the murmur of voices in the other room, then a few moments later, the front door opened and closed.

Then the bedroom door opened.

The bed creaked and sagged. Bob. She turned her head and cracked one eyelid in his direction.

"I'm sorry. I never should have done that." Bob reached a hand to her but stopped midway, dropped it back into his lap.

She rolled over. Sighed. "I wanted to give you that privately."

He nodded, his mouth a grim line. "I thought I was being funny."

"Well, har har. That was super funny."

"No need to get sarcastic."

He wasn't the one humiliated in front of her daughter, and suddenly the fact that she'd had to go to…such lengths to…well, save their doomed marriage rose up inside her and simply ignited everything simmering inside.

"Don't tell me how to be!" She sat up, nearly sliding off the bed in her haste. "I'm sure Stella is mortified. She doesn't want to think about us in that way."

"Stella will be fine. She can't really be that ignorant about her parents." Bob shifted on the bed, turning to her. "If you'd told me it was private, I wouldn't have teased you."

Of all the…

"So now it's my fault?" Her jaw hurt from clenching it so hard.

"Of course not. I just meant…it *was* with the other gifts." He stared at the ceiling.

"Fine. Whatever. It's over now." She stood and crossed to the small bureau against the wall. Opened a drawer and threw the stupid garment in.

"It's not even close to over. In fact, you've been mad this entire trip. Talk to me. What's going on?"

Oh, that was rich. "Talk to you? All you've done these past few days is ignore me. Why should I talk to you now?"

"I don't really understand what is going on here."

"I thought maybe I could add some romance to our trip, is all. Clearly I was way off base."

He ran a hand through his hair, making it stand on end. "Romance is the last thing on my mind."

She snorted. "I noticed."

He held out a hand to her. "Seriously, Marilyn, I don't think a nightie will fix anything."

A beat. Because yes, right then, he'd just confirmed…well, maybe her worst fears weren't just a nightmare, but real. Her eyes started to burn, her voice cutting soft, ragged.

"I just wanted to do something fun and spontaneous. I didn't want to end up like the Wilsons." She took a breath. Held it.

He blinked at her, then, "Jeff and Wendy? What does…this gift have to do with them?"

She shook her head. "Are you serious right now? You have been acting strange since we heard about them."

Now he stood. "I really don't know what you're talking about. We are nothing like the Wilsons."

Fine. Whatever. A weariness crept over her.

"I guess it's nothing." She picked up the clothes she'd been wearing at nighttime. "I'm going to go change for bed."

"At six thirty?" Bob's eyebrows crept nearly to his hairline.

She pushed past him and out the bedroom door. "I'm tired."

When she came out of the bathroom, Bob was in his pjs and had slipped under the covers. She climbed into her side of the bed and rolled away from him.

So much for romance. So much for connection.

Maybe they were headed exactly in the direction of the Wilsons.

CHAPTER 7

There was no chasm so wide as the foot of space in bed between a married couple who were angry at each other. No bedcover as small, either.

Marilyn had spent the night tugging on her share of the duvet, refusing to roll closer to Bob. She woke, shivering in the dark dawn of a northern morning. On the other side of the bed, Bob's deep breathing told her he was still sleeping soundly. Probably because he'd won the tug-of-war with the blanket and was now wrapped like a burrito.

Might as well get up. A cup of coffee would fix some of what ailed her.

She pulled on a pair of fuzzy socks and padded out to the kitchen. The door to Stella's room stood open. Bed made. Hmm. That was strange. She must've gotten up even earlier than Marilyn.

Maybe Stella had texted Bob her early-morning whereabouts. She would ask him when he got up.

Except…right. She wasn't speaking to Bob right now. She sent her own text to Stella.

Where are you? After a few moments, she gave up on watching for an immediate answer.

She wrapped up in her coat and took her coffee outside. The sun was valiantly trying to creep over the horizon, its feeble rays poking at the clouds.

After plucking her cell out of her coat pocket, she dialed her sister.

Her sister answered on the second ring. "Mars! What are you doing calling me on your vacation?"

"Good morning, Liz. Are you ready for Christmas?" She pictured her sister in her signature reindeer slippers and the elf sweater she always broke out of the closet this time of year, probably sitting with a cup of coffee by her hearth in her Minneapolis home.

"I think I've gotten every Christmas cookie baked, and my turkey is thawing. Should be ready just in time for Christmas Day on Sunday. How is your getaway?"

"It's beautiful up here."

"Not what I meant. What about the…you know…"

Now she regretted telling her sister about the negligee. But she'd needed some advice on what size to buy. "The gift exchange was a complete disaster." She relayed a little of what had happened. By the end of the story, Liz's laughter echoed through the phone.

At least someone could laugh.

Through her chuckles she asked, "What did Stella say?"

"She didn't say anything. She just had this horrified look on her face. She sat there barely blinking. I snatched the nightie away and fled."

"Poor Stella." Another chuckle.

"Poor Stella? I think you mean poor Marilyn. What was I thinking, trying to get him to notice me that way, anyway? All it got me was a big fight."

On the other end of the line, a sound like a spoon clinking echoed. "Sorry, just adding a little creamer to my coffee. What do you mean a fight? Didn't Bob, ahem, appreciate the gift?"

"I don't know if he even really realized what it was. We got into a verbal disagreement about who should have done what and then fell asleep. He never got a good look at the thing."

Across the lake, a wind stirred the tops of the pines, their gentle dance a testament to their resilience.

"You know, you're never going to fix what's wrong between you with a little bedroom time. It kind of sounds like there's more going on with Bob."

Her sister's words poked at a sensitive spot in her heart. Marilyn kicked at a clod of snow. It broke into several satisfying pieces. "What do you mean?"

"Think about some of the things he said. He usually is so in tune with you—you guys are practically a hive mind sometimes. Remember that time we played Catch Phrase and he would shout out the answer before you even finished giving him the clue? You guys wiped the floor with us that day. For him not to see how he hurt you is out of character."

Yeah, she had to admit it was. "So you think I'm in the wrong."

"I'm not saying he's totally off the hook, but I do think you owe him an apology for being so angry. You caught him off guard."

Huh. "Maybe you're right. Of course you're right. It was my pride that was hurt, nothing else."

"Your big sis is always right."

From behind her, a thump-bump sounded in the cabin. "I think Bob is up. Time to go face the music."

"Go get 'em, tiger. Love ya, Mars."

"Love you too."

Inside the cabin, Bob stood at the counter pouring himself a cup of coffee, his gray sweatpants on again, one pant leg hitched up at the calf. His hair stuck up wildly around his head, and his face was grizzled with three days' stubble. Her heart skipped a beat. After everything, even in his sweatpants he was handsome.

She thought about his other qualities—his kindness, concern for others, his desire to always do the right thing. The way he could make her laugh. Dear Lord, she loved this man.

Her harsh words from the night before poked at her.

He looked at her over the rim of his coffee cup. "You're up early."

"Couldn't sleep. Thought I'd call Liz." She raised her cell phone as though she needed to prove herself.

"Cold outside?"

"Not as bad as earlier in the week." She moved a step closer to him. "I'm sorry about yesterday."

He turned and leaned against the countertop. "Don't worry about it."

"No, really. I'm sorry we fought."

He took a drink of his coffee. "It's really no big deal."

"My pride was hurt, and I lashed out."

"I said I forgive you, and I do. I'm sorry too. It takes two to tango and all that."

"Thank you. I forgive you too." She reached around him and refilled her coffee cup. "Any idea where Stella is?"

He glanced around the small room as though Stella might magically appear. Bless his heart.

"Never mind." She picked up her cell phone again to text Stella. "I know she's a grown woman and can do what she wants, but I'd feel better knowing she's safe."

Sorry for the weirdness yesterday. Hope you're doing okay.

The three little dots indicating a reply was coming appeared, disappeared, then appeared again. Finally a response from Stella.

No problem. You and Dad have a good day. I'll be gone most of it.

Well, she was alive at least. That was something. A pang of regret shot through Marilyn. It was Christmas and she hadn't spent much time with Stella. Even though they weren't separated by an ocean like they had anticipated, the distance between them seemed to be growing. Marilyn would have to figure out how to patch up that relationship another time.

Meanwhile, she *was* grateful for the time alone with Bob.

In the few minutes of the texting exchange, Bob had moved to the table and was focused on his puzzle again. She went around behind him and put her hand on his shoulder.

"Looks like it's just the two of us for the day. What do you want to do?" She lowered her voice an octave. "All alone. In this cozy cabin." She gave his back a rub.

"I thought I'd finish this puzzle, then maybe start that Jack Ryan novel. It's been so long since I've been able to just read for pleasure."

Right. And she got that. "How about I make us a special lunch. We can eat it in front of the fire."

Bob grunted a reply that she took to mean yes.

In the bedroom, she unzipped a pocket in her purse and pulled out a recipe for a red ginseng and chili pepper beef short rib stew she'd found online. She'd spent a long time trying to find a recipe to match the one they'd eaten several times at the only restaurant within fifty miles of their honeymoon cabin. From the same pocket she unearthed the small bottle of dried red ginseng she'd bought on Amazon. She hoped Stella had found the rest of the ingredients when she went shopping the other day.

The nostalgia of this dish would be so overwhelming Bob wouldn't know what hit him.

All a man needed for happiness was a warm fire, good food, and an engaging jigsaw puzzle.

The coffee table in the cabin, pockmarked and rustic, was just big enough for a puzzle. Bob fitted another piece into the one lying in front of him. A tricky 1,000-piece work of art, the puzzle featured Van Gogh's *Café Terrace at Night*. The subtle shading contrasted with vivid colors made for an exciting puzzle.

Bob had always been partial to Van Gogh's work. Something about the whirling stars wheeling through *Starry Night* and the otherworldliness of his landscapes twanged Bob's soul. He knew what it was like to look at the world through an impassioned lens.

The stew Marilyn was busy with smelled divine. She must have added something spicy, because his nose tickled with every sniff. He heard her open the oven and slide something in.

"Is there an ETA on lunch?" And yeah, he probably could have toned his voice down. He hadn't realized it would come out so loud in the quiet of the cabin.

"Sorry," Marilyn said. "It needs to cook in the oven for another few minutes for the flavors to meld. I told you it would be a while."

"It's not a problem. I didn't mean to snap." He found another yellow piece and added it to the window he was working on. "Did I see you using a Dutch oven? Lucky they had one here. I wouldn't have thought a cabin like this would stock something like that."

Marilyn turned on the water in the sink and scrubbed at something. He couldn't hear her reply.

"What was that?"

"I said, I brought my own." Marilyn used the back of her hand to wipe a hair off her face. She shot him a sheepish glance, which held a note of…something. Almost…shyness?

He couldn't help the wry smile turning up his mouth. "You brought your own?" The woman was a marvel.

She gave a small shrug, turned back to the sink. "I had a recipe I really wanted to try, and I couldn't risk that they wouldn't have the right pans here."

Her words from last night about the Wilsons pinged inside him. Did she really think that he would be like Jeff Wilson and completely abandon his marriage and ministry?

Except, if he were honest, that was exactly what seemed to be stirring in his soul. And frankly, it was time to talk to her about it. But he didn't want to spoil the peace that had grown between them.

"The food is ready." Marilyn brought two steaming bowls to the table and sat next to him.

He took a spoonful. The scent, peppery and smoky, reminded him of something he couldn't put his finger on. His stomach roared to life. The bite in his mouth held a hint of heat and something piquant in the background. "This is incredible. What did you say this was called?" He spooned another bite of the beef into his mouth, and the flavor filled his senses.

"Short rib stew." Marilyn beamed. "I found the recipe on the internet." She stirred her food but didn't eat any. "Remember that venison stew we had at the lodge during our honeymoon? I wanted to try to recreate it. Except without the venison." She crinkled her nose.

"Oh, right! What was that place called again? Rusty Waters?"

"Rustic Lake." She sprinkled a little salt over the top of her bowl.

"This is better than theirs. You should make it back home. I'm loving this." He reached out and put his hand over hers. Her gaze warmed.

"Some of the ingredients are kind of expensive. I don't know that I will be making it very often." She flipped her hand over and twined her fingers between his. Her thumb stroked his forefinger. Pulling his gaze away, he fished out a bite of pepper to eat next. Heat flooded him. This meal was doing funny things to him. He scraped the last bite out of his bowl, savoring the spice.

"I'm not sure if I care how expensive it is. This might be the best thing you've ever made for me. And you know I love your cooking."

Still holding his hand, Marilyn scooted her chair closer to him. She spooned another helping into his bowl.

Tell her now. This quiet moment was ripe for spilling secrets. He took a deep breath. *Marilyn, we need to talk.*

"Have I said how delicious this is?" *Quit stalling and tell her.*

"Must be the exotic spices."

He leaned closer to her. "Or the beautiful chef."

With his free hand, he reached up and tucked a strand of hair behind her ear. She wore it shorter than when they first married, but something about the look in her eye reminded him of the day of their wedding. His fingertips tingled as he ran them across her cheek.

"I did add an extra portion of love."

He gave her a wink. "Oh, I can taste that."

She blushed.

He took a breath. "Marilyn, we need to talk." Now.

Except suddenly, his entire stomach convulsed. He dropped her hand and pressed his fist into his stomach. It gurgled in response. "I don't feel quite right."

Marilyn put her hand to his forehead. "You don't look very good. But you're not running a fever."

His insides ate at him. His stomach roiled. He stood so fast his chair tipped over. "Bathroom." He gasped. Then lurched toward it.

Suddenly he wondered if this had been a good time to give up prayer.

CHAPTER 8

Okay, she was officially done with being sexy. Like, forever.

Every time she'd heard a horrible noise from the bathroom the day before, Marilyn's heart had clenched.

Turned out, red ginseng came with a side of stomach issues. Who knew? Guess she should have warned her husband before he took his second helping. She thanked the Lord she hadn't eaten much herself—that bathroom wasn't big enough for two.

Now, sitting in the car next to him on their way into town, the space between them filled with the chilly December morning air that even the noisy car heater couldn't blast away.

Sigh. So much for romance. Now she was sure she had imagined the spark of interest Bob had shown yesterday. Must have just been the heat from the stove.

And then she'd gotten the phone call from the hospital about Stella. Her heart had nearly stopped. Thank goodness her daughter's injuries weren't serious. Just some minor smoke inhalation from a fire in town.

Marilyn shuddered imagining how much worse that event could have turned out.

Bob had been asleep when she got the call, and she'd almost shaken him awake to drive them to the hospital, but in the end, she hadn't wanted to wake him. He'd slept right through the night, so now she had to add her concerns about Stella to the list of things unsaid between them.

Stella hadn't come home again last night. She must have slipped out after Marilyn brought her home. Marilyn couldn't find it within herself to get too worked up about it. Bob was right. Stella was a grown woman and had to make her own decisions. Marilyn was too emotionally weary to deal with it anyway.

Marilyn, we need to talk.

Those ominous words had sat inside her all night. By morning, she'd resigned herself to hearing whatever Bob wanted to tell her today. She couldn't imagine he was going to bring up the d-word, but maybe he wanted a separation or to live separately at home. A divorce wasn't in his good-natured character.

When he'd gotten up before dawn, feeling fully recovered, and announced they needed some of the Flashy Fox's famous cinnamon rolls, she'd decided that maybe whatever bomb he was going to drop might be softened by fresh coffee and something sweet.

Oh, who was she kidding? But here she was, as usual, by his side, bracing herself for whatever was ahead.

Merry Christmas Eve to the Brown family.

The car was filled with a thick silence. She missed the quick wit and gentle teasing they usually engaged in while on car trips. She blinked rapidly, but the tears threatened anyway.

Bob parked the car in front of a small storefront. An image of a stylized fox danced across the plate glass.

"I'm hungry," Bob said. "It's kind of a good feeling, actually. I wasn't sure how things would be this morning."

Marilyn put on a pleasant face. "I'm glad you're feeling better. I hope these cinnamon rolls live up to their hype."

They pushed through the door to the bakery, and a warm, yeasty gust of air swept over them. Beside her, Bob took a big breath.

They'd entered a small dining area with a long bakery display lining the back. A swinging door hung at one side of the display. Several small tables were scattered around the space. Warm reds and creams made the room feel intimate and welcoming.

Just then, Elaine came through the swinging doors carrying a tray. "Oh! Hello! Sorry, I didn't hear the door." She slid the tray into the bakery case. "You're Marilyn and Bob, right? We met during the snowshoe event?"

"Yes." Marilyn kept her smile in place. "That's us. We've come to try your famous rolls."

"You're in luck. I've just pulled a fresh batch out of the oven." She gestured to the back. "I'll go grab a few."

"We'll take a couple of coffees too, if you have any," Bob said.

"Coming right up." Elaine's singsong voice played an annoying tune across Marilyn's tightly strung nerves.

She forced herself to breathe deeply. She was a woman of faith. And she could handle whatever Bob had to say.

How foolish she'd been to think a nightie and a few days of romance would fix whatever this was between them.

"Let's sit." Bob indicated a table with two chairs near the cash register. She slipped off her winter coat and sat. Bob sat kitty-corner from her. He laid his gloves on the table.

Elaine came bustling back through the swinging door, carrying two plates. "Jim is coming out to say hi too." She set the plates in front of them. A heady aroma of warm cinnamon enveloped them. "I'll get those coffees. Since you'll be here a while, I'll put them in real cups. I think it enhances the experience." She gave them a wink and went behind the counter to where the coffeepot sang a song of caffeine.

Jim came through from the kitchen, wiping his hands on a towel. "I'm glad you stopped by. I was just in the back making a batch of our famous walnut raisin bread. If you hang around long enough, I'll send a fresh loaf with you."

Elaine brought over two coffee mugs.

"Will you join us?" Typical Bob. Once again, his invitation indicated his desire to never be alone with her, even here at the bakery.

Jim and Elaine exchanged a look. Jim smiled. "We'd love that. I have a few loaves to put into the oven, but then we'd be free to join you for a few minutes."

"It's been slow today. I'll grab two more coffees." Elaine walked back behind the counter.

Bob reached out and took Marilyn's hand. Sighed.

Right here? Right now? He was going to end their relationship in the space of pouring a cup of coffee? She had nothing.

"Honey, lately I've been having a hard time—" Bob's cell phone jangled. He broke off and checked the screen. "I should probably take this. It's Dan Matthews."

Whatever. "Go ahead." Bob stepped away from the table and answered the call.

A second later he returned to the table and grabbed his jacket and tossed it on before heading outside. "No, it's fine. Yes, I was up. No, I wasn't doing anything important." His words wafted back as the door shut behind him.

Nothing important.

Nope. Nothing.

Suddenly, all her efforts at keeping the tears at bay were in vain. They began rolling down her face in fat drops of despair.

"Oh no! What's wrong?" Elaine came back from around the counter. She put a hand on Marilyn's shoulder, then dropped into a chair next to her.

Marilyn grabbed a few napkins from the dispenser and mopped at her face.

"I'm sorry. It's just that I think my marriage is falling apart." And just like that, the words out of her mouth took her under. She was going to need more napkins. "Forty-one years, and now it's ending."

"Is it really that bad?"

"Yes, it is. Bob can't stand to be alone with me anymore. He doesn't initiate conversation or interaction or...or *anything*." She wasn't going to tell this virtual stranger about the bedroom stuff. No matter how delicious her cinnamon rolls were.

Elaine gave her a soft smile, something of compassion in it. "I won't pretend to know what you are going through, but Jim and I have been married about ten years longer than you and Bob. We went through a rough patch too. A few of them, really. It seems to hit every couple sometime."

"You seem so happy now. How did you get through it?" She tore the side of her napkin into bits.

"It took a lot of work and a lot of honesty with each other. I'm glad we did it too. Not that long ago we had a bad scare. Jim had a heart attack, and I thought I'd lose him forever." Now Elaine, too, grabbed a napkin.

"Oh, I'm sorry. He looks so good. I wouldn't have guessed."

Elaine dabbed at her eyes. "He's made a great recovery." She took a shuddering breath. "Anyway. I believe there comes a time in every marriage where you have to decide if you're going to stick it out, if what you've built together is worth it. I think a good marriage is worth fighting for."

Marilyn nodded. Attempted a smile.

Elaine began ticking things off on her fingers. "Do you love your husband? Is he good to you? Fun to be around? Does he show care for the people around him?"

Marilyn nodded at each question. He did all of that and more.

"Then my advice is to fight for him. Keep pursuing unity with him. Show him that you'll love and respect him through thick and thin."

Good advice that Marilyn had probably even given herself at some point.

Problem was, the fight seemed already over.

Talk about being saved by the bell, or rather his cell phone's ringtone.

The drive into town with Marilyn had seemed to last two lifetimes. Sure, yesterday's lunch could have gone better. But he'd been too miserable to reassure her that he didn't hold the accidental food poisoning against her. Plus, the news that he was quitting the ministry...well, that needed to be done right.

He needed to explain himself, tell her how he got here.

Although, honestly, even he wasn't sure. Just that...the idea of returning to the pulpit filled him with a heaviness he didn't know how to escape.

But if he explained it, or tried to, then maybe she'd understand.

Who knew? Maybe she'd even agree with him.

When Dan's name had popped up on his screen, well, call him a coward, but he'd jumped at the moment. Still, yes. He had to talk to her. He'd never kept a decision this big from Marilyn before, and he didn't like doing it now. He could feel the distance between them growing wider, and he hated that.

So he couldn't help the relief he'd felt at answering the phone and avoiding the inevitable. When he had heard Dan's raspy voice, he'd known cinnamon rolls were not more important in that moment than finishing the call. He'd headed outside for some privacy.

Bob pressed the phone closer to his ear, Dan's voice a thin croak on the other end. "You sound terrible. What's up?"

"Smoke inhalation, among other things," Dan said. "I fought a fire in town last night. I'm actually calling you from the hospital."

"I'm sorry to hear that. Can I stop by and visit you?"

"I'm sorry to call you so early, but I have a request." Dan coughed, groaned. Bob heard him take a sip of something. Water probably. "I was supposed to officiate a wedding today." Dan paused to breathe. "Obviously, I'm unable to talk long enough to do the ceremony, and even if I could, they want me in here for another night of observation."

"I'm glad they're being cautious. But where do I come in?" A growing sense of unease filled him. There was only one way he could imagine being involved.

Dan confirmed it. "I want you to do the ceremony. I trust you to do right by them. They're a special couple—they deserve a great pastor."

"Oh. Dan. I…" He took a breath. "I'm sorry, but—"

"I wouldn't ask if it weren't important. I know how much you needed this time off."

"It's not that." Bob rubbed at a spot on his temple. Good thing he'd stepped outside. The sun had just cleared the horizon, the sky a glorious blue. A perfect day for a wedding. So long as he wasn't the one doing it. "Look. I haven't even talked to Marilyn about this yet, but I'm thinking about leaving the ministry."

"What?" Dan's voice broke on the word. "Why?"

"Remember when we had our conversation before you offered us this vacation?" Bob took Dan's raspy wheeze as a yes. "You were right. I needed to get away." Then, in a quiet voice, he told Dan about the ways he'd been messing up in the pulpit. All the errors he'd made. How he felt like he couldn't get up the gumption to stand in front of his congregation anymore.

That maybe he'd even, well, lost his calling.

"Oh, Bob. You haven't lost your calling. Every pastor has lost his place in the service or messed up wording in the pulpit. Even me. Usually it's when I'm not focused. Maybe that's what happened."

Bob shut his eyes. "Yeah, maybe I let my mind wander." But it felt deeper than that.

"I can guarantee that every pastor has off days."

He rubbed a hand across his eyelids. "I really think I'm losing it." What would his friend think if Bob told him how stepping into the pulpit was giving him hives? This whole conversation was confirmation of what he'd decided.

What kind of pastor let his hospitalized friend counsel him?

Shouldn't Bob be the one giving comfort in this moment?

"I think you just needed a break. There's no shame in that."

Every word Dan spoke sounded like it had been dragged across a field of broken glass. "Every person in ministry needs a break sometimes. And look, maybe it is time for you to take a different path, but I wouldn't be a very good friend if I didn't remind you that God loves you. He has not forsaken you." He coughed again. "You're going through a rough patch. But I believe you'll get through."

"No, Dan. I've been feeling this for a while, and I…don't have it in me to do this anymore."

A sigh. "Okay. I'll try and find someone else. Maybe one of the pastors from Two Harbors can come up."

And now he was just a jerk. "There isn't another preacher in the entire county?"

"I just thought, with you in town… It's fine. I'll keep calling."

And losing his voice.

And he didn't know why, but suddenly, the entire thing just sat in his craw. He was on vacation. And yes, it did…mess everything up.

Remind him of his failures. And the fact that, despite everything, God was still giving him the silent treatment.

And as Bob wished Dan well and hung up and stood there in the cold, that fact pinged inside him.

He wasn't the one who'd walked away from his calling.

God had walked away from him. Or at least…at least, it felt like it. Because hours of prayer hadn't given him one answer from heaven.

And he was tired of waiting.

He went inside.

Marilyn and Elaine looked startled when he burst back through the door. "We're leaving."

"I haven't finished my cinnamon roll yet." A red blotch appeared on each of Marilyn's cheeks.

"If you can wait just a minute, I'll put these in a box for you." Elaine scooped up their plates and took them behind the counter.

Marilyn opened her mouth, then closed it again. She stood and pulled on her jacket. "What was that all about?"

"Nothing. I want to get back." His chest itched. Heck, his everything itched.

Elaine came back with a white pastry box with a fox dancing across the top. "These will keep for a while. Put them in the microwave for fifteen seconds and they'll be delicious."

"Thank you. What do we owe you?" Marilyn accepted the box.

"It's our treat. If you're ever back in the area, stop by to see us. I'll be praying for you."

With a quiet "Thank you," Marilyn told Elaine goodbye before leading Bob to the car.

The seats crackled from the cold. Bob cranked up the heater, but it only blew cold air at them.

"Why are we leaving? Was there something wrong with Dan?"

He pressed his lips together. "No. Well, actually, yes. He helped fight a fire last night and ended up in the hospital. Smoke inhalation."

Marilyn stifled a gasp. "I'm sorry to hear it. Should we head over there?"

"Absolutely not."

"Don't you want to go visit him?"

"Nope."

"I don't get it. Why are you acting so weird?"

"He asked me to officiate a wedding. I told him no."

"You told your friend, who needs your help because he's in the hospital, no?" Marilyn's voice held another question. He almost wished she would just come out and ask it, that she would just say she was disappointed in him.

"I came here to get out of those kinds of responsibilities, so what makes you think I want to take them on for a bunch of strangers?"

"But Dan needs your help."

He thought Marilyn was going to touch his arm, but she pulled back. He glared out the window at the road in front of them. "He can find someone else. I'm not doing it."

"He's your friend." Her eyes pierced him, but he hardened his heart against the arrows.

"He should know better than to ask. This time off was his idea, for crying out loud."

She crossed her arms and fell silent. The car tires whirred over the icy roads. Mounds of snow from the recent storm towered around them.

And all around him, the world was white, silent, and cold.

CHAPTER 9

SATURDAY, 8:00 A.M.

*B*ob could measure the distance between them in miles in the two steps to the cabin door.

Once inside, they shucked off their coats and dodged each other in the small space, avoiding eye contact, bodily contact, and any other possible contact as only two people who are angry know how to do.

"I'll put these in the fridge." Marilyn tossed the bakery box alongside the last of their groceries on the top shelf.

Bob sat at the puzzle again. None of the pieces he picked up fit into the gap he was trying to fill. Marilyn sat across from him with a huff.

"I don't get what is up with you."

He kept his eyes on the puzzle. The right piece would appear if he looked long enough. "What do you mean?"

"Just everything." She waved her arms to encompass the room. "The hiding out in the cabin. The excessive puzzles. Anytime I even hint at doing something with just the two of us, you find some random stranger to join in. It's like you're afraid to be alone with me."

Her accusation hung in the air. Next she would be saying that she'd also noticed he was no longer fit for the ministry. He didn't want to hear it.

Not when he already knew the truth.

"It's Christmas Eve. Let's not fight."

She stood, her eyes fierce. "Not fight? You'd like that. All you've been doing lately is avoiding things. Something is wrong with Stella, and you won't see it. Not to mention, I picked her up from the hospital last night. Something is wrong with us, and you won't acknowledge it. But yes. Let's. Not. Fight."

He stilled. Frowned. Something was wrong with Stella? What hospital? But also… "What do you mean something is wrong with us? I think we're doing fine." He sighed. "It's not you, it's me."

"Oh. Classic. Just gonna quote rom-coms now, eh?"

Wow, she was really mad. He kept his voice steady. "No, I mean it." Saying these words took guts he didn't think he possessed. "I'm losing my grip. I think I need to quit the ministry." Each word came out quieter than the last.

Silence. A beat.

Then, "I'm sorry, what did you say?"

He couldn't look at her and instead stared at the puzzle in front of him. "I understand if you're upset at me. I haven't been myself lately. I think I need to leave the ministry. I'm tired and I keep screwing things up."

She slid into the chair opposite him. "What, because you don't remember the words to the Lord's Prayer, you're somehow doomed?"

He gave her a sharp look.

She raised an eyebrow. "You don't think I noticed? I'm a pastor's wife." Her voice softened. "But it really wasn't a big deal."

"What about the other times?" he said softly.

She touched his hand. "You mean when you lost your place in your sermon notes? I'm not trying to be dismissive, but I think you might be blowing those events out of proportion. Sure, you messed up a few times. I'd like to see the pastor who hasn't."

"I feel like a fool every time I step into the pulpit." He looked away again. "These last few months have been torture."

"Why didn't you say anything?"

"I didn't want you to look at me any differently."

"And you thought freezing me out would do the trick?"

Something in her tone caused him to finally look at her.

Wow, she was pretty, the way the sun streaming in through the window touched her face. She still wore kindness in her blue eyes, and frankly, he'd spent the night longing to reach out to her, pull her against himself and tell her that she was every bit as beautiful as the day he'd married her.

That he couldn't bear to disappoint her.

He swallowed. "I'm just not cut out for ministry anymore."

"What do you mean…not cut out for ministry anymore?" She drew in a breath. "Have you prayed about this?"

"What's the Lord going to say? 'Sure, Bob, I don't need another pastor. I only have all these lost souls to save'? I'm not off the hook." Bob shook his head. "Isn't it our duty as Christians to serve Him and His purposes? Isn't mine preaching?"

"It might be. But it might not be. It's not an all-or-nothing game. You can be a Christian and not preach," Marilyn said. "You don't know until you pray about it."

His jaw tightened. "It doesn't matter. He doesn't answer me anyway."

She just stared at him.

He swallowed.

"So you're giving God the silent treatment?"

He frowned. "No, He's giving *me* the silent treatment."

She got up and went over to the table where he'd found the puzzle. Pulled out the Bible from the drawer. Came back and set it on the table. "God is not silent. He just might not be moving in your spirit right now. But His words are always here, Bob. He is always here."

He put his hand on the Bible, the worn leather beneath his palm.

"Why didn't you tell me?" She sank down into the chair. "What about 'In good times and bad'? What about our vows? Aren't we supposed to help each other carry our burdens?"

"I didn't want to bother you with this burden."

"So, like with God, you decided to give me the silent treatment?"

He looked away.

She sighed, and with it her voice turned tender. "Don't you know that I would support you whatever you decided? I would never think less of you." Her voice shook. "I would have suggested we pray for God's leading together and then move forward. Together."

His throat ached as the silence pulsed between them.

"But maybe you don't want that."

"I'm not even sure what I want," he said softly. "I just know that I can't live like this."

"Oh."

He turned as she got up.

"I see."

"Marilyn—"

"No, I get it. I think I just need...some fresh air." She grabbed her jacket, and before he could stop her, had put on her boots. And left.

Walking out on him, just the way God had.

SATURDAY, 9:30 A.M.

He couldn't live like this? What*ever*.

Enough was enough. Marilyn had thought when they got up this morning that they'd turned a corner. She and Bob had clicked right along. Then that disastrous trip into Deep Haven, and now this fight.

I'm not even sure what I want.

She was over trying to fix this. He didn't even want to pray with her.

I didn't want to bother you. His words worked their way under her skin as she tromped out into the snow—into the too-glorious morning—creating a canker she couldn't quite soothe.

Didn't want to bother her?

Wasn't that what marriage was? Well, not a bother, but the sharing of worries and burdens?

Whatever. The wind shivered off snow from the nearby pine trees. From the lake, the snow glistened.

I think I need to leave the ministry. Wasn't that something you discussed with your wife?

Yeah. That hurt.

He'd decided to uproot their entire life without a word to her.

Not one word.

Maybe this was worse than the demise of her marriage, because—and her steps slowed as she came upon the realization—it seemed that Bob's faith, his very soul, was at stake.

But then again, he didn't want to talk about it with her, right? She would get someone to drive her into town. She could take a shuttle to Minneapolis and then an Uber home. It would be expensive, but anything was better than staying in this romantic cabin, which mocked her every minute.

Elaine's advice from earlier came back to her: *I think a good marriage is worth fighting for.* Well, this soldier was tired of fighting for something that, clearly, Bob didn't want. She was throwing in the towel, waving the white flag, saying uncle, and any other cliché that fit.

She came closer to the lodge, not sure where she was going, and through the trees she spotted…wait. Was that a castle?

Made of ice?

And then, in the breeze, the sound of a cello drifted toward her.

What?

She'd recognize that brio anywhere.

Stella was playing her cello.

She followed the sound, the path down to the dock. There. What looked like a church, or maybe a cathedral, rose from the ice. Built with ice blocks, it featured a rounded altar at the front, and a doorway covered in evergreen boughs at the rear. Twinkle lights winked along the top.

And inside, on a wooden block, sat her beautiful daughter. She held her cello between her knees, her body bent into the music, her eyes closed.

Marilyn held her breath. The music was at once lonely and mournful, then strident, then rich and full, and with a start, she recognized the recital piece Stella had played in Duluth.

This time without a hitch. Except now, she morphed the music into another song, something romantic—yes, Pachelbel's Canon in D.

She easily transitioned into "A Thousand Years," and then an Elvis song. And by then, Marilyn had stowed away in the woods outside the chapel so her daughter couldn't see her.

Whatever had been haunting her this week, however, seemed to have vanished from her face.

More songs, Christmas carols, and then a hymn.

"How Firm a Foundation."

The words stirred inside Marilyn, as if awakening her from slumber or shaking her free from the clutch of cold.

When through the deep waters I call thee to go,

The rivers of sorrow shall not overflow;

For I will be near thee, thy troubles to bless,

And sanctify to thee thy deepest distress.

She shook with the power of the song.

This water she forded just now loomed deep, threatening to sweep her away. Could it be possible that within the river of sorrow, the Lord was with her?

A soprano she and Bob went to school with had sung this song at their wedding so many years ago.

If she had known then the troubles ahead of them, maybe she wouldn't have gone through with it. Sure, she would have missed the pain, but then she would have missed the beautiful parts too.

"Lord," she whispered, "You promised to be with me in deep waters. Be with me now." Her heart stilled, filled with peace, and she smiled.

CHAPTER 10

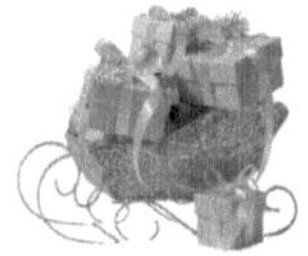

*H*e was such a fool.

Bob stood for a moment holding the scrap of red fabric his wife had tossed on the top of the pile in her suitcase.

In his preoccupation with his own slipups and fatigue and his distraction with the job offer from Planting Hope, he'd not noticed the rift developing between them.

So, like with God, you decided to give me the silent treatment?

Oh, Marilyn. In a horrible burst of clarity, he saw all the efforts Marilyn had been making lately. Efforts he'd been ignoring or outright rejecting.

Yeah, he'd been a jerk. Probably, he didn't even belong in a pulpit.

Worse, if he were honest with himself, he *knew*.

A few times there had been advances toward unity and connection on Marilyn's part that he just hadn't been up to reciprocating. He'd thought that, well, someday he'd figure out how to fix them.

Instead, those cracks had turned into a chasm.

Between him and his wife.

Him and God.

He stared at the Bible on the table. Heard his wife's words. *God is not silent. He just might not be moving in your spirit right now. But His words are always here, Bob. He is always here.*

Too easily he could hear Stella reading the Luke 2 passage. The story of God not being silent. Of sending the Word of Life to earth. To walk among us, to be with a people who had rejected Him. Emmanuel.

Not silent at all.

Maybe it wasn't that God had stopped talking, but that in all his busyness, Bob had stopped listening. Really listening.

Or maybe he feared what God had to say. What if it was over?

I'm sorry, Lord. I...

God loves you.

Dan's soft, raspy voice was suddenly in his head.

He has not forsaken you.

He didn't know why he reached for the Bible and sat on the couch. Muscle memory, maybe. It opened easily to the Luke 2 passage, where the angel of God appeared to the cold and tired shepherds, and he found himself reading aloud. "And the angel said unto them, Fear not: for, behold, I bring you good tidings of great joy, which shall be to all people. For unto you is born this day in the city of David a Savior, which is Christ the Lord.'"

A Savior, proclaimed to the lonely shepherds, to remind them they weren't forsaken.

A Savior, to prove to the world that God loved them.

A Savior, to save them from their darkness.

He looked out the window, to the sunlight on the snow, the glint of light against the ice.

And a God who, out of the silence, broke through to give mankind what they needed.

Himself.

Maybe he didn't need answers. He just needed a Savior.

Lord, forgive me for thinking I have to carry all this alone. Or at all. He got up. Closed the Bible and pressed his hand against it. *Forgive me for giving You the silent treatment. Please give me ears to listen.* Then he reached for his boots.

Time to fight for this marriage.

As he opened his door, he heard…music? A cello, and he recognized the end of the song.

"Can't Help Falling in Love" by Elvis.

Oh, that was Stella. But what was she doing playing outside?

He hurried out the door. Marilyn had headed down the snowy path, and now he followed it. As he passed by cabin six, Tom stepped out onto the deck. "Bob!"

Bob didn't want to slow, but Tom caught up to him. Gerald had come out behind him.

"Thank you for that sleigh ride you took my grandpa on. He talked about Grandma for hours, and we spent the evening writing down stories about their adventures. Thank you for suggesting it. Our whole family will benefit from remembering Grandma that way."

Gerald caught up and now squeezed Bob's bicep. "Cherish that wife of yours. She's a rare treasure."

Indeed.

"It seems the skies are singing," Gerald said, pulling his coat on. He put his arm around his grandson.

A medley of familiar tunes now filled the air as Stella transitioned quickly between many songs. Bob didn't recognize all of them until—

"Sounds like a hymn," Tom said.

"How Firm a Foundation." The song seemed to hang in the wind, drawing him, along with another couple down the path. As he neared the lake, a familiar coat caught his eye. Marilyn stood outside what looked like a large ice building.

No, a chapel, complete with an altar and a bower.

And playing at the front of the church, as if she belonged there, his beautiful, miraculous daughter.

Oh, how he was blessed. He looked at his wife. Her eyes were shut, listening.

He stepped up behind her, the words sinking through him.

When through fiery trials thy pathway shall lie,

My grace, all sufficient, shall be thy supply;
The flame shall not hurt thee; I only design
Thy dross to consume, and thy gold to refine.

Yes. God hadn't forsaken him. He'd refined him. Was still refining him.

He caught Marilyn's hand on the refrain, and then, as the last of the song faded, leaned in.

"Never, no, never, no, never forsake."

Her eyes opened and she turned her face up to him. Her cheeks were wet.

"They sang that at our wedding," he said.

She nodded.

"I'm sorry, honey." How could he have missed how much he was hurting her? "I was an idiot. I never should have thought I could just not let you in. One flesh, right?"

She nodded, wiped a hand across her cheek. "For better or worse."

"You were right. I was carrying this burden alone. When I shouldn't have been carrying it at all."

"Methinks someone should listen to his own preaching."

"Naw. That's what I have you for." He swallowed. "Right?"

The music had faded out, and in the silence, he just heard the thunder of his heart.

Then, "Right."

The music changed, and Stella began playing a new song. But it was sweet and romantic, and suddenly, he was on his knees.

"Will you forgive me for my neglect these past few weeks? Will you do me the honor of continuing to be my bride?"

Marilyn let out a choked sob-laugh that turned into a smile. "I do. I will." She cupped his cheek with her free hand. "I'm sorry I jumped to conclusions. I was just... I let my fears get ahold of me. I should have believed in you. In us."

He stood and wrapped his arms around her. "All is forgiven." She rested against his chest, her arms tightening around him. "I know we have more to talk through, but from here forward we will do it together."

"You know I will follow you anywhere." Marilyn raised her head, her gaze a promise.

"How about Botswana?"

He chuckled at her confused look, something in his chest unraveling. He could trust this woman with his heart. He'd lost sight of that. He'd lost sight of *her*. Never again. "I'll explain later, I promise."

He closed his eyes for an instant, then looked over to Stella, who had finished her piece.

Romeo walked over to her, was talking to her, and even from here, he could see that the smile on his daughter's face seemed— "Is there something going on between Stella and Romeo?"

"Oh, Bob. Bob!" Marilyn laughed, her hands on his chest.

What?

Just then, a man walked by him, his gloved hand holding the mittened hand of a pretty Christmas elf, given her red hat topped with a pom-pom and her red jacket. "Duke!" He knew him from the coffee shop.

"Preacher," Duke said.

He didn't mind. "Did you ever find that car?"

"Sure did." Duke's grin stretched wide. "Thanks for your advice."

The beginnings of a revelation took hold in Bob's mind. His advice to Duke, his care for Gerald—these had not been because he was a pastor. He'd served God in those moments because of who he was, not because of an office he held.

It's not an all-or-nothing game. Marilyn's words rang true. He didn't have to keep doing ministry the same way. He was called to serve, and he would do just that, in whatever way God had laid out for him.

Next to him, Marilyn and Duke chatted, Duke outlining the disasters they'd been overcoming this past week, his arm around the woman next to him. She was beaming up at the man. So maybe love was in the air up here.

"Now we just need to find a pastor for this wedding." Duke gestured around. "Or all this effort will be for nothing."

Right. The wedding.

Dan's words about friendship haunted him. Dan had made the

hard call to confront Bob about his actions. Bob owed him an apology phone call.

And maybe something else.

Marilyn grabbed his arm. She speared him with a look. And yeah, he'd felt the tug in his own heart too. "Duke," she said. "You're in luck."

A flurry of activity and several hours later, Bob waited by the makeshift altar flanked by tulle and birch branches. Spread out in front of him, a congregation watched for the bride to walk down the aisle.

After agreeing to do the wedding, he'd met with the bride, Vivien Calhoun, and the groom, Boone Buckam, who'd confirmed they'd be grateful for his help. They'd spent some time getting to know each other over a cup of hot chocolate in the Evergreen lodge. Then they'd held a rehearsal for the wedding party before the bridesmaids changed into their gowns.

Bob had run through the order of service and jotted a few notes for an impromptu sermon. He'd put on something nicer than his sweats and combed his hair, slipping into a familiar pastoral uniform that felt just right—called, even.

The bridal march began, and Vivien appeared at the end of the aisle in a white dress, a fur wrapped around her shoulders.

"Would the congregation please stand," he called out. As one, the group stood.

Near the back, he saw Marilyn. She met his eyes and smiled.

The bride joined her groom.

"Dearly beloved…" The words of a traditional wedding service flowed from him like warmed honey from a jar. Boone held Vivien's hand as they moved through the elements of the ceremony.

Bob's hands felt slick in his gloves. Time to take the plunge into the sermon. He prayed he could keep it together. "Some of you may know how hard Boone and Vivien have fought for this day and the many mishaps they've conquered along the way. In fact, this whole week is a fitting metaphor for the adventure that is marriage."

As Bob gave his sermon, he alternated between looking at the couple and looking at his own wife. He wanted this message to reach her heart too.

"We strive for perfection but find something else, usually something better. A winter wonderland wedding, for example." He pointed at the snow structure around them, the twinkle lights reflected a million times over in the ice until the whole place was lit like starlight. A few people in the crowd chuckled. His heart soared. This was the first message he'd given in a while that just felt right. "Maybe we lose some things along the way." He grinned at Duke, who gave him a little salute in return. "We try to hold it all together..." This with a quick glance at where Romeo and Stella sat next to each other. "But in the end, we find that keeping Christ as our foundation is what holds our marriages together. A wise man recently admonished me to cherish my wife. I intend to do that, and I in turn admonish you to do the same, Boone. Cherish your wife."

He blinked back unexpected tears. The old familiar thrill of being part of birthing a new family came over him.

"If we could have the rings." He led Boone and Vivien through the exchange of rings, but his eyes kept returning to Marilyn, who mouthed the vows along with the bridal couple. He winked at her. She blushed and ducked her head.

They reached the end of the ceremony, and now for the best part. "Ladies and Gentlemen, I present to you for the first time, Mr. and Mrs. Boone Buckam. Boone, you may kiss your bride!"

The crowd erupted in hoots and hollers as Boone dipped Vivien into a deep kiss. Bob joined the rest of the congregation in clapping and cheering.

He couldn't wait to do the same thing to his own bride.

She always cried at weddings.

Marilyn swiped at her cheeks. Happy tears this time. The swell of the music had filled her heart as the bride walked down the aisle in a fitted lace dress that flared at her knees, a small train following behind.

Vivien's bridesmaids in their slate-blue dresses made the ice chapel take on the hues of the sky. And the groomsmen, standing tall and proud beside their friend Boone, all looked so handsome. She felt it was safe to admit that, because she was old enough to be their mother.

The pomp and circumstance of weddings always danced in her heart. This one was made even more special by the looks Bob kept throwing her way. She'd held his gaze as often as she could. She hoped no one else noticed that he looked at her more than at the couple he was marrying.

They'd stolen a few moments together while he was changing, and he'd told her about LeRoy's job offer. "It's just for a year, but I think it could be really fun. Stella doesn't need us as much anymore, and I bet the church would give us the time."

Excitement built in her. "Of course, we'll have to pray about it, but I'm game for an adventure." She'd laughed at his bemused expression and kissed him on the cheek. "What, did you think I was too much of a homebody to want to try something new?"

"I don't know what I thought, but I'm never doubting you again."

Botswana. The word whispered through her.

Of course, they'd pray about it, but she already felt a tug in her heart to Africa. She could hardly wait until they had time to really talk about it.

Earlier, she had gone to the main house—she supposed it belonged to John and Ingrid Christiansen—to help Stella fix her hair. The wedding party had been in there laughing and getting ready.

She'd spared a quick look at her daughter. With her golden hair piled on her head and in a stunning dress she must have borrowed from someone, she looked like a princess. The look of contentment on her face told Marilyn that her decision to put off going to Vienna was the right one.

Bob's voice rang out. "A wise man recently admonished me to cherish my wife. I intend to do that…"

She met his eyes again. He gave a slight nod. Yep. That line was for her.

Soon the vows were being said. Marilyn felt she said them along with Vivien. She didn't miss the wink Bob threw her way.

"Boone, you may kiss your bride!"

Under the starry sky and the twinkle lights, Boone dipped Vivien for a deep kiss. The congregation erupted in applause.

She remembered Bob dipping her at their wedding. At the time she'd been both exhilarated and slightly embarrassed.

Tears threatened again.

She'd come so close to losing him this time. She should go compose herself. No need to be sobbing in the middle of a wedding celebration.

Now, in the hubbub of the processional and the dismissing of the congregation, she slipped away. From past experience, she knew Bob would be tied up for a while getting the license signed and making sure the bridal couple was taken care of.

Head down, she almost ran into Elaine Fox.

"Marilyn! Hi! Taking off so soon?"

"Good to see you again." Her voice choked up. "I'm glad you're here. Turns out, my marriage isn't falling apart." The words blurted out of her.

"I'm so happy to hear that." Elaine touched her shoulder.

"Thank you again for your advice. It meant so much to me." She left Jim and Elaine and made her way back to cabin five. She needed to make it in the door, then she could let herself go.

In the kitchenette, she'd just begun taking off her jacket when she noticed a glow coming from the bedroom.

Her tears dried up and she stared in wonder at the twinkle lights she'd brought from home, now strung in a zigzag over the bed. From one low-hanging strand dangled a sprig. Mistletoe. She reached for it.

"I hope Boone and Vivien don't mind that I swiped a little of the extra mistletoe from their supplies."

She whirled. Bob leaned a hip against the doorframe.

"Don't you need to be out there taking care of things?" She put her jacket on the chair, but it slid to the floor.

"They can handle it." Bob's slow smile warmed her from head to toe. "The entire Deep Haven police department and Crisis Response Team are out there. I think they can figure it out." He pushed off the doorframe and unzipped his jacket. Taking it off, he threw it to the bed. Missed.

"Did you do this?" She motioned to the lights.

In a step, he was beside her. "The lights outside looked so romantic I thought it would have a similar effect in here too."

Her heart sped up. "I like it."

He reached for her hand and tugged her closer. Wrapping an arm around her waist, he picked up a small bag she hadn't noticed before.

"I really think we need to give this a trial run."

She dug in the bag and slipped out a scrap of red satin-and-lace. Low in her belly, heat pooled.

"What about Stella?" It was hard to breathe.

He tightened the arm around her waist. "I'm sure she will be busy with wedding stuff for a while longer. She told me she was going to play a few songs for the reception too."

Marilyn reached up and pulled his face down for a kiss. "I love you, Parson Brown," she whispered against his lips.

He tasted of hot cocoa and cinnamon. She wound her arms around his neck, the red fabric clutched in her hand skimming across his back.

"What about the reception?" she said softly.

His lips whispered against hers. "We'll skip it."

In the distance, or maybe just in her mind, Marilyn heard sleigh bells ringing a chorus of joy.

EPILOGUE

*H*ow Romeo loved the magic of a Christmas Eve in Deep Haven. With snow drifting from the sky as if stars falling, and tonight, especially, with wedding guests lingering on the deck of the lodge or warming themselves around the bonfire near the lake, their mitten-clad hands cupped around hot mugs of cocoa, with music—Bing or Sinatra—serenading the night.

Yes, magical.

Romeo stood on the deck, the massive deck heaters pumping out enough heat to melt the snow and cut through the deep cold of the north.

Beyond the shoreline, the ice cathedral sparkled with the lights strung from it. Vivien and Boone had donned skates and were dancing in the middle of the ice, the bride wrapped in a parka over her vintage, white fur-lined dress.

Not far from them, Duke, the cop from Minneapolis, was dancing with the guest who wore a Santa hat with a white puffy pom-pom, both swaying on skates also.

In fact, the whole day, maybe even week, had felt magical. Yes, with a few bumps, but really, the happy ending seemed worth it.

"You okay?"

He turned to find Stella holding a mug of cocoa and a donut from World's Best. She handed him the mug. "I swiped the last powdered donut. Want to split it?"

"You're the best." He took his half and let the crumbs mix with the soft powder of snow.

"Nice wedding." She stepped up next to him at the railing, looking out at the spectacle on the lake.

"Nice save by your dad."

"He did well."

"Where are they?"

She raised an eyebrow, smiled.

"Oh. So, everything okay between them?"

"I think so. But maybe I'll sleep on your sofa again."

He laughed. "I'll probably be up late cleaning all this up anyway."

"The work of a resort manager is never done."

He raised his mug.

"It's Christmas Eve." She turned back to the railing. "I thought I'd be spending it in Vienna."

"Are you disappointed?"

She looked up at him. "Not in the least."

Then she lifted herself on her toes, and he couldn't stop himself from kissing her. She tasted sweet, like chocolate, and tempting, and maybe it wasn't a great idea for her to sleep on the sofa.

But maybe he'd spend the night at the lodge, in front of the fireplace, remembering his first Christmas here when he'd been broken and alone and unwanted. And then, suddenly, not alone. Not unwanted.

God is in the business of miracles. Taking on the impossible.

Yes. Romeo pulled Stella into a hug and held on.

In her pocket, her phone dinged. Stella pulled away and retrieved it. "Oh my. Someone posted a video of me playing the cello." She clicked on it. "It's from an Instagram account, and they tagged the resort." She scrolled down the post. "And I have a message from the Fritz Kreisler Institute."

She opened it and turned so he could read it too.

Oh. Wow. "They reversed their decision," he said quietly. Swallowed.

"And they've extended me a scholarship."

She looked up at him. A pulse, a beat.

"It's only two semesters," he said.

"You'll wait for me?"

He leaned his forehead to hers. "Of course."

She closed her eyes, then stepped back.

"But what about smokejumping, and…will you still be here?"

"Of course he will."

Romeo looked up at the voice, his body stilling.

Owen?

His cousin seemed to have materialized out of the night, standing next to him, holding his four-month-old son in his arms. He wore a stocking cap, his parka open, and a grin. "I have to admit, Romeo, when we left the place in your hands, I didn't think you were going to throw a rager."

Romeo simply gaped at him. "When did you get here?"

"Just now. We were worried about—well, I guess nothing." He hoisted Paxten to his other arm. The little boy slumped against his father's shoulder. "Is that Vivien and Boone out there in…what is that? An ice palace?"

"Cathedral," Stella said, grinning up at him.

"And you are…"

"One of the—" Romeo started.

"Evergreen Resort event coordinators," Stella finished.

Owen raised an eyebrow. Romeo didn't correct her.

"We had to move the wedding here—"

"Romeo!" The voice of his older cousin Casper rang out as he came onto the deck. "This is awesome." Casper walked over and pulled Romeo into a hug.

Huh.

Casper looked at Owen. "See? You were all worried that Romeo was going to be alone on Christmas Eve."

Romeo stared at him. Really?

Owen made a face. "I felt like a jerk leaving you alone on Christmas Eve—"

"We all did," Casper said. "So Owen made us rent a van, and he drove like a maniac—"

"You were the one who nearly drove us off the road in Iowa—"

Casper held up his hand. "Okay, so we all wanted to get back. But I guess you don't need us."

Romeo drew in a breath, the Ghost of Christmas Past rising to his lips. He didn't need any—

"Thanks, guys."

Casper grinned, winked.

"Is that an ice castle?" The question rose from behind them, and Romeo's throat thickened to see his aunt Ingrid close the sliding glass door behind her and walk out onto the deck.

She went right to Romeo and pulled him into a hug. "Merry Christmas, nephew."

He hugged her back. "What are you doing here?"

She let him go. "Someone had to hang the stockings on the banister. How else will Santa find us?"

He didn't know what to do with the swell of emotions inside.

She caught his face in her hands. "You're family. And family doesn't let family spend Christmas alone."

He leaned down and kissed her cheek.

Sweet. But he wasn't alone.

He'd never been alone. *Especially* on Christmas Eve.

Still. "I really hope you brought cookies."

"Always." She laughed. "John's in the garage. He needs your help to find a tree."

Owen headed into the house as Casper left for the bonfire.

Romeo looked at Stella. Took her hand. She smiled, nodded.

He stepped off the deck into the night, the crunch of the snow at his feet, a song in his heart, unafraid of tomorrow.

Walking in a winter wonderland.

CONNECT WITH SUNRISE

Thank you so much for reading *Once Upon a Winter Wonderland.* We hope you enjoyed the stories. If you did, would you be willing to do us a favor and leave a review? It doesn't have to be long—just a few words to help other readers know what they're getting. (But no spoilers! We don't want to wreck the fun!) Thank you again for reading!

We'd love to hear from you—not only about this book, but about any characters or stories you'd like to read in the future. Contact us at www.sunrisepublishing.com/contact.

We also have a monthly update that contains sneak peeks, reviews, upcoming releases, and fun stuff for our reader friends. Sign up at www.sunrisepublishing.com.

You're the One That I Want

For other books by Susan May Warren, visit her website at http://www.
susanmaywarren.com.

ABOUT THE AUTHORS

USA Today bestselling, RITA, Christy and Carol award-winning novelist **Susan May Warren** is the author of over 85 novels, most of them contemporary romance with a touch of suspense. One of her strongest selling series has been the Deep Haven series, a collection of books set in Northern Minnesota, off the shore of Lake Superior. Visit her at www.susanmaywarren.com.

Rachel D. Russell is a member of Oregon Christian Writers, My Book Therapy's Novel Academy, and is a regular contributor to the Learn How to Write a Novel blog. When Rachel's not cheering on one of her two teens at sporting events, she's often interrogating her husband on his own military and law enforcement experience to craft believable heroes in uniform. The rest of her time is spent cantering her horse down the Oregon trails and redirecting her three keyboard-hogging cats. Visit her at www.racheldrussell.com.

❊

After growing up on both the east and west coasts, **Michelle Sass Aleckson** now lives the country life in central Minnesota with her own hero and their four kids. She loves rocking out to 80's music on a Saturday night, playing Balderdash with the fam, and getting lost in good stories. Especially stories that shine grace. And if you're wondering, yes, Sass is her maiden name. Visit her at www.michellealeckson.com.

Andrea Christenson lives in Western Wisconsin with her husband and two daughters. When she is not busy homeschooling her girls, she loves to read anything she can get her hands on, bake bread, eat cheese, and watch Netflix—though not usually all at the same time. Andrea's prayer is to write stories revealing God's love. Visit her at www.andreachristenson.com.